PASSION'S DECOY

"Easy, easy," Colter whispered, brushing his lips across her mouth. Sabrina gasped, parting her lips. Her jacket fell open as he pressed against her, almost dizzy from the feel of her full breasts. For a long senseless moment, he forgot what he'd started out to do as the kiss meant to distract Sabrina had an unexpected effect on him.

Sabrina pulled back and slapped him. "Why did you do that?" she asked as she backed away.

"I don't know," he admitted ruefully, "but I think it was a mistake."

"Then I don't suppose you'll need this now, will you?" She reached down and pulled the knife from her boot.

"No. I guess I won't."

"Preventing me from discovering this knife in your bedroll was what this was about, wasn't it? Don't ever try something like that again, Captain Colter, or I'll use the knife on you."

"Before or after you kiss me back?"

"During!" she snapped, her entire body trembling like a snow rabbit caught in the gaze of a mountain lion. . . .

BANTAM BOOKS BY SANDRA CHASTAIN

Rebel in Silk
Scandal in Silver

SCANDAL IN SILVER

SANDRA CHASTAIN

BANTAM BOOKS
New York • Toronto • London • Sydney • Auckland

SCANDAL IN SILVER

A Bantam Fanfare Book / November 1994

ISBN 0-553-56465-X

Published simultaneously in the United States and Canada

PRINTED IN THE UNITED STATES OF AMERICA

OPM 0 9 8 7 6 5 4 3 2 1

For all the booksellers who
have been so supportive.
Especially for Benny, Michelle,
Cheryl, Vivian, Pam, Barbara,
and Harriet.

My special thanks to Ms. Agnes Dix, Curator of Interpretation, Fort Collins Museum, Fort Collins, Colorado for all the information she supplied about the fort and army life during the time of the book.

Dear Reader:

Is there a true romantic who hasn't watched the wonderful musical *Seven Brides for Seven Brothers*? The characters, the music, the wonderful premise of being kidnapped by, and falling in love with, a beautiful, loving man, is the stuff of which romantic fantasies are created.

I wonder how many readers know that this movie is based on a Roman myth about the founding of Rome in which Romulus went into the Land of the Sabine and kidnapped women to be brides for his soldiers. Years later, when the army of the Sabine finally invaded the city, the women refused to leave the men they'd grown to love.

My second Once Upon a Time Romance, set in the Colorado territory, is based on this legend, with a modern twist. Instead of brides, it's the grooms who are kidnapped. I hope you like the Alexander sisters and the prisoners who fall in love with them. I especially hope you enjoy the sizzling romance between Sabrina and Colter and the love affair that results in *Scandal in Silver*.

Sandra Chastain

1

"Brina, darlin', you'd better get outside the mine while I set the charge."

"Papa, are you sure this is a good idea? Maybe we ought to cut some more timber and shore up the tunnel better first."

"Nonsense. We've hit pure rock, girl. It ain't going nowhere except where I tell it to. I've been blasting rock for more years than you've been here."

Cullen Alexander packed the charge into a hole he'd made in the tunnel wall and began to string the fuse. "Blast, too short." He stopped and let out a chuckle as he slapped his knee good-naturedly.

"What's so funny?" Sabrina Alexander had never been able to understand her father's whimsical sense of humor.

"Miners ought not to use words like 'blast,' had they?" He didn't wait for an answer as he stepped back and studied the stubborn wall of rock they'd encountered after weeks of digging. "Well, no matter, I move fast."

Not as fast as you used to, Sabrina thought. She didn't know why she was so uneasy. Following her father around, making sure he didn't do something foolish, had been her self-appointed duty from the time she was only six years old. Nothing had changed in the years since, even though he'd sired four more daughters and outlived three wives. But this afternoon she couldn't shake a feeling of impending disaster. God knew, they'd set off enough dynamite charges in the past. At one time or another Cullen had been convinced that every hill in Colorado's Front Mountains was hiding gold, and he'd blown up a good portion of them.

But today was different.

Sabrina was tired. They'd been digging for six hours straight, with little or no results, until her father had uncovered two gray knobs of what he immediately pronounced to be silver. Sabrina couldn't be sure; they'd been fooled before. But Cullen was exuberant, and his enthusiasm had been known to lead to carelessness. Sabrina prepared herself to reassure her father when this new mine turned out to be the latest in a long list of Cullen Alexander's pipe dreams.

"Papa, please," she said, inspired with a thought that might slow his action. "Let's stop and have a cup of coffee first, just to get our breath, maybe add a wee drop of spirits to warm ourselves. I'll run to the house and get it."

"Irish whiskey?"

"Of course."

"Capital idea, my girl. We'll celebrate a new beginning. Like Columbus when he discovered America."

"Except Columbus made a small error in geography and ended up claiming the wrong country."

Sabrina smiled. Historical debates with her father were always lively, and often her father adjusted the facts to fit his own interpretation. If Sabrina hadn't swapped a pig with a trader for a set of history books she would never have been able to hold her own in their frequent discussions.

But Cullen wasn't ready to give up yet. He came

up with still another dramatic comparison. "Like Romulus when he founded the city that became Rome, this site will be the start of Alexander City, Colorado. There's a bottle under me mattress that I've been saving for a special occasion. Go fetch it, Brina, my girl, and make sure your sisters have done the chores. Looks like it's gonna come another snow before night."

Sabrina nodded her head. She didn't have to see to her sisters; quiet, gentle Lauren would already have done so. And unless there was something to distract her, Isabella always brought the cow in, and Mary always fed the chickens. Sabrina couldn't be certain about Raven; she was the sister who fit no pattern.

Cullen Alexander was a whimsical ne'er-do-well who deluded himself into believing that he was the kind of man who brought up his daughters to assume responsibility. In truth he'd had little to do with that. Sabrina had been both mother and father to her sisters since the death of her second stepmother fifteen years ago. All Cullen had done was isolate them so that they would never experience the ills of the world.

At that moment, Sabrina was giving her father a worried look. Satisfied that the only way she could delay his frantic hurry to fire the charge was by bribing him with coffee and whiskey, she pulled her coat tight against the wind and started off down the valley to the house nestled in the spruce trees below.

She resisted the urge to remind her father that the only reason Rome succeeded was because Romulus hedged his bet by raiding a country called the Sabine for workers and wives. So far the City of Alexander was limited to one man and five women.

"Wait for me, Papa."

"Just get the whiskey, girl. I feel a need to christen our mine, hereafter to be known as the Silver Dream."

As Sabrina made her mad dash down the valley, she wished she felt as confident. A curl of smoke beckoned from the rock chimney ahead. Sabrina reminded herself to check the wood supply. From the looks of the sky Pa was right. The weather was going to turn nasty. She sighed. Wood was what Pa ought to be worried about, not gold or silver. And he always meant to, but he knew that his girls would see to the tasks of day-to-day living. If he could strike it rich, he could give them the kind of life they ought to have, in a real house in town.

With a sense of dread still dogging her steps, Sabrina hurried, picking her way through the bare rocks and hard ground that had once made up the bed of a long-lost, mighty river. She was only a few hundred yards away from the mine when the explosion set off a tremor in the earth beneath her feet. A sharp pain knifed through her.

"Papa!"

She whirled around and climbed back up the slope, losing her hat and tearing her glove in her mad flight to get back to her father. The sound of the blast was still echoing up the canyon, bouncing off the sides of the mountains like cannon shots in a battle. A cloud of dust billowed from the mine entrance. Loose rocks tumbled out, rolling down the incline, biting her feet and ankles as she made her way back inside the tunnel. But she knew what she'd find, even before she encountered the thick, choking air inside.

A wall of dirt and rock sealed the entrance.

"Papa! Answer me, Papa! Are you all right?"

But all she could hear was the settling of twisted timbers and debris.

"Damn you, Papa!"

He hadn't waited. Cullen Alexander never waited. He never believed that anything could happen to him. Others might be unlucky, but he was protected by God and the little people, protected and inspired. Beyond the next shovel of dirt was a gold nugget the size of a dinner plate. Beyond the next rock was the mother lode. Beyond all of these was heaven, and he wasn't welcome there yet.

Sabrina grabbed a shovel leaning against the side of the mine and began to dig. Frantically, furiously, she shoveled, only to have each space filled by new dirt sliding down the mound of earth that had sealed her father inside the mountain he'd spent weeks hollowing out.

Other hands joined hers at some point, and time passed in a haze of dust and pain, until finally— "Brina? Brina! Stop, Brina! We can't do it alone." Lauren was shaking Sabrina's shoulder.

Sabrina finally stepped back and let out a deep, ragged breath. She looked up and turned slowly around, her lips pressed firmly together in that familiar way she had of daring anyone to disagree with her.

Mary was crying softly, her arms around Isabella and Raven, who'd pressed their faces against her ample chest.

"He's gone, Brina," Lauren said quietly. "He couldn't have survived the cave-in."

Sabrina pulled her father's old sheepskin-lined coat tighter and shook her head hopelessly. "No! It can't be true. I won't let it be true. Papa is back there, behind the wall, waiting for us to dig him out. We have to keep going!"

But this time it was the sisters who comforted Sabrina. Hollow-eyed and beaten, they made a circle around the person who'd always been their strength.

Sabrina swayed as the truth washed over her. Lauren was right. Two flickering lamps lit the cave. The black night sky was giving way to a pasty gray dawn. They'd worked through the night. Still, after hours of digging, they'd made little progress in moving the earth. She was long past any feeling at all, and her sisters were exhausted. Lauren was right; it was hopeless. Five women couldn't get through the rock.

"It isn't fair," Sabrina said. "Finally, after twenty years of searching, Papa really thought he'd found his pot of gold at the end of the rainbow."

"I know," Lauren said, swaying as she leaned on her shovel. He had always been so sure.

Sabrina swallowed hard, her throat hoarse from calling out, begging for some response, some hope that he was still alive. But from the beginning there'd been only silence, broken by the occasional rattle of a loose stone echoing through the dusty darkness.

Once he'd lit the fuse, he would have made his way forward and the tunnel had collapsed just inside the opening. He should have had time. Why didn't he get out? Who knew how far back the cave-in went? Even if the rocks hadn't killed him, the air supply wouldn't last.

She'd known that he was dead, but she refused to admit defeat. It was because of her sisters, she told herself. They were young. They'd be devastated. She had to protect them.

But as she looked at her sisters, she knew that she was wrong. The Alexander women weren't that young. It wasn't just that the events of the night had aged them; all of the five women were old enough to be married, except perhaps Raven, who was only fifteen. But Cullen had refused any attempt at courtship by the few men in the territory who happened by their isolated cabin. At twenty-eight Sabrina was content with her spinsterhood, but perhaps keeping the others so isolated had been a mistake.

"Why wasn't I born a man?" Sabrina asked. "Maybe I could have done something—"

Lauren gave the answer that they'd all come to accept long ago. "You've always been Papa's son, Sabrina, performing the tasks that he never quite had time to do. Now," she added, "you must do the most painful thing of all—accept what has happened. He's dead, Brina."

"But we can't—I can't let him go."

"Lauren is right, Brina." Golden-haired Isabella sniffed and pulled away from Mary, arguing in what was for her a rare moment of calm responsibility. "The sun is rising. But the sky still looks like snow."

"Please, Brina." Mary, the peacemaker, seemed more torn by Sabrina's raw pain than she was over dealing with the death of their father. "You have to rest."

But the decision was ultimately made by Raven, the beautiful youngest sister, the child who was a mirror image of Cullen's third wife, the half-Indian mother who'd died giving Raven birth. "I think we should go and leave Brina here. Like Papa always said, we must let the mountain speak before we can accept its actions."

"Yes, please go. I need to think for a bit." Sabrina nodded and watched as Lauren, Isabella, Mary, and Raven reluctantly started down the hillside. They were united, but the four women were so very different.

The cold wind whipped through the crevices at the end of the canyon and pushed against their backs, shoving the girls forward through the gray light of morning, sending the dry balls of tumbleweed ahead of them like giant shadow marbles flying across the patchy snow.

Sabrina was the only one who'd believed in her father's dream of finding the legendary River of Gold. She could still hear his excitement: "Any fool can see, Brina. Look at the shape of the land; it's like a giant curled finger inviting me inside." And he'd followed, only to have the finger kill him.

Perhaps, Sabrina though wearily, Raven was right about the spirits of the mountains. Even Cullen swore he'd heard them. But he'd said the little people were speaking to him, whispering promises that the practical, level-headed Sabrina never heard. Perhaps it was time she listened.

Sabrina settled down on a red-colored boulder, staring out at the valley her father had claimed, and watched a watery sun steal silently over the ridge in the distance. As it cast a drab light over their tiny valley, she slowly let go of her stoic resolve. Exhausted from the digging and numb from the pain, she didn't feel the cold, only a strange vibration of the rocks beneath her feet. She didn't know whether she actually heard music or whether she felt it drumming through her veins.

"Ah, Papa," Brina said, listening to strange new wind sounds outside the cave. Air currents whistled down the valley, through the spruce trees, creating lyrical musical sounds as they gathered up loose rocks and flung them against canyon walls. "The mountain is speaking to me, but it isn't telling me what to do."

The light turned saffron as she sat and watched.

To the southeast she could see a strip of open plains, dotted with brown buffalo grass that became fodder for Isabella's animals. Here and there patches of wind-blown snow lay across the brown grass like the coat of a pinto pony.

Ruffled by the wind that swept down the valley, the brown grass lay flat for a moment, then, like a mischievous child playing tag with the tumbleweed, sprang back and bent in a different direction. Sabrina never tired of watching the changing landscape. She'd always loved this bare, unyielding land.

Until now.

A strong gust of wind howled past the cave entrance, picking with icy fingers at Sabrina, unleashing strands of auburn hair that caught in her thick lashes, tugging at her, almost as if it were urging her to go. As the seriousness of their situation ate through her pain, Sabrina realized that they were truly alone, a day and a half from Boulder City to the south and a day's ride from Fort Collins to the north. They were facing weeks of cold and snow before the arrival of spring.

A renegade band of Ute had been raiding the few settlers who were left, and these attacks, along with the skirmishes between the Union and the Confederate soldiers in the area, had brought to a stop all the stage-coach lines, except those along the Overland Trail. Few new people came to the territory now, unless they were fleeing the war.

With only a few gold nuggets and some slivers of silver to buy flour and bacon, Sabrina knew they could be in serious trouble. For now she was faced with the responsibility of feeding her sisters without help. But when had that been any different?

Suddenly, digging through the cave-in became more than recovering her father's body for burial; it meant their very survival, for their precious ore was hidden in the cave beyond the wall.

Sabrina pulled off her gloves, wincing as the blisters beneath ruptured and stuck to the sheepskin, ripping away the flesh and leaving her fingers in bloody agony. She looked down at her hands, allowing her mind to focus on the red rivulets that began to freeze, then cracked as she flexed her fingers.

Her hands hurt. Her back hurt. Her heart hurt with such pain. And as she sat, she took in that pain and used it to shore up her faltering courage. After a long minute she swore and leaned forward, propping her elbows loosely on her knees. She wasn't Cullen Alexander's daughter for nothing. There had to be a way.

No one else knew about the two knobs of silver in the red rock that had excited Cullen Alexander so that he'd blasted without first making the tunnel safe. He believed he'd found not the River of Gold he'd been searching for, but a vein of pure silver, the Silver Dream, he'd christened his find. Mining the silver was their only answer. Sabrina had to find a way to get at it without the outside world learning of his discovery.

But she couldn't do it alone. She had no way to get to it without help. If only she had someone to talk to. But she didn't. She never had. And through the years she'd learned to keep her thoughts to herself.

Wearily, she pulled herself to her feet and walked away from the mine. A fine stinging snow began to fall, whirling down the canyon, catching the granitelike dirt and blowing red swirls of snow through the air. Colorado, the Indian word for "red earth," had become red death to Cullen Alexander.

As she walked, Sabrina considered and rejected several possibilities: moving her sisters back east; searching for charitable families who would take them in. But there were too many widows and children left behind by the war between the North and the South. They could move into Boulder City and find work as seamstresses or cooks. But the war had claimed so many of the men, and those who were left in Boulder City were either deserters, thieves, or poor men with little money to spend on clothing and fancy meals.

The most practical place to go was north, to Fort Collins, where the Union troops were stationed to control the Indians and to fight any Confederates who tried to claim the routes between the gold fields of California and the eastern banking interests. But Papa hadn't believed in war and had made his feeling clear about exposing his daughters to the kind of men who served in this wilderness. This valley was their home, where they belonged, where they'd be safe.

Eventually, when she had it all worked out, she'd call a family meeting.

The moisture in Sabrina's mouth turned into ice as she drew in the cold air. Even her face hurt, and she realized that the crust on her cheeks was formed by the freezing of her tears. She stopped, swallowed hard, and forced the tears back. She couldn't be weak now. She had too much to do.

Sabrina intended to mine the silver.

But she needed help. She needed a man, someone who would protect their interests as his own. There was only one answer.

One of the Alexander women had to marry.

Quinton Colter and his group of ragtag misfits waited behind the rocks, muscles cramped from the frigid ground and the enforced stillness. Bitter cold seeped through their clothes, numbing their fingertips and turning their toes into chunks of ice. The fine, blowing snow hung on their eyelashes, freezing there, turning them into old-world pictures of ruddy-faced Father Christmases.

A movement caught Colter's eye as a huge jackrabbit loped across the valley and disappeared in the rocks.

"Figures," a serious voice whispered behind chattering teeth. "The only food we've seen in days and we can't shoot. Maybe I could trap it."

"Keep still, Tyler," Colter said. "It's gone."

"How much longer, do you think, me lads?" The third man's musical accent was Irish and oddly out of place with his fierce looks. Even so, nobody knew better than Irish that caution and slow movements lulled not only the wildlife, but the enemy, into complacency. A lifetime as a farmer had taught him patience if not military skills.

"Not long," Colter answered. "Those Yanks left Denver this morning heading for Boulder City. They'll be along pretty soon."

From beyond the smaller outcropping to Colter's left came movement. "Careful, boys, the South needs the munitions they're carrying, and I could use a few coins or two from that new mint in Denver." Carl Arnstine, the fourth member of the team, allowed a grin to show. He'd known he was a good soldier; he'd just never tried until Colter found him.

Colter shook his head slightly. Waiting never had been Carl's way. If there was a fight to be had, he'd start it and finish it too, more often than not. It had surprised Colter that the fast-talking ex–saloon keeper had taken a fancy to Tyler Kurtz, the scholarly member of their group. Tyler never asserted himself, and Carl had become the serious, educated soldier's fierce protector. Dane, the point man, the lookout, was the loner, a fancy dresser who kept to himself. And Irish, big, burly Irish, was mother hen to them all.

"Where's Dane?" Tyler asked quietly.

"He's down the trail, keeping watch," Colter answered.

Irish gave a soft chuckle. "Knowing Dane, he's probably found himself a place to build a fire and he's cooking that rabbit if he could figure out how to do it without getting his clothes dirty. Want me to take a look?"

"No. Keep quiet and don't move."

Colter would feel better if he could see Dane, but that would require movement, and their cover wasn't good enough to chance that. They were in the rocks above the trail just south of Boulder City with little ammunition, and they were outnumbered. They needed the guns and ammunition the Yanks were carrying. As for Carl's wish for gold, most of it was shipped along the Overland Trail, the gold that didn't go west to California.

They waited, five Confederate soldiers, rejects from other units, who were dubbed the misfits. They were outfitted as drifters and sent west to find guns, ammunition, gold, anything that would help the struggling southern armies who were running out of hope and help. Colter's men badly needed to capture this cargo to send back to Virginia, where Lee was playing cat and mouse with Grant's army.

The temperature was well below freezing, a biting, bone-chilling cold that turned a man's blood into slush and made him think about August in Carolina, when the cotton fields were heavy with white. For a moment Colter was back there, a boy again, on his father's farm, the hot black dirt squishing between his toes.

Big Moe, his black skin slick with sweat in the sun, was moving back and forth along the cotton rows, hoeing weeds, singing in that deep voice that made the world seem right. Colter knew that come late afternoon he and Moe would slip down to the river and fish into the evening. He could still hear the tree frogs and see the lightning bugs blinking their signals across the black night sky.

But there was no family now, no farm and no life back home to protect. Not even Big Moe, who'd followed Colter into battle, had survived. There was nothing to return to, for Colter or any of his men. That's why they'd volunteered for assignment in the West. Their lives, as they'd known them, were gone, and they wanted to leave the South behind, find a new place for themselves. They'd done well attacking patrols, recovering small numbers of weapons and money, which Colter got to Wiley, who ran the trading post for shipment back to the South. To protect Wiley's identity, only Colter knew that he was their contact.

But Colter was tired and so were his men. The war hadn't ended in a few months as their leaders had expected. It had ground on, choking out every symbol of the life they'd fought for, turning gentle farmers and patriotic young men into killers.

Suddenly the wind swept down the valley, wailing like the sound of bagpipes accompanying some ghostly regiment into battle. Colter lifted his head, listening for a moment. Then the wind dropped. The music was gone and a silence fell over the hillside.

Colter cursed his sudden loss of concentration. There'd been no signal from Dane. If Colter hadn't allowed his mind to wander, he would have heard the soldiers approaching sooner. He didn't hear the soldiers moving toward them even now; rather, he felt them, at least the pounding of hooves on the ground. The others heard too and responded with the sound of weapons being readied for shooting.

With his heart pounding Colter rose to take a quick look down the canyon. It was that movement that saved him from the arrow that whizzed past his arm and embedded itself in the snow in the spot where his chin had rested moments earlier.

His men had no chance. Before they could get off a shot, they'd all been wounded, then surrounded by tall men with painted faces, wearing capes made of bear fur and buffalo skins.

"Indians!" It was Tyler, breathing raggedly. "We're watching for Yankees and we get captured by Indians. It figures."

"Gray Warrior's Ghosts!" the tallest of the Indians said contemptuously.

Colter cursed. Because of a rare moment of weak sentimentality, he'd allowed his men to be surrounded, wounded, captured.

Except for Dane, who wasn't in the rocks beyond Tyler as he was supposed to be.

Maybe Dane *had* found a safe place to build a fire. Maybe he'd managed to escape. If so, with any luck they weren't dead yet.

Then again, maybe their luck had finally run out.

For the Indian let out a bloodcurdling yell and signaled to the Union soldiers riding up the trail.

2

Quinton Colter rattled the door to the makeshift Boulder City jail where they were being held while the detachment of Union soldiers found a wagon to transport the men injured too badly to ride.

He'd never felt as helpless as he did now looking at his wounded men. Helplessness wasn't a condition he would accept, even when he'd been outnumbered in a fight. Death had become a familiar sight, and with each loss the pain had numbed a bit more, until he'd thought that he was immune to suffering.

Maybe that was why he'd grown careless, because duty had become a matter of survival, not a cause to be defended. Out here, in this wild, untamed land, fighting had seemed more personal. One man was equal to another, and the color of the uniform mattered little; it was simply one will against another.

Now the men who depended on him were suffering. A bullet had passed through Irish's upper thigh. He'd lost a great deal of blood, and even if they could get away, he couldn't walk without starting the bleeding anew. Tyler's head wound appeared to be minor, but every time he stood up, he nearly fainted, and Carl was unconscious. Whether he'd passed out from loss of blood from his shoulder wound, or from something else, Colter didn't know.

He rattled the door again.

"Simmer down back there," yelled the burly proprietor of the livery stable, who'd become their jailer.

"We need a doctor," Colter demanded.

"There ain't one. He's over at the fort looking after a group of settlers them Ute attacked last week, and ain't nobody moving during this storm, including you."

"At least bring some hot water and bandages," Colter pleaded.

There was no answer. There hadn't been an answer through all of yesterday and most of today. "Damn!" Colter slammed his hand against the log post that formed the door frame to the dark, cold room. He still couldn't believe the ease with which they'd been captured. It was almost as if the Indians had known exactly where they were. After their capture, as if by appointment Gray Warrior's Ghosts had handed Colter's men over to the Union troops carrying the munitions.

Once the wagon arrived, they'd be taken by the troops escorting the munitions to Fort Collins, where, more likely than not, Colter and his men would be hanged, if they lived long enough to get there. He couldn't figure out why it was taking the soldiers so long.

Colter had thought he was ready to die. When South Carolina seceded from the Union, he'd expected to die in battle. But he'd led a charmed life. Everyone else had been destroyed—his entire family, his friends, his land. Finally, when there seemed to be no reason to keep fighting, he'd volunteered for General Lee's assignment to go west in search of badly needed weapons and funds. Captain Quinton Colter had been ready for, even welcomed, death, but he'd never envisioned being ambushed. For now he was certain that was what had happened. They'd been set up.

In the darkness Tyler groaned. Poor Tyler. A more unlikely soldier had never donned a uniform. Fighting had never come naturally to the quiet, slender man nicknamed the professor. Now he was about to die for a cause he supported from his heart, knowing that the rationale was flawed.

"Pretty bad spot, eh, Captain?" the big immigrant nicknamed Irish said softly. "But we've been in worse."

"Not bloody damn lately," was Colter's reply. And, he could have added, never with so little hope. If they managed to overpower the store owner, three badly wounded men on the run stood little chance of escape.

Even Carl, who was willing to gamble on which way the wind would blow, wouldn't have taken a bet that they'd survive.

"Think our contact knows we're here?" Tyler asked.

"He probably heard about what happened."

"Maybe Dane got word to him," Irish said.

"He doesn't know who our contact is," Colter said. "General Lee thought it would be safer if he gave us each a piece of the puzzle. Dane knew the territory. Tyler knew the codes. Carl knew the contacts. Irish knew the escape plans. Nobody except me knew it all."

"Then," Carl asked weakly, "where the hell is Dane?"

For two days the snow fell, piling up around the Alexanders' crude log house and outbuildings, preventing Sabrina from returning to the mine. She kept her mind occupied by working to the point of exhaustion shoveling a path between the house and the barn, fastening the cow, their two horses, and the chickens inside.

Wrapping strips of cloth around her blisters to protect them, she kept working. She needed the pain, needed to be reminded that the strength she'd always relied on was gone. She couldn't talk about it. She didn't try. Her sisters wept in secret, wiping their eyes and feigning some kind of busy task whenever she appeared. Sabrina couldn't cry. She needed to hurt physically to contain the pain in her heart, so she continued to use her hands, deliberately interfering with healing.

Isabella had found a calf, left behind by soldiers herding cattle to the fort. She insisted on bringing it into the house, coaxing it into accepting a gruel Lauren made up to substitute for milk. Now it followed Isabella every step. Sabrina didn't want to remind her sisters, but the corn for the chickens and the cut grass Isabella had stored for the horses and the cow were almost gone. Until the snow let up, there'd be no more grass gathered.

Still the snow fell.

Dear God, why are you punishing us? You've taken everything, what more do you want?

Dusk fell early on the third day, closing out the purity of the white mountainside as it cloaked the house in purple darkness. Sabrina made a final check of the outbuildings, returning to the house half-frozen from the vicious wind that continued to blow down the valley. The snow had finally stopped.

Inside, she dropped into the crude rocker by the fireplace, her hands folded around the tin cup someone handed her, the heat of the liquid, which was little more than coffee-flavored water, thawing out her hands so that the blisters ached and her frozen fingers tingled. For a long time she sat, staring into the fire unaware of the silence.

"Come and sit down," she finally said to her sisters, who'd hovered uneasily behind her. "We have to talk."

The sisters took their normal places on the splint-pine benches, carefully avoiding any mention of the empty seat at the head of the table.

"We're listening, Brina," Lauren said softly. "What have you decided?"

"It isn't up to her to decide," Isabella protested

with a pout. "We're all adults. We ought to have a say in what happens to us."

Plump Mary, with her shock of carrot-colored hair, shook her head in disagreement. "Sabrina is head of the family now, Isabella. She'll know best."

Sabrina put down her cup. "Isabella is right. We must all agree, for what I'm about to suggest will change our lives forever."

"We're going into Boulder City?" Isabella's voice was filled with cautious awe.

"One of us must go," Sabrina agreed. "You see, Papa didn't have a chance to tell you, but he believed that he'd finally found his vein. There is a possibility that we're rich."

"Whoopee!" Isabella shouted.

"Really?" Mary asked quietly.

"Rich." Lauren said in the careful, measured tone she always used when faced with something new, something she didn't yet believe. "Brina, Papa *always* thought we'd be rich."

Raven, the youngest sister, only listened.

Sabrina felt her way. The last thing she wanted to do was build up her sisters' hopes and have them end in failure, as Papa always had. "There were two knobs of what Papa said was silver lodged in the wall. That might be all there is. Papa couldn't be sure. That's why he set off the charge that caused the cave-in. To follow the vein."

"Silver?" Mary repeated the word, turning it into a question.

"That's what Papa said." Sabrina didn't voice the possibility that he could have been wrong. For now, in the midst of disaster, her sisters badly needed the hope of a better life.

"Perhaps the earth will not give up its treasure," Raven said.

"Of course it will," Isabella snapped at her youngest sister. "Stop talking like an Indian."

"But I am Indian—at least one-fourth Indian."

Isabella chortled. "And you're three-quarters white. You are more white than Arapaho. Think, Raven, we could be rich. All we need is—someone to help us—a man."

"Yes," Sabrina agreed slowly. "But first we have to bury Papa."

The sisters looked at each other in shame. Just for a moment they'd been distracted by the unexpected thought, not only of wealth, but of bringing a man into their lives. Now they lowered their eyes in guilt at having forgotten the reason for that need.

Lauren brought a crushed handkerchief from her pocket and dabbed at her brown eyes. "Of course you're right, Sabrina. Isabella doesn't mean to be unkind. She's just afraid. We must give Papa a proper burial. For that we need outside help. What do you mean to do?"

As long as she could, in the wake of her sister's censure, Isabella held back her excitement, then sprang to her feet, adding a log to the fire. She paced back and forth in front of the hearth. "I don't mean to be a terrible, uncaring person, Brina. But you aren't teasing us, are you? You are actually going to hire someone?"

"How will we pay him?" Lauren asked.

"Where will we find—someone?" Mary chimed in.

"That's the problem I've been studying," Sabrina said. "Papa never wanted any outsiders to know his business, our business. He thought, as I do, that family matters ought to be kept in the family."

"But we never had any family matters to discuss, did we?" Mary asked. "I mean, if we did, nobody ever told me."

"You're right, Mary. But Papa always believed that we would. He never wanted anyone to know where he was digging or what he'd found. He always expected someone to try to steal his claim."

Lauren replaced her handkerchief and smoothed her apron. "And now we do, or we *may*, have something to steal, and we must try to find someone who'll help us without taking advantage. How, Sabrina?"

"I'd considered hiring one of the men who used to prospect with Papa," Sabrina began, forcing herself to share her thoughts with her sisters.

"But we haven't seen a prospector in months," Isabella cut in with a pout in her voice. "Besides, they're old and they smell bad!" The bright expression on Isabella's face changed into one of disappointment. "We'll never get off this mountain, never meet—anyone."

"Perhaps one of my mother's people," Raven suggested. "I could ask my grandfather, Flying Cloud."

Sabrina took in and let out a deep breath. She'd wrestled with that question for three days until she'd finally faced the inevitable truth. "No, Flying Cloud wouldn't help us mine our silver. That would bring more people into his mountains. We can't ask that of him. We must help ourselves."

"How?" all four sisters asked at once.

"A hired hand won't do. Family matters must be kept private, in the Alexander family. The only answer to our problem is for one of us to—to—marry."

There was a long, breathless silence.

Then Isabella turned, lifted her chin dramatically, and announced, "You're right, Brina, it's the only thing to do. I will take a husband."

"No," Lauren said quickly. "Sabrina is the oldest and the wisest in the ways of the world. She must be the one to pick a mate."

"I don't know," Sabrina answered honestly. "Perhaps you would be a better choice, Lauren. You've always wanted a home of your own and children."

Lauren shook her head. "No, Isabella was right about one thing. I am not brave enough and she's far too impulsive. Mary isn't ready yet. As for Raven, she's too young, and finding the right husband for her might be more difficult. I believe that is why Papa tried to protect us from the cruelty of outsiders."

Sabrina stared at Lauren in surprise. Lauren, Mary, and Isabella's mother had been white, as had been Sabrina's mother. It was true that Raven's mother had been the daughter of a French trader and an Arapaho woman, but none of them had ever considered that a problem.

"You mean because of Pale Raven?" Mary's voice was filled with disbelief.

Mary had been only three years old when Pale Raven had died giving birth to Raven. All of the Alexander women had loved and respected their father's third wife, never considering that others might not share their lack of prejudice. There was no denying that Raven was a mirror image of her mother, but Cullen's isolation of his family had prevented any of the sisters from ever encountering hostility over their father's choice of a wife.

"Lauren is right," Mary agreed. "If we are to find a man to look after us, it cannot be one who would look down on any of us or treat us badly. We must rely on you to make the choice, Brina."

Sabrina had known from the first that the final decision would be hers, just as the responsibility for making a home and caring for her sisters had fallen on her shoulders.

"Yes," Sabrina finally agreed. "I would not have you mistreated. It must be me, then."

The four sisters were staring at Sabrina in disbelief.

She could see the questions in their eyes. Sabrina married? Sabrina taking a husband? Sabrina, who didn't even own a dress? It was beyond comprehension that it would be Sabrina when any one of the other sisters would be happy to have a husband.

Isabella didn't hesitate to voice her feelings, even resorting to a temper fit. She tossed her fair hair and pursed her trembling lips. "But, Brina, it isn't fair. You never wanted to wed. All you ever wanted to do was dig in the dirt. It ought to be one of us! Lauren, or Mary, or . . . me."

Her words trailed off into a sob, and Sabrina realized for the first time the dilemma Cullen Alexander had faced. "You are right, Isabella, it should be one of you. Of course you want husbands and homes of your own, and I promise you, you shall have them. But we don't have the time to look, and you wouldn't have the vaguest notion about how to pick a man. Letting the three of you go husband hunting would be like feeding three lambs to a pack of wolves."

"And you know about husbands?" Mary's question came as a surprise. She was usually the peacemaker, the agreeable one, always ready to see someone else's side.

"No, but then I would never search for a husband. I'm not the kind of woman any man would want. A real marriage is out of the question. I'll be looking for a miner, a hired hand who is strong and willing to work hard. Perhaps a man who isn't too bright. That, I will recognize."

"But, sister," Raven asked softly. "why would you not want a real husband?"

Sabrina looked at her sister with genuine shock in her eyes. "Raven, look at me. I'm more Papa's son than I ever was a daughter. I have no social skills. I'm a poor cook and don't know how to sew. What kind of man would want me?"

"A wise man," Lauren answered.

"And that isn't what I'm looking for."

Isabella stood and let out a sound of frustration. "But, Brina, how will you convince this man to marry you? Papa said the man always does the asking."

Isabella was right. Why on earth would any man want to take her as a wife? Aside from the limitations she'd already voiced, she was far too outspoken, too bossy, too accustomed to running the mine and her family. Her father had told her that often enough. She didn't have to have him around chastising her for the way she looked; she knew she was tall and shapeless.

The russet color of her hair was outrageous, and her skin was burnished from the elements. Somewhere between hazel and green, her eyes were more odd than appealing. And she didn't even own a dress. To his credit Papa had often tried to soften her, telling Sabrina that all men liked their women to be a little more gentle. But she'd never seen a need. And for the last years he'd seemed content with the life they led.

As for the more personal part of marriage, it wasn't that she didn't have some understanding of what was expected. As a child she'd seen too many men in too many mining camps not to, but that wasn't something she intended to allow. Her husband would have a home and a family, and if the silver was there, he'd be rich. If her husband wanted more he could find it elsewhere, so long as he didn't bring shame to the Alexander household.

"I don't know," she admitted honestly, "but I'll cross that bridge when I come to it. I'll be leaving for Boulder City at first light. I figure I should be back in six days."

Lauren rose and started to bank the fire for the night. "Will you wed him here, or in town?"

"In town. Mary, see that the shed is made livable while I'm gone, and get Papa's burial suit ready."

Mary raised a questioning eyebrow. "The shed?"

"He has to sleep somewhere," Sabrina answered.

"Then you're not going to . . ." Lauren's voice trailed off in uncertainty. "To bring him in the house?"

"No, I'm not. Now get to bed, all of you. I need to make a plan."

Lauren, Mary, Isabella, and Raven slept in the loft over the big room used for everyday living. On the main floor, in the corners on either side of the front door, like sentries, were two bunks on which Sabrina and her father slept. Tonight as she lay watching the flames die down, Sabrina wondered how she would find a man who would be willing to take on the life she was offering.

She was still wondering the next morning as her mount picked its way down the valley through the sporadic falling snow, pulling the packhorse behind.

When she judged it to be near noon, she found a leaning rock surrounded by others and climbed down, leading her horse inside the enclosure away from the blowing wind. From a pouch she carried next to her skin to keep its contents from freezing, she poured a small amount of water into her hat and offered it to the horses.

A quick check beyond the rocks revealed the clear blown snow. She'd be safe for a rest. No hoofprints revealed her position. She perched on the side of one of the rocks and chewed on a piece of dried beef and some corn bread. She allowed her fears to run free.

Suppose she failed? Suppose she couldn't find a man willing to wed? Without telling him about the mine, she couldn't think of one reason why any decent man would agree to her terms. Yet she couldn't tell him the truth—not until they were married. Perhaps not even then, if her choice turned out not to be a wise one.

It was good the wind was beginning to die, for she'd planned to make camp for the night farther down the trail in a cave near the stream. Traveling in the blowing snow was risky; she might miss the spot she had in mind. Just as she started to rise, she heard the sound of another horse approaching. Sabrina froze. Being discovered by some Indian hunting party was always a possibility, and she couldn't be certain that the hunters would be friendly Arapaho, now that the Ute were raiding the territory.

The strange horse reined in and stood just beyond the rocks where she was hidden, pawing the ground nervously. To keep her own horses quiet, Sabrina took her precious supply of bread and began feeding it to them a crumb at a time. Moments later she heard a whistle, answered by another whistle. Now there were two men.

"Gray Warrior, it's good to see you."

"I am here, Long Rifle."

Gray Warrior was an Indian, and if she could interpret what she was hearing, the second man was a white man, carrying a rifle. There was nothing unusual about bearing arms, but being called by that name indicated that the rifle was in some way special.

Sabrina curled her fingers around the pistol she carried in her pocket, praying that she wouldn't be discovered. Her sisters were depending on her. They would never be able to take care of themselves if she didn't return. She'd been gone only half of one day, and already her mission was in jeopardy. "Where are your little people, Papa?" she whispered. "I may need some help."

"The escorts will camp by the stream, beneath the cedar tree," the man called Long Rifle was saying. "Don't kill anybody, just take the supplies."

"It will be done. The rifles and horses will be mine."

"Yes. The mules carrying the saddlebags are mine. Everything else is yours."

There was a grunt of acknowledgment and the men rode away. Sabrina let out a deep sigh of relief. She would be hungry without her bread, but at least she hadn't been discovered. One man she might have taken, but two would have been difficult.

Sabrina piled her auburn hair beneath her hat, tied a scarf made from a flour sack around her head, covering her hat and her ears, and remounted, cautiously leaving her place of hiding. One set of footprints in the deep snow headed off in the direction she was going; the other went toward the stream. Not wishing to encounter either, she directed her horses away from the trail and into the rockier area at the base of the mountains. The going was more treacherous and slowed her considerably, but she felt safer.

As night fell, she reached the stream just north of Cedar Bend and began to search for the cave. She wished she knew how far downstream the escort would be camped. But there was no way of knowing. The stream ran all the way down the gorge until it met the river that flowed by Boulder City. She'd have to be careful come morning not to run into the Union soldiers. Since she knew they were ahead of her, she'd just find a way around.

But dark was falling quickly now, and she had to make camp. On the occasions when she'd accompanied her father into town to fetch supplies, they'd always made camp in the caves at the curve of the stream where the grass was plentiful. The grass was covered with snow now, but at least the water was still flowing beneath its crystal cover.

First she tied the horses in the trees near the water,

where they'd be protected from the wind. Next she broke the ice so that they could drink, then fed them a handful of the cut grass she carried in her pocket. Finally she dug away the snow as best she could to expose the frozen grass below. Had Isabella been along, she'd have insisted that the horses be draped with a wool blanket. For a quick moment Sabrina wished one of her sisters had come with her. She'd made many journeys though these mountains, but Papa had always been with her.

Sabrina gave a quick sigh, then moved her supplies up the side of the hill, where she quickly checked out the cave for any wild animal who might not be willing to share its shelter. She was lining it with her bedroll when a blast of wind brought the sound of laughter from downstream.

The little people? No, this was real. There were men camped down the trail. The ones the man called Long Rifle had mentioned? Sabrina looked ruefully at her bed, then decided that there was to be no sleep until she checked out the source of the sound. Perhaps she should warn them of what she'd overheard.

She drew her pistol and quietly crept farther up into the rocks at the base of the mountain. In the fading light she was able to move about easily from one patch of shadow to the next. A hundred yards down the draw she spotted a wagon in a stand of trees by the stream. For a long time she studied the object until she could make out the men inside.

A wagon filled with dead bodies? That made no sense. They were lying down, dark shadows, frosted with snow. Perhaps they were dead. Then she heard a moan and sensed movement. One man struggled to lean forward, cursed, and slammed his hand against the side of the wagon. He couldn't see her, but she felt his eyes burning into her skin, felt the hate, the anger, and for a moment she ducked behind a rock, feeling as if she'd been buffeted in a storm of raw emotion.

Then she heard the laughter again, farther downstream. She worked her way along the rocky overhang until finally she was above the main campsite.

She counted eight blue-uniformed men huddled around the fire. They were passing several bottles back and forth and laughing loudly. She could see only one lookout at the far side of the camp. The soldiers had chosen a poor site for a camp, but she suspected the prospect of drinking the whiskey had influenced their choice. She was debating the wisdom of warning them about what she'd heard when she saw the lookout drop silently to the ground.

At that moment the savage cry of an Indian split the night, followed by a barrage of gunfire.

Sabrina dropped down behind the rocks and peered through a crack between, watching wide-eyed as a band of Ute in full war paint descended on the campsite. The Union soldiers returned fire, but it was obvious that the Indians were disregarding the order not to hurt anyone.

Sabrina scooted away, moving back down the side of the mountain toward her camp. If the savages discovered her, she might not be able to hide. Then she heard voices from the wagon. They weren't all dead.

"We're sitting ducks, Cap'n," one of the men said. "If the Yanks don't get us, the Indians will."

"Yeah, might as well get ready to kiss the Blarney stone," the voice of an Irishman said weakly. "It ain't fair that a man don't even have a fighting chance."

An Irishman, like Papa. Before she thought, Sabrina scampered down the hill, dodging from tree to tree until she reached the wagon. There were four of them. With her hunting knife she quickly cut the ropes binding them to the wagon and to each other.

Sabrina didn't know who the captives were, but every man deserved a fighting chance. "Be quick," she said, "follow me."

For a moment the men were startled, then began to slide to the end of the wagon.

As quickly as he could, the leader climbed out, then as gently as possible assisted a second man to the ground. "Careful," he said. Awkwardly the first two managed to drag the other two from the wagon. Supporting a man on either side, the leader fell in behind

Sabrina. Followed by the Irishman, who was limping badly, they climbed the windswept rocks until they reached Sabrina's cave above the stream.

Leaving the men behind, Sabrina headed back to obliterate their footprints in the snow as best she could. Carefully she worked her way back down the gorge to the spot above the Union soldier's camp and watched as the Indians systematically erased all signs that the attack had been made by Indians.

It was almost full dark now. She could see only the silhouette of the Indian leader who rode back to the wagon, studied it, then looked around curiously before returning to the white man waiting out of sight beneath the cedar tree just below where she was watching. There was no attempt to keep their conversation quiet. They couldn't have, in any case. The Indians were making far too much noise in their glee over discovering the remaining whiskey.

"I told you not to kill them," the leader said, his voice obviously shaken. Sabrina couldn't get a good look at him, but she recognized the voice as that of Long Rifle.

"Dead men don't talk."

"What about the prisoners? You didn't kill *them*?"

"Not see prisoners," the Indian insisted, more interested in the boots of the enlisted man at his feet than in the escapees. "Prisoners gone."

"Damn, I didn't want—no, maybe that's better. The commander will think that the prisoners escaped, then killed the guards and stole the horses and the munitions."

"Not take horses!" the Indian said. "Horses belong to Gray Warrior now!"

"Fine," Long Rifle agreed, anxious now to get away from the sight of the dead and dying men. "You take the horses. All I want is the pack mules. I can't worry about the prisoners. They won't survive without food and shelter anyway."

Sabrina could tell that the speaker was still disturbed. Gray Warrior gave a harsh laugh and set about directing the collecting of the horses.

Sabrina watched as the white man rode away, only his back visible in the light of the campfire. The Indians were passing the bottles around as they strapped the captured weapons and knapsacks to their horses.

Sabrina waited until they gave a savage cry of victory and rode away. She didn't understand what she'd just seen, and she couldn't desert the Union soldiers any more than she could have left the men inside the wagon. But a quick check appeared to confirm that they'd all been killed and everything of value taken.

Prisoners. Long Rifle had said "prisoners." It made sense now. The wagon wasn't for corpses, it was to transport men, a prison wagon. And she'd set them free. Now the army would be searching for them, and for her as well. She wondered what they had done, why they were wanted, and what would happen to them now. Still, she couldn't just walk off and leave them out there, wounded, with no horses, no food.

Sabrina let out an impatient groan and thought of her mission, of her father still trapped in the cave-in. She needed to be on her way to Boulder City at sunup, not shackled with a bunch of wounded prisoners.

With her pistol still drawn, she returned to the cave.

Colter was quietly caring for his men, making them as comfortable as possible. When he heard her step, he turned.

"Looks like they've gone," she said in a low voice. "You're free to go."

"Free, yes. For that I thank you. But Irish can barely walk. Carl has passed out, and Tyler's head wound has left him addled. I'm afraid we'll have to have your horse."

"No, I have an important mission in Boulder City. I need my horse."

His face was hidden by the darkness, but his size and deceptively loose stance spoke of danger. Sabrina was only now considering the risk she'd taken, allowing herself to be alone with men guilty of heaven only knew what kind of crimes. The one consolation she had was that they thought she was a man. And she did have her gun.

For all the good that would do if the leader of the criminals wanted to take it from her. He seemed physically unimpaired. He could have waited at the entrance of the cave and overpowered her when she returned, and he hadn't.

Now he studied her with a long, searching look. "I don't know what your mission is, but if you'll help us, we'll do whatever we can to help you in return."

She heard the faint drawl in his voice—a man from the South, no doubt. But it was the stern expression on an unreadable face that stopped her—that, and an odd sense of tension that flared when his gaze touched hers. "Your men don't look as if they can help themselves."

"Not my men. Me. I'll—I'll repay your kindness. There must be something you need, something other than killing, that I can do. I give you my word, you will come to no harm."

He was tired. For just a moment he let his composure slip, and she caught a flash of pain in his eyes. Even criminals cared for their own. And who was she to judge what a man had to do when he was threatened? For just a moment she wanted to reach out and comfort him, just as she might one of her sisters.

Her sisters. Papa. Then it came to her—the answer—the way out of the dilemma. The wounded needed care. That took time. This man was offering his services in return. There didn't have to be a wedding. She had four men dependent on her, and one was willing to do whatever was necessary to repay her for her help.

Four prison escapees, with no place to go. Four men who'd just swapped one set of jailers for another. Maybe the little people had heard her. Maybe she'd been given an answer to her prayers.

She didn't have to take a husband. All she had to do was take four prisoners.

"All right," she said, making her decision. "I'll help you. Get your men back to the wagon while I get my horses."

"Horses? More than one?"

"I have my mount and a packhorse. We'll hitch them to the wagon and pull you to a safe place."

"That might not be safe for you," he said.

"Why wouldn't it be? You said I would come to no harm."

"Not from me or my men. But I fear that the soldiers from the fort will be looking for us."

"Aye," the man called Irish agreed. " 'Twould be a risk. Let her go, Captain. I heard the bagpipes playing, and just before we were captured, the little people moved the ground beneath my feet. We'll manage if we're meant to."

Sabrina gasped. Bagpipes? The Irishman had felt the earth move beneath his feet? He'd experienced the same sensation she had earlier at the mine when she'd asked for help. And she'd been sent help. Four men instead of one. If she'd been uncertain before, she was no longer. Now she had to get them home.

"What have you done? What crime?" she asked, her mind already made up that it didn't matter.

"No more than any other soldier in a war," the captain answered, his voice weary and low. "But that doesn't matter now. Just help us get away. No harm will come to you."

"Then let us leave. I'll take you to a place of safety."

He stopped and swore again. "Hell, there is no safe place."

"Put your men in the wagon," Sabrina snapped. "You're in Colorado Territory, not hell."

At least not yet.

3

The expression on the captain's face was unreadable. But the tight lines at the corner of his eyes and the plant of his shoulders clearly said that he would never have returned to the wagon had it not been for his men. He helped each of them back inside, doing what he could to make them comfortable.

Sabrina didn't offer to help. The tension between the two of them had already become so great that she mounted her horse in order to put distance between the officer and herself. At least on the horse she was in a position of authority; she could look down on her captive when he approached her, as he was doing now.

At that moment the moon seemed to vault over the mountain as shiny as one of Lauren's tin dishpans, hanging there as if it were emptying moonlight over them.

His gaze locked with hers and she felt a flutter of unease in her chest. For just a moment there was an open challenge in his eyes, that and more, anger maybe, smoldering and looking for a target.

His gloves were gone, as was his scarf, and she suspected that he'd given both to his men. Wearing a fur-lined canvas jacket with the collar turned up beneath his ears, he pulled his stained Stetson lower so that all she could see were the corded veins in his neck. Still, visible or not, his eyes were watching her defiantly, melded to her gaze as if they were connected. He had a scruffy, light-colored beard, though she decided that he hadn't been able to shave rather than that he consciously chose not to. He was too tall, too lean, and too stern. Standing there in the moonlight, he seemed coiled, like some wild animal ready to strike.

"We'd better not waste any time," she said uneasily. It was well enough that he promised her that no harm would come to her, but he was a criminal, and she would be wise not to trust him, not yet. "There's always the possibility that one of those Indians will decide to come back."

"Indians don't usually attack at night." He continued to stand as if he were jockeying for position, accustomed to and waiting for her to defer control. That, she didn't intend to do. She needed prisoners, not challengers—men who would follow her instructions, not give them.

Sabrina moved her hand into the pocket of her father's oversize coat and clasped the pistol. "Don't give me any trouble, Captain . . . What is your name?"

"Colter, just Colter," he said, his voice almost a dare. "Of the Confederate States of America. Why are you doing this, ma'am?"

She flinched from the raw, hard set of his lips at the mention of the word "ma'am." He knew. "I'd do as much for a hurt animal—even if it didn't have the good manners to appreciate having its life saved."

"Seems to me that the difference between a wild animal and a human being is more than manners. But if that's your measure, I might remind you that I told you my name."

She started, both from the intensity that seemed to flow between them and the truth of his logic. She was equally guilty, it seemed, of being an ill-mannered savage.

"You're right, Captain Colter. I'm Sabrina Alexander, and I'm about to drive this wagon north, into the mountains. If you'd rather walk, I'm certain the horses would appreciate it."

She gave a cluck to the horse and it began to strain, inching the wagon forward. After a few minutes it became obvious that the task was going to be more difficult than Sabrina had realized. The two horses weren't pulling together; they hadn't been trained to share the load of a heavy wagon.

Captain Colter closed the back of the wagon and fastened it shut, then walked around to the other side, where he took the packhorse's reins. By coaxing him he managed to lead them in the proper direction so that they were pulling together. Feeling the bite of pride nudging her, Sabrina slid down to walk along the other side, removing her weight from that which was being pulled.

"Why don't you get inside the wagon, and I'll lead them?" Colter said.

"That would be fine, if you knew where to go."

"Then I assume that you have a destination in mind?"

"I do."

"And how long will it take us to get there? My men are wounded, cold, and hungry. They can't take much more exposure."

"We'll be—there—by breakfast, if we don't have any trouble. Just keep quiet and walk."

He jerked his face to the front, and she could see the grim line of his lips as he bit back his reply. He might take orders to save his men, but Captain Colter wasn't a man used to following instructions. Sabrina suspected it had little to do with the fact that she was a woman. She was beginning to wonder if she'd been as smart as she'd first thought in rescuing the prisoners. Maybe marriage might have been a better choice.

Marriage?

What if she'd picked a man like the captain?

No, this was infinitely better. And she did have the gun. And the other three men were wounded.

Still, there were other problems. If feeding her sisters and the livestock was a problem before, she'd just made it worse. Not only that, but she had no idea how she'd control the man who was fighting her every step of the way.

Papa. She had to focus on her original mission: free Papa so that they could give him a proper burial. Then she'd retrieve their gold nuggets and use them to buy supplies. Once that was done, she'd consider her next move. Until then she'd find a way to keep the prisoners in line.

Mile after mile, one foot after another, they made their way through the snow back to the valley. Sabrina was exhausted. She didn't dare stop or the horses might not be able to move again. It had been hours since she'd even heard a moan from the wagon. The men might be dead for all she could tell, and the captain didn't seem to be inclined to investigate. Rather, it was as if he were caught in some kind of spell that drove him. At last the moon set and the pale fingers of sunlight began to pull themselves over the sides of the valley that was Sabrina's destination.

The horses, catching sight of the barn, drew on the last of their strength and moved briskly toward food and shelter, coming to a stop at the barn door.

The captain stumbled as the packhorse drew to a halt. He'd walked for most of the night on sheer determination, knowing that if he even thought about the next step, he'd collapse. There'd been no food or sleep since they'd camped along the trail in wait for the Union soldiers carrying munitions and the captured weapons the South needed so badly.

How many days ago? Two, three? They'd been given water in Boulder City, but no medical care. Tyler and Carl might be dead by now. And Irish, the burly farmer who'd taken the wound in the leg—had he survived?

Colter gathered the last of his strength and looked around. The strange-looking woman who'd rescued them was opening the barn door, leading the horses inside. He forced himself to follow her, walking on feet that had long lost their feeling, flexing fingers that wouldn't even clasp the reins now dangling by the big packhorse's neck.

"See to your men," the woman directed. "I'll get help."

Colter replayed her words, trying to recall the name she'd given as she walked past him. "Ma'am," he managed, and took a step toward her. Then everything blurred, and like a whirlwind that suddenly deflated, he slumped against her. She stumbled backward against a stall.

Suddenly she was face-to-face with the prisoner, his haggard features closer than she'd ever before seen any man other than her father. She couldn't breathe; she couldn't move. All there was, was the shape of his body pressing against her, the wiry feel of his whiskers tickling her face.

"Captain!" she managed to say sharply. "Don't pass out on me now!"

He didn't fall, but he didn't seem to hear her either. Sabrina braced herself against him, using the stall to keep him upright. Although he was tall, she'd thought him much leaner than the weight she was suddenly supporting. If she let him go, he'd collapse.

"Help!" she called out. "Lauren! Mary!" Surely one of them had heard her drive up. Where were they?

"Sabrina?" It was Lauren who answered. "We didn't recognize the wagon. We weren't sure it was you."

Isabella's stunned voice cut through their shock. "What are you doing, Brina?"

"Trying to hold this man up," Sabrina said. "He is half-unconscious!"

"Oh, I thought you were—I mean it looked like—"

Sabrina didn't want to know what Isabella had thought. She was too confused and exhausted.

"Somebody help me before I drop him."

Moments later Lauren and Mary were helping

Captain Colter to the floor of the barn. They looked at the man and the wagon in disbelief, still unsure of what they were seeing.

"Is he your husband, Sabrina?" Mary finally asked.

"No! He's my prisoner, as are the others. Isabella, don't get too close!"

She was too late with her warning; Isabella was already peering at the men. "There are three more men. Oh, Mary, she's brought one for us. But they're hurt. Brina, did you have to shoot them?"

"I didn't bring them for you, and I certainly didn't shoot them. You're not to touch them. They're prisoners. Stay away!"

"Nonsense, Brina," Lauren was saying. "They're hurt and they need help. Girls, help me get them to the house."

"But the shed," Mary said. "I thought Sabrina said get the shed ready."

Isabella was unfastening the back of the wagon. "There's no heat in the shed. These men need warmth."

Before Sabrina could stop them, Lauren, Isabella, and Mary were inside the wagon, evaluating the men's conditions and making plans. Raven was the only one who'd followed Sabrina's directions. From the doorway where she was standing, she walked over to Sabrina, who was hanging on to the side of one of the stalls, silently cursing her weakness. "Sister, shall I see to the horses?"

"Oh, yes, Raven. They're exhausted and hungry."

"And what about him?"

Sabrina followed the direction of Raven's gaze and fastened on the captain, who seemed to have revived and was struggling to get to his feet. Sabrina swore, used the last of her strength, and moved to his side, adding her weight as a brace while he stood.

"I beg your pardon, ma'am. I suppose it's considered ill-mannered to pass out, but I seem to have exhausted my endurance."

"As have we all," she said, wondering if he, like

her, was still suffering from the shock of his collapse. "Let's get your men inside, where my sisters can see to their wounds."

"Sisters?" Colter allowed the chatter of the women to cut through his confusion. They were pulling Irish to his feet, a petite, brown-haired woman planting herself under the big man's shoulder to help him walk.

"Can you make it, Irish?" the captain asked.

"With the help of these colleens," he managed in a tight voice.

Mary looked up from her examination of the thin, dark man with the head wound. "An Irishman, Isabella, like Papa."

"I think this one is unconscious," Isabella said, cradling the fourth man in her lap. Peeling back his hat, she found a mass of dark curls and a face that was cold and unresponsive. The front of his shirt was stiff with dried blood, and a quick assessment of the wound beneath took her breath away.

"He's lost a lot of blood," Colter said, finding strength that he didn't have to move toward his friend. "We need to get him warm."

The man Mary was tending to forced himself to a sitting position. "Just give me a minute and I'll help."

"Stay put, Tyler, you'll do good to get your own self inside."

In the meantime Raven came toward the wagon dragging a child's homemade sled. "You could use this, but his feet will hang over."

Colter nodded. With the help of the women he managed to pull Carl out of the wagon and lower him to the sled.

Isabella leaned over, took his hand, and squeezed it. "You're going to be all right," she whispered.

For a moment Carl's eyes opened. "An angel with golden hair," he said. "I'm in heaven after all."

Over Carl's body Colter's eyes caught Sabrina's. "Not yet, Carl. I have it on good authority we're still in Colorado."

* * *

Sabrina watched helplessly as Isabella, Mary, and Lauren each appointed herself responsible for one of the men, Raven remaining behind in the barn with the horses.

In spite of what she'd just told the captain, bringing them inside the cabin wasn't what she had planned. Until she had a clear idea of their crimes, she had to restrain her sisters' kind-hearted ministrations.

"Stop it! Stop this minute!"

The girls turned around and stared in disbelief at their older sister.

"But they're hurt," Isabella said. "They need our help."

"These men could be—" *Dangerous.* But she couldn't say it, couldn't put her sisters in a position of fear. They'd been taught to be kind and caring to anything injured, and Sabrina knew they wouldn't understand the risk.

"They're soldiers," Captain Colter said. "Confederate soldiers who will be grateful for your help no matter which side you support."

"We take no sides," Sabrina blurted out. "We have no concern for your futile war."

"And we will offer you safe haven," Lauren said positively, "no matter what Sabrina says. Papa wouldn't have allowed us to behave badly."

"Papa wouldn't turn away anyone who was hurt," Mary added solemnly, making a pallet of quilts near the fire.

They were right. But Papa would never have exposed them to criminals, as she had. Now her sisters began to take on their normal roles: Lauren the mother figure, Mary the peacemaker, Isabella the adventurer. Sabrina shook her head wearily. How could she explain that the men had been held as prisoners, guilty of God knew what? In her mind they were to be miners, hired hands who would perform badly needed tasks around the cabin. She hadn't considered their appeal to her sisters. She hadn't considered anything beyond a profound relief that she wouldn't have to marry.

"Don't worry," a tired voice said in her ear. "We

won't harm you or you sisters. I promised you that we'd return your kindness, and I'll see that my men behave like true southern gentlemen."

Frustration swept over Sabrina—frustration and a strange, achy feeling of uncertainty that she couldn't identify. This was what she wanted. But dare she trust Captain Colter? Did she have any other choice?

No was her answer to both questions.

"All right, I'll hold you to that," she said, "and I'll shoot you myself if you or your men harm my family in any way. Do you understand?"

"I understand, but now I think that I need to sit down before I fall again. Point me to a place where I won't be in the way."

Sabrina glanced at his face and saw the glazed look in his eyes. Blue eyes, she noted, weary blue eyes that were trying valiantly to hold on to her face as he waited.

"There, you may take Papa's bunk." She inclined her head to indicate the bunk in the corner, then made a move to assist him, only to catch the frosty disdain of his frown.

"Fine, get there under your own power, Captain." She didn't have to be told that he would. This man obviously traveled alone, and had for a long time. A man might become one of his band, but not without proving himself first, and she was sure that he never allowed anyone to get close.

Stiffly, as if he'd been starched and hung out to dry in the desert sun, he moved toward the bunk, collapsing into it without a word. He wanted to inquire about the man whose bed he was to occupy. Where was he? What would he do when he returned? But he was too tired to think about anything. Now he needed rest. Now he'd sleep.

Sabrina watched him collapse into the rope bed and close his eyes. She ought to tie him up, she thought. Then Raven was there, taking her arm. "You rest too, Brina. You've done what you set out to do."

"But I can't. I have to make sure that these men

don't—I mean, I don't dare leave soldiers alone with our sisters."

"They're half-dead, Brina. They can do nothing now. Besides, I think the only man in this group we might have to fear is too tired to be a threat."

Raven covered the captain with a wool blanket and turned back to see that her sister was complying with her directions. For once Sabrina obeyed, stretching out on her bunk fully clothed. She was asleep before Raven removed her boots and her hat.

Raven watched as Lauren, Mary, and Isabella ministered to the injured men. She nodded her head and turned to go back to the barn. As she had for most of her life, she felt now there was no place for her here.

The smell of coffee woke Sabrina, that and the sound of whispers, followed by an admonishment from Mary.

"I think you'd better be careful, Isabella. He might wake up."

"If he didn't wake while I was washing and treating his wound, I don't think he's going to now. I wish he would. I don't want to lose him."

Mary gasped. "You mean he might die?"

"I don't think so. He seems warmer and his color is better. What color do you suppose his eyes are? I'll bet they're blue. No, green, like the moss that grows by the creek in summer."

Sabrina cracked her eyelids and took in the scene by the fireplace. The three wounded men were stretched out on pallets; the big Irishman was sitting up, leaning against the wall of the cabin, an unusually solemn Lauren feeding him from a bowl. Mary was crouched beside the tall, slim soldier with the scalp wound, and Isabella was holding the third man's head in her lap while she wiped his face. Fresh bandages covered his bare chest, bandages that looked suspiciously like the ruffle from Isabella's best petticoat.

Sabrina cast a swift glance around the room. What kind of caretaker was she? Her entire plan had likely fallen apart while she'd been sleeping. The girls were mooning over the soldiers, and nowhere in the room could she see Captain Colter. He was gone.

"Isabella!" Sabrina said, coming to a sitting position faster than her body approved. An arrow of pain sliced across her shoulders, ran down her arms, and culminated in her hands as a sharp reminder of her activities for the last five days, since the cave-in. "Get away from that man, Isabella. Lauren, where is Captain Colter?"

Isabella gave the soldier with the dark, curly hair a final dab with the rag she'd been holding and slipped his head to the goosedown-stuffed pillow on the floor. "I don't know why you have to be so sharp, Brina. He doesn't know I'm here, anyway."

Lauren lowered the bowl she was holding and turned to look at Sabrina with a concerned frown. "The captain has gone hunting, Brina, to find a rabbit for a stew."

Sabrina forced herself to stand, reaching for her jacket at the same time. "I'll just bet he has. I suppose you gave him a gun?"

Mary came to Sabrina's assistance as she stood. "We gave him Papa's rifle, Sabrina. There's little left to eat, we couldn't refuse his kind offer."

Sabrina bit back a sharp reprimand. How could her sisters be expected to understand the danger in arming a man like Colter? She hadn't been honest with them. She wasn't even certain how she felt about the officer. She didn't fool herself; he could have overpowered her if he'd really wanted to. His willpower and strength were obvious. Through the night he'd accompanied her every step of the way and still gone after food this morning.

She wasn't entirely sure whether it was his being gone that bothered her, or the idea that he was looking after her sisters when she should be doing so herself. Even Papa had been loath to go hunting in bad weather. Only Sabrina knew that her father's eyesight in the last years kept him from hitting the broad side of a barn unless he was within five feet of it. Sabrina alone was the hunter, the woodcutter, the provider.

Now someone else was filling her shoes, and it left her feeling a little empty inside.

If that was, in fact, what he was doing.

"You don't have to worry, ma'am," Irish said in a reassuring voice. "The captain is a trustworthy man."

Honorable? Maybe. But he'd been a prisoner, under arrest for God only knew what, and now he had a rifle. She'd better go out and check on his whereabouts. She looked around for a weapon until she realized that Papa's pistol was still in her jacket pocket, and that she was still wearing her gloves. Heading for the door, she struggled into her coat and glanced at the wounded men only long enough to decide that at the moment the prisoners were little threat. More likely, the threat was of their being nursed to death.

"Brina, don't you want something to eat first?" Lauren took the corner of her apron and wiped Irish's mouth.

"Not now. Where's Raven?"

The three sisters looked around in surprise. "I don't know," Lauren admitted. "I'm sorry, Sabrina. I guess we weren't paying attention. You know how she is about disappearing. Maybe she's gone with the captain."

Sabrina felt her heart lurch. Raven routinely went into the mountains and visited with her Arapaho mother's tribe. They'd long ago ceased to worry about her safety. But Raven out in the snow with Colter? That was different. Sabrina hurried out the door, leaving her shamefaced sisters behind.

The path to the barn had been cleared, and she could see the evidence of a man's boot print and Raven's smaller step behind him. Sabrina hurried, feeling stiff and clumsy from muscles that ached with every step.

In the barn Raven had spread the last of the grass for the horses and the cow. She was holding the bucket of precious seed that they'd planned to plant for next summer's kitchen garden. The chickens were gathered around, pecking at the few pieces of grain she'd thrown to them.

"Brina!" Raven said quietly. "Are you all right?"

"I'm worried right now, Raven. Where is Captain Colter?"

"He went out to find a squirrel or a rabbit."

"And how long has he been gone?"

"Since early morning. It seems that you selected well, Sabrina. He's not only concerned about feeding us, but about our safety."

"Safety? What do you mean?"

"He asked all kinds of questions about the valley, the distance to Boulder City, and the fort. He wants to scout the area so we won't be caught by surprise if the soldiers come looking for them."

Questions? About the valley, Boulder City, and the fort? That bothered Sabrina. Why would he care about their safety? Fear of the soldiers searching for their prisoners was the reasonable answer. Or perhaps he was already planning his escape. "Raven, the captain can't be trusted. If he has questions, let him ask me."

"But, Brina, the captain seems honorable. Why are you so suspicious?"

"I don't know," Sabrina admitted. She just knew that he seemed too good to be true. "I don't think he's to be trusted. We don't know enough about him. Not yet."

"It is your decision, Brina, but I think he has a kind heart. I trust him. He said he'd return as soon as he could. After he brings food for us, he's going to find feed for the animals."

He was winning over her sisters, even Raven, who normally reserved judgment by maintaining silence. It wasn't like Raven to voice open approval.

"And after that he's going to part the waters of the Red Sea and lead us to the Promised Land!" Sabrina's sharp voice came from pure frustration.

"Don't have to, not this morning," an amused male voice said as its owner stamped his boots on the floor behind Sabrina. "I can walk on any water in this area, and I can't claim credit for that. It's all frozen."

Sabrina whirled around, her hand safely in her pocket if the pistol was needed. The captain was holding two rabbits out to Raven, and across his back was a small deer.

"Oh," Sabrina said, both relieved and chagrined. She should be thanking him, but something held her back, something akin to envy that someone other than herself had provided for the family. She considered what Isabella was going to say when he took the deer inside, and felt secretly pleased at what was likely to occur. Food was necessary, but if her golden-haired sister could manage to avoid killing to eat, she would. The animals' sad, accusing eyes always bothered Isabella. As Sabrina watched, Colter's own eyes lost their amusement, and he cast a look of sad accusation on Sabrina.

"Rabbits and a deer," Raven said. "Mother Earth was generous today. I'll dress the rabbits for a nice stew." She took the animals and started toward the house.

There was a long silence as the captain watched Raven walk away. "She has a strange way of speaking," he finally said, "as if she's older than we are. Why is that?"

"It's her Indian ancestry. She never knew her mother, but she visits often with her grandfather and his tribe, where she learns the Indian ways. And somehow she seems to sense certain things that the rest of us don't. Pale Raven was like that. Papa said that as she was dying, she transferred her Indian self to Raven."

His eyebrows lifted. "Her mother was an Indian?"

"Yes."

"And she's your sister?"

Before the cave-in Sabrina would never have discussed her family, but this morning it seemed the safest topic they could address. "My father had three wives. My mother was his first. She died when I was five years old."

"And your name is Sabrina. Tyler says that means 'from the Land of the Sabine.' "

It was Sabrina's turn to be surprised. The two men must have discussed her this morning while she was still sleeping.

"Yes," she said without elaboration. She knew, of course, of the land of the Sabine women; it had been one of her Papa's favorite tales, the one he always recalled when he was justifying the site for his newest mine, the Rome of the West. Sabrina would be the first lady of the City of Alexander. Cullen Alexander had chosen all his children's names. Lauren had been named for his first mining partner, Mary for his mother, Isabella for a dance hall girl who'd once been kind to him, and Raven for his third wife.

Sabrina didn't like knowing that Colter had been discussing her with his men. What else had they talked about? Escape? That was to be expected. But the meaning of her name—that was personal. It rattled her and she didn't understand why.

"I'd prefer that your men not talk about me, Captain. I . . . I appreciate what you did this morning, hunting for food, but I'll take the rifle now. As my prisoner, you understand that I can't allow you to keep a weapon."

She knew how ineffectual that sounded, declaring him to be her prisoner while he towered over her with a gun in his hand. But Sabrina refused to exhibit any sign of weakness. He had to agree to her wishes. If he would not, she might as well know it now.

"Your prisoner?" He finally said, his expression reflecting the impossibility of her claim. "I may be here because you rescued my men and I promised to repay you. I may stay because you need my help. But make no mistake, I am not now, nor will I ever again be, a prisoner."

He handed her the rifle, glancing at her gloved hands without comment as he let the deer drop to the floor. "I'll dress the beast and tie him out of the reach of wild animals. My guess is that the storm has ended, but the cold will linger for several days before the snow melts."

And just as quickly the confrontation was over. It

wasn't settled, but it was temporarily put aside for the good of all. Sabrina had no choice but to go along for now.

"And how much experience have you had with snow, Captain Colter? Your voice sounds very southern."

"I was southern once."

"What are you now?"

"I don't know, and at this moment I can't say I give much of a damn."

"Oh, I think you do, Colter. Otherwise you'd be long gone. You just hide your emotions very well."

He looked as if he were going to argue, then frowned and picked up the deer once more. "Go back inside, Miss Sabrina Alexander, unless you intend to butcher this deer yourself, not that I doubt that you could."

"I could, I generally do."

"You chop the wood, get the food, and care for the women. In short, you're a paragon of virtue. Well, let me tell you, lady, if you want to be a man, you're halfway there. You look like hell!"

Her reply was quick, born of hurt, and of determination not to let him rattle her. " 'Hell'—that's one of your favorite words, isn't it, Captain? I hope you don't think I intend to allow you to take over and give your men free rein. My sisters are very inexperienced with men, and I won't let them be hurt!"

"You think my men will hurt your sisters?"

"I don't know anything about you or your men. Until I do, I'll make certain that they don't."

Colter didn't want to admit it, but he was beginning to feel a grudging respect for the woman standing before him. He didn't doubt that she'd been the man of the house. Whatever she'd been doing was hard work that had left her physically exhausted. Still, she'd led the horses to safety, saved his men without complaint. He didn't doubt for a minute that she'd defend her sisters with her dying breath.

Her eyes, a curious hazel color, almost green, were large and grave, staring at him now, daring him to

challenge her authority. A strand of auburn hair had
worked itself from beneath the stained hat she was
wearing, and hung down by her cheek. Its rich color
seemed out of place on the plain, gawky woman, a
misdirection even, as if she wanted to confuse a man.

Whatever the reason for her stubbornness, the tension continued to flare between them, tension that was
out of place in a life that long ago had been carefully
purged of emotion. He didn't like the way she made
him feel. He didn't want to be responsible for five
women. Directing a fighting unit was a mechanical,
emotionless duty. But the bareness of the shelves over
the cookstove this morning had brought back memories of his mother and his sisters, and those memories
struck at the icy core of his being.

Looking after five women was opening a pathway
to the past, and that, he'd sworn never to do. Were it
not for his men, he'd gone before dark, heading for
California or the frozen tundra of the far north. But he
couldn't do that. Not yet. The failure of his mission
gnawed at him. And failure was one thing he couldn't
tolerate.

Sharing the women's cabin would be a necessary
evil while he avoided the Yankee soldiers who were
certain to be searching for him and his men. Their losing the munitions and the guns to the Indians did not
mean Colter's mission had been canceled—it had just
been temporarily postponed. They were still under
orders to find weapons and supplies for General Lee.

Until his men were ready to move out, he was going to consider the arrangement an exchange of services. Finding food had seemed the logical first step
toward payment for a place of refuge. But he'd expected some kind of appreciation. Instead the woman
had seemed disturbed, angry that he'd brought food.

"Look, Miss Alexander, you're in a bad way
around here, and I really don't think you're in a position to be choosy about accepting my help. Until your
father comes back from wherever he is, I'll keep you in
food and wood. In return I'll expect you to care for my
men."

"My father isn't—"' She broke off. She needed to be careful. His belief that Papa would be coming back was a kind of protection, but that deception defeated the purpose of her bringing him to the valley. He couldn't help free her father from the cave-in unless she told him he was there.

"Your father isn't what?"

She'd gone this far, she might as well go all the way. If she couldn't count on his help, there was no point in keeping those men around. In fact, from what she'd already seen back in the cabin, their staying might be a greater risk than trusting the captain.

"My father isn't coming back. That's why you're here."

Colter watched her face turn white. Then, as if she were a prisoner ready to mount the steps to the gallows, she straightened her shoulders and braced herself.

"Was he in the war? If so, he might not be dead. There are hundreds of men in prison camps. Once the war is over . . ."

"No, he wasn't in the war. Come with me, Captain. I'll show you the real reason why I brought you here. It wasn't because of my kind heart."

"I wondered when you'd get around to it."

"It will be a bit of a hike. Are you physically up to it?"

He smiled. "After what I've been through in the last four years, Miss Alexander, there isn't much I can't handle. After all, didn't you choose a man who can part the Red Sea *and* walk on water?"

4
─

Colter's trousers were smeared with icy streaks from the fresh snow deposited during the night. As he moved up the valley he felt as if his lungs were bursting as he drew in the crisp Colorado mountain air.

Even Sabrina, who was accustomed to making the climb, was breathing hard. She'd weathered the aftermath of such storms before, but never had one come at a worse time. First the cave-in, then more snow. The elements, fate, or even Papa's little people seemed to be conspiring against her. Now she raised her eyes, measuring the route up the valley to the side of the mountain where the mine entrance was located.

Because of her exhaustion she'd slept far too long this morning. Then, after she'd found the captain, she'd had to wait for him to clean and store the deer. Now it was late morning and there was no more reason for delay.

More than ever she wished that she'd never brought the wounded men to the valley. As unkind as it seemed, perhaps it would have been better to leave

Papa where he was and forget the silver. She was sure that if he'd been allowed to choose, he couldn't have wished for a more fitting burial spot.

But that would mean forgoing the possibility of mining the silver, and leaving their only money buried along with Papa. She knew that doing so wouldn't please him. She was only trying to justify her cowardice, trying without success. There were her sisters to consider and her responsibility for providing for them. And there was her father's claim that he'd found silver. She could almost hear Papa admonishing her to hurry, to dig through the rubble and prove that the Silver Dream wasn't a dream any longer; Alexander City was just ahead.

Sabrina let out a big sigh and moved forward. The wind currents in the valley pushed against her, blowing the snow away from the rocks and down toward the house, then died down again. The sun-splattered snow was so bright that she had to squint her eyes against the glare. A few more feet and they'd leave most of the drifts behind. Then a fresh current swept down the canyon, setting off the familiar sound that Papa had likened to bagpipe music.

"What's that?" Captain Colter asked as he stopped and listened.

"You heard it?"

She looked surprised when he nodded.

"Papa said it was the little people playing their pipes. I think it's the wind hitting some rock formation that makes the sound."

Colter gave her a quick, startled look. "Little people? Sounds like something Irish said the other day—that he heard the sound of bagpipes and felt the earth move."

Sabrina gave the captain a quick glance. She hadn't really believed in her father's yarns, and she tried not to give them life by admitting that she too had heard the sound of the bagpipes. Now this stranger had heard them. "Yes, well," she admitted reluctantly, "he's Irish. Perhaps he and my father kissed the same Blarney stone."

She started forward again.

"You don't believe in legends?"

"I believe in reality, Captain Colter. That's the only thing that you can count on."

He simply nodded. He understood that kind of logic; he'd adopted that philosophy a long time ago. For two reluctant companions, they shared a remarkable similarity of views. She took on life and fought it for her family, and he was doing much the same thing for his men.

Seeing her in the daylight, from behind, was having an odd effect on his opinion of her gawky body. He realized that the bulky men's trousers and jacket she habitually wore hid her figure well. He felt his pulse quicken and forced his mind away from her physical attributes. He'd simply been too long without a woman. Even this sharp-tongued shrew was beginning to look good.

"Where are we going?" he asked.

Sabrina looked up at the mountain. "Up there."

"Any particular reason why we're going mountain climbing in snowdrifts?"

"Yes."

"Are you going to explain?"

"Presently."

They made the rest of the climb in silence. Colter understood that Sabrina wasn't used to casual conversation. She wasn't used to dealing with outsiders, and he was beginning to understand that though her heart was kind, she would never have brought him here out of simple altruism. She was a woman who knew what she wanted, made a plan, and moved relentlessly toward her goal. He wondered if her single-mindedness was born of dedication or of necessity, then decided that they were one and the same.

Colter wondered what in hell she did to keep herself from going crazy up here. Apparently her family had been here since Raven was born. Fifteen years without friends or neighbors, or normal conveniences like a well or a second room on the house. He hadn't stayed in one place for long since the war had started.

He'd expected one day to get back to the plantation, and to take up its management when his father decided it was time.

There was no father now, no plantation, no family. The storms of war had burned the Colters out and their dream along with it. Now he was like the wind hurling first one way, then another. Movement suited him. It made the forgetting easier. His self-proclaimed jailer, on the other hand, took her pain with her, corseting it silently and tightly inside.

Sabrina came to a stop at the burrowed-out tunnel in the side of the mountain. There were piles of dirt and rock deposited near the entrance, as if they'd been dropped there in the interest of speed rather than practicality. For a long moment the woman just stood there, as if she'd forgotten he was behind her.

He'd seen reluctance before, but never accompanied by such regret, not even during the war. Whatever her purpose, she was fulfilling it with a struggle. He found himself trying to make it easy for her.

"Is there something wrong, Miss Alexander?"

"Yes! No! Not wrong, but I will ask you to make a promise before I explain."

"A promise without an explanation? That's asking me to take a big chance, don't you think?"

"I took a big chance," she said. "There is nothing you can ever do that will be as risky as the chance I've taken. My sisters' futures depend on you and whether I've chosen wisely, and God help me, I don't know."

"What's the problem?"

"That what you see will remain here. That you won't try to take advantage of me or my family. That you'll do what I ask."

He studied her without comment. If she expected him to ask questions or to bargain, she was going to be disappointed. He'd already learned enough about Miss Sabrina Alexander to know that there was no pretense about her. If she'd been a man, she'd be known as a handshake man, whose word was his bond. Then, as if she'd accepted his silence as his consent, or decided that ultimately it didn't matter, she took a step inside and waited for him to follow.

He did, straight into a wall of dirt, from which two shovels protruded and a crude wheelbarrow on which a pick had been laid.

"This is why you're here," she said simply. "My father is caught in that wall of dirt. I need help in freeing him."

"My God. How long ago did this happen?"

"Five days. He set off a charge of dynamite and the tunnel collapsed. I—we couldn't get to him."

"That's why you brought us here."

"Yes, in part." She felt the bravado melt away as desperation overcame her. "Will you help me?"

Colter walked back and forth in front of the mound of dirt. "Where did he set the charge, which side?"

"In the wall on the right, leading deeper into the mountain."

"Then he would have most likely moved away from the charge, which should put him on this side." He picked up the shovel and began to fill the crude wheelbarrow with earth. Sabrina fell in beside him, moving rocks and emptying the wheelbarrow when it was full.

Noon came and they were joined by Mary, who brought a pail of rabbit stew and bread. "Stop and eat," she urged. "It won't do for both of you to get sick; we already have enough patients."

"How are the—*prisoners*?" Sabrina asked.

"They're not prisoners, Brina. They explained what happened. They're just soldiers who were captured by other soldiers, all fighting over something they don't even want."

"Oh?" Captain Colter's voice lifted in dry amusement. "What's that, Miss Mary?"

"Worn-out land that won't belong to any of you, no matter what you do. At least that's what Papa said the country was destroying itself over."

"That's about as good an interpretation of what

we were doing as I've heard," the captain agreed, and helped himself to a dipper of the stew.

Mary handed a bowl to Sabrina and filled it. "Mr. Irish has made himself a crutch. Mr. Arnstine has finally awakened, though he's pretty weak."

"And Tyler?" Captain Colter asked.

Sabrina couldn't help but notice Mary's blush. "Tyler, I mean Mr. Kurtz, has a lump on his head. He's got a big headache, but he's able to move about now without keeling over. What about—Papa?"

"No sign of him yet," Sabrina answered, turning up her bowl and drinking the last of the stew before she handed the container back to Mary.

Captain Colter copied her action, drinking from the bowl and resuming his own digging.

"Shall I help, Brina?" Mary asked.

Sabrina only shook her head in refusal. There was little room, and as slowly as they seemed to be moving, Mary would only get in the way.

"Are you sure? Your hands must be hurting something awful," Mary argued.

"I'm fine, sister. Go back to the house and keep an eye on the prisoners."

"Soldiers," Mary corrected, gathering up her soup bucket. "You'll change your mind about them, Brina, once you get to know them. Mr. Kurtz was a professor. He's a very nice man."

Sabrina wanted to reprimand her sister, remind her that they knew only what they were being told, but she refrained. The best thing for her to do was to get the job done as quickly as possible, get rid of the men, and then she and her sisters could get on with their lives.

Filled with frustration, she grabbed a rock that was too heavy. It twisted in her hands, and she let out a groan and dropped it.

Colter drove his shovel into the dirt and turned back to Sabrina. He pulled a package of matches from his boot and lit the lantern hanging from an exposed tree root. Then he set it down beside Sabrina and held out his hand.

"Let me see them."

Sabrina's eyes opened wide, both at the nearness of the man and the firm command in his voice. "What? What are you doing? Get back to work!"

"Your hands, let me see them."

When she made no effort to comply, he reached down and jerked her wrist forward, into the light. Carefully he removed the glove, then the strips of cloth she'd wrapped around her palms.

"Good God, woman, your hands are a bloody mess!"

"Release me, Captain Colter. They're my hands, and I'll take care of them when Papa is free."

She didn't want to feel the tenderness of his touch, the gentleness in his grasp as he ran one fingertip over the broken blisters.

He ignored her. Stripping the bandages from the other hand to reveal more raw skin, he swore. He couldn't begin to understand this kind of courage from a woman. She'd obviously done this to herself, trying to free her father. Then she'd ridden for help, found the prisoner's wagon, and spent the night pulling the reins of the horse to guide them back here.

What kind of pain must she have felt? And she'd never given any indication of the extent of her problem. He wasn't certain he could have done that. Now she'd spent the morning lifting rocks and emptying the wheelbarrow.

Moving his fingertips from her open palms, he lifted her chin so that he could see into the eyes of Sabrina Alexander. In the hazy light of the lantern, hazel eyes and blue-gray eyes caught and held for a long, silent moment.

He'd been wrong about her lack of grace. She was tall, but not clumsy. She'd simply been exhausted and forcing herself to keep moving—a woman who was accustomed to hard physical work and didn't know how to stop.

Back in South Carolina, with her face shielded by a bonnet, her skin would have been that pale, alabaster shade of a redhead. But here her skin was bronzed from the elements, the color deepening as she became aware of his scrutiny. He ought to move away, let go of her hand and step back. But he continued to look down at her.

Then, surprising himself, he ripped the stained brown hat from her head, allowing the mass of auburn hair to fall across her shoulders. The woman was—

"Beautiful," he said, the word slipping out without his being aware that he'd spoken.

Sabrina stared at him blankly, feeling as if she were two people, the one standing back and watching the other caught in some fantasy dream spell that Raven's Indian people might have talked of.

"You must have loved your father very much to do this to yourself," he went on as if he were unaware of his startling reaction to her hair.

"Yes. Please release me." Her voice had softened into a kind of whimper that even she didn't recognize.

"You need a doctor."

She gave a light laugh. "That seems a little strange, considering our situation. Four wounded men being treated by Indian medicines, administered by simple women."

He grimaced and let out a deep sigh. "Damn this war and what it's done to innocent people."

"The war didn't kill my father," she said. "He did it himself, because he—" She stopped herself. Whether or not she allowed the captain to know everything depended on so many things she wasn't ready to decide yet. "Because he wasn't always a careful man. He was inclined to be impulsive, like Isabella."

"Carl is like that. I have to keep a tight rein on him."

"Carl, the one with the shoulder wound, the one Isabella seems to have taken as her patient?"

"Yes. Strange, isn't it, how they chose each other without knowing how well matched they are?"

"Don't say that!"

There was a sound at the entrance to the cave. "Captain?"

Colter dropped the woman's hand, glad for the interruption. Intimate moments laced with tension and need were forbidden. He didn't know how he'd allowed himself to drop his guard.

He wouldn't have, if he hadn't seen her hands.

He'd seen hands like that before, slaves' hands, Moe's back when he'd been whipped. Moe had suffered in silence, just like Sabrina.

"Tyler? Come in. How'd you get up here?"

"Mary, I mean Miss Mary Alexander, sent me. We decided that I was steady enough to give you a hand. She sent this to you, Miss Sabrina." He handed Sabrina a tin. "For your hands."

"What is it?" Colter asked.

Sabrina opened the tin, took a whiff, and groaned. "Some of Raven's concoctions—probably bear grease with healing herbs added to the brew."

Sabrina took the ointment and began to spread it on her palms. Only now had they begun to hurt. They felt as if they'd been frozen until Colter had taken them in his large hands and thawed them out. She didn't welcome this pain, for it came from intimacy, from this connection between them that continued to simmer, then burst powerfully alive on contact.

She had rescued him, true. Now he was coming to her aid, but that was all. It was the same as an eye for an eye in the Bible. One deed in exchange for another. There was no warmth in the exchange and no need for dependency. Still, she wasn't foolish enough not to recognize that there was something between them, something unnamed and unwanted. And she'd do well to keep herself from touching the man, or allowing him to touch her.

She watched him now as his strong arms slammed the shovel into the narrowing wall of dirt and pulled back, his trousers tight against the whipcord muscles in his thighs, his body still firm, though it was obvious that he too had suffered. In another time, if she'd seen him in town, or passing by in one of the express wagons, she might have noticed a strong face filled with resolve. Colter was not a man given to frivolous notions. But a part of her wondered if once, in some other time, he might have joined her papa in a drink of Irish whiskey and a tall tale or two.

Colter. She'd tried not to refer to the prisoner by name. So long as he was "the captain," he was anonymous. Now, in spite of her efforts, he had a name. It was a crisp, clean name that matched the sharp, finely chiseled lines of his face.

Throughout the afternoon the two men dug, with Tyler resting frequently and Colter moving steadily. Then he stopped and moved back.

"Tyler, help me."

"What is it?" Sabrina came to her feet.

"No, stay back, Miss Alexander. I think we've reached your father. Let's move the rest of the dirt away at the top, Tyler."

Carefully, shovelful by shovelful, they uncovered the crushed body of Cullen Alexander until they were able to pull him out.

"Go to the house, Sabrina, and prepare a place," Colter said. "We'll bring him down."

"Then he is—"

"Yes, he's dead. My guess from the bruise on his head is that he fell and knocked himself out. He never knew what happened."

"He couldn't move fast enough," Sabrina said softly. He'd fallen and hit his head as he tried to hurry.

Until that moment Sabrina had harbored some secret hope that he might have been caught behind the wall of dirt, that there might have been a pocket of air that could sustain him. But he was dead. At least he hadn't suffered. Sabrina didn't know whether the lick on the head had been responsible or not, but she clung to that thought as she hurried down the valley. That, and Colter's words, which had been meant to comfort her. She hadn't expected as much.

The shed that the women had prepared for Sabrina's husband would be used instead to hold Cullen Alexander until they could thaw the ground

enough to dig a grave. A spot was selected and the
snow was dug away. Dismantling the army wagon on
the grave site, Colter set it afire.

Tyler seemed to be back to normal, and while the
fire burned, he brought in a haunch of the deer to be
roasted. Sabrina, unusually submissive, sat in her father's chair before the fire and allowed her hands to be
treated and wrapped.

The fat from the deer sizzled as it hit the coals,
sending off a good smell. The heat warmed the room
and the quiet whispers of the women created a kind of
reverence in the house, until Lauren handed Irish his
evening meal.

"Broth! By all the saints, woman, I need food! Cut
me off a chunk of that meat and some bread."

"You need nourishment and liquid, Mr. McBride,
and this is what I'm giving you. Drink it down, every
drop. I'm going to stand over you until you do."

Sabrina hadn't often heard her sister raise her
voice, and she was surprised to hear it directed toward the giant-size man she was leaning over. He
could send her flying with a flick of his wrist. Sabrina
started to her feet, prepared to defend her sister
against the bully.

To her surprise he grinned sheepishly and took the
cup, draining it in one long gulp. "Now, darlin'," he
said softly, "would you be so kind as to give me a
smidgen of that meat? I'm certain 'twould do me great
good."

Lauren smiled and, taking a cloth in her hand,
loosened one end of the spit so that she could swing
the rod out of the fire. She sliced off chunks of the outside meat, then moved the meat back over the fire to
continue to cook. With the deer she served a bowl of
hominy corn and biscuits made from the last of their
flour.

The other men ate hungrily, including the one Colter had identified as Carl, the saloon keeper, who was
allowed only broth.

"How is he?" Sabrina asked Lauren.

"Like Irish's leg, the bullet passed through his

shoulder. It's a miracle. He lost a lot of blood, but it must have missed the lungs."

"No infection?" Colter's voice was quiet. It was obvious that he didn't want the answer to carry.

Lauren poured hot water into her dishpan and began to wash the dishes with sand from a box by the stove. The last of her soap was being saved for more important purposes. "Nothing that Raven can't handle," she answered.

"Raven?" He'd heard the earlier reference to Raven's concoctions. Of the sisters she seemed the one most unlike the others. Still, this confidence in a younger sister caught the captain by surprise.

"Raven has learned a great deal from her mother's tribe. She slipped off this morning while you were in the mine and came back with some moss and roots."

Colter walked over to where Carl was being spoonfed by Isabella. The firelight danced across her hair, turning the golden color into a crown. From the look in Carl's eyes, Colter decided that Sabrina was right to worry. Carl liked the ladies and the ladies liked him. And this one was vulnerable and asking for trouble each time she leaned over to put the spoon in Carl's mouth.

"I'll do that," he said, inserting himself between Carl and the girl. "How are you?" he asked his friend, scooping up broth into the spoon.

"Guess we'll have to change my name to Lucky," he managed weakly, "though your sour puss isn't as easy on the digestion as the angel who's been caring for me."

"Never mind angels, just get well. You're in no condition to be chasing women, and this one definitely isn't one you should be interested in."

"Chasing may be a bit beyond me for now, but I'm afraid you're too late with the warning. I've fallen in love."

Colter shoved the spoon into the friend's mouth with more force than necessary. "You've been unconscious. You don't know what love is."

Carl's weak smile vanished, replaced with a surprisingly firm scowl. "Sometimes, you know," he insisted, "only a fool folds when he draws an ace to complete a full house."

Sabrina, sitting quietly in the rocking chair, suddenly stood, grabbed her jacket from the peg by the door, and left the cabin. She'd heard every word exchanged between Colter and the soldier who'd called himself Lucky. She'd seen the look in Isabella's eyes, and she didn't like what she saw. The situation was volatile. And for the first time Sabrina was beginning to understand that her sisters were truly grown women with needs of their own.

It was only then that she realized the significance of Colter's actions. In order to bury her father, he'd destroyed the wagon he could have used to transport his men.

She suddenly felt small, vulnerable, like Pandora, the woman in one of the stories in Mama's book.

And she'd just opened the box.

Three days later they held a quiet service and buried Cullen Alexander on a small hill beneath a cottonwood tree.

There were no flowers, just a spray of swelled pussy willows broken off a bush protected by the thick limbs of the spruce trees beside the stream.

Tyler Kurtz recited a sonnet, and Irish surprised them all when he began singing, his beautiful tenor voice sending Cullen to his final resting with an Irish lullaby. To an outsider it might have seemed out of place, but Sabrina knew that her father would pronounce it as just right.

The ground was still half-frozen, but Colter's men managed to fill the hole. In another month the earth could be tamped and the mound evened up. A cross had been fashioned from tree limbs, and Tyler hammered it into the ground.

Afterward everyone walked down the hill, back toward the house, leaving Sabrina staring down at the grave.

"I can't believe you're gone, Papa," she whispered. 'You're the one who was always there. No matter how many times you left us, you always came back."

But he was gone. And Sabrina was alone, and there was so much to decide.

"When are you going to tell me the rest of it?"

Sabrina whirled around. "I thought you left with the others, Captain."

"That's what I wanted to tell you. I plan to go, at first light."

"Go? Where?"

"The animals have to have food. Your sisters are cooking the last chicken. There is no more flour and the only beans are in the pot. We've exhausted your means by coming here."

"But you've hunted for meat."

"Cows and horses don't eat meat. They need oats. I didn't want you to think I was trying to *escape*," he said sternly. "That's why I'm telling you."

Sabrina dropped her head, guilt flushing her face. That was exactly what she would have imagined. Suddenly the unwanted thought welled up inside her. Suppose he didn't come back? She pushed that idea away, refusing to consider what prompted it. She couldn't let him leave yet. There was still the rest of the cave-in to be removed so that they could begin to shore up the mine.

There was no way she could go out and recruit another man. More than ever she was convinced that no man would have her for a wife, and judging a man was nothing like studying rock formations. She simply didn't have the knowledge to go in search of a replacement for Colter. She couldn't allow him to leave.

"I'm going with you," she announced, startling even herself with that pronouncement.

"That wouldn't be smart, Miss Alexander, traveling with an escaped prisoner—alone."

"I'll take my chances. Besides, if someone asks, I can always say I captured you."

"That wasn't exactly what I was thinking about. Of course"—his lip quirked for a second, then straightened out—"if someone asks, I could say that you've run away with me."

"Be serious, Colter. Nobody who knows me would ever believe that."

"And how many people are we likely to run into who know you that well?"

"Unless we cross paths with some of Pale Raven's tribe, or one of the traders, probably nobody," she admitted. "Pa went to Wiley's Trading Post mostly, sometimes on into Boulder City to get supplies, but we didn't know the people. We've always stayed to ourselves, and that's the way I intend to keep it."

"Looking at your sisters, I can see why. If the men in the Colorado territory ever got a look at them, the Overland Trail would head straight for your valley. But my men need help. Until they can leave, I intend to do what I can."

She glossed over his reference to leaving. "How? You have no money and you have nothing to trade."

"Don't ask me and I won't be forced to lie to you."

"You intend to steal?"

"If I have to. It won't be the first time. Unless you have a better idea."

Sabrina thought about the pouch containing the gold nuggets her father had picked up along the floor of the dry riverbed and the two knobs of silver he'd discovered in the mine. No need to mention that just yet. Still, if Colter was going out after supplies for her family, she intended to go with him.

"No," she said. "I don't have a better idea—not now. But I will come along, whether you like it or not. I know more about this territory than you do."

"You're right about that. Most of our assignments have been in Texas. This is about as far north as we've been sent."

"Will they be looking for you?"

"The Yankees? Hell, yes. One thing about a Yankee commander, he'll move heaven and earth to find anybody who kills one of his men."

"But you didn't kill his men."

"I only hope he knows that, though I'm not sure it will matter. We're escapees now, wanted men, regardless."

"That's all the more reason for us to travel together. They won't expect to find a man and woman. If they do, they'll think . . ."

"That we're husband and wife?" This time he did let his lips curl into a smile. A wife was the last thing he wanted. "Hell, why not? I've used a lot of disguises in this war, but being married hasn't been one of them."

Maybe her idea wasn't such a bad one. Wiley's Trading Post was exactly where Colter was heading. He couldn't be certain that the post wasn't being watched. But on the off chance that Wiley hadn't learned their fate, word about their capture had to be sent back to General Lee. And there was still the matter of the missing Dane.

The ever-present wind sprang up and died down again. Colter had found a spot uphill of the grave during the ceremony and studied the woman. Seemingly oblivious to his presence, she'd stood with the house and the mountain behind her, her eyes closed and her head bowed. For a moment he'd experienced the odd feeling that he'd been there before. But of course he hadn't. It wasn't the place, it was death he'd seen too much of, and funerals. His father, his sisters, his mother, and finally, on the side of some bloody battlefield in some snow-covered field in Pennsylvania, he'd buried Moe. After that it seemed that he'd buried his grief and his feelings.

Until now.

"All right," he agreed, "come with me. I've been thinking about taking a wife. Guess it won't hurt to practice it before I make up my mind."

Besides, he told himself, his men weren't ready to move yet. Traveling alone, he couldn't be certain that someone on the trail wouldn't recognize him as one of the prisoners who'd been held in the general store. Having Sabrina along might be a good military move; he wasn't so sure about his personal feelings.

He was beginning to find Miss Sabrina Alexander, with the stoic manner and big hazel eyes, entirely too appealing.

5

The next morning Sabrina had to work quickly. It was still dark as she made her way inside the mine. Her breath came fast and shallow, her heart beating like distant tomtoms. She forced herself to stop and slow her breathing.

Captain Colter would be rising soon, and she had to complete her mission and be back before he left. He'd made his plans clear: leave at first light, get food and supplies any way he could. But after the questions he'd asked Raven, Sabrina couldn't be certain of his true motive, and she wanted to be sure that she could take care of the mission if need be. The pouch containing the last of their gold nuggets and the silver was still in the cave, and she intended to retrieve it.

With that in mind she lit the lantern, shored up her courage, and stepped past the remaining mound of dirt into the small cavern beyond. Holding the light high, she swung it around, reassured to discover that the hiding place was accessible. Quickly she moved the rock away from the hollowed-out space behind and felt for the pouch.

It was still there. She didn't know how tense she'd been until she had the lumpy bag in her grasp. Removing the gold, she decided to leave the silver knobs, taking only some slivers of silver ore; then she shoved the pouch back into its hiding place. What she had wasn't much, but at least she could buy food rather than steal it. She didn't know yet how she'd handle her transactions without the captain knowing about the silver, but she'd worry about that when the time came.

Replacing the rock, she stood, shining the light from the lantern around the walls again. And then she saw it, the chunk of shiny ore at her feet. Silver, in the shape of a bolt of lightning, branded the rock and reflected the glow of the lantern. More silver.

Papa had been right. He'd found his bonanza and it had killed him. Sabrina stood, looking at the ore for a long moment. This decided everything. Once she got the dirt cleared away, she could mine the silver and provide for her sisters. Studying the mound of debris and the walls of the mine, she decided that there was no evidence of the vein. The cave-in had concealed the vein, if there was one, dislodging this one telltale sign of what was hidden. Quickly she added the chunk of silver to the pouch, blew out the lantern, and backed out of the mine.

The first faint signs of light were coloring the sky as she scurried back down the valley toward the cabin.

Colter, standing in the shadow of the trees below, watched curiously. He'd known there was more to Sabrina Alexander than she pretended. But he couldn't figure out what had taken her back to the mine. From what he'd seen in the digging, there'd been nothing there but dirt. From what he'd seen at the cabin, he accepted Cullen Alexander's failure as a miner without question.

Maybe he'd underestimated Sabrina.

Maybe this trip would be more interesting than he'd thought. Maybe he'd better rethink his plan.

* * *

"She'll be safe, Miss Lauren." The big Irishman had been watching the russet-haired beauty for days as she went quietly about her routine. In the time he'd been her patient, he'd recognized her gentle but firm control of her sisters. The women deferred to Sabrina as head of the family, but beyond that it was Lauren who directed the daily activities that made up their simple lives.

"I'm sure you're right, Mr. McBride, but Sabrina has never been to Boulder City without Papa."

"The captain will look after her."

"I doubt she'll let him. My guess is that it will be Sabrina overseeing the trip. Besides, how will they get supplies without money?"

Irish gave a soft laugh. "Money. The captain is an expert at that. We haven't seen real money since the war started. There was plenty of worthless paper money, especially in the South. Only occasionally did we have a few gold coins. He'll manage."

Lauren put down the shirt she'd washed and was now mending for Carl, the soldier who'd been shot in the shoulder. "And how did you come across those coins, Mr. McBride?"

"Couldn't you call me Irish? You make me feel like I ought to hold out my hand and let you slap my palm with a ruler."

"Maybe I ought to do just that, Mr. Irish."

Lauren wasn't about to drop the "mister." She didn't trust her instinct where he was concerned. He appeared to be a kind and sympathetic man—his simple Irish ballad at the funeral proved that. But that image didn't match Sabrina's having discovered the wounded men in a prison wagon. Sabrina had warned Lauren to keep an eye on Isabella and Mary.

Lauren told herself that she was bothered by the knowledge that her patient was a prisoner; she didn't want to think that she was uneasy about the man. But Irish McBride's simple kindness was disturbing. She wanted to trust him, wanted to believe that the worshipful look in his eyes was genuine. But she didn't dare.

Irish sensed her uncertainty. His ability to move about on his handmade crutch seemed to unsettle Lauren, and other than treating his wound, she kept her distance. But she was aware of him and that pleased him. Irish liked the way her face flushed so prettily. She was a shy woman, who knew little about talking to a man. If he moved his chair closer to hers, he had no doubt that she'd suddenly find some chore that would take her away. He couldn't blame her; he'd never had much experience in conversing properly with a lady. Conversation didn't come easy, and after his embarrassing reaction to her touch this morning when she changed his bandage, he decided that Tyler would perform that chore in the future.

"How long have you lived up here, Miss Lauren?"

"Fifteen years. Since Raven was born."

Irish looked around and winced. What kind of man must her father have been to allow his family to spend fifteen years in a one-room cabin? In his country a man was considered to be a hard worker or a ne'er-do-well. It wasn't hard to know which Cullen Alexander was. But his daughters spoke of him fondly, and that said something about the man.

"Before that," Lauren went on, "Papa traveled about. He prospected from here to California before he married Pale Raven, and her family helped him build this house."

"Pale Raven? An Indian?"

"Yes, she was a member of the Arapaho tribe. We lived with them for a time, when Papa was having a spell of bad luck. When he married Pale Raven, they came here, to the mountains where her ancestors lived."

"What happened to her?"

"She died giving birth to Raven. I don't think Papa ever quite got over that. Either that, or he just couldn't figure out how to move us again. Mary was only three and Isabella was five."

"And Sabrina was thirteen?"

"Yes. Though she always seemed older. I guess

Papa never realized how hard it was for her. He always intended to take us back east one day, but it—it never happened. Tell me about your family, Mr. Irish."

"I guess I know something about being without a mother. Mine passed on when I was a babe. By the time I was six years old, I was working along with my other brothers in the mine."

"Oh, you were a miner, like Papa?"

"No, ma'am. I was a coal miner, working for someone else, not like your papa. It was a . . . hard life, a lot like yours, I'm thinking."

Lauren sat up straight, rocking a little faster for a moment, then slowing her motion with her foot. "Papa tried very hard, Mr. McBride. It wasn't his fault he never found a big strike. And we had a good life. My own mother was a Christian woman who loved us very much."

"I'm sure she did. Her gentle touch shows in all of you, except maybe Miss Sabrina. What happened to your mother?"

"She was killed in an Indian attack."

Irish didn't know how to respond to that. But he knew she was waiting for more questions, and he asked, "Indian attack? Not the Arapaho."

"No, Ute. The Arapaho found us and took us in. The Ute have always been more warlike. But that was a long time ago, when the Indians were trying to protect their land from the settlers. Papa never blamed them. He said he'd fight for his land if he had to. But it was hard, until he married Pale Raven."

Irish nodded. Life without a mother was hard. Life in Ireland was hard anyhow. At sixteen he'd signed on with a sea captain and made his way to this country. Once he'd set foot on American soil, he'd known that he'd found his pot of gold. Then the war came, and he'd had to fight for the little piece of Georgia land that he'd farmed. He wondered if someone else had claimed it.

But five women? Alone? He frowned. A man ought not to let his women live like this in a country that had so much to give. Tilling the soil in the sunshine was the way to care for a family, not grubbing in the bowels of the earth. He'd done both, and farming was better, though the land up here was poor and dry.

"Have you ever thought about moving away from here? There's land along the Rio Grande where cotton plants grow as big as trees. A cool breeze blows, and they say the river never runs dry."

Lauren stopped her rocking and leaned back with her eyes closed. For a moment there was a comfortable silence. The sound of melting snow dropped off the ends of the icicles along the roof in musical plops.

"And it's warm there?" she finally said.

"Oh, yes. It's always warm."

"I dream about being warm always. About fields of growing things and clear water to bathe in. But"— she looked down at her mending guiltily—"Colorado Territory is beautiful too, in a different way."

"But don't you want a family of your own?"

"I couldn't leave my sisters. They need me."

Irish noticed that she didn't answer the question, not really. But perhaps she did. Her needs weren't important. She had to care for her sisters. Still, the bittersweet expression on her face revealed the truth of his observation. Lauren Alexander was a woman who needed her own home and children—and husband.

This time Irish didn't have to feel her hands on his thigh to respond to the picture of Lauren as a wife and mother. His physical reaction to her was instant and overwhelming. This was a new experience for Irish, potent and embarrassing. The silence that fell between them this time was cold and sharp, like a reprimand.

"What about you, Mr. McBride?" she finally asked. "Don't you want a family?"

"Me?" He gave a disbelieving laugh. "If the Yanks don't hang me, I'll have another farm one day. But a wife? I doubt there's a woman anywhere who would be interested in an overgrown oaf like me."

"But of course there is," Lauren responded, then felt her face flame at the forwardness of her remark. To cover her confusion, she stood, moved to the stove, and stirred the beans. As she tried to sort out her feelings, she heard the door open and Isabella's laughter fill the room.

"Oh, Carl, I don't know how you were a bartender if you weren't better at filling a glass than hitting the milk bucket."

With Tyler on one side and Isabella on the other, the curly-haired man, still pale from losing so much blood, was being half carried to the fire. He coughed, and there was a new rattle in his chest that hadn't been there. Lauren didn't like the sound of that. They needed him to get well, not take a fever.

The man could die or he could recover. Either way Isabella could be hurt. Lauren took one look at the stars in her sister's eyes and the expression on the bartender's face and knew she had to intercede. "Isabella, what are you doing?"

"I'm helping Carl—Mr. Arnstine."

"And where is the milk?"

The sharpness in Lauren's voice surprised Isabella, whose laughter quickly died in her throat. "Mary is bringing it, Lauren. Mr. Arnstine is still weak from his wound."

"Too weak to be helping with the milking. Sit down, Mr. Arnstine, and I'll pour you a cup of coffee. Isabella, take Mary and Raven with you and see if you can find some range grass beneath the melting snow."

"I'm afraid you're right, Miss Lauren," Carl admitted. "I apologized to the cow and I apologize to you for causing you concern. We'll find food for the animals. It's too cold outside for you ladies."

Lauren heard the resignation in his voice as well as the pain. Lashing out was unnecessary. The man had almost died. He still might. His brave show of recuperative powers was more show than substance. For all she knew, they were all in danger of starving, of freezing, of being found by the soldiers who had to be searching for the men. A little laughter could be forgiven. Even she'd been tempted into seeing Mr. McBride as a gentle man; why shouldn't her sisters find the prisoners just as appealing?

"Right you are, my boy," Irish said. He clambered

to his feet and steadied his crutch beneath his arm. He too had heard the cough and seen the pallor of his friend's face. "I'll find grass. You'd better stay here and protect the women. A trip to the barn is enough for one day."

"No," Carl argued, standing and trying to steady himself by holding on to the arm of the chair. "I'll go."

It was Tyler's voice that stopped him. "Irish is right, Carl. I don't think we ought to leave the women alone. You stay here."

Carl gave his friends a sheepish look. "And how am I supposed to protect them? With my bare hands?"

"Use that silver tongue," Irish said, thumping to the door. "I'm thinking you can just outtalk the devil, if you set your mind to it. We'll be back before dark, Miss Lauren. We'll get some grass."

Lauren looked at him for a long moment. She wasn't Sabrina. She didn't know how to judge people or make hard choices. All she knew was to trust her own instincts, and those instincts told her that Irish McBride would look after them. If she was wrong, she'd just have to suffer the consequences.

"Will you be all right?" he asked. His words were meant to be a question. Instead, the graveness of his gaze was more like a promise, from him to her. "Will you?"

She nodded.

They headed down the valley, toward Boulder City, Sabrina leading the way. This was her land, her territory, her past.

Colter let her, relaxing as the quietness of the early morning gave way to midday. Though it was still cold by Georgia standards, the snow was beginning to melt, giving the air a fresh smell that was almost springlike. Overhead the sky was Carolina-cornfield blue, the kind of day he and Moe had once enjoyed, a day for catching catfish in the pond, for sailing leaf boats across the still water. A day before the conflict and the pain took away the peace.

For a time Colter let his mind wander, before pulling it back to the present. He rarely relaxed anymore, certainly not with a woman. Being with Sabrina seemed to trigger old memories, and he didn't like that. There was a mission to complete, and there was no room for softness in his life. He made up his mind that he'd talk to the men as soon as he returned. They couldn't be allowed to think of the Alexander sisters as anything other than jailers. They were wanted men who would probably be hanged if the Yanks won the war.

Colter would never voice his opinion to the others, but he saw no way the South could win. Colter's misfits were dead men; it was just a matter of time and luck. Best if they didn't leave widows and children behind. They knew that, but perhaps it was time he reminded them.

Now there was the distraction of four women—four desirable, beautiful women. Rather, there were two who fit into that category. There was one child and there was Sabrina. The verdict was still out on her. By coming to the cabin they'd bought a little time. But luck?

He'd never thought much about luck. A man reaped the results of his efforts, or lack thereof. But he guessed he'd had plenty of luck in his time, certainly in recent years. He wasn't dead yet, though he'd lost everything a man wanted to live for.

Hell, he was getting maudlin. It was the woman. She made him ashamed of his motives. She was only trying to keep her family together. He was using her to protect his men. But when he was gone, her problem would still exist—except her sisters wouldn't be the same, not if Carl had anything to do with it. He only hoped that Tyler could keep the Casanova of the group in line.

By the time the sun was directly overhead, they'd reached the spot where the massacre of the Union soldiers had taken place. Colter reined his horse, pausing to study the remains of the campfire, the scuffed marked where bodies had fallen and been dragged away. There was no sign of either hoofprints or moccasins. Only boot heels dug into the damp earth.

The melting snow left the ground muddy. The ruts left by the wagon wheels filled with water, some pink-colored from the blood. Bloody earth. He'd thought by coming west he'd left that scene behind. He was wrong. If it hadn't been for Sabrina Alexander, it could have been his blood seeping into the soil.

Sabrina waited beyond the campsite, watching Colter.

His scruffy beard had grown fuller, concealing more of his thin, angular face. She wondered how many meals he'd skipped to see that his men had been fed. His blue eyes were brooding now, his brows drawn into a line of consternation. He might be considered a renegade but apparently death didn't come easy to the captain.

There was tragedy in his face, and Sabrina felt a return of that compelling urge to comfort him. But she knew her intrusion wouldn't be welcome, and she wouldn't know what to say.

When he finally joined her, she didn't speak. Instead she allowed her horse to fall back until they were riding side by side. She didn't know much about war, but she recognized pain and she understood responsibility. God knew she'd spent her life trying to care for her family, trying to be there when they needed her.

She didn't know how Colter felt about failure. He kept everything inside, allowing none of his emotions to show. Yet it couldn't be easy to see your men hurt, captured, and hauled away.

She hadn't been any more successful. She hadn't been able to keep her mother safe. And Bessie— Lauren, Isabella, and Mary's mother—had died in spite of Sabrina's efforts. Then Papa. A shiver ripped down Sabrina's back, a shiver of fear. What if she couldn't protect her sisters? What if she lost them like the others she'd loved?

"Do you have a family somewhere, Colter?" Her question was a surprise, even to herself.

"Not anymore."

"So where are you heading, when this fighting is over?"

He looked off in the distance as though he might be remembering a place. "Anyplace," he finally said. "Anyplace where the rain at midnight is warm."

A warm rain at midnight. Curious, Sabrina thought. Though in a crazy way she understood. A picture of a warm summer night, two people protected by entwined tree limbs overhead, and the sound of rain falling. Peace.

"That sounds like one of your friend Tyler's observations. Is he really a scholar?"

"He was once."

"And Mr. Arnstine? Tell me about him."

"Carl is—well, Carl is the kind of man who keeps the world loose. He gives the impression of being a joker, but he's deceptively quick, and he can size up a man before he hears his name."

"He sounds like a man who goes his own way. But he's a soldier."

"We're all soldiers, now, Miss Alexander. It's hard to remember the men we once were. Maybe you don't want to know."

After that they were silent. Sabrina, riding into less familiar territory, allowed her horse to fall back, and Colter took command. The move was subtle, but he understood her message. He was in charge, but she was right behind him, watching every move he made. The rifle was strapped onto her saddle. And the bulge in her jacket said that she carried a pistol as well. He might not be her prisoner, but it was a standoff he didn't choose to debate.

Not now. Fort Collins and the Union Army were behind him. Wiley's Trading Post was ahead, and Boulder City was just beyond. He felt confident he could arrange for supplies at Wiley's. At the same time he'd have to find a way to get information to Wiley without Sabrina knowing what he was doing. He'd play it by ear. He only hoped that his companion and would-be jailer could be fooled.

Finally, as the open plains beyond the valley ap-

peared in the late-afternoon shadows, Colter left the
trail and rode into a stand of fir trees beside a small
stream. "We'll make camp here," he said, dismounting.

"Why stop? Couldn't we do better under the cover
of darkness?"

"We don't know what we'll find, and I don't fancy
riding into trouble in the dark. Give me the rifle and
I'll find some food. You make a fire."

"You make the fire," she snapped. "I'll find the
food."

'Suit yourself. I just thought you'd rather stay with
the horses than trust me with them."

Her throat tightened at the dry amusement in his
voice. He was right. If she left him with the horses, he
could ride away in a heartbeat. On the other hand, if
she gave him a gun, he was close enough to civilization
to find his own horse.

The unmistakable growl of her stomach prompted
her decision. She'd have to trust him, and he'd have to
learn that she wouldn't be dictated to. Sliding from her
horse, she handed him the reins and took the rifle from
its place on the saddle.

"Don't set the woods on fire, Colter. I'll be back
with our supper."

Colter watched her stretch the muscles in her
shoulders as she walked away. The ride had been long,
and neither of them had slept much since the first time
they'd ridden this trail. He pushed back the brim of his
hat and kept his eyes on her until she disappeared.

He'd already decided that she wasn't as bulky as
her clothing indicated. And her hair was a wonder: Almost a russet color, it was thick and luscious, the kind
a man liked to run his fingers through. Nevertheless,
she rode like a man and she refused to be intimidated.
And you never knew what she was thinking. Truth
was, she'd make a good soldier. He'd fight alongside
her anytime.

He couldn't say he didn't consider riding off, leaving her behind. It would make what he had to do
easier. But something held him back. Honor maybe, or

just plain contrariness. She'd expect him to disappear. And he wouldn't.

By the time Sabrina returned with the squirrels she'd shot, a fire was blazing. The horses had been bedded down for the night, and the bedrolls had been laid out.

Side by side.

She felt a sudden infusion of warmth as her eyes took in the scene. She hadn't been sure he'd still be there. She wasn't certain that she wanted him to be. No matter that she understood her limitations as a woman, she was also beginning to understand that having a virile man close by was a temptation.

And a threat.

Colter came lazily to his feet. "I suppose it would be foolish of me to offer to clean those, wouldn't it?"

He had her there. While she'd shot the squirrels to prove a point, she hadn't intended her independence to carry that far. One look at the expression on his face, and she knew that he was enjoying her little show of power.

"It would," she was forced to agree, "for you have no knife with which to dress the animals."

Wisely, Colter didn't mention the hunting knife Raven had secretly given him. Raven had understood that he'd protect Sabrina, even if Sabrina was still not sure of his motives. He'd concealed the knife in his bedroll while she was hunting. He wanted it close at hand if he needed it during the night. Sabrina wanted to be in charge, so he'd just let her. Maybe, while she was distracted, this would be a good time to question her further about the Indian attack on the guards.

As she skinned the puny, furry creatures, he asked his first question. "Miss Alexander, tell me again what happened the day of the ambush."

"What do you mean?"

"Where were you? How did you know the Yanks were camped down stream?"

"I heard them. I'd already seen one of them meeting with the Indian earlier in the day, when I stopped to eat."

His head jerked up. "You'd already seen one of the soldiers meeting with an Indian?"

"Yes. At least I heard him. He was a white man. He called the Indian Gray Warrior and the Indian called him Long Rifle." Sabrina split open the animals, dressing them as skillfully as any man. "They met beyond the rocks where I had stopped to rest."

"What did he look like?"

"I can't tell you that. I never really saw him. I only heard them. They were talking about where the soldiers would camp."

"You think the soldier was in on the massacre?"

"Oh, yes. But he told the Indian not to hurt anybody. They could have the horses and guns. All he wanted was the pack mules. And he was there, after the attack."

"Bloody hell! I wish we *had* escaped and stolen the ammunition. What would he want with the mules?"

Sabrina fed the meat onto a spit that Colter had fashioned from tree limbs. She buried the remains and headed for the stream. "Watch the food while I clean my hands," she instructed.

"Yes, ma'am! Shall I set the table and pour the wine?"

"Don't be smart, Colter! Just do what you're told."

He could have argued, but he didn't. Biding his time would serve him better. Besides, he wanted to think about what she'd just said. The killing of the detachment wasn't planned. All the man called Long Rifle wanted was the mules. But something had gone wrong.

Killing a detachment would only set the military against the Indians. Why would the white man take such a chance? What were the mules carrying? Since the Federal Government set up the munitions plant outside of Boulder, weapons and explosives were easier to come by. It had to be something more. Somebody who wanted Colter's misfits to take the blame.

Long Rifle and Gray Warrior. He had names, though they didn't mean anything yet. They would.

The weapons and supplies were important to the Indians, who would turn them back against the people moving west. But the man called Long Rifle was a mystery. What did he stand to gain? It made no sense. Except that now, in addition to failure, his men would be accused of cold-blooded murder.

Colter fingered the knife and frowned. There was still a question Sabrina hadn't answered. Sabrina had been on her way to Boulder City when she crossed their path. Was she somehow involved? He had only her word for what had happened. Why didn't she go to the fort for help in freeing her father?

He was reaching, looking for reasons to distance himself from this woman. He'd learned to bury his emotions beneath layers of protection. Still, she had come to their rescue. The question was, Why? She had no loyalty to the South. He rotated the meat, then sat down on the bedroll. It had been a long time since he'd slept with a woman, never with a woman who was as good a man as he was—and never without touching her.

He lay listening to the screech of an owl in the distance. A yellow moon tiptoed across the treetops, playing hide-and-seek with the tall silver aspens. Behind him towered the snow-covered peaks of the mountain, and ahead was the unknown.

As the fat fell into the fire and sizzled, it came to him that there was a certain appeal to this rugged country. It was harsh and demanding. But it endured. In the scheme of life the buffalo disappeared. The Indians were being pushed forever back. Brothers were fighting brothers in a war that nobody would win. But this land survived.

Just like Sabrina Alexander.

6

Sabrina and Colter ate, dismantled the spit, and walked to the spring, where they washed their hands and mouths in the icy mountain stream.

Colter gathered more dead limbs to feed the fire through the night. When he moved back toward the camp, he noticed that the bedrolls had been separated. One had been pulled to the other side of the fire.

"Damn! Why did you do that?"

"What's wrong, Captain? Surely you aren't afraid of the dark?"

It wasn't the dark he was afraid of, it was what Sabrina Alexander would do when she discovered the knife he'd hidden beneath the blanket she was about to climb under. Sabrina would be angry, and he wasn't certain he was ready for that. He had to think fast. He was not anxious for her to learn the extent to which he'd enjoyed his little joke about cleaning the squirrels.

"What was that?" he said, and came to a full stop, his action suggesting imminent danger.

To her credit she didn't jump up or cry out. Instead

she looked slowly around, tilting her head to listen to the sounds of the night.

"I don't hear anything, Colter."

"We're being watched. Stand up slowly. Hold out your hand and smile."

She followed his directions, but the smiling was hard. She was certain there was nothing out there and that he knew it. This was some kind of ruse. She'd known not to trust him; this proved it. "Now what?"

He returned his smile, dropped his wood, and started toward her, speaking under his breath. "When I take your hand, I'm going to put my arms around you and we'll walk deeper into the trees."

"Why?"

"I don't know what's going to happen, and I don't want to be out in the open." He hoped she didn't stop to examine that bit of inane logic.

"Shall I bring the rifle?"

"No, that would give us away."

He clasped her hand and pulled her close, sliding his arm around her and turning her away from the fire. After an awkward moment she fitted herself against him and matched her steps to his.

"Like this?" she asked, taking a page from Isabella's book, throwing her head back and widening her smile recklessly. Her motion allowed her hat to fall behind her, freeing her hair and exposing her face to the light. She was rewarded by the astonished expression on his face. Two could play games, she decided.

His smile vanished. "Yes!" he said hoarsely. "You're getting the idea. In fact—"

"Don't you dare say I'm beautiful again, Captain Colter. Even a fool would know you are only trying to frighten me." Now she was looking up at him with eyes storming with intensity, her mouth soft and inviting, lips parted in anticipation. "Why?"

"I'm not trying to frighten you," he answered. She couldn't know how appealing she was, or that her expression invited him to kiss her. And he couldn't refuse the invitation. He curled his arm, bringing her around in front of him as he lowered his head. His lips touched hers. She froze.

"Easy, easy," he whispered, brushing his lips back and forth against a mouth now clamped tight. She gasped, parting her lips, and he thrust his tongue inside. Her jacket fell open as he pressed against her, almost dizzy from the feel of her full breasts. He felt her arm creep around him. Her unconscious attempt to hold herself up had the effect of pulling him down closer. For a long, senseless moment he forgot what he'd started out to do, as the kiss meant to distract Sabrina had an unexpected effect on him.

Then she pulled back, letting go of the curls she was holding with one hand. She looked stunned; then reality set in, followed by fear and finally anger. She slapped him, hard, with the bare palm of her healing hand.

Her eyes were wide. "What was all that about?" she asked as she backed away, one hand protectively across her chest, the other behind her.

"It didn't work," he said ruefully, "but I was trying to distract you."

"I see. Then I don't suppose you'll need this now, will you?" She reached down and pulled the knife from her boot.

"No. I guess I won't."

"Concealing the knife in your bedroll was what this was about, wasn't it? Don't ever try something like that again, Captain Colter, or I'll use the knife on you."

"Before or after you kiss me back?"

"During!" she snapped, and whirled around. Moments later she was inside the blanket, eyes closed, her entire body trembling like a snow rabbit caught in the gaze of a mountain lion.

She'd known there was nothing out there, but she'd let him play out his plan, wondering how far he'd go. She hadn't expected him to kiss her. But more than that, she hadn't expected the blaze of fire that the kiss ignited, the way her body had reached out, begging to be touched, the way her lips parted, inviting him inside.

Sabrina was only fooling herself, believing that she could control this man. Though she'd expected him to try to rid himself of her, this physical connection had come at her from the darkness like a spell conjured up by one of Papa's little people. Concentrating with every ounce of her willpower, she forced the spasms in the back of her knees to still. Her breathing finally slowed, and the burning heat inside her body met the night air and cooled.

Colter was still stunned by the heated, though brief response of the woman. Just hours earlier he'd pronounced her as good a man as any he'd ridden with. She carried herself like a man, thought like a man, even talked like a man.

But tall and gangly as she was, this was no man. Neither, however, was she a cool, calculating female. Damned if he knew what she was. But his encounter with her had left his body hot and heavy, and as uncomfortable as a porcupine in full alert with no enemy target for his quills.

"Guess you're not going to take the first watch," he finally said.

"You guessed right, soldier," she said in a voice that should have been one of irritation. Instead her throat was so tight that her words came out in a breathless rush.

"Got to you, did I?" he teased, surprising himself with the lightness of his tone. "The truth is, you got to me too. But both of us know that nothing can come of it. No two people could ever be more unsuited to each other. It won't happen again."

"You're right, Colter. It won't. As for why I responded, perhaps I have my own ways of distraction."

Her claim was brave, but he didn't for a minute believe she'd kissed him intentionally. He didn't even try to analyze his kiss. Giving thought to the combustion only fueled the flame. Best to put it behind them, wrap it in a layer of ice that froze emotions.

"Sweet dreams, madam jailer. I hope you don't have nightmares. I'm unarmed."

Sabrina didn't answer. He was wrong. He had a weapon, a new and powerful one against which she had no defense. He'd started a wildfire, and Sabrina felt as if she were burning up. What she needed now was some of that rain at midnight.

Except she needed it cold and hard and quick.

The next morning they broke camp and headed toward the trading post. There was a wariness between them that was different from the distrust of the day before. Sabrina didn't look at Captain Colter; yet the not looking made the remembering more vivid.

Finally she reined in her horse and turned to face him.

"I don't know what you're planning when we get to Wiley's, Colter, but I think you owe me at least one straightforward answer."

"Oh? What's that?" The adversary was back, in control, her authority fully restored.

"I want to know the truth about your crimes. Why were you in that prison wagon? And don't lie to me."

"I don't intend to. Your sisters already asked. We were about to ambush the fort's supply wagon. They were carrying badly needed shells and gunpowder from the factory in Boulder City. Except it looks like somebody else had his own plans for the munitions."

"So how were you captured?"

"I'm still trying to figure that out. We were pretty well hidden, above the trail the wagon and pack animals were taking. Then suddenly there were Indians everywhere and we didn't have a chance."

"Would you have killed the escort?"

"Yes," he said, "if I had to. I'm a soldier, remember."

But he didn't look like a soldier. He looked like an outlaw—not dark and forbidding, but steely, like granite. Gone was the warmth and fire she'd felt last night.

Colter was like the silver of Papa's ore sample, jagged and unreachable.

"How did you know about the supplies?"

"Does it matter?"

"No, I suppose not. Of course, you'd have to have someone around, some contact, someone to whom you had to report."

He didn't answer. She was smart. Knowing too much could endanger her, even more than their presence already had. Still, leaving her to try to outguess him could be a risk. She might make a wrong move and give him away. There was even a possibility that was what she had in mind. After all, he'd freed her father and helped her bury him. What further use did she have for a fugitive Confederate captain?

"I answered your question, Sabrina. Now you answer mine. Where were you heading when you found us?"

"To Boulder City."

"Why?"

Like Colter, she saw no reason to lie about her original purpose, and telling the truth had always been important to her. It was a trait that kept a person out of trouble, a trait her father had never acquired. "I was going to find a husband."

That stunned him. "Why?" he repeated.

"Why else? I needed a man to help me free Papa."

"But surely a neighbor would have been glad to help you. Or one of the soldiers from the fort. Why resort to marriage?"

"Papa never allowed us to go to the fort, and we have no neighbors. There was a time when the stage stopped, before Fort Collins was built, but we haven't seen a stage in a long time, not since the commander at the fort started paying the Ute to fight for them."

"I don't understand. How does that affect the stage-line business?"

"The stagecoaches are great targets. The Indians need horses. After they took our last team, the stage didn't return. By that time they'd built the fort, and the stagecoaches didn't need to go out of their way to stop here."

"So how have you lived?"

There was a pained expression on her face that she quickly hid. "Not very well. Papa kept on with his prospecting, but it hasn't been easy. The Arapaho brought us meat and pelts, which we traded. We had a small garden. But after Papa was killed, I—we decided that we needed a man—for protection."

Colter took a long look at his companion. "I find it hard to believe that you'd admit to needing a man, Sabrina Alexander."

"I didn't—don't. But my sisters do. Looking after them is my responsibility, and I'll do whatever I have to do."

"So you went after a man for yourself. Instead you found four. What made you change your mind about finding a husband?"

She gave him a long, hard look. "Prisoners are disposable, husbands are permanent."

"What about the future?" Colter didn't know why he was pushing her. Hell, the last thing he wanted to hear about was a bunch of fool women looking for husbands.

"I don't know. I suppose I'll still have to consider a—a man at some point in time."

"From what I saw back in your cabin, I'd say we're going to have to deal with at least three potential suitors. I don't think that's good."

"Neither do I, at least not good for me. For my sisters, I don't know. We will need help getting the ranch started and later to drive the cattle."

He couldn't hold back a laugh. "Ranch?"

"It will be, once I buy some cattle. I always wanted to raise beef cattle. Now I will."

A sudden unpleasant thought washed over him. "Surely you don't intend to keep my men prisoners to work your ranch."

This time it was her turn to laugh. "As you said, from what I could see, I don't think it will take much to convince them to help us out. Do you?"

"My men are soldiers, Miss Alexander, not cow-boys."

"Your men like my sisters, Captain. And the war is going to end someday." Sabrina was probably more worried about that situation than the captain was. But for now she'd keep that thought to herself.

"Lorelei," he suddenly said. "We've fallen into a trap set by Loreleis."

"Loreleis?" she questioned.

"Another of Tyler's tales. Lorelei was a mythical siren who posed on the rocks, singing to the passing sailors, luring them and their ships to be shipwrecked.

"I suppose," she admitted, more worried than she was pleased at the comparison. She'd left her sisters because she'd had to, but not before warning Lauren to keep a sharp watch on the others. Nursing the men was the Christian thing to do, but this talk of sirens was even more unsettling than husbands, particularly after what had happened between her and Colter. The important thing was to get supplies and get back.

"Now," she said sharply, "let's decide how you intend to proceed. What's your plan?"

"Don't have one. I guess we'll just have to see how it goes." Colter didn't intend to tell her that Wiley was his contact in the area, that he was the one who supplied the information about the goods being moved and got them back to Confederate forces when Colter captured them.

Sabrina groaned at his response. One of the ways she'd been able to keep her mind off him as they rode was to work out possible scenarios for getting food for her sisters and the stock. She hadn't yet considered one she thought would work. To find out now that he had no plan was even more discouraging.

"If you don't have an idea, you'd better leave it up to me," she said.

"Fine. I don't suppose you have an account with Wiley?"

"Not that I know of, but I might have a way."

The trading post came into view. It was a crude structure at best, but it had been the only sign of civilization for miles since the War Between the States began and Wiley suddenly turned up.

"Just out of curiosity, Miss Alexander, why were you going on into Boulder City instead of doing your husband hunting at Wiley's?"

"Because I wanted a special kind of man, and I wanted a choice. Wiley's is a one-man operation. I'm convinced that he's a crook, and the kind of people who would trade with him aren't that reliable either."

She was a lot closer to the truth about Wiley than she knew. "Looks like he's got company today. Maybe we ought to keep going."

Sabrina took a good look. There were three horses tied to the hitching rail, and a battered covered wagon. One of the horses bore military trappings.

"Settlers, and one soldier," Sabrina said, wondering how she could use that to her advantage. If she was going to spend some of her precious silver for goods, she didn't want the captain to know. Maybe the soldier would keep the captain outside, where he wouldn't witness the exchange of payment.

There was no ice this morning. The bright sun had almost thawed the ground surface. They allowed their horses to drink from the trough, then tied them to the rail on the other side. "You go inside," Colter directed. "I'll stay out here and keep watch."

That was what she wanted. But now that Colter suggested as much, she wasn't certain it was a good idea to leave him alone. "I don't think so, Colter. We stay together, for protection's sake." She'd started up the steps to the porch when the door opened and a man wearing a blue uniform stepped out.

"Howdy, ma'am," he said, his eyes raking Sabrina's body intimately. "Ain't seen you around before."

"Haven't been around," she said, and tried to move past. "Step aside, please."

"Just hold on there, ma'am," the man said, stepping in front of her and placing his hand on his pistol. He transferred his gaze from Sabrina to Colter, his eyes narrowing suspiciously. "I'm Sergeant Nealey, the federal officer in charge here, and we're looking for some escaped prisoners. I'll need to know who you are."

"I'm Sabrina Alexander and I'll thank you to let us pass!"

"And this fella? What'd be your name, mister? You look like you've been without a few meals lately."

"He's—"

"With the lady," Colter said, daring the soldier to push the matter. "Don't you have better things to do than worry about a few prisoners?"

"Not now. What with Grant about to take Richmond and Sherman burning everything south of Virginia, don't look like we're gonna have too much fighting left to do."

Colter tried not to let his surprise show. It had been weeks since he'd had any news of the war. He'd known for months that it had to be over soon; the South was out of manpower, supplies, and will to fight. But he hadn't known the end was this close. He swore silently. If they'd completed their mission, those supplies might have made things easier for the Confederacy. But ending the war wouldn't erase the warrants for his men. They were still wanted for a crime they didn't commit.

Behind the officer a man who looked to be a farmer and his wife appeared, followed by another man wearing an ill-fitting black suit with a too-tight collar.

"Morning, folks," the suited man said, moving toward them with his hand extended. "I'm Brother Seaton and this is Brother William and his wife. We just call her Mrs. William. These good people and I are on the way to the Indian territory to minister to the heathens."

"You are?" Sabrina couldn't keep the disbelief from her voice. "I mean, how nice to meet you. I'm Sabrina Alexander."

"And this is your husband?" the minister asked.

"This is—" She faltered. She couldn't give Colter's name, and in the awkwardness of the moment she was unable to find a logical conclusion to her statement. She didn't get a chance to finish.

"You know, you match the description of one of the men I'm looking for," the sharp-nosed sergeant said, taking a step forward to study Colter.

Sabrina felt Colter stiffen. She didn't want a confrontation here now, not with her holding both weapons. It was obvious that the sergeant had no such compunction.

"Nonsense! This is—my—my husband," Sabrina finally said, reaching back and linking her arm with Colter's.

"Mr. and Mrs. Alexander." The minister took Colter's hand and shook it vigorously. "God has sent us a beginning to our flock. I hope you'll come to Sunday services as soon as we get our church built."

"Where are you planning to build, Reverend?" Sabrina asked, trying to maneuver past the sergeant and the missionaries blocking the door.

"I don't know yet. Sergeant Nealey has promised to escort us to the camp of the great Ute leader, Gray Warrior."

Gray Warrior was the name of the Indian from the attack. Colter removed his hand from the energetic clasp. "Are you sure baptizing a renegade band of Ute is the best place to start, Reverend? I understand that Gray Warrior is a violent man."

"But we're on a mission for God," Brother Seaton pronounced, "and He's on our side." The minister started down the steps, followed by his companions. "Are you ready to depart, Sergeant?"

"Yeah, I'm ready." The sergeant turned away, obviously reluctant to leave. "Just where is your place, Mr. Alexander?"

"Beyond the mountains," Sabrina said, moving through the door with Colter behind her. "Far beyond."

"Better be careful," he called out, "those prisoners are out there somewhere. There are four of them, and they're cold-blooded killers."

Sabrina shivered.

"Don't worry, darling," Colter said, dropping his voice to a whisper as they stepped into the store, "your husband will protect you with his life."

She might have let that statement pass if he hadn't taken the charade one step too far. His hand, resting protectively on the small of her back, slid around her waist and pulled her close in mock reassurance.

His touch wasn't reassuring. It was like being branded, and she jerked away. "If he lives long enough," she hissed, "and still has the use of his—faculties!"

"His faculties work very well," Colter answered. "At least I think they do. It's been a long time since he's been tested."

"Morning. What can I do for you folks?" The proprietor stepped forward, eyeing them curiously, especially Sabrina. "This is the day for strangers. The name's Wiley."

"Mr. Wiley," Sabrina said sweetly, "I'm Sabrina Alexander and I've—we've come for some supplies."

"You say your name is Alexander?" Wiley said, glancing from Sabrina toward the captain and back again.

"Yes," Sabrina said, "my name is Alexander."

"Only Alexanders I ever heard of in these parts is that crazy miner who lives up in the hills. Didn't you come in here once or twice with him?"

"Cullen Alexander wasn't—isn't crazy!" Sabrina raised her voice in fury. She was ready to whirl around and leave.

Colter was almost inclined to let her. There were other general stores in Boulder City that would be a lot safer for her than the trading post. Once he'd passed his message, moving on might be wise, even if it was another's day's travel away.

"Maybe not," Wiley agreed, backing down, though from the expression on his face still not convinced. "Sorry, didn't mean to offend you, ma'am. Can't be too careful these days. Why, just the other day I heard they found a drifter, dead in the woods. The

Union major that found him said he'd been shot and robbed."

Colter shot a quick look at the store owner. "Any idea who he was?"

"Word from the fort was there wasn't a piece of identification on the man and nobody recognized him. Folks figured he might be another deserter."

"One of those Rebs who've been giving the Yanks hell?" Colter asked.

"That's what I'm guessing, but he didn't match the description of any of the missing Rebs," Wiley answered. "What can I get for you?"

Colter frowned. Dane? Surely Wiley would know if it was Dane. But what other explanation was there? If he wasn't dead, where was he? "We need supplies."

The store owner glanced at Sabrina again, as if trying to make up his mind, then caught Colter's slight shake of the head and said, "Yeah. How many folks you got at home to feed?"

Colter was pleased that Wiley seemed to understand what he was saying. "Three hungry men and four women, plus some livestock."

Sabrina didn't understand what Colter was saying. Why was he telling this man how many people were in the cabin? Was he up to some kind of flimflam?

"I'll take care of the supplies," Sabrina said in a low voice. "We want flour, meal, beans, bacon, coffee, and some oats for our cattle. Do you have those things?"

Wiley looked at Colter for a long moment, then shrugged his shoulders. "Yes, ma'am. I'll get them right away." He began to assemble the supplies.

"What do you mean, you'll take care of the supplies?" Colter growled under his breath as the trader moved away. "Are you telling me you have money?"

"I told you I had my ways. Now get out to the barn with Wiley and make sure he doesn't cheat us."

"Did you bring a wagon to haul these supplies, Mrs. Alexander?"

Sabrina was startled. She hadn't thought that far ahead. They'd burned the army wagon, and Papa had used the wheels on their own wagon to shore up the tunnel. He'd intended to replace them, but like so many other intentions, he never quite got to it.

"We'll haul the supplies on horseback," Colter said.

"Unless you have a cart for sale," Sabrina said, mentally counting the pieces of silver ore she had in her pouch.

"No cart, but there is an old Indian travois made out of poles and possum belly. I could let you use it, maybe. You can store your goods on the possum belly and pull it with the horses like the Indians do."

"Possum belly?" Colter looked at Sabrina, who nodded. "Fine," he said, trusting that she knew what Wiley meant. "Let's see it."

Sabrina was torn between wanting to wait to pay for the goods after Colter left, and worrying about letting the two men out of her sight. She decided it was better that they stay together.

Wiley put the food into coarse woven sacks and figured the total. "That comes to thirty dollars. I'll throw in the travois. Return it next time you come."

He waited.

Colter waited. With the price of goods skyrocketing because of the war, he knew the price was very low. Wiley was making certain that Colter's men got what they needed. From the expression on Sabrina's face, Colter couldn't be sure whether or not she understood what Wiley was doing, but she didn't comment.

Sabrina knew the price was too low. Thirty dollars for two sacks of supplies and a travois was pure charity. None of this made any sense unless the goods were stolen. Suddenly Sabrina wanted to get out of there, back to the valley, where she felt safe. She pulled a small drawstring purse from her pocket and, placing herself between Colter and the storekeeper, took out several pieces of the silver ore. In a low voice she asked, "You'll take this?"

There was no concealing the surprise in Wiley's eyes. Sabrina knew that she'd made a mistake offering far more than the supplies were worth. She should have let Colter handle the transaction. But nobody had ever acted in her behalf before, and Sabrina refused to allow it to happen now.

"Yes, ma'am," Wiley said. "I'm always glad to make a fair trade, specially with a woman who knows a good deal and comes prepared. Want to give me a hand with the oats—*Alexander*?"

7

"Why do you always find something else to do when I try to talk to you, Miss Alexander?"

Tyler had finally managed to find Mary alone at the spring. She was kneeling by the water hole, filling her bucket.

"I don't. I mean, why would you want to talk to me?"

"Why not?"

Mary ducked her head and blushed. "I'm not very experienced at conversation. I don't know much at all. And you're so smart, with books and things like that. I've never even been outside the valley."

"I'm not sure you've missed much," Tyler said, his mind running back across the last years. War and pain and hunger were things a man fought against so that women like Mary could be safe. And when it was all over, what then? He'd attended his share of soirees and balls in Savannah. He'd even gone away to school at the University of Virginia. But it all seemed so shallow now.

Looking at the slightly plump girl with the carrot-colored curls, he felt a kind of peace he hadn't known for a long time. She wasn't being a coquette. She simply didn't know how to flirt. She was real in a world that no longer was; she was like a clean piece of writing paper ready for beautiful words. But he'd seen few women like Mary in his travels.

"Tell me about your home," she said softly, setting her bucket on a level section of ground and sitting on a rock nearby. "Did you live in a big house, with servants?"

"You mean slaves? Yes, my father owned a big house. He inherited it from his father, who took it from an Englishman who returned home after the Revolution."

Mary closed her eyes, barely allowing herself to breathe as he talked. His voice was gentle and melodious, like the song of the stream in summer.

"There was a gazebo near the river, where the women would sit and watch for my father to come home."

"Come home?" Mary opened her eyes and leaned forward. "Where would he go?"

"He was a ship captain, carrying cotton and tobacco from Savannah to England. He loved the sea."

"And you? Did you never want to go to sea? I think it would be wonderful to see such a great body of water, to feel warm breezes and see new lands."

Suddenly the thought caught his fancy. He would like to travel, if he had someone like Mary with him. "I'll take you," he said, surprising himself as much as her, "after this is over."

"Oh, I don't think so. I wouldn't fit in a world like yours."

"You'd fit as well as me," he said with a trace of bitterness in his voice. "Surely you must have guessed by now, Miss Mary, we're all a bunch of misfits."

"You don't understand, Mr. Kurtz. I've been raised in mining camps. My stepmother, Raven's mother, was half-Indian. I've never had much schooling. There are many who would think I didn't belong."

"I'll teach you."

"Thank you, but I couldn't leave my sisters."

Tyler looked into Mary's eyes and saw nothing but honesty. He laughed silently. He'd told her about his beautiful house and his sea-captain father. He'd just failed to mention that his father's legal wife lived back in England, and that both his education at the university and the trust fund his father had left him were unusual for an illegitimate son.

Tyler held out his hand, waiting until she placed hers in it. "I think you'd fit anywhere you wanted to go, Mary. The measure of a person is what's inside the heart. And yours is as pure as the stream bubbling from the center of the earth."

Gallantly, Tyler tucked her arm in his and lifted her pail of water. No woman could have felt more treasured than eighteen-year-old Miss Mary Alexander as they sauntered back toward the cabin.

Lauren, watching through the window, grimaced. Sabrina had made it clear that the girls were to be prevented from spending time with the prisoners. She'd tried to keep them occupied, creating work when there was none. But there was little food to prepare and the mending was all done. She'd finally sent a reluctant Isabella with Mr. McBride to the creek where Sabrina had set the fish trap. Now that the sun was melting the ice, with any luck they'd find a trout that would give them a change from the deer meat they'd been eating for the last two days.

Truth was, it was Isabella she was most concerned about. Mr. Arnstine was the slowest to heal, and perhaps the most untrustworthy. She'd heard his bragging, his stories about San Francisco and New York City, places he'd been and sights he'd seen. And Isabella was soaking up every word of it. She wished that Sabrina were home.

Two days. She glanced at the bright-blue sky and tried not to worry. Sabrina was on the trail alone with the captain. And Lauren was as worried about Sabrina as she was the sisters left in her charge. No matter how much the big Irishman tried to defend his superior officer, Lauren knew that Captain Colter was a man to be reckoned with.

The captain was the only one of the men not wounded when they were captured. But Lauren need only look at him to know that there were wounds on the inside that ate away at him. He was dangerous and he was alone with Sabrina.

Still, she couldn't help but be aware that there was something between her sister and the man she'd rescued. It was there—obvious, yet invisible. Both avoided looking at each other. If one sat by the fire, the other sought the shadows of the room. If one spoke, the other remained silent. Yet the tension was ever present.

Captain Colter was nothing like Mr. McBride. Lauren felt her lips curl into a smile. The Irishman always ducked his head, like a little boy who'd been caught with his fingers in the honey pot. Shy, yes, but his demeanor was one of respect. As a soldier he'd been wounded and taken prisoner, but Lauren had the feeling that killing didn't come easily to Irish McBride. He considered himself unappealing as a man because of his size. But Lauren found that size and earnestness reassuring.

She glanced at the sky again. He and Isabella had been gone a long time.

Lauren wasn't the only one counting the time. Carl Arnstine had been sitting up too long. He felt as if he'd never regain his strength. Weakness was something new to Carl. Not being able to go after what he wanted was also new. And he wanted Miss Isabella Alexander. For days her golden hair had skimmed along his chest as she'd changed his dressing. Her hands had planted little fingerprints of heat across his skin and sent chills down his spine.

Now she, and the calf who was her shadow, were off with Irish, and he was imagining all kinds of unspeakable things. Imagining them with a groan of impatience, anticipation, frustration.

Raven, her senses alive to the undercurrents inside her house, finally stood and pulled on her bearskin jacket. "I'm going up the valley, Lauren," she said. "Perhaps I'll find some grass where the snow has melted."

"I wish you wouldn't," Lauren said, finding something on which to focus her concern. "Until Sabrina returns, we ought to stay close to the cabin."

"I'll be safe, sister. You know that Mother Earth always protects me."

The dark-eyed girl waited politely by the door for Lauren's approval. Lauren couldn't push aside the nagging concern she felt, but she couldn't say no. Raven was right. Of all the Alexander women she seemed the most comfortable in this harsh land. Besides, the cow was lowing, asking for food. The range grass Isabella gathered was growing harder and harder to find. If Sabrina didn't return with supplies, the stock would have to be turned loose to fend for themselves.

Lauren sighed and nodded. Everything was changing since Papa died.

Then she heard the sound of laughter and the rollicking Irish folk song that announced the return of her Irishman.

Her Irishman? Lauren hurried to open the door.

Colter didn't mention the payment for their supplies, and neither did Sabrina. Still, she felt his eyes on her as they rode side by side, dragging the Indian travois behind them.

They passed the spot where they'd camped the night before and kept moving. Progress was slower now. Captain Colter gave every appearance of being relaxed as they rode, but his eyes were anything but. She could tell that he was constantly watching and listening. For what?

There was an intensity about him that seemed to encompass her as well, and with every hour it grew. By midafternoon clouds were gathering above the mountains in the distance—dark, angry clouds containing rain, not snow.

"We'd better start thinking about making camp,"

he said. "We need a place where we can keep our supplies dry if that storm keeps building."

"Up ahead, the cave where I hid you from the Indians."

"That's good." He picked up the pace. The snowstorm they'd weathered was giving way to another kind of storm, the kind that came in the spring, the kind that brought great whirlwinds to the plains, and floods to the flatlands. He hadn't expected the temperature to rise enough to melt the snow, but it was doing just that. Strange weather for March.

By the time they finally reached the place where they left the trail and climbed up, the wind was blowing wildly and the day was as dark as night. It took three trips up the side of the mountain to stash the supplies inside the cave.

"Find something for a fire before it starts to rain," Colter said. "I'll see what I can do about the horses."

"There's a ledge just below us, around behind that boulder. If you can get them up there, they'll be protected."

He turned and began the descent. "Cover their eyes," she called out, only to have her words caught by the wind and carried away.

For the next few minutes she didn't have time to worry. Finding wood was important, for the wind was cold and damp. She dragged several dead limbs inside the cave, then went back for twigs and smaller pieces to start the fire. Finally, convinced that she had enough, she started back to the cave. The rain began to fall just as she reached the entrance.

Piling the twigs and grass near the cave opening, she went about setting a fire. From their packs she took one of the precious matches and, shielding it from the wind, touched the damp grass. It wouldn't catch. She didn't want to chance using another match unsuccessfully and searched for something dry enough to burn.

Nothing, except the oats for the cattle, which had to be protected. Desperately she looked around, reaching inside her pocket for another match. Then she noticed a strand of her hair. Quickly she peeled off her hat and, with the Indian hunting knife, cut a swatch of her own hair and covered it with the twigs. This time the match caught the hair, and in seconds her little fire began to crackle.

The cave opening sucked the smoke and the smell of burning hair away, and some of the heat as well. She laid out the blankets and located the coffeepot. From the steady downpour she was able to fill the pot without leaving the cave. Colter would be wet and cold. She used his need to justify dipping into their new supply of coffee. Just this once she'd made it strong enough so that they could tell what they were drinking.

Using a small amount of flour mixed with rainwater, she placed it in the greasy skillet, covered it, and buried it in the fire. She knew enough about cooking to know that it probably would be hard as the boulders outside, but it would be filling.

Moments later Colter stepped into the cave and came to an abrupt stop. "What the hell?"

Sabrina glanced up. "What's wrong? Don't you like my fire?"

"Your hair, damn it! What happened to your hair?"

"Oh, I used a hunk of it to start the fire. It's an old Indian trick. Raven told me."

He only stared. She looked—wounded. Without her hat, her hair spilled down across her shoulders like liquid fire, except for the missing gap. He was caught by the reflection of the flames, turning her auburn tresses into fire. Suddenly, tonight, she seemed younger, less certain of herself, more feminine.

"Did you get the horses settled?"

"Yes, but I had to leave our 'possum belly' on the trail. Surely they didn't really make that rawhide pouch from possum bellies."

"I don't know. I just know the Indians tie hide between the poles and use it for carrying everything from tepees to children. Before they had horses, they used dogs to pull them."

"This is a good spot. The rain will wash away our tracks. And we're high enough to see and hear anyone approaching."

Colter shivered and moved nearer the fire. It wasn't just the cold that bothered him—the setting was entirely too intimate. They were alone, inside a burrow in the earth. He took off his hat and slung the water from its brim. The raindrops hit the fire and hissed.

"You're soaked," she said. "Take off your wet jacket and hand it to me. I'll throw it over that rock to dry."

He hesitated for a moment, then removed his gloves and, with icy fingers, took off his jacket and draped it over the rock, turning back to find that Sabrina had unfolded one of the blankets.

"Come sit by the fire and get warm."

Colter couldn't tell whether he was just cold, or whether he was reacting to the same tension that had grown with every mile they'd covered through the afternoon. Her words kept coming back to him. "He's my husband," she'd said, not from necessity, but willingly protecting his identity by turning him into the husband she'd started out to find.

"What about you?" he asked. "You're wet, too."

She was. In her attempts to set up camp and be ready for Colter, she'd hardly even noticed. Now she did, and she started to tremble. Under his intense gaze she unfastened her coat and laid it out next to Colter's.

Colter warmed the blanket by holding it close to the fire. Then he draped it around Sabrina's shoulders and pushed her down on the bedroll.

He covered himself with the other blanket, then sank down beside her. "Is that coffee I smell?"

"Yes. Sorry, all I can offer you along with it is some very hard bread." She reached for the handle of the pan submerged in the fire, swore, and dropped it.

Colter, still holding his glove, took the handle and pulled it back. He lifted the lid and sniffed. "Smells good. Is it ready?"

"Not yet. Turn it over and put it back in the coals for a few more minutes."

Colter followed her instructions, or tried, finally resorting to the Indian knife to turn the bread over. "Now, let me see your hand. Did you burn it?"

"No, my hand is fine. The skin is just a little tender."

"Sabrina, let me see your hand."

Sabrina reached out, holding her breath when Colter's hand enclosed hers, then turned her palm to the light of the fire. The blisters had formed scabs. A few were almost healed, leaving large pink splotches of tender new skin. The captain studied her for a long time before speaking.

"When I was a little boy, my mother used to kiss my wounds and make them well."

"Your wounds?" she said, her voice barely more than a squeak. He was still holding her hand.

"Yes. My father was very strict. When I misbehaved, which was often, he'd punish me. Sometimes he—paddled me."

Sabrina gave a nervous laugh. "I find that hard to believe."

"What? That my mother kissed it well, or that I was punished?"

"That you were merely paddled. I doubt that Colter ever simply misbehaved."

"You're right. It was a strap and there was nothing simple about it. I did things that I knew were bad for me. But if I wanted a thing that much, I took a chance on the consequences. Didn't you ever do something you knew was foolish?"

"Yes." The squeak turned into a whisper, and her heart was beating so hard that she thought surely Colter could hear it.

"Was it worth it?"

"I don't know—yet."

His eyes weren't blue, she thought. They were silver. Yet they were no longer cold. Somehow the ice seemed to melt and blur so that she could feel gentleness in the man she'd thought made of granite. Suddenly she knew that the little punishments he'd suffered were much more than little.

Sabrina reversed their position, turning Colter's hand up and examining his palm. "Strong hands," she said. "Hands that protect and defend."

This time he didn't attempt to conceal the tremor that ran through him. "Hands that kill," he said quietly, and pulled it away, as if he were afraid for her to see more. "How about that coffee?"

She knew too that if she let herself care, her hurt would be just as great. Colter had already said there could be nothing between them. He was first, last, and always a soldier. And she knew she had nothing to offer that he needed. Once his men were well, he'd be gone. Colter wasn't a man to stay in one place.

Suddenly the silver in his eyes turned back into granite, as if a barrier had once again been erected. Sabrina reached back and found two tin cups in the pack. This time when she pulled the skillet from the fire, she used a corner of her blanket. Tearing the bread into two pieces, she handed the largest one to Colter. Then she filled the silence by pouring their cups full of the fragrant, hot liquid.

Neither spoke as they ate. The moment of touching had at first broken the tension, then seemed to sear their vocal cords, destroying the ease of their conversation and changing the moment of warm sharing into one of awkwardness.

After they drank a second cup of coffee, Sabrina held the pot outside the entrance to the cave and collected enough rainwater to rinse the cups. She set the pot outside and let it refill, so that she'd have water for the morning.

Colter built up the fire and stretched out on the bedroll, covering himself with his blanket. This time there was no room to separate the blankets, and Sabrina was forced to lie down beside him, feet to the fire, heads away.

The flickering flames danced across the roof of the cave like probing fingers. Sabrina watched, trying desperately to still her breathing. What would happen when they returned to the valley? They had food and supplies to last for a while. But she'd been forced to use a good portion of the silver ore Cullen had hoarded over the last months. She would have to begin mining the Silver Dream right away.

Colter had gone to great lengths to make her understand that he wasn't a prisoner. Yet he was tied to her valley, at least until his men were capable of travel. That was assuming that he could find mounts for them and that he wasn't captured by the military. Then he'd leave, going back to his secret assignment, risking his life for ideals that seemed lost and a future that no longer belonged to him.

Everything was such a muddle. She sighed and turned over on her side. Her feet were too warm and her shoulders were freezing. But if they changed the position of the blankets, there was room for only one beside the fire.

Colter wasn't asleep. She knew that he was as wide awake as she. The rain continued to drone against the rocks, and the wind howled.

Colter heard her inadvertent sniff. That surprised him. *Ah, no, don't start crying, woman.* He was no good with women, certainly not crying women. The sound of tears would bring him to his knees in a heartbeat. Still, it made his companion seem softer, in need of the comfort he had no intention of offering. He didn't blame Sabrina. She'd lost her father and overnight had become saddled with the burden of her sisters. Then she'd rescued four prisoners, and with all the risks that brought, he didn't think she'd considered the danger of being thought an accomplice. The future looked bleak. But he hadn't expected her to cry.

There was only one sniff, followed by complete stillness and breathing so shallow that he knew she was consciously controlling it. Clearly she hadn't wanted him to know that the formidable Sabrina Alexander had a weakness.

The rain had slowed to a rhythm that was almost hypnotic. Warm rain at midnight, Sabrina thought longingly, not like the one she was hearing. Tonight the rain was cold and lonely, and for the first time since she was a very little girl, Sabrina wanted someone to kiss away the hurt.

The morning brought clear skies, a muddy trail, and even slower travel.

It was midday when they rounded the clump of rocks behind which Sabrina had hidden when she heard the man called Long Rifle talking to Gray Warrior. There in the middle of the trail was Brother Seaton's wagon with one wheel dismantled and leaning against a tree.

"Praise the Lord," Brother Seaton said. "God is truly good to send up a second miracle in the wilderness."

Colter took in the scene and groaned inwardly. "If we're the second one, I'm afraid to ask what was the first."

"Sergeant Nealey, of course. He's gone to the fort for help. But he said it would be two days before he could ride there and back."

This time it was Sabrina who voiced the concern. "Sergeant Nealey has gone for troops? Why?"

"To repair our wagon, of course," Brother William explained. "We're disabled here. Can't you see we've lost a wheel?"

It didn't take Colter long to see that the linchpin holding the tire on the axle had broken. He glanced at Sabrina, then back at the misguided missionaries. "Maybe we can help you." He lifted the wheel, examined it carefully, and motioned the two men closer.

"What can we do to help?" Brother Seaton asked.

"You two lift the wagon and let me slide the wheel back on the axle."

"We tried that, but it kept working its way off. You see the linchpin that holds it in place seems to be broken off inside."

"Yes, I see that. Give me the knife, Sabrina."

Sabrina climbed down from her horse and handed the knife to Colter. Using it as a wedge, he gave a strong chuck to the end of the knife and drove the broken piece out of the hole.

"I'll find something to use as a wedge," she said, looking along the trail. It took three tries before she found a limb small and green enough to fit through the hole. Now the wheel was mounted on the shaft, and the stick held it in place.

"How can we ever thank you folks?" Brother Seaton asked.

"Just turn this wagon around and head back for Boulder City," Colter said. "You got no business out here alone."

"Oh, we're not alone now," the cheerful little man said. "We're with you. Perhaps we'll just visit with you folks a spell while we wait for the sergeant to return."

"No!" both Sabrina and Colter said at the same time.

"I mean, you can't," Sabrina said. "You wouldn't want to. We have a very small cabin, one room, and a loft—and there are nine of us."

Shocked disbelief washed across Mrs. William's face. "You have seven children?"

"No, of course not. They're not my children; they're my sisters. I mean four of them are my sisters, the others are—"

"Hired hands," Colter finished for her. "But you can see that we don't have much room."

"That's quite all right," Brother Seaton said confidently. "The Lord will provide."

Sabrina looked at Colter and felt sick. She'd lied to protect the man, and now that lie was about to lead to more lies. The missionary thought she and the captain were married. If that wasn't enough, he was about to find out that the hired hands were the escaped killers the military was searching for. How could she explain their injuries? Sergeant Nealey would definitely return with troops. She couldn't allow that to happen. She had to do something quick.

"I'm sorry, Brother Seaton, I'm afraid we've misled you. This man and I aren't married. We're . . . we're living in sin. It would be morally wrong to welcome you into our home under false pretenses. I'm certain the Lord would punish us severely. Under these conditions you'd do better to wait here for the sergeant."

Sabrina started to remount.

"You poor thing," Mrs. William said, coming to put her arms around Sabrina, holding her back. "I know about men who lie to their women. And we won't let this man get away with taking advantage of you. We'll remedy your problem right now. Brother Seaton will marry you, and the world will never know of your transgressions."

"No! I mean that isn't necessary. I mean we can't. We're—waiting for someone else."

"Well, the only one who's likely to come along here is the sergeant, and I really don't think he's empowered to perform marriage ceremonies." Mrs. William eyed Sabrina with concern. "If you're being held against your will, child, you can just come along with us to the fort and we'll protect you. I'm sure that once we explain it to the fort commander, he won't allow this man to escape his duty."

"No, that won't be necessary," Colter said, coming to the conclusion that the missionaries were rapidly deciding he was misusing Sabrina, and that the only way to protect her virtue was to take her to the fort along with them. If that happened, it would mean death warrants for his men. He didn't have a choice except to sacrifice himself.

"Yes, that isn't necessary," Sabrina chimed in. "Mr. . . . I mean Cullen isn't interested in marrying me. I don't want him as a husband. Tell them why . . . Cullen."

"Of course I'm going to marry you, darling. But I insist it be done properly. When Brother Seaton gets his church built, we'll be the first bride and groom to walk down the aisle."

"Nonsense! God's house is everywhere," the minister proclaimed, opening his Bible. "Let us pray."

Sabrina and Colter had no choice but to bow their head and listen to Brother Seaton plead for God's forgiveness for their living in sin. He rashly promised that the couple would earnestly work toward achieving salvation, beginning with today.

"Now, join hands," he instructed.

Unable to figure out how to avoid following his orders, they complied, eyes still pressed closed.

Oh, Papa, send the little people, Sabrina prayed. *Mother Earth, send a flood.*

"Now, do you, Sabrina, take this man to be your husband?"

Sabrina's eyes flew open. "No, of course not. I mean later . . . I will. I promise I will."

"And you, do you, sir, take this woman to be your wedded wife?"

Sabrina's promise became a consent to Brother Seaton, and Colter couldn't see any way out. If he confessed the truth, he'd be sentencing his men to certain death. If he continued to lie, the minister would certainly spread that juicy bit of information to Sergeant Nealey. The only way out was to marry this woman. The ceremony would never be legal, anyway, he rationalized. The missionary was marrying a woman named Sabrina and a man he thought was Cullen Alexander, who was dead and buried.

Finally, in a pious voice, Colter said, "I do."

Sabrina gasped.

Mrs. William clapped.

Brother William said, "Praise the Lord!"

Brother Seaton smiled. "Now, young man, you may kiss your bride."

Sabrina's mouth was still parted in astonishment. Her hazel eyes were wide, and her voice caught back somewhere in the vicinity of her rib cage.

"You're not," she said in a strangled voice, "actually going to kiss me before God and everybody?"

"I think I have to," Colter said, and quite firmly planted his lips on hers.

The kiss was brief, but somehow it sealed the ceremony, marking it with a finality that seemed reverent.

"Now," Brother Seaton said briskly, "let us move on. Mrs. Alexander, will we reach your place by dark?"

Sabrina, still dazed by what had happened, couldn't speak a word.

8

"What do we do now, *husband*?" Sabrina was so angry that she could barely speak. She had to force herself to lean close to Colter to keep her conversation private.

"Have a honeymoon?" he offered, curling the corners of his mouth into a big smile for the benefit of the missionaries following them.

"I was thinking more of a hanging," she snapped.

"You know," Colter observed seriously, "you probably saved us from just that. Thank you for not giving us away. You could have easily."

"There had to have been another way, other than a—wedding. We could have . . . ."

"Maybe, but short of holding the brothers Seaton and William prisoners, I couldn't think of one. Don't worry, Sabrina, I won't hold you to your vow."

"I never made a vow, except a private one to shoot you at the first opportunity!" She forced herself to hold her voice down.

Colter didn't know why he was teasing her. This

kind of interplay was totally out of place, given their situation. The last thing he wanted was a wife, though the thought of a wedding trip with this woman raised his temperature a degree or two. What he'd done was draw the women even further into his plans by building a web of deceit.

It was time to be honest. "You're right to be angry," he admitted. "But given our situation, I thought it would be well for us to go along with Brother Seaton. The alternative could be worse."

"What alternative?"

"Your having to go to the fort to protect your honor. Of course, if you'd rather, you may go. That might be the best way to keep the missionaries away from the valley. I'll even escort you. I assure you that my men will look after your sisters."

"That's exactly what I'm afraid of!" This time her voice rose in anger. "I have no intention of leaving my sisters in your care. I didn't need your protection before, and nothing has changed."

"Don't worry," Mrs. William called out from the rear. "The men always take a time to adjust, but I'm sure Cullen will make you a good husband."

"I'm not worried," Sabrina snapped, without thinking.

"Of course, it does help if you try to be gracious and loving," the missionary's wife chided gently. "It's a woman's duty to put aside her wishes and follow those of her husband. You'll be blessed with a fine life and many children."

Colter chuckled.

Sabrina swallowed her retort, then pursed her lips, let out a long breath, and said, "I wouldn't want the Lord to punish us any more than He already has. I promise you that I intend to give my husband just what he deserves."

For the rest of the afternoon Sabrina and Colter exchanged cloyingly sweet glances meant to reassure their witnesses, while they each tried to think of a way to ward off the impending disaster ahead. The answer came through no effort on either Sabrina's or Colter's part. Just after they turned off the main trail and headed toward the valley, the make-do linchpin snapped, sending the wheel off its axle.

"Thank you, Lord," Colter whispered. He dismounted and untied the rope pulling their sling. "Sabrina, you go on ahead to the cabin and prepare for our guests."

"And what are you going to do, *husband*?"

"I'm going back and"—he hesitated, formulating the lie he was about to tell—"leave a clear trail for Sergeant Nealey. After all, *wife*, we don't want him to go the wrong way, do we?"

"Of course not," she said sweetly. "I trust you'll direct him properly."

"But what about us?" Brother Seaton asked, puzzled at the exaggerated interchange between the newly united couple.

"You wait right here, Brother Seaton," Colter directed. "Sabrina will send one of my—our hands back to repair your wagon."

"But we'll just walk along with Sabrina," Mrs. William said agreeably. "Surely it isn't too far now."

"Oh, but it is," Sabrina said, giving her horse a nudge. "I'll be back soon."

Before their unwelcome guests could protest, Sabrina had ridden off into the canyon and Colter was backtracking down the trail.

"But what if hostile Indians come?" Brother Seaton called out to his retreating rescuer.

"Pray for a burning bush," Colter said, and rode away.

"Look, it's Sabrina. She's alone." Raven started toward the door, followed by her sisters and Tyler.

Sabrina rode hell-bent for leather, sending her horse into the barn and meeting her anxious family at the porch. "I don't have time to answer any questions, so listen close. There are three missionaries on their way up here, and we have to convince them that—I mean they think that—"

Mary took her sister's hand, as if to slow her speech. "What, Sabrina? Why are missionaries coming here?"

"Where's the captain?" Tyler asked, surveying the valley anxiously.

"He's trying to erase our trail so the troops won't come. Oh, it's too complicated to explain right now. We just have to convince them the captain and I are— married and that you men are hired hands."

"Married?"

Their surprise was so great that Sabrina didn't know which of her sisters had spoken.

Finally Mary asked the question. "You want us to pretend that you and the captain are married?"

"Yes, it's important."

"And," Lauren repeated dutifully, "that Carl and Tyler and Mr. McBride are hired hands?"

"Yes!" Sabrina snapped. "If you want these men to remain free, you'll do as I say."

"But, Brina," Isabella argued, as though she hadn't heard Sabrina's startling confession, "Carl isn't well enough yet to be a hired hand. Nobody is going to believe it. They'll see he's been shot."

"Then he'll have to be a sick hired hand," Sabrina said, the worry in her voice galvanizing the women into action. "We'll move Mr. Arnstine to the shed. All of you will have to move to the shed until we can get rid of our *guests*."

"Of course, we'll do whatever you say," Mary said, and began gathering up the blankets. There was a hint of a smile at the corner of her lips as she said, "And we won't tell them you aren't married to the captain."

Irish, who was standing in the doorway, turned immediately back inside. "Help me with Carl, Tyler."

"You can't carry him, Mr. McBride," Isabella said, biting back her curiosity and directing the others with a second surprising show of maturity. "I'll do it. You bring the blankets and help me build a fire out there."

"That's right," Lauren agreed. "Nobody's going to

believe that you stay in a shed with no heat and no sleeping facilities."

Isabella waited while Irish and Tyler helped Carl to stand. "They're about as likely to believe that," she said, "as they are to believe that Sabrina is married to anybody. But I'll keep her secret."

To their credit the women followed orders without any more questions. Moments later they'd made the move. Raven and Mary were building a fire and bringing wood inside to keep it going.

Sabrina ignored the questions in her sisters' glances. "All right," she said, trying to see the cabin through the eyes of the missionaries, "this is what we have to do now. The linchpin holding one of the wheels on their wagon has been sheared. There are some spares on the barn wall. Tyler, you take my horse and go down the valley, and bring the visitors back here."

Tyler nodded. "Is there anything else I need to know?"

"Just this: The missionaries think that Colter's name is Cullen Alexander and that he's my husband. The reason that I—that—we—never mind, Colter will explain. I can't even begin to, not now."

Tyler eyed her curiously, then nodded and moved off into the barn. She could only hope her sisters would continue to follow her directions without asking questions. Sooner or later, she knew, she'd have to explain—as soon as she figured out how.

Sabrina went to the shed. Carl looked ashen by the time they got him settled. Isabella looked as if she had no intention of leaving him, and Mary was sneaking worried glances toward the barn as Tyler rode way. Sabrina looked around. The shed didn't look lived in, but it would have to do. "Let's get to the cabin now. We're going to have to house these people until we figure out what to do."

Lauren lifted an eyebrow in question. "Can't they stay in the shed with the others?"

"No, two of them are husband and wife."

"Then they'll have to share the loft. We'll come

down and sleep in Papa's bed and on pallets by the fire. Come along, Isabella. Irish will look after Mr. Arnstine."

Sabrina noted briefly her sister's easy use of Mr. McBride's nickname. At the same time, she saw a flash of rebellion in Isabella's eyes.

"We have to do this, Isabella. If the missionaries don't believe us, they'll tell the soldiers about our prisoners. I don't think you want that to happen, do you?"

Torn between what she wanted and what she had to do, Isabella shook her head and followed her sisters. "I'll leave the calf here, Carl," she said. "She'll lie down beside you and keep you warm."

The injured man managed a weak smile. So far his prolonged recovery had one good result. The golden-haired angel was putty in his hands, and soon enough she'd be in his bed. That is, if he could get past the irrational pangs of conscience that had so far, unaccountably, held him back.

"There's just one problem, Sabrina," Lauren was saying. "We don't have enough blankets, and what about food?"

"Brother Seaton and Brother William have their own, and they have a pipeline to heaven. Whatever they need, they'll just ask for."

"And Captain Colter?" Raven said softly. "Will he be returning?"

"Damnation! I don't know. Maybe he'll run into a Ute war party and be scalped. That will save me the trouble of giving him what he deserves."

Lauren, caught by the simmering fury in her sister's voice, glanced at her. She got the distinct impression that Sabrina was having trouble deciding just what the captain deserved.

"The trip," Lauren ventured. "Did it go well?"

"The trip?"

"Yes, the trip into Boulder City for supplies. Did you get what you went after?"

"I did. That, and something I didn't go after."

Mary scurried along beside her older sister, not

even trying to hide her excitement. "Are you going to tell us what happened?"

Sabrina went inside the cabin and looked around. Without the men the cabin looked the same as it always had. Perhaps it was the only thing unchanged.

"All right," she said reluctantly, and told them about the charade she and Colter had created—that she and the captain were Mr. and Mrs. Cullen Alexander. She just couldn't bring herself to tell them about the marriage ceremony.

Captain Holland pushed back his chair and studied Sergeant Nealey. "You mean you left three helpless missionaries to the mercy of that renegade, Gray Warrior? You know we can't control his raids."

"Ah, they're all right. They're on the trail not more than a day's ride out. Besides, Gray Warrior is more concerned about settlers than he is a couple of missionaries."

"Why?" the captain questioned.

"Because the settlers claim the land and the animals. Missionaries are no threat."

"So what is so important that you left them behind?"

"I couldn't fix a broken axle," the sergeant explained, trying to decide how to make his suspicions seem important enough to excuse what the captain obviously felt was poor judgment on his part. "And I thought you ought to know about the Alexander woman and her husband."

Dane Beckworth, wearing shiny black boots, leather gloves, and the blue uniform of a Union officer, stood beside the captain, all his attention focused on Sergeant Nealey. Anything that bothered the sergeant might give a clue. He'd spent the better part of the last three days scouring the territory for the missing prisoners, not because of duty and perseverance, but as self-protection. "You say there's something about the girl's husband that bothers you?" he asked.

"Yes, sir, Lieutenant. I don't know the Alexanders,

but I've heard talk about the old man, crazy old Irishman hiding off up there in the hills looking for gold."

"Nothing new about that, Sergeant," Lieutenant Garland, the captain's aide, said. "What did the husband look like?"

"He was tall, thin, blond, a cold-looking character. Even I knew he wasn't a miner. He was just too quiet, trying too hard not to call attention to himself."

Captain Holland closed the book he'd been writing in. "So what are you telling me, Nealey? I've got four escaped killers, a missing supply wagon, and a renegade Indian band to worry about, not to mention a wife who expects to be back in Boston before the summer's over." He raised his eyes in a gesture of helplessness. "Boston! Balls! Double balls, Sergeant. I'd rather go into battle than to a fancy ball. Get back there and fetch those fool preachers before Gray Warrior finds them."

"But, Captain, you don't understand. They're heading for Ute territory, to minister to the heathens."

"The Ute territory is one thing; Gray Warrior is another thing altogether. He and his renegades refuse to follow orders. They continually go off raiding on their own. Something is going to have to be done about that. In the meantime, get those missionaries, Sergeant."

Dane stepped around the corner of the desk. "What if I accompany Sergeant Nealey, in case he runs into either the escaped prisoners or renegades?"

"Fine, don't take too long. The way the news is going, Grant is going to overrun Lee, and he's the last holdout. If that happens, I'll need you here to notify the settlers."

"What happens to the escaped prisoners if the war ends?" Lieutenant Garland asked.

"If they're still in Colorado Territory, they'll be caught and tried. Let's find them, gentlemen."

Dane nodded. He had every intention of finding them and Cullen Alexander. He didn't know who this miner was, but Dane made it a practice to follow his instincts, and they were telling him to check the man

out. Nobody alive could connect him to Dane
Beckworth the fifth member of Colter's misfits.

Even Captain Holland didn't know that the man
presenting his orders a week ago was not Union officer
Lieutenant David Littlejohn, but an escaped Confederate soldier. Lieutenant Littlejohn, reporting to Fort
Collins after completing a secret mission in the West,
had the misfortune to cross paths with Dane as he was
leading the pack mule away from the massacre. When
Littlejohn saw Dane's civilian clothing and the army
markings on the mule's packs, Dane had no choice but
to kill him.

Once the man was dead, it occurred to Dane that
he could change places with the Yankee, say that he
came along just after the massacre, that he learned
about the prisoners' part in the killings from one of the
dying soldiers. Dane left his clothing on the dead officer and, after hiding his loot, released the mules and
reported to the fort. He figured he had enough money
so that he could live comfortably for the rest of his life,
compliments of the U.S Army, once he made certain
that Colter's men weren't roaming around out there.
So far there'd been no trace of them beyond the missing prison wagon. Dane hoped they'd escaped and
were long gone from Colorado. He regretted blaming
his former comrades, but he'd had no choice.

Hiding out, being on the run in the West, had
never been his preferred assignment, but when General
Lee had ordered him to Colter's misfits, he'd gone,
knowing that it meant glory or, better still, a chance to
stay alive. He hadn't counted on being accepted by the
team. And even now he wished there'd been another
way.

Stolen supplies and intercepted gold shipments
were being wasted on the South. The Rebels were going to lose anyway. Dane finally decided that the spoils
of war would be better appreciated by him. Recruiting
Gray Warrior had been a risk, but he'd used the Indian
before, when he'd worked with the surveyors mapping
the territory. They'd both profited from that venture,
and it hadn't been hard to convince Gray Warrior and

his band of renegades to join forces with Dane rather than work for the Union.

Now the war was ending. Dane had money and, under the name of David Littlejohn, the promise of a new life.

Except for Quinton Colter and his misfits.

Colter studied the wagon tracks. There was no way he could conceal them, not as deeply as the wheels had sunk into the mud. However, his and Sabrina's prints were almost entirely obliterated, what with their horses and the travois traveling in front and the missionaries' wagon following. All he had to do was unload the sling and drag it forward until he hit a bare spot. Then he'd hide it. With any luck Sergeant Nealey would think that the Indians took both it and the missionaries away. He worked his way back to the turnoff and toward the missionaries' wagon. They were gone.

Apparently they'd decided not to wait for Sabrina's return. Good—he wouldn't have to explain what he was doing. Like Sabrina, lying to a man of God didn't come easily to Colter. In no time he'd loaded their supplies into Brother Seaton's wagon and fashioned a way to tie the poles together with one line. Without the weight, his horse was able to move the sling. For several miles he pulled the empty travois, until he reached a place where he had to cross the stream. Halfway into it he dropped the poles, and the connecting hide ripped away, washing downstream. By the time the military returned, they would believe that the goods had been stolen or pilfered by wild animals. Colter remounted and rode back to the turnoff, where he covered the wheel marks with leaves and branches. It wasn't perfect, but it was the best he could do, and night was coming.

Maybe he'd ask Brother Seaton to pray for more rain.

* * *

Tyler met the two men and the woman walking along the trail.

"Hello, pilgrims," he said, giving the odd trio a smile. "I was told you needed help."

Brother Seaton glanced expectantly around Tyler. "Are you alone?"

"I am. Where's the wagon?"

"Back there a ways. Mr. Alexander seemed to think we would be a target for an Indian named Gray Warrior, so we decided that we'd try to put some distance between us and our wagon. Did Mrs. Alexander get home safely?"

"*Mrs.* Alexander?" Tyler bit back a smile. "Yes, she sent me back with a linchpin for your axle." He took a look at the weary travelers and realized that they were as out of place here as Mary thought she'd be in Tyler's world. "Why don't you wait here and let me have a look?"

The round little man, who was obviously the leader, gave a nod of agreement and sank down on a rock. "Thank you, son. May God bless your efforts."

By the time Tyler reached the wagon, Colter was loading the last of Sabrina's supplies inside. "Understand we're having company, Captain."

"Did Sabrina explain?"

"Not much, only that you were married and that we are now ranch hands who live in the shed. She sent me to rescue three lost souls."

"Yes, well, that's the abbreviated version. At the trading post we ran into a Sergeant Nealey, who was escorting the missionaries to the Ute's encampment. When the linchpin broke on the missionaries' wagon, he abandoned them on the trail while he took off to the fort for help."

"Did he know who you were?"

"No. I've never seen him before, but I got the feeling that something spooked him. When he came on the disabled wagon, Brother Seaton invited himself home for supper. Bringing them to the valley seemed the safest thing to do. How near to being ready to leave are Irish and Carl?"

Tyler tied his horse to the back of the wagon and climbed into the driver's seat before he answered. "It'll be a few more days. Irish is making good progress on his crutches, he can take a step or two without them. But Carl—well, he's getting pretty randy over Isabella, but he's still too weak to do anything about it."

"That's what I was afraid of. My guess is that Raven will know where the Ute are camped. The best we can do is take the missionaries there ourselves. But we've got to do it without running into the Yanks."

"Yeah, well, I don't think any of us are in a big hurry to move on. I mean, the women need our help. It isn't safe for them to stay out here alone."

"You too, huh?"

Tyler ducked his head. "What do you mean?"

"Is it the little redhead?"

"I do like Mary, very much. She's so innocent, and I'd hate to have anything happen to her. Which brings me to this wagon and those people. Couldn't you have just left them back there somewhere?"

Colter slowed his horse and gave his friend a long, measured look. "I could have, but our hostess couldn't bring herself to abandon them. If it weren't for the Alexander women's kind hearts, we'd be hanging from the nearest pole by now, wouldn't we?"

Tyler nodded and moved the horses off at a measured clip. He heard his friend's stiff reference to "the Alexander women" and wondered at the odd choice of words. In showing his concern for Mary, Tyler wasn't doing anything that Colter hadn't already done. He just wasn't having the same trouble that the captain was admitting his interest.

A short time later they caught up with the missionaries, who were waiting patiently for their ride. Transferring the reins to Brother William, Tyler remounted his horse and fell in beside.

"Brother Seaton," Colter began, "I think you ought to know that our hands are new to the valley. They're travelers, like yourself, taken in by—Sabrina for the winter."

"Of course. A kind and generous woman you have there, Alexander. What do you raise?"

Colter had to do some quick thinking. "The ranch has been a way station for a stagecoach line, but the war interrupted service and it's—we're—come spring, we're going to raise cattle."

"We've seen some splendid animals along the way," Brother William added, "with great long horns. Do you have cattle like this?"

Colter thought about Isabella's cow and calf and smothered a smile. "Not yet, but we intend to once the snow melts and we can build the proper facilities."

"Mr. Alexander, did you get the trail marked for the sergeant?" Mrs. William asked. "I mean, we wouldn't want to impose on you and Mrs. Alexander unnecessarily."

"*Mr. Alexander?*" This time Tyler didn't try to conceal his amusement.

Colter merely frowned. "I took care of the trail. Don't worry, we'll get you to the Ute if the sergeant doesn't get here by morning." That would accomplish two purposes: get rid of the missionaries, and put him in touch with the Indians responsible for the massacre.

"I'm certain you won't impose on *Mrs.* Alexander," Tyler said. "She's very capable."

"Yes," Mrs. William agreed. "Of course I could never ride a horse like she does, or wear men's clothing, but I expect she has adjusted to living under primitive conditions. I'm sure that underneath she's a real lady."

Colter flicked his reins and picked up the pace. It riled him more than he could imagine that this paragon of Christian virtue would say anything disparaging about Sabrina. "Any man would be glad to have a wife like Sabrina—any man with good sense, that is."

"Of course," Brother Seaton was quick to agree, and directed a frown on his companions, who seemed properly chastised. For the moment conversation ceased.

The cabin came into view, and Colter wondered what kind of arrangements Sabrina had made for their visitors. Lauren came outside, wiping her hands on her apron, and giving the three tired missionaries a broad smile.

"Welcome. You must be exhausted. Do come in by the fire and have something hot to drink."

Mrs. William caught sight of Lauren's gingham dress and allowed herself to be led inside. Mary, standing to the side, hurried to the wagon and sought the coffee and flour. Tyler gave her a quick smile and went to her assistance, bringing in the remaining supplies.

"Brother Seaton here. This is Brother William and his wife, Grace. But most people just think of them as Brother and Mrs. William."

"We don't have much room," Lauren said, "but we're ready to share what we have with you. Where are you from?"

"Tennessee. Our home church was destroyed in a battle, and being servants of God, we couldn't join in the fighting. No, we're answering a higher calling, that of saving the heathens in the name of the Holy Spirit."

Colter glanced inside the house and saw that the injured men were gone. So were Isabella and Raven. He pulled the wagon toward the barn, where he unhitched the horses and turned them into a newly repaired corral with Isabella's cow. The oats were stored, with a small measure added to the range grass and fed to each animal.

A glance inside the wagon confirmed that the missionaries' goods were stored in strong boxes that should protect them from wild animals. He'd leave them there.

The sound of laughter caught Colter's attention, and he stepped to the doorway in time to see Isabella slip out of the shed and dance toward the cabin. So that's where his men were.

A quick check of the shed revealed sparse but adequate accommodations for the still immobile Carl and the barely mobile Irish. "You men going to be all right out here?" Colter asked.

"We'll manage, Cap'n," Carl said, his voice still weak. "If that big hulk doesn't hog all the heat." Carl coughed, lost his breath, and let out a long, rattled breath. "Where's Tyler?"

"He's getting the supplies into the cabin. I guess you heard that we have visitors, a couple of missionaries."

"Missionaries!" Irish said in disgust. "Couldn't you have run up on a good Catholic priest? I feel a great need to confess my sins."

"I hope you haven't sinned, at least not here, Irish, and I'd be happier if we hadn't run into anybody. Just stay put. And be ready to move if we have to. The missionaries think you're hired hands, and I'm hoping they don't know enough about cattle to realize this isn't a ranch."

Carl rose suddenly. "You think trouble's coming, Colter?"

Colter thought about the last twenty-four hours and pondered an answer. "Trouble, my friends, is already here."

9

While Lauren managed to get the missionaries settled and fed, Sabrina found work in the barn, reasoning that if she weren't present, the subject of her husband wouldn't come up. She was torn between fear that her marriage claim would be questioned and guilt over the lie she'd told to bring it about.

The trouble was that she felt obligated to protect the men. Trying to pretend she was Colter's wife wouldn't work, for the missionaries would surely see right through the charade. Subtlety had never been Sabrina's strong point. Either a thing was or it wasn't. The only time she'd ever allowed herself or her sisters to indulge in fantasy was when her father talked about finding his treasure at the end of the rainbow.

Cullen Alexander had never meant to lie, and he didn't consider himself a dreamer. It was just his nature to see things in a different way. Sabrina saw the glass half-empty while her father saw it half-full. Nothing could ever have changed him; Sabrina had seen his first two wives try and fail. Only Raven seemed to believe in the kind, gentle man who lived through his dreams.

Now this man Colter had come into their lives, and Sabrina hadn't been able to decide what to do about him. He certainly wouldn't want her as a wife, even if he were inclined to marry. She was simply a means to protect himself and his men until they could formulate an escape plan. She knew without being told that he'd do whatever was necessary, including kissing her. But marriage seemed extreme, even for him.

The truth was that the marriage wasn't legal. They both knew that. But, dear God, it felt legal, and maybe that was what was bothering her, her conscience. She didn't like not knowing where she stood. Marriage wasn't like a drinking glass. It couldn't be a halfway measure. She'd learned that from her father. He'd loved all his wives, just as he'd loved his daughters. And they'd forgiven him any shortcomings and loved him in return. Sabrina had never thought to share that with a man; therefore, she'd never seen herself with a husband. She didn't know why this deception was bothering her.

It was obvious that Colter didn't consider the dilemma worth worrying about. He neither mentioned it, nor avoided contact with their guests. Why, then, was she out here in the cold, after dark, sweeping the barn?

"Don't you think you've hidden out here long enough?" Colter was leaning against the barn door, his arms crossed over his chest.

"How long have you been standing there?"

"Long enough to know that there's no more trash to be swept. I think it's time you came in, unless you're planning on sleeping out here with the cow. You can't claim the calf. Isabella left it with Carl."

"I don't plan on sleeping out here," she said sharply, "though it wouldn't bother me if I had to." As if to prove her statement, she hung the broom on a peg in the corner and blew out the lamp.

"You don't have to worry. Your sisters have been very cooperative."

"That isn't it."

"Then what?" he asked. "I think you're avoiding me."

"I don't know what you mean," she said, walking toward him, but stopping short of the door.

"I mean you really don't have to worry," he said, bringing it all out into the open. "Both of us know that the wedding ceremony was a sham. I'm not Cullen Alexander, therefore the whole thing is illegal."

"I know!" she railed out, then wondered at the sharpness of her reaction. "There is no way I'd ever marry a man like you. You're everything I wouldn't choose in a husband—arrogant, dictatorial!"

"That I am. You aren't the first to tell me that, though I haven't heard it in a long time."

What she hadn't said, but felt, was that he was filled with so much pain and anger that nobody could ever expect any kind of tenderness from him.

Still, there'd been moments when he'd shown concern. She remembered his reaction to her blistered hands. An unwelcome shiver ran through her as she thought about the gentle way he examined her palms. And he had freed her father from the cave-in and helped bury him. He cared for his men and—and damn it, underneath it all, she liked him. Even if he was a thief. Too bad he couldn't really be a hired hand. They would work well together, if they ever decided who was boss. "Colter, we need to talk about what we're going to do."

"Agreed."

"Your men aren't ready to travel yet, and even if they were, you don't have horses. The army is looking for you, and you still need a place to hide. I have a proposition for you."

"I'm listening."

"I might be willing to offer you a job. Since the stagecoach stopped running, nobody ever comes up here. I think you'd be safe."

He gave a dry laugh. "Nobody comes up here? What do you call the three missionaries up in the cabin?"

"Well, they're the first."

"But probably not the last. I doubt that my feeble attempts to cover our tracks will keep Sergeant Nealey away for long."

"Then we'll hide you. They won't know you're here. After they're satisfied, they'll go away."

"And there's Gray Warrior, who has to have some kind of inside connection. I'll bet Long Rifle has sent him out to search for us. Then there's Raven's mother's tribe, who could, according to Lauren, come for a visit anytime."

"Pale Raven's family. The Arapaho. Of course. That's our answer. The missionaries want to convert the heathens. We'll let them. Pale Raven's family probably won't give up their beliefs, but they won't kill the missionaries either. We'll take them to the Arapaho. Tomorrow."

"We?" Colter asked wryly.

"We. You, me, and Raven. I'll tell Raven to prepare for the journey. Good night, Colter."

As she started to pass him, Colter stepped out of the darkness into a patch of moonlight and took her arm. "There's just one thing."

"Oh? What?"

"Where do *I* sleep tonight?"

"Why, in the shed with your men, of course." His fingertips were biting into her flesh. He took a step closer. She could feel the warmth of his breath on her face. "Where else would you expect to sleep?"

"It isn't me, but the good missionaries might expect me to sleep with my wife."

"You've been into the locoweed, Colter."

"Don't you think my staying out here will look a little odd to Brother Seaton?"

"Hang Brother Seaton. You're not sleeping in my bed!"

"Just a thought, ma'am. You might want to get your story together before you get back to the cabin. We are supposed to be married, though I guess we wouldn't be newlyweds, would we?"

"We're not anything, Colter. I thought we both understood that."

Sabrina felt as if she were being split in half. Part of her wanted to lean against him, allow the sheer strength of him to protect her. The other part wanted to jerk away, put distance between them, reach a safe space where her mind could stop the jumbling physical reaction his touch invoked.

"I understand, Mrs. Alexander. You just have to decide how we're going to play this, since we have an audience."

Colter realized he was prolonging her departure. Why? What in hell did he expect to accomplish by touching her? The way he'd felt since he'd been rescued was like being half-dead, or more accurately half-alive. Something about this plain woman seemed to slither beneath his skin and touch a part of him that had been lost for so long, he didn't know how to find it.

He didn't know why he continued to bait her. She was just so quick to respond, like some scraggly alley cat with her claws half-extended. Scratch her back and she wouldn't purr. If you insisted on touching her, you'd probably draw back a mass of bleeding flesh.

"This is not playacting, Colter. I don't know how to do that. I've never had the time," she said in a low voice, pulling herself away from his grip. "Good night, Captain."

As she headed for the cabin, he wondered if anybody had ever scratched her back or said sweet words meant to tease. More, he wondered what kind of woman Miss Sabrina Alexander would be if she ever let go that iron will and learned to play.

He could believe that she'd never been a child. Being forced to shoulder the responsibility for all this, her sisters and her father, had turned a somber child into a somber adult. Sabrina thought her father hung the moon, but it hadn't taken Colter long to decide that Cullen Alexander was a dreamer who was damned good at little else. He was beginning to see that not only had the man been irresponsible, he'd isolated the women up here so they would be unlikely to leave.

Hell! Cullen might have been right. If Colter had a choice, in protecting his daughters, wouldn't he? His father had done the same thing to his children, only he'd done it through intimidation, not isolation. Colter got away, but he wasn't certain the Alexander women even wanted to leave.

Now their world had been invaded, and he had the feeling that nothing would ever be the same for them again.

"Brother William and Mrs. William can have the loft," Sabrina said. "Tyler and—" She faltered. She couldn't say "Colter," she couldn't say "Cullen," and she was having great difficulty calling Colter her husband.

"Tyler and I," Colter spoke up, filling in the rest of her sentence as he stepped into the cabin, "will sleep in the shed with the hands. We have to keep watch."

"For what?" Brother William's eyes grew as large as saucers.

"Indians," Colter said.

"Wild animals," Tyler said at the same time.

Sabrina was beginning to believe they might escape any further playacting when Mrs. William suddenly questioned the arrangements. "What about Brother Seaton?"

"I'll go to the shed, too," he said quickly.

"No!" Sabrina glanced at Colter helplessly. "I mean, there isn't room."

Mrs. William glanced up at the sleeping loft. "Then there is only one answer. The women will share the loft and the men will sleep down here. I'll feel a lot safer, Mrs. Alexander, if your husband takes the bunk by the door."

"Husband?" Isabella said. The word slipped out, and she covered it by pretending to choke.

"Husband," Lauren repeated, looking at Isabella in warning.

"But, Sabrina—" Mary began.

"That's enough talk, girls!" Colter said in a voice

that brooked no rebuttal. "There will be *no* further discussion! Besides," he added as he came to stand beside Sabrina, "my *wife* and I don't always—sleep together, do we, darling?"

Sabrina's unexpectedly loud cough came out sounding more like "Humph!" It covered her sisters' collective gasp while she quickly added, "Not another word! Mary, Raven, Isabella, get the loft ready for us. Lauren, we'll make a pallet on the floor for Brother William, and Brother Seaton can have—Papa's bed."

Isabella's smile widened into pure mischief. "But, Brina, surely the captain—"

Sabrina turned toward Isabella, flashing a look guaranteed to shrivel the hide on a grizzly and said, "Now, Isabella. Raven, Mary, get up the ladder—silently!"

The girls looked at each other in amazement. Sabrina had never spoken to them in such a way. Of course, they'd never seen a man apparently so possessive of their sister, either. And even back when the stage stopped, they'd never, ever seen so many men inside their house at one time.

With barely contained excitement Isabella, Raven, and Mary climbed the ladder, spread the pallets, and waited for their sisters to join them. Their curiosity sheathed in silence, they peered over the edge of the loft, watching as Lauren and Mrs. William prepared a pallet for Brother Seaton.

Sabrina was doing some hard thinking. She didn't want Colter down below, near the door. She knew that he'd already had any number of chances to escape, but now there was a wagon in the barn and horses enough to carry his men. With her upstairs and him downstairs, he'd be in a position to disappear into the night. She couldn't allow that to happen. Colter already knew about the mine, though he couldn't know about the silver strike. Or did he? He knew she'd paid for their supplies and he had been out alone, hunting.

No, she couldn't allow him to leave. Not only did she have to protect her secret, she needed him to help her. It was too late to bring anybody else into her plans.

Captain Colter was going to help her make the mine operational, and she'd keep him here any way she could. He owed her a debt and he was going to repay it. She could feel his gaze burning into her. He thought he had the upper hand here, and it was time she exerted her own authority.

"I always sleep here, by the door," Sabrina said, daring anyone to disagree.

Mrs. William sidled over close and spoke in a low voice. "I know, Mrs. Alexander, and I believe I understand."

Sabrina couldn't conceal her surprise. "You do? Why?"

"I'm thinking we may have come along just in time to help you save your sister from making the same mistake you did."

Sabrina gasped. "Save my sister?"

"Lower your voice. Let's just keep this between us for now," Mrs. William whispered. "Surely you see that there is something between your sister Mary and that nice young man who came after us. I don't blame you for wanting to keep watch. But never fear, I'll alert my husband to keep an eye out. She won't be slipping out of this cabin with William at watch."

"Mary . . . and . . . Tyler?" Sabrina repeated helplessly. "You think I'm worried about Mary slipping out?"

"Of course, but tonight we'll put all the women in the loft with you on one side and me on the other. I know about these things. We must make certain that we protect Mary from depravity."

Sabrina tried not to see Colter's amused smile. She could only nod at the woman in the black dress, who was gathering up her things as Sabrina opened the door.

" 'Depravity' isn't the word," she whispered furiously to Colter, who'd followed her.

"No. I think I'd call it lust," Colter said under his breath. "Don't worry, darling, I'll let you have the bed by the door, and I'll sleep in the barn and keep a watch on Tyler and the other hands."

Lauren waited until Sabrina closed the door behind Colter and Tyler, then came along beside her sister and helped secure the door by laying a pole across it and into the slots on either side. "Sabrina, I'd like to have a private word with you."

"No! Not tonight." She gave Lauren a guarded look and inclined her head toward the missionaries. "We'll discuss the situation privately in the morning. Do you understand what I'm saying?"

"Of course, Sabrina," Lauren said, and turned to assist Mrs. William up the ladder. "Good night, Brina. Sleep well."

But Sabrina couldn't sleep. She lay wide-eyed, listening. But there was no sound of horses moving, or of a wagon being loaded or driven past the cabin. The world was silent except for Brother William, whose snoring was enough to make Mrs. William glad to be sleeping upstairs.

Finally Sabrina gave up. She couldn't rest easy until she knew what Captain Colter was doing. When she was convinced that everyone was sound asleep, she slipped out of bed, still wearing the trousers and shirt she'd worn all day. Threading her feet into Papa's Indian moccasins, she reached under the bed, found the bottle of Irish whiskey he kept hidden there, and tiptoed to the door.

She donned her jacket, put the whiskey in one pocket, and checked to make certain that her pistol was still in the other. Then she lifted the pole and pushed open the door, holding her breath for fear that it would creak and rouse the sleepers.

There was no sound except for the occasional crackle of a coal in the fireplace. Letting out a long breath, she scooted out into the night, feeling the blast of cold air hit her face, bringing her back to reality. She walked toward the barn, arguing with herself every step.

What in hell are you doing out here, Sabrina Alexander? she asked herself.

"You have to make certain that the captain hasn't absconded with the wagon and the horses," she whispered in answer to her own question.

And suppose he has. What will you do?

Her footsteps beat a rhythm that matched her reply. "Be glad. I don't need him."

Are you sure?

"Papa and I managed all these years alone, and I'll keep on," she argued.

But isn't it time you considered your sisters? Her footsteps slowed, as did her thoughts. *You can't do this alone.*

"I *will* do it alone, if I must."

Both her feet and her conversation came to a stop.

The next voice that came through the darkness wasn't hers. "You know, Sabrina, it might be easier if you told me what it is you're trying so hard to do alone."

It was Colter. He was leaning against the side of the barn, Cullen's rifle resting in the crook of his arm.

"What are you doing out here?" She was a clear target in the moonlight, while he was only a shadow.

"Keeping watch. I wouldn't want a wild animal to get you—or your guests."

"There are no wild animals up here." *Except you.*

"I don't know. I've heard some strange noises in the last few minutes. You may be in danger."

"If I encounter a wild animal, I'll take care of it."

"Oh? How?"

She slid her hand into her pocket and pulled out her weapon with a flourish. "I'll have you know I can use this as good as you can."

"Fine, open it up and I'll match you, drink for drink."

Only then did she realize that she'd brought out the Irish whiskey instead of her pistol. "Oh. Wrong pocket."

"And what did you plan to do with the whiskey?"

"I—I thought you and your men might like a

drink," she stammered. "For medicinal purposes, of course."

"Of course," he said gravely. "I didn't suppose that you were going to try to club a bear with a bottle. Relax, Sabrina, and let's find a place to sit down."

"I don't think I trust you, Captain Colter."

"That's the first smart thing you've said since you started that strange conversation with yourself. Are the Shepherds asleep?"

"Yes, of course. You don't think I'd come out here if anyone knew."

Colter slid along the barn until he reached a spot where they would be protected from the wind and sat down, leaning against the barn wall. "Why, Mrs. Alexander, you're being downright sneaky. And I don't think you've had much practice."

"Oh, you! Get up!"

"Don't run away, Sabrina. Come and sit down. I'm tired tonight, tired of doing things I don't like to people I do. Tired of second-guessing and covering up. Tonight I'd like us just to be two normal people who meet and talk about normal things. Tell me why you're really here."

Something in his voice drew her. That, and the knowledge that he had been keeping watch, guarding his men and her family. She wasn't foolish enough to think it was a vigil of protection from wild animals. But whether it was Indians or the army didn't matter; he was there.

He hadn't loaded up his men and run away.

She walked over and sat down beside him.

"I was afraid you might be gone."

"You thought I'd leave Carl and Irish?"

"I—I didn't know." But she had worried about it. Deep inside she'd wanted him to be there, and she was strangely comforted by his presence. And she, too, could use a little normal adult conversation.

"Well, I'm still here. Now, are you going to share that whiskey or just hold it?"

"I didn't bring a glass," she said shyly.

"Never use one when I'm doing serious drinking anyway."

He took the bottle and pulled out the cork, taking a long drink of the liquid. Then he handed it back to Sabrina. "Drink up."

Sabrina had watched her papa do enough drinking in his lifetime to know how it was done. She'd just never done any herself. Tonight she didn't want to break the fragile thread of friendship Colter seemed to be inviting her to share. She needed friendship and sharing. She raised the bottle and took a swallow.

Pure fire raced down her throat and hit her stomach like an avalanche of hot coals. When she finally managed to draw in a breath of air, she let out a long, "Whee! How do you drink this stuff?"

Colter took another long pull on the bottle. "A couple of slugs of this, and you'll forget all your troubles, darling. Drink up."

Darling. Of course he was just being clever, but it sounded almost wistful. Sabrina reached for the bottle, her fingers brushing his.

Colter decided that her touch was as powerful as her determination. He felt the return of tension within him that seemed to simmer always, just below the surface, then flare up every time Sabrina appeared.

He flinched.

She felt his involuntary move.

"I'm sorry, Colter. I don't understand what happens when I touch you."

"I'm sorry, too, Sabrina. I think it's called 'desire.' Haven't you ever been with a man, a man who wasn't your father or someone here to take care of business?"

"No. I've never had the time. I wouldn't know what to do. I'd probably think he was crazy and shoot him."

"Under other conditions I'd show you how good it feels. But I can't go down any more wrong roads."

"Why?"

"Life isn't that simple, not for me."

"You think it's simpler for me?"

"It could be. Why don't you and your sisters just load up your things and get the hell out of here?"

"There it is again, that word 'hell.' "

"Sorry, it's just that I've spent so much time there that it's become my home. Heaven is just an illusion."

"But we have to keep believing, don't we?"

"Believe, yes, but face the truth. You and your sisters could move into Boulder City. There are three men for every woman there. I figure it ought not to take more than an hour to pick out one for each of your sisters, if that's your idea of heaven."

"It isn't." She tilted the bottle and drank again. The warmth in her stomach spread through the rest of her body, freeing her tongue. "To me heaven would be having things back like they were."

"Half the world is saying that, Sabrina. And they aren't going to get it any more than you."

"So what do you suggest, Captain Colter?"

Recognizing potential trouble, he forced himself to give the only right answer. "I suggest that you go to the house and get some rest. The best way to keep your sisters hidden is to get rid of the honey that draws the bees."

"Honey?" she said, as if she couldn't quite focus on the word.

"The missionaries and us. Mrs. William was right about Tyler and your sister Mary. And I don't like it any more than you do. My unit still has a mission to complete."

"You aren't going after more guns and supplies, are you?"

"I'm still a soldier under orders, Sabrina. Once I accept an order, I don't give up just because I don't want to do it anymore."

"But you're a wanted man, an escaped prisoner."

"I was already a wanted man. This doesn't change anything except that now I have a face and a name. I'll speak to Tyler. In the meantime, you talk to Mary."

"Mary wouldn't let any man take advantage of her," Sabrina said confidently.

"Somehow I don't think she'd look at it that way.

She seems too honest and too giving. If she and Tyler wanted each other, I don't believe she'd think it was wrong."

"Then you'd better speak to Tyler, and Irish as well. I won't allow either of my sisters to be compromised." Sabrina started to stand. What was wrong with her? The ground seemed to be moving. No, her feet and legs were asleep.

"Damn it to hell! I can't get up."

Colter chuckled and climbed to his feet. "And you admonished me for saying 'hell.' "

"I never said it before," she protested, "not until you came around, messing up my mind."

Reaching down, Colter took the bottle and recorked it. Then he clasped Sabrina's hand and pulled her to her feet.

She felt like a feather being caught in the wind and slammed into his hard chest. "Goodness," she whispered.

Colter groaned as his arm snaked around her. It was good, feeling her against him—too good.

She giggled, then swallowed the sound. "You are very strong and tall, Captain. I'll bet you could take on a bear if you had to."

"If I had to. I learned a long time ago to do what I had to, to survive until tomorrow."

"A man ought to have a bigger purpose in life than just to survive until tomorrow."

"And what was your father's purpose?" He was making inane conversation, conscious only of the forbidden needs being broadcast by his body.

"To find the mother lode."

"And he never did. So why is the way I live less acceptable?"

"There's no focus. Isn't there something you want in life?"

"There was once. What about you?"

"Oh, yes," she sighed, leaning fully against him. "I want to finish his dream. And . . ." Her "I want you" was a whisper.

Sabrina's arms slid around his waist. She was clinging to him like a tree frog in a hurricane.

"Why did you come out here, Sabrina?"

"To make sure you were still here."

"I don't think so," he said in a hoarse voice tightened by the surging of his pulse. "I think you came for this."

The link between them was hot with promise. And this time, when he lowered his head, she was ready. The feeling was like lightning on a hot summer day, ready to strike, its power dancing like wildfire around them.

"You know this can't be," he said, his lips only inches from hers.

"I don't seem to know anything tonight, Colter. My mind is filled with sweet mush, and my body feels like the desert in July."

"I'll be leaving here as soon as I can," Colter argued.

"Don't go. We'll mine Papa's claim together. I'll share—whatever we find."

"Share?" He was losing the battle with himself as he jerked her up and savagely claimed her lips.

He never knew there could be such sweetness in a kiss. But he felt her opening up to him, like a flower to the sun, matching his needs with her own. The bottle fell to the ground as arms enclosed and bodies melded.

She gave a startled cry as she felt his fingertips brush her breast. Every move was sheer pleasure, a pain more exquisite than she'd ever imagined. And she gave over to his kiss and his touch.

For a moment Colter forgot where he was and why. Then, as the door of the cabin opened, he brought himself back to the present. "Sabrina, someone is coming."

"What?"

"From the cabin." He transferred her from his arms to his side, helping to support her while she regained her control.

"Mrs. Alexander?"

It was Brother Seaton.

"Yes?"

"Is everything all right?"

"Yes, of course," she stammered. "I just thought I heard something and I came out to check."

"Everything is fine, Brother Seaton," Colter said. "Tomorrow morning we'll be taking you to the Indian encampment. Better get back to bed now."

Colter started walking Sabrina back to the house slowly, so that the icy air could clear her mind and put out the fire that had raged between them only moments ago.

At the porch he stopped, planted a last quick kiss on her lips, and whispered. "Dreams are never real, my make-believe wife, even if we want them to be. Don't let your father's dream spoil your sisters' lives."

"But it isn't a dream, Colter," she said as she scooted out of his embrace and to the door. "At least I don't think it is. This time Papa found what he was looking for."

It was only later, when he changed shifts with Tyler, that he remembered what she'd said about Cullen's mine. Could that old man really have found it, the mother lode? She'd offered him a share in the mine, in whatever they found. She'd been around her father too long. She sounded just like a hundred other miners he'd heard. The gold was there, just a little deeper, just a bit farther up the river, just a day or two away.

Unless—

Suddenly everything fell into place. That's why she needed him to stay, because of the mine. It wasn't her sisters keeping her here, and she wasn't concerned about his men. That's why she'd come out with the bottle. She needed him, desperately, but not as a man.

She wanted a miner.

Miss Sabrina Alexander might not know much about the ways of being a woman, but she was learning. She was like a spider, instinctively weaving her web and setting it with a chunk of silver. And he'd come close to being caught.

Colter swore. He'd better get rid of those missionaries and get back to looking for the supplies. Dealing with the enemy was easier. It was impersonal. It was honest. It didn't hurt.

Getting tangled up with the Alexander women was the kind of commitment his men couldn't make. There was a price on their heads, both as Confederate soldiers and now as escaped prisoners. Tomorrow he'd consult Raven for a way to get the missionaries to her people while avoiding the soldiers. He'd take Carl somewhere to be cared for, and then he'd get back to his assignment.

Tonight was gone, forgotten, relegated to that place where dreams go to die.

Tonight the loneliness swept back over him like the wind roaring down the valley, and he felt the heavy weight of his responsibility. He shouldn't have kissed Sabrina. He shouldn't have let down his guard.

Tomorrow he'd find a way to leave, before it happened again.

In the cabin Sabrina's eyes closed almost immediately, her body still warm and pulsating. Being close to a man was like nothing she'd ever imagined. She just wished that Colter could be trusted. She wished he'd stayed because he wanted to, not because his men weren't ready to move out yet. Still, he was out there. He could have gone and he didn't.

And he did kiss her and touch her. She went to sleep reliving those few moments, refusing to allow any foreboding thoughts to spoil her one moment of passion. There would never be any more. But she'd worry about that tomorrow.

It was the next morning when she remembered that Colter had said he was leaving. He just hadn't said when.

10

Lauren was stirring a pot of mush the next morning when Sabrina came to the stove. Without turning she said, "I still find it hard to believe that you and the captain are married."

"We're not! It's just playacting, for the benefit of the missionaries and that soldier we met."

"Some kind of playacting." Lauren caught Sabrina's arm and forced her to look up. "You're not fooling me. I've seen this same kind of guilty look in Papa's eyes when there was something he didn't want to fess up to. You can fool the others, but not me. Tell me again, all of it."

"Well, the store owner got the idea that Colter was my husband, and with that soldier watching, I thought it was safer to let him believe it—to protect Colter."

"I can see that. Protecting these men would be the Christian thing to do. What happened then?"

"Then we ran up on Brother Seaton and the others broken down on the trail. They wanted to come here until we could get the wagon fixed. I couldn't let them."

"But they did come, didn't they? What aren't you telling me?"

"You don't understand. I'm not clever like Papa or Isabella. I tried to tell them we didn't have room, but that didn't work. I had to think of something that would make them want to go, make them believe they weren't welcome."

"Why would you do that, Sabrina? Don't you think that Papa would have welcomed them?"

"Papa never really welcomed any outsiders, Lauren. I knew the preacher wouldn't approve. I—I told them that this was a house of sin—that Colter and I weren't really married."

Lauren averted her eyes so that Sabrina wouldn't see the laughter there. Her sister was trying so hard to hold back the truth. It was painfully obvious that she was rattled.

"Well," Lauren observed, "it isn't a house of sin, and you aren't married."

Sabrina closed her eyes and dropped her chin. "We are now. Brother Seaton felt called to save us from hell by performing a ceremony right there on the trail."

Lauren couldn't hold back her reaction. She gasped. "You're actually married?"

"Not exactly. I mean, hang it all, I don't know. Brother Seaton thought that Colter was Papa. I mean not Papa, but that his name was Cullen. So he married Cullen Alexander to Sabrina. We said the words, but I don't know if we're married or not."

It was all Lauren could do to remain serious. She'd seen her sister go through every kind of trouble and keep her composure. She'd even seen her slip out the door last night, stay for a very long time, and come back unsteady on her feet. But looking at her now was like viewing Isabella's calf the first morning she found it. Sabrina's lips were swollen, her eyes red and puffy, and she walked as if she had sore feet from being too long on the trail. The only thing she wasn't doing was crying. She was truly upset.

Sabrina, trying to gather her senses, poured a cup of coffee and sipped it greedily. The way her head was pounding, she couldn't begin to explain the situation to Lauren. She didn't even want to think about the mess she'd made out of everything. She felt as if she were caught up in one of those terrible winds that bounced off the valley walls and back again without end.

Now she was about to leave her sisters alone with three soldiers whom she barely trusted and take three missionaries where they shouldn't even go. She was still trying to decide which was safer, accompanying Colter so that she could be certain he'd return to help in the mine, or staying put and hoping he wouldn't come back.

And there was Raven. Though she'd danced all over these mountains alone without Sabrina's concern, this was different. She'd be with the missionaries, certainly, but Colter was a wanted criminal.

"Lauren, we're going to take the missionaries to the Arapaho winter camp. They'll be safe there. After I'm gone, please find a way to explain to Mary and Isabella what really happened."

"Colter is going with you?"

"Yes, and Raven."

"Will you be safe?" Lauren asked. "What if that awful Gray Warrior finds you?"

"He won't. You know Raven. She can hear somebody coming for miles. And nothing ever seems to harm her."

"I know. She believes that the spirits of the mountains keep her safe. But those mountains haven't had to defend her from Gray Warrior."

"That's one of the reasons I'm going along. While I'm gone, I'm counting on you to make sure that everything—everybody—is safe. Don't forget that Tyler, Irish, and Carl are wanted men, not husband prospects."

"I'm sorry, Brina, no matter what you say. I just can't believe that these men are dangerous criminals."

"Oh, Lauren, don't think like that. No matter how much we want them to be something else, they're wanted men. Please, don't take any chances. Do you want me to leave you one of the guns?"

"Good heavens, Sabrina, we'll be all right, I promise. You're the one I'm worried about. You and Raven. How long will you be gone?"

"About four or five days, depending on whether they've moved their camp."

Lauren hugged Sabrina and held her for just a minute. There was more to her sister's dilemma than simply concern. For the first time Sabrina wasn't sure of herself, and Lauren hurt for the sister who'd never let herself be a woman—until now.

Colter and Tyler talked as they hitched up the missionaries' wagon.

"If Nealey returns," Colter instructed Tyler, "get Carl and Irish up to the mine. Don't try to take on the Yank. We don't want him to know we're here."

"He already knows you're here," Tyler argued.

"Yes, but he thinks that I'm Cullen Alexander's son."

Tyler smiled. "And that you're Sabrina's husband, I'm told. I'm really confused. Don't suppose you'd like to tell me how that happened, would you?"

"It's not important. It—well, it couldn't be avoided."

"Yeah, maybe."

"Tyler, I'm counting on you." Colter's voice was lethal, bringing an immediate end to any amusements. "Once we get these fool missionaries out of our hair, we'll get back to our assignment. I managed to let our contact know that you are here. He thinks Dane is dead."

"Why?"

"The Army found a drifter, shot dead in the woods. One of the army mules was nearby."

Tyler swore softly. "That's too bad. I've been thinking, Captain. I don't look forward to any more secret raids. It's one thing to fight as a soldier, wearing a uniform. I don't like it, but it's honest. This is too close to being an outlaw for my taste."

"According to our contact, the South is defeated. We knew it was over when General Sherman started in Tennessee and burned everything in sight between there and Savannah. Once they defeat Lee in Virginia, they'll capture President Davis and it will be over."

Tyler didn't answer. Colter understood his feelings. On the one hand, they were all tired of bloodshed. On the other, no man wanted to admit defeat. Win or lose, either road would take them a direction they didn't want to go.

"Maybe this is better, Captain. Out here it seems like every man is his own person. These mountains have survived longer than the men who live on them. I like the thought of surviving."

"Sounds like you're considering staying, Tyler."

"No. I don't belong here, and I have nothing to go back to in Carolina. I think I might travel to England and see the land of my father."

"That sounds good, Tyler. I've been giving some thought to our future myself. Carl can operate a saloon anywhere, if he can find a stake. Irish already has his eye on land on the Rio Grande. As for me—well I've always had an urge to see California, if we survive. But I guess it won't much matter what we'd like. We'll be like the rest of the South, defeated and too poor to start again."

Tyler frowned. "I haven't thought that far. I always had money before the war, from my trust fund. But money doesn't mean much out here. I think maybe Mary is right. She says a person just needs to care and be cared for."

Colter didn't want to think that way. That kind of thinking bred weakness, just like loving a woman. He shook his head. "Look after everything until I get back, Tyler. I'm counting on you."

"Get back, Captain. We'll be here."

* * *

Mrs. William was sitting on the wagon seat between her husband and Brother Seaton. It was obvious that she wasn't eager to leave the cabin and the company of the Alexander women. "Are you sure we ought not to wait for Sergeant Nealey?"

"I'm sure," Colter said. "With Raven to lead us, we'll be much safer than you will be traveling with one soldier. Raven knows these mountains like you know Scripture."

"But the Arapaho?" Brother William questioned. "I thought we were going to save the Ute."

"Don't worry, you'll bring a lot more souls to God by converting the Arapaho than the Ute, and you'll live longer, too. The Arapaho will welcome Mrs. William as a teacher for the children."

Sabrina, already mounted, rode her horse over to the minister. "Don't worry, Brother Seaton, Raven has been traveling through these mountains since she was a child. The Indians believe that the land is their mother, and that if they honor it, they'll be protected in return."

"That sounds almost blasphemous," Brother William said.

"Do not concern yourself about my safety," Raven said. "I go now to visit Flying Cloud, my mother's father, and the old ones. You may come or not, as you choose."

Raven turned and walked away from the cabin without waiting to see whether the wagon followed. And the matter was settled.

Mrs. William was horrified. "She's going to walk?"

Sabrina answered, "Most Indian women walk, or run. Only the men have horses. Don't worry, she's used to it."

Colter didn't worry about Raven, but he too was subdued this morning. He was growing soft. Instead of being concerned about the missionaries, he ought to be confiscating their wagon and using it to take his men to a place of safety. If there was such a place.

Then it was too late. They were headed back down

the valley by another trail, running along the far side of the valley, Raven in front, Sabrina beside the wagon, and Colter behind.

Colter hadn't wanted Sabrina to make the trip. But even with the missionaries along, traveling alone with Raven hadn't seemed like a wise idea. He'd have preferred to have Tyler along, but that would have left the women too vulnerable.

Instead of heading down the valley and following the trail toward Fort Collins, Raven headed due west and led them through the foothills along a rocky path that was hardly wide enough for the wagon.

"Are you sure you know where you're going, young lady?" Mrs. William asked as she almost bounced off the wagon seat.

"I know. By nightfall we will reach the lake of the moon and we'll stop. I go then to tell my grandfather that you come."

Brother William seemed bewildered. "You mean you're going to leave us up here in the middle of this wilderness?"

"Just think of yourself as Moses," Colter said dryly. "You're waiting for a sign from God."

"You're giving up that role?" Sabrina quipped, allowing her gaze to fall on her heretofore silent companion. He didn't look much better than she felt. His beard badly needed trimming, and his face was drawn and tired. Neither of them had had much sleep since she'd rescued the men from the prison wagon. At the rate they were going, the entire Ute nation could slip up on them and they wouldn't know it.

"Gladly," he answered. "I never pretended to be anything more than what I am."

And what is that? she wondered.

"Moses?" Brother Seaton repeated. "Yes, that is a good comparison. We will lead these poor heathens to the Promised Land. Very well, Miss Raven. We'll wait by the water as did the Disciples, except we wait for the arrival of an earthly being."

But Raven didn't answer. She was already around the next boulder, out of sight.

The day passed. The higher they rode, the more snow they encountered and the colder it became. By the time they reached the lake, even Colter was exhausted. Raven, who'd walked all the way, seemed barely winded.

"You make camp here and wait. I will return at daylight."

"Wait, Raven." Sabrina dismounted, forcing her stiff muscles to support her. She walked away from the others to where her sister was waiting. "Are you sure you'll be all right alone?"

"My grandfather knows we are here. He has sent my cousin to escort me. He is waiting at the head of the lake. Do you not see him?"

Sabrina hadn't. Now she looked and saw the lone figure silhouetted against the setting sun.

"Be careful, Raven. I know this is your land and these are your mother's people, but you're my sister and I worry about you."

"That is as it should be, Sabrina. We will come for the missionaries in the morning. If they do not wish to visit with the Arapaho, then we will take them where they want to go."

"But they won't be safe with the Ute."

Raven looked at Sabrina, then glanced at the brave waiting. "Their fate is already written, Sabrina. It will be as it will be. Do not worry about a watch tonight. The Arapaho will keep you safe until the morning."

Sabrina hugged the small, dark girl who seemed so much wiser than her fifteen years. Each time Raven left, Sabrina had the feeling that she would never see her again. And yet she always returned. But this time an unexpected shiver rippled down Sabrina's back.

Until she could see Raven no more, Sabrina watched her, then turned back to the campsite. Colter had already watered the horses and tethered them in a secluded place. He was hand-feeding them a swatch of grass and allowing them to eat from the half-filled sack of oats. Sabrina began to gather sticks and limbs to build a fire.

Colter directed Mrs. William to fill her iron coffeepot with water from the lake and sent the two men to find more wood.

Sabrina and Colter worked well together. For the first time she allowed herself to think what it would mean to have someone beside her, shouldering the burdens, making decisions. But she couldn't allow herself to think like that. Colter would be gone, and she didn't want to lose any of herself when he went.

By the time Mrs. William returned, Sabrina had the fire going. Colter produced an iron skillet, and Mrs. William cut thick slices of bacon, which she fried. The smell wafted through the night sky, and Sabrina realized how hungry she was.

Bread and bacon and then to sleep. As they cleared away the remains of the meal, Sabrina stole a glance at Colter. He was watching her. She felt a flush spread up her cheeks and quickly averted her gaze. By tomorrow they would have delivered the Christians and she could get back to the mine. By tomorrow she'd be back on familiar ground where she belonged. But first she had to get through the night.

"I'll take the first watch," Brother Seaton said confidently.

"That won't be necessary," Sabrina answered. "Raven said that the Arapaho would stay close by to keep an eye on us. For tonight we'll be safe."

"In that case," Colter said, "I'm for turning in. I know we're all tired."

He unrolled the bedrolls he'd laid out beside the fire and began to smooth the ground beneath them. Across the fire Brother and Mrs. William would sleep in the wagon. Brother Seaton took his customary spot beneath it.

Sabrina took a look at the bedrolls and felt a quiver in the back of her legs. She hadn't thought about sleeping. But the missionaries would expect her to sleep near her husband. Inwardly she groaned. Colter was right. She needed this night's sleep. But she knew, even as she came to her knees on her blanket, that she would never rest—not sleeping beside the man who was slowly driving her crazy.

* * *

Colter knew he should be pleased that they were about to complete their mission. He wasn't foolish enough to think that the sergeant wouldn't find his way to the cabin; he would. But with any luck he'd come while they were gone, and Lauren would explain that he and Sabrina were taking the missionaries to the Arapaho.

There was no reason for Sergeant Nealey not to believe what was true. Colter and Sabrina wouldn't have to face the soldier, and with any luck the man would go on about his business and leave the Alexanders alone.

Why, then, was he so tense that his eyes felt like dinner plates in the Colorado sun? For days he'd fought his growing attraction to his captor. His need baffled him. Sabrina Alexander wasn't a soft, gentle woman, the kind of companion he might once have wished for. She wasn't a bawdy, sensual woman who knew about life and men, and how to satisfy them.

Yet he was lying there seeing russet hair and hazel eyes in the darkness, feeling shame for his deceiving the missionaries, and responsibility for the women back at the cabin.

"Tell me about Carl," Sabrina said softly in the darkness. "Is he—can he . . ."

Her voice trailed away, and he lost the last of her question. He understood that she didn't want the others to know what she was saying. Thank God there were others present. Colter wasn't certain that he could spend the night with his pretend wife without touching her.

"I didn't hear you, Sabrina," he whispered in a voice that carried like the splash of a fish in the lake water beyond.

Damn! She saw no need to let the others know what she was asking. She might not like the situation she'd created, but it was done, and there was a certain comfort in knowing the man beside her was there.

She scurried closer, rising on one arm to speak in

his ears. "What I wanted to ask is—do you trust Carl?"

"A hell of a lot more than I trust me," he murmured.

"Trust is hard," Sabrina said in understanding.

"You don't know how hard, darling wife. And I don't think you want to be so close to me, or you're likely to find out. Go to sleep. We'll talk after the missionaries are delivered."

He turned over on his side, hoping that she wouldn't try to prolong the conversation.

"Please, Colter. I don't think I can sleep. I'm worried about my sisters. I should never have brought your men to the cabin. It seemed so simple then."

He didn't answer. What could he say?

"I should never have talked about taking a husband. It made them think about what they're missing. They want to lead normal lives, with families of their own. I never thought about what would happen."

"You can't blame them, Sabrina. It's natural for a woman to want marriage and a home. Haven't you ever thought about it?"

"No, at least not until now. I never thought that a man would want me."

He rose, caught by the mysticism in her voice. In spite of his best intentions he couldn't let her go on thinking that she was undesirable. "You'd be wrong," he said in a gravelly voice.

"I would?"

Not thinking, he rolled onto his back.

She held her breath for a long minute, then dropped back to her blanket and let out a long, sad sigh. "I feel all shaky inside, Colter. I'm not sure of what I'm doing now. Maybe, in trying to make my sisters' lives safe, I've brought a snake into the Garden of Eden."

"Well, if you did," he drawled as he sat up, "I think it's biting my bottom." He slid his hand under the blanket, pulled out a rock, and flung it into the water, where it made a big splash.

"What's wrong?" Brother Seaton came to his feet.

"Nothing," Colter said sheepishly. "It was just a fish jumping." He made a great show of smoothing his blanket, all the while he was resetting himself as far away from Sabrina as he could.

It didn't work.

Sometime after moonset he woke and found her head lying trustingly on his chest. For a moment he allowed himself to enjoy the rare feeling of belonging. Beneath the blankets her leg was thrown intimately across his body. Sabrina shifted, drawing attention to the portion of her anatomy at the juncture of her legs, the section pressed warmly against his thigh.

As she clung to him, he realized that his arm encircled her back, his hand anchoring her by clasping her breast. There was no chemise, no corset, no frilly woman's clothes beneath her shirt. Instead, if his touch didn't fail him, she was wearing wool underwear.

Wool underwear, against soft skin that teased his fingertips. *Don't torture me, Sabrina. Don't make me admit that I want you, that I care about the pain you feel.* Wool underwear. He wanted to laugh. He wanted to find the buttons and slip his fingers through, to touch bare skin, to discover what lay hidden beneath this rough exterior. But he couldn't move. He didn't dare. She might wake, and how could he explain their position?

Instead he pulled the blanket higher, covering them from prying eyes that might awaken early. She let out a little moan and snuggled closer, wiggling like the kitten he'd compared her to as she sought the heat of his body. When her hand stole around him, inadvertently brushing his male organ, he couldn't hold back a groan. Another few minutes of this, and he'd become one of those wild creatures he'd warned her against, and she'd know what it meant to become joined in the flesh.

He lay, forcing himself little by little to relax. When next he woke, he was alone. Sabrina's bedroll was empty, and the sun was making watery ripples in a sky of morning gray.

Colter stayed very still for a long moment. The

smell of Sabrina still lingered, a curious smell, like that of green leaves in the spring, or perhaps a crushed berry in the woods. Her scent mingled with the icy crispness of the mountain air as it ruffled the water, slapping it against the banks.

He came to his feet, seeing Brother Seaton beneath his blanket like a lumpy sack of brown sugar. Turning around, he caught sight of Sabrina, walking from the far side of the lake with a string of fish in her hand. He started toward her, then came to a stop, the memory of last night still nudging his body with warmth.

He wondered what she'd thought when she awoke. Did she lie there embarrassed that their bodies had reached out, seeking the warmth of each other? Colter adjusted his clothes and turned to collect more wood to build up the fire.

By the time the fire was ready, Mrs. William had made coffee and Sabrina was threading the scaled fish across a green limb staked across the coals.

"Brisk wind this morning," Brother Seaton said as he rubbed his bare hands together.

"Yes indeed," Brother William responded, "but God is good. He's sent us a fine mess of fish for our breakfast."

"Too bad He isn't here to divide them," Colter said, letting his frayed composure show.

"Divide them?" Mrs. William questioned.

"We could do with a few loaves of bread too. Surely you're familiar with the feeding of the multitudes." Colter's voice was little more than a growl.

"You seem to have more than a passing acquaintance with the Good Book," Brother Seaton commented. "Would you like to give thanks, my son?"

"He's be glad to," Sabrina answered brightly, and bowed her head.

If looks could kill, Sabrina knew she'd be dead. She'd decided when she woke and found herself wrapped in Colter's arms that if unclean thoughts were dangerous, she was already headed for the hell that Colter seemed so well acquainted with.

Surprising the campers, Colter bowed his head and

said a quiet and simple thank-you for the food and the earth that had provided it.

The ministers were pleased.

Sabrina couldn't decide whether he'd given a prayer or an incantation. Either way, the moment of truth was still there. If Colter knew how they'd spent the night, he didn't allude to it. If he didn't, she certainly never would.

By the time they were finished with the fish and ready to continue their journey, Raven and two members of the Arapaho tribe were waiting on the other side of the lake.

Brother Seaton started forward on foot, ready to meet his challenge with enthusiasm. "Look, Brother William, look how magnificent they are. Surely bringing these savages to God is the task He's laid out for a man like me."

Mrs. William took a long look at the two braves and averted her eyes. "My, my," she said. "They don't wear many clothes, even in the winter, do they? They'll have to be told about godly ways."

"I knew this was a mistake," Colter said as he moved his horse on down the trail. The two braves with Raven were wearing bearskin capes and fur-lined boots extending halfway up their legs, wrapped with strips of leather.

"This was your idea," Sabrina reminded him.

"I know," he said in a tight voice. "So was ambushing the munitions train, and look where that got me."

"You could always go back."

"I know. God knows why I'm not."

"I'm beginning to think that you're a lot closer to heaven than you are to hell, Captain Colter. Who knows? This might be the beginning of a new civilization out here."

"I guess I've listened to too many of Tyler's tales. I'm no Romulus founding a new city."

Sabrina winced. Her father's dream was still her dream, and the man she was beginning to rely on was warning her once more that he was there temporarily.

Instead she greeted Raven and her escorts as they arrived. "Good morning, sister," she said. "Thank your cousins for keeping us safe through the night and welcoming us to their mountains with a fresh catch of fish."

"You are safe, but you must hurry. A large war party approaches from the west, and we do not yet know their purpose."

Colter kicked his horse into a gallop, motioning for Brother Seaton to do the same. Soon the small party was making its way rapidly toward what looked to be a blind canyon. Raven's companions were emptying animal skins laden with snow across the trail, erasing any trace of the wagon and the shod horses.

"Surely nobody would harm a peaceful man of God," Mrs. William said in a worried voice.

"The problem," Sabrina said, "is that those who approach may honor a different God."

Brother William began to pray. Mrs. William held to the sides of the wagon seat and stared straight ahead.

Colter slowed his horse so that Sabrina's could come alongside. "If this doesn't go well, find some way to hide yourself and Raven. I'll lead whoever it is away from here."

"Colter, look ahead. There is no exit. I think it's time for Moses to rap his staff against the rock."

"What will that do?"

"Make a door where there isn't one."

"I think, wife, that you have me confused with Ali Baba and the forty thieves, which, now that I think of it, is a more accurate representation than a biblical figure."

She laughed, surprised to find that she could in the midst of pending disaster. "Well, the profession is right. If you're trying to escape capture, who better to lead than a thief?"

They didn't have to ask for a miracle. Just as they reached the end of the canyon, Raven cut behind a rock and disappeared into the mountain. The others followed before they had time to think. The animals plunged headlong into the darkness, following the sound of the leader. Ahead they saw a pale oval glow of light beyond a sheet of falling water. Bursting through the spray, they found themselves in a valley surrounded by steep cliffs and dotted with cone-shaped tepees beside a snakelike creek fed by the waterfall.

"Oh, my goodness," Mrs. William exclaimed, straightening her black bonnet.

"This is the village of my people," Raven said to the disheveled group. "And they bid you welcome."

"I don't believe it," Colter said, looking around in amazement. "The spirits of the mountains seem to have provided a door, water, and sanctuary."

Still wet from the trip through the waterfall, Sabrina shivered. "Yes. Now all we need is the burning bush."

11

Carl was definitely stronger. Isabella could tell from the way he held himself up as they made their way back to the house. He still leaned heavily against her, his hand digging into her ribs as he let her support him.

With Tyler on the other side, they made the move from the house to the shed with much more ease than the trip yesterday. "Only a little farther," she said.

"Oh, I thought we'd take a turn around the park before lunch, Miss Isabella," Carl said with forced lightness. "Then later we'll go to Brooklyn and watch a baseball game."

"I'd love to go to Brooklyn, though I've never been there, and I'd love to watch a baseball game with you—but I don't know what that is. Besides, I don't think your body is quite up to the trip," Isabella answered, flinging her head back so that she could give him a reassuring smile.

Carl quickly forgot about explaining baseball as he considered the inaccurate description of the condition of his body. "I keep trying to tell it that," he said seriously, "but it insists on rising valiantly to the occasion."

"Humph! Sorry!" Tyler said as he stumbled, digging into Carl's rib cage with the fingers supporting him. "Guess I stepped on something hard—like your head!"

"Something hard?" Carl chuckled weakly. "Ah, yes. I suppose you'd recognize that condition," Carl admitted. "Seems to me you're becoming something of an expert on the same subject yourself lately."

Isabella caught the teasing between the two old friends and felt a lightness fill her. She'd never been this close to a man before, not even with Papa. Papa had teased her about going to London to visit the queen, so she recognized the quick wit of the conversation between the two men, but she wasn't certain she understood the underlying meaning to their words. She only knew that Carl made her feel good. No, not just good—special, important. Sabrina and Lauren never understood how much she needed that. They mostly humored her, giving little thought to the frustration she carried around inside her.

This morning as she'd looked out over their little valley, she felt as if she wanted to sprout wings and fly. There was a whole world out there waiting for her, calling to her, and for the first time someone understood her need to experience it.

Inadvertently she gave Carl a squeeze with the arm she'd threaded around his waist. He tightened his grip on her, slipping his fingers higher until he was just touching the edge of her breasts. Her pulse quickened as a shiver rippled across her chest.

Carl felt her respond to his touch. He swallowed hard. "Hard" was definitely the word of choice here. Hard and ready. She was ready. And damn it all to hell and back, he was more than ready. He was twitching with impatience to peel that simple little frock away from that luscious body and sink himself deep inside. He'd already have taken her, except for the fluid that invaded his lungs and brought back the weakness. But that was improving. Soon he'd bed Miss Isabella Alexander and teach her all the things she'd been asking for since the first time he'd opened his eyes and seen those golden curls skimming his bare chest.

He let out a groan, bringing the movement to a stop. "Are you okay, Carl?" Tyler dropped the teasing. Concern wrinkled his face.

"Fine," Carl managed, concealing the fact that his problem was one of severe want, not weakness. "Get me inside and feed me, people, and I'll survive."

Isabella gave a light laugh. "That's what I plan to do, Mr. Arnstine. What would you like?"

"Don't answer that, friend," Tyler's interjection came just as they reached the doorway. "Just give him a bowl of snow and some strong coffee."

"Snow and coffee?" Mary said as she opened the door for them to come inside. "What kind of breakfast is that?"

"Don't pay any attention to Tyler, Miss Mary. He is a man who hides behind pretty words instead of taking on his demons and conquering them."

Mary smiled. "I don't believe a word you're saying. Mr. Kurtz doesn't know any demons, and I love to hear all those pretty words."

Carl's groan was loud and disbelieving.

Tyler's groan was silent and deep.

Lauren watched from her place by the stove and wished that Sabrina were there. She couldn't seem to stop her sisters from finding reasons to spend time with the prisoners. In truth, she was having a hard time staying away from Mr. McBride. He didn't talk, or tease, or spend a lot of time engaging her attention. Rather, he stayed busy, anticipating their needs before they became evident. He kept them in meat and wood for the fire.

Tyler cared for the animals, leaving Isabella free to see to Carl's medical care. Lauren had no reason to chastise Isabella, who had always been the same with her animals. If they were sick or hurt, she never left their side. What she lacked in medical expertise she made up for with compassion, and her patients always responded.

Now she was helping Carl sit by the fire, leaning against the wall while she wrapped him in a blanket and piled a second one across his long legs. Lauren didn't miss the quick kiss Carl planted on her wrist, or Isabella's bright laugh in response.

Carl was the man Lauren was most concerned about. Sabrina was right. These men should never have been allowed in the house. They weren't suitors, no matter how much her sisters wanted them to be. They should have been treated as prisoners and kept locked away from the Alexander women.

This lack of propriety had all come about because of Sabrina's plan to take a husband. When that thought dropped into their isolated lives, each of them had let their fantasies run free. If Sabrina had brought only Captain Colter back, they might have gone on as usual.

But she'd brought four men.

Captain Colter was Sabrina's. The other three seemed destined for the sisters. It never occurred to Sabrina that they would interpret it that way, but secretly each of the sisters quickly paired with one of the men. Sabrina had kidnapped one husband. Lauren was very much afraid that what she'd found was four.

Except for Carl Arnstine. Lauren kept coming back to that. She wasn't at all certain that his intentions were honorable. Isabella was young, trusting, and she'd always reached out for life with every bit of energy she could find. Now it was obvious that she was reaching out to Carl Arnstine. Lauren frowned.

"Don't worry, Miss Lauren," Tyler said from behind her. "I'll make certain that Carl doesn't take advantage of your sister."

Lauren blushed, covering her concern by reaching for the coffeepot. "Thank you, Mr. Kurtz. I'm afraid that Isabella has had little experience with men."

"I'm thinking that's true of all of you, isn't it, ma'am?"

"Yes, I suppose. We must seem—unsophisticated to a man like you."

"Sophistication is only a matter of knowledge

gained and used. Your family is warm and giving. These qualities are more to be treasured."

Lauren turned to look at Tyler, who was watching Mary tidying up the sleeping loft. "You like Mary, don't you?"

"I do. She gives me hope, and I hadn't thought to feel that again, ever."

"I guess you know, after Papa died, Sabrina went to Boulder City to find a husband. When she discovered you in the wagon, she thought that meant she didn't have to marry. She intended to keep you as our prisoners and use you."

"Sabrina, from the Land of the Sabine. Such irony."

"I don't understand, Mr. Kurtz."

"The Greeks believed that the founding of Rome came about when one of their gods, Romulus, tried to make his father proud by building a city of his own. He soon found that he needed women to people his city, and there were none. He and his men went into the Land of the Sabine, captured many of the women, and brought them back to their city."

"What happened to the women?"

"The men took them to wife."

"And was that a satisfactory solution?"

"Not for the families and husbands back in the Sabine."

"Oh." Lauren hadn't considered that their prisoners might have families, even wives, back home. She felt a great weight fall over her.

"The story was that the families of the women tried unsuccessfully, for years, to take them back. When finally they mounted an army and captured Romulus's city, the women refused to go. The men went home empty-handed, and the city of Rome was the result."

"How sad."

"Sad?"

"Yes, the women must have been torn between returning to their families and staying with the new families they'd made. I couldn't make such a choice, I don't think."

Tyler gave a wry laugh. "No? Think about our situation here."

"Are you—are there wives somewhere, waiting for you?"

Tyler gave a dry laugh. "Wives? Not likely. All of us are castoffs, chosen for this mission because nobody would ever miss us if we disappeared from the face of the earth."

Lauren lowered her eyes. "I don't think your story signifies, Mr. Kurtz. We would never keep you against your will."

"Maybe not you, but what about your sister? She went out and captured four men, brought them to her valley with the idea of using them. What happens when the army comes for us?"

Lauren had no answer. She had considered Sabrina's action a rescue. But the comparison to Mr. Kurtz's story about the women of the Sabine was too close to the truth. The Greeks had kidnapped wives. Sabrina had kidnapped—whom had she kidnapped? Perhaps Sabrina had been wrong from the start. Were these men prisoners, or were they, like the women of the Sabine, potential spouses?

"Do you really think the army will come, Mr. Kurtz?"

"I think the army will come. The question is, What will the Alexander women do?"

"Do?" Lauren said with a sharp pain in her chest. "The question isn't whether we *can* protect you and ourselves. The question is how."

"I thought you could track anything," Dane Beckworth said to Sergeant Nealey as the soldiers studied the creek bank.

"I never claimed to be as good as those Indians. But I know that travois was pulled into this creek. This is one of the poles. The goods either got swept downstream, or the Indians took them."

"So where are the missionaries you left back there?"

"My guess is that Gray Warrior got 'em all. He likes taking prisoners, making them slaves."

Dane tugged at his gloves and swore. He was beginning to doubt the sergeant's entire story. Dane and Sergeant Nealey had spent the better part of two days making the trek to the trading post and back along the trail. There were wagon tracks indicating that at least part of his story had validity. But of more than that, Dane remained unconvinced. For all he knew, the man had taken the missionaries' horses and wagon himself. Many of the men sent out here to protect the gold being sent back east were little more than thieves themselves.

"Well, they'll have a hard time with that gray-eyed miner if they took him," the sergeant said, leaving the creek and remounting his horse.

"What was that you said?"

"I said they'd have a hard time with Alexander."

"No, I mean about the eyes."

"They're a silver-gray, like granite, and he scarcely blinks."

"How tall was he?"

"About six feet, maybe a couple of inches more, and lean. Light-colored hair, scraggly beard. Why? You know him?"

"I think I do," Dane said, a dread settling around his heart. "Where do the Alexanders live?"

"Up in the mountains somewhere. Don't know exactly where."

"I want you to find out, Sergeant Nealey. You go back to the trading post and see what else you can learn from the proprietor."

"Where you going?"

"I'm going to study the trail a bit, then head back to the fort. I'll see you there."

Not bothering to conceal his reluctance, Sergeant Nealey turned his horse and started back to Wiley's. The lieutenant's concern for the Alexanders seemed greater than his concern for the missionaries. Nealey would have to think about that. He wasn't a man to miss an opportunity, and he'd had his eye on Little-john. There was something odd about his sudden appearance alone, with orders from Grant himself. The man was up to something.

Dane waited until Sergeant Nealey was out of sight, then cut across the creek and rode in the same direction as Nealey, along the edge of the trees. When he reached the spot where the rocks tilted crazily together to form a natural tepee, he climbed from his horse, hiding him in the woods. He built a fire inside the tepee and sat down to wait. He didn't know how long it would take, but Gray Warrior would be along. The Indian wouldn't explain how he always knew when Dane was waiting, only that he was a Spirit Warrior who saw all things. Dane hoped that he'd seen the silver-eyed man.

"Don't worry," Raven said. "This valley has existed undisturbed for hundreds of years."

The sheer rock walls dropped almost straight down, ending in a snow-edged valley interspersed with fir and cottonwood trees. A corral held a number of horses and three fat cows. Tepees made from tanned animal skins dotted the landscape like cone-shaped anthills.

The strange group followed Raven along the stream and into the center of the village, the wagon carrying Brother Seaton, Brother William, and Mrs. William, Sabrina and Colter riding along on either side.

Brown-skinned children hung back, eying the strangers from behind the legs of the women, who lowered their eyes as the wagon and the horses passed. Finally they reached the largest tepee, where Raven stopped and dropped to her knees.

Momentarily a very old man, wearing simple deer-skin leggings and a red flannel shirt, stepped out. His gray hair was woven into a long plait and hung down his back.

"Welcome," he said, touching Raven affectionately on her bowed head as he spoke. "I am Flying Cloud. Please know that any friend of my granddaughter is welcome at my fire."

"Oh, my," Mrs. William whispered.

"God sends his blessings," Brother Seaton said, climbing down from the wagon and holding out his hand in greeting.

Flying Cloud looked at Brother Seaton for a long time, as though seeking some unwritten message in his eyes. Finally he nodded and placed his hand against the missionary's palm.

"The gods bless all who honor them, even the white man."

"Oh, my," Mrs. William said again, looking at Brother William as if she expected him to object. When he didn't, she reached behind her and pulled a flour sack from the wagon. She waited, staring at Colter impatiently until he understood that she wanted assistance in dismounting.

Colter looked at Sabrina and lifted an eyebrow. When no response was forthcoming, he shrugged his shoulders, then slid from his horse. "May I help you, Mrs. William?"

The tall woman in the dusty black dress and bonnet stepped down and took a purposeful step toward Flying Cloud. "I, too, am a servant of God, Mr. Flying Cloud, called to work with the children. I have brought hard candies. May I share them?"

The chief, at first taken aback, glanced at the brazen woman, then down at the sack being held open for display, and smiled broadly. "I accept your gift, Death Woman. You may share." With that he took the bag, reached inside for a candy, and placed it in his mouth.

"But—"

"That was a generous gesture," Raven said, cutting off Mrs. William's rebuke. "How could you know that my grandfather has a sweet tooth? He also likes Irish whiskey, Brother Seaton, if you would like to share. It is appropriate to offer the host gifts."

Sabrina bit back a smile, glanced at Colter, and

saw that he too was pursing his lips in merriment. She suspected, from the innocent look on Flying Cloud's face, that he knew very well what he was doing. He'd been willing to accept the presence of the outsiders when he learned that Mrs. William would teach the children. But they didn't need to know how much he understood.

Flying Cloud wanted his people to learn. The Arapaho were a peaceful people. They could no longer fight the white man who came like an unending snake across the prairie. They had learned that once you cut off its tail, it grows another and continues to sidle forward. No, he decided, when Raven explained the quest of the outsiders, it was best to learn of the enemy, and if these strange people would teach, so be it.

"Daughter of Pale Raven, take the people who wear black to the lodge where they may stay. Daughter of Alexander, I would speak with you and the man with silver eyes."

With that Flying Cloud dismissed the missionaries and turned back to his shelter, assuming correctly that Colter and Sabrina would follow.

Once inside, they were shown to skins of fur placed around the fire, where they were instructed to sit. Moments later hollowed buffalo horns filled with hot liquid were brought in by two timid Arapaho women.

Sabrina lowered her eyelids, holding her drink, until the chief took a sip. He smiled broadly and nodded that the guests should do likewise. Sabrina had never been given this honor before, but her father had explained the potency of the brew they were about to drink. Taking a deep breath, she tipped her horn, as did Colter. Her small sip went down easier than Colter's. She pretended not to see the bruising look of accusation from her new husband.

At least he understood enough to wait until Flying Cloud emptied his horn and handed it to the waiting woman. "You escaped from blue soldiers?" he finally asked.

Colter glanced at Sabrina, who showed no surprise at the old man's knowledge.

"Yes. My men and I were captured by Union soldiers."

"Blue soldiers dead."

"Yes."

"Killed by hand of Gray Warrior."

Colter didn't know enough about Indian relationships to be certain how Flying Cloud would look at Gray Warrior's actions, so he waited.

The chief pretended to study the fire as he said, "Gray Warrior wears two feathers. Not good for man to wear two feathers."

Colter wondered how much the old chief knew about Colter's misfits and their actions, then decided that it served no purpose to deceive this man. "Sometimes a man is forced to act in the shadows when he'd rather live in the light."

Flying Cloud nodded.

Colter went on. "He must follow the orders of his leader, though in his heart he would be true to himself."

"Yes." Flying Cloud raised his eyes and turned a sharp glance at Colter. "You take daughter of Alexander as your woman?"

"No!" Sabrina began, trying to decide how to explain.

"Yes," Colter answered for her. "All Alexander's daughters share my protection now. I thank you for allowing the daughter of Cullen Alexander and Pale Raven to lodge with you and your people."

"It is good," Flying Cloud said, rising to his feet. "Now you go to your place of sleep and rest. Long Rifle has set off the spirits in the mountains today. They are restless."

"Long Rifle? You know this man?"

"I know of many men. Long Rifle also wears two feathers, while underneath he hides his own. You will wait here until it is safe."

Colter also stood. "Thank you for your warning,

but if there is danger, my duty is to protect the house of Alexander. I must return."

Flying Cloud nodded once. "Yes. But daughter of Pale Raven will stay here, at her grandfather's side, until I say she may go."

"It is agreed," Colter said. "Perhaps I should also leave my woman—Sabrina."

"In a pig's eye," Sabrina said sharply, then swallowed the rest of her argument. Flying Cloud's women might not make their own decisions, but Sabrina Alexander did.

The flap of Flying Cloud's tepee was suddenly opened by one of the silent women, who motioned for Colter and Sabrina to follow.

Sabrina contained her fury until they were away from the center of the circle. "How dare you speak for me, Captain Colter?"

"Be quiet, Sabrina."

"I will not be quiet. If I choose to go, I will, and you won't stop me. If you think for one minute that I'll stay here while you go back to the valley, you've got another think coming."

"Quiet, Sabrina!" Colter's voice was low and threatening. "I don't think the chief will look favorably on a man who allows his woman to talk back."

"So what do I care what the chief thinks?" she protested, knowing all the while that Colter was right.

"Because we're in his valley, under his protection, and he has taken our horses away. However, if you really want to leave on foot, I won't stop you."

Sabrina looked around. Colter was right. Their horses were gone. Only the missionaries' wagon was left. A circle of braves stood beyond the village, legs spread apart, rifles and bows in their arms. She swallowed hard. "Oh, Papa, where are your little people now?"

"Brina, do not worry." Raven fell into step beside her sister. "I will be safe. It is well that I stay here until the missionaries understand the ways of the Arapaho. I am not needed at home."

Sabrina looked at Mrs. William unloading her

trunks and supplies, considered the adjustment the woman would have to make, and agreed. Besides, if the soldiers came to the valley searching for Colter's men, it would be better if Raven was safe here.

"All right, Raven. But Papa wouldn't want anything to happen to you. Come back to us as soon as you can."

"I will. This will be your tepee. Grandfather says that you will rest through the day and leave by the light of the moon. Little Fox will bring you food."

Raven lifted the flap to the tepee and waited for Sabrina and Captain Colter to enter. She smiled tentatively. "This is the tepee used by those who have just married. They live here while the new wife sews the skins to make her own home. It would be well for you to stay inside until my grandfather says for you to come out."

Sabrina started to argue. Having Colter give her orders was one thing, but Raven was only a child. "Raven, you listen to me. I refuse—"

Colter took Sabrina's arm and shoved her inside, sliding his hand across her mouth and pulling her back close against his chest as he followed her inside. "Sabrina, I thought you were a woman who had some degree of intelligence. Yelling at your husband isn't acceptable action and should be punished by a beating. Verbally abusing the chief's granddaughter could be even worse."

Sabrina's eyes flashed lightning bolts. Her breasts heaved as she struggled to free herself from his grasp. In the melee her hat fell off and her russet hair fell over her shoulders, draping across his arm behind her head.

When she finally stopped fighting him, he slowly moved his hand from her mouth, his fingertips tangling in her hair as he slid them behind her neck.

"Are you going to be quiet now?" he asked, allowing her to turn inside the tight enclosure of his arm.

She nodded, leaning back, trying to move away from the closeness of his face. Even in the shadows of the enclosure she could see the tiny weathered lines at the corner of his eyes, the weather-roughened skin that was pulled taut against finely honed cheekbones. He was a warrior who brooked no argument from any man. A woman was in even greater danger. For she could feel the strength of his body and the beat of his pulse.

For a moment she forgot their disagreement, forgot that her authority was being displaced. He was going to kiss her. She felt herself sway toward him, parting her lips, waiting. His head lowered. The sounds of the village disappeared and a warm quiet fell over her, like the heavy feeling that precedes a summer storm.

"Ah, Sabrina," he said in a tight, rough voice, "what have I gotten myself into?"

"You?" she whispered back. "What have you gotten my family into? All I wanted was a temporary husband, to free my father and—"

"Work your mine?"

"No. I mean yes. But not like this. Please, let me go. This wasn't supposed to happen."

"Nobody knows that better than I," he said, catching the long strands of her hair between his fingers and pulling her head back. "You're going to ruin my mission if I don't figure a way to stop you."

"How?" Her voice was so tight that the word barely escaped. Her heart was pounding and her body seemed to have turned into gruel more watery than that Isabella fed to the calf.

"By filling my mind with thoughts of you—and—this."

Then he kissed her. He couldn't stop himself. He didn't even want to. Instead of pulling back, or fighting like some wild creature caught in a trap, Sabrina felt suspended, caught up in new feelings that she had no knowledge of. She allowed him to pull her body close.

Someone moaned.

Someone closed the flap to the tent, and a half darkness swept over them, surrounding them, hiding them from the sunlight.

"We all wear two feathers," she heard Colter say. "What we want and what we are."

"No. I don't know anything about feathers. I only know that a stone can only be what it is."

"A stone? Is that an Indian saying?" he asked, pulling back.

"No, that's Irish."

"I don't understand."

"Simple. Fool's gold looks like the real thing if you've never seen it. Papa told me a long time ago not to let myself be fooled by what a thing calls itself. Let me go, Colter. I'm not your wife." She pulled herself from his grasp and backed away.

"We're not married and you don't want to be, right?"

"Right!" she retorted, and felt the cold air of separation surround her, taking away the warmth and bringing her back to the moment. "Right. Now, let's get that rest. I'll take this bed here."

"There isn't another, Sabrina. This is the honeymoon tepee, remember?"

In the darkness she hadn't noticed. "There's a fire laid. You'd better light it. Then if you're cold, you can huddle near its warmth."

"As you did last night?" he said, and heard her gasp. He knew now that she'd found herself in his arms when she awoke.

"Never mind, Colter," she said unsteadily. "There are two skins, a top and a bottom. You take one. I wouldn't want you to do something to keep warm that we'll both regret."

"I wouldn't. Regret comes only when one's desire for something is thwarted. I don't allow myself to feel desire for anything I can't have."

Sabrina sank to the floor of the tepee and wrapped herself in her fur skin. She didn't want to hear the warning in the thick hoarseness of his voice. She didn't want to ask how a body knew desire. She was afraid that the trembling of her limbs was telling her.

Colter squatted beside the fire as he touched it with a match. He watched it ignite. After using one of the poles designed to open the top of the tepee and draw the smoke through the hole, he waited.

He didn't know what he was waiting for; he only knew that he understood what Flying Cloud had meant when he said the spirits were restless.

Keeping the Alexander women safe had suddenly come between his men and their mission. He was beginning to understand that there comes a time when a man's duty to his country turns into a war with his own personal needs. And Colter didn't know whether he wanted to win that war, or lose it.

12

"Captain," Raven said, "the war party searching the mountain has gone now. It is safe for you and my sister to leave."

Colter and Sabrina followed the young woman from the tepee out into the moonlit night. "Who were they, Indians or soldiers?"

"Both. A party of Ute were traveling with the soldiers from the fort."

"Ute! Gray Warrior," Colter said, wishing he'd been alone. Alone, he could have seen for himself, maybe even learned more about Long Rifle, who could be the key to finding answers to the massacre for which they were being blamed. Being considered a soldier who confiscated goods from the enemy was one thing, but Colter chafed at being declared a wanted criminal.

Sabrina's worried voice came from the darkness. "Raven, how is it that the Ute don't know about this place?"

"I do not know. Flying Cloud says that this is a

sacred place for the Arapaho, known only to our tribe."

"How close did the—war party come?" Colter asked.

"You don't need to worry, husband of my sister. You will be safe if you do not tarry."

"He's not my husband, Raven. I wish you'd stop sounding like some medicine woman. Any minute I expect you to shake your ceremonial shells at me and start a chant."

"I am sorry I offend you. I only wish to honor both my white and my Indian heritage."

"Just you remember, you're more white than Indian. Papa was an Irishman, not an Arapaho!" Sabrina knew that she was being unduly cross. The older Raven grew, the more Indian she became. Still, Papa hadn't thought it was wrong; he loved the Arapaho. Why should Sabrina worry?

She was just tired. Instead of resting throughout the afternoon, she'd lain in the shadows, tense and wide-eyed. That strange feeling of being pulled in different directions seemed to accompany her even when Colter wasn't present. When he was close by, she felt as if her body were being slowly barbecued, like the fish being turned on the spit over the fire.

Raven was still speaking, and Sabrina realized that she hadn't even heard what younger sister said. She forced herself to listen.

"Yes, Captain Colter. But there are so many more of you than the Arapaho. Besides, I think my grandfather needs me. My sisters have you and your men. Please do not be angry, Sabrina."

Sabrina put her arms around Raven and hugged her. She didn't understand this allegiance, but here, in this place, she felt closer to her sister than she had before.

"I'm not angry, Raven. You must do what you feel is right. Just as I must. Will you thank Flying Cloud for us?"

"I will. He is pleased that I will stay for a time,

and Captain Colter, he wishes to give you a parting gift of two horses."

Sabrina's heart sank. How could they feed more livestock than they had? On the other hand, how could they refuse such a generous gift?

"And you will thank Flying Cloud for his generosity. When my men are well enough to leave, we will have need of horses."

When we leave. Of course, Colter had something to do with the gift. She should have known. Raven handed over the reins to the two animals.

The missionaries' lodge was dark as they mounted their horses.

"We have prepared food for your journey. Be careful, Sabrina," Raven said.

"You'll come home as soon as you can?"

"I will. Captain Colter, take care of my sisters."

"I will, Raven," he promised, then realized the commitment he'd just made. He hadn't thought he'd ever feel needed again, not as a man. Being a soldier was a different kind of commitment. Assuming the responsibility for a woman was personal, and as he watched Sabrina, strong and tall in her saddle, he knew the feelings that he'd kept tamped were in danger of escape.

For a moment Sabrina's gaze melded with his, and he thought she must have felt something of the same thing, for she quickly averted her eyes. "Take care of the missionaries," Sabrina said.

"We will. Flying Cloud believes they've been sent by the spirits to protect us from death."

"That may be what they believe, too," Colter said dryly. "But I'm curious to know why Flying Cloud thinks that."

"Because of their black clothing. He thinks they walk in both worlds. Don't worry. He'll look after them. And perhaps they will learn from us as well."

The same guides who'd accompanied them into the valley escorted them out and led them back to a spot where they could find their own way back to the lake. Sabrina had the strange feeling that she'd never see

Raven again. Twice she reined in her horse and looked back, drawn both to the valley behind her and to the one below.

"You can't change it, Sabrina," Colter said. "Events occur that take us away from the lives we thought we'd live, and we can never go back again."

"I suppose. But somehow I don't think that Brother Seaton is going to take up wearing a bearskin, and I find it hard to imagine Flying Cloud in a black suit and hat."

Colter gave a dry laugh. "Try imagining Mrs. William in a leather dress and moccasins."

"Mrs. William. I can't fathom going through life being called by my husband's first name. Do you suppose the woman has one of her own?"

"I think Mrs. William might surprise all of us one day. She seems to have a mind of her own. When she decides to use it, Brother William may learn about the patience of Job."

By first light they'd reached the lake. This time when Colter built a fire, he found a hidden spot among the cottonwood trees. "To protect us from the wind," he explained, without mentioning the eyes of the Arapaho who might be watching.

Sabrina made coffee and meal cakes. She spread their blankets near the fire. The sun warmed the morning, continuing to melt the snow so that the horses could graze. After they'd eaten, Sabrina and Colter lay down to rest, neither speaking.

There was a rare feeling of camaraderie between them. And rather than risk renewing the tension, or discussing things Sabrina did not wish to address, she remained quiet and Colter followed her lead.

Eventually Colter broke the silence. "I wouldn't have expected the snow to melt so quickly, not after such a bad storm."

"People are usually surprised. Sometimes in the spring we have spells where the snow melts and wildflowers cover the mountains."

"Will you always live up here, Sabrina?"

"I never thought about not being here. Why would I leave?"

"Oh, I don't know. There is so much of the country that you haven't seen. New York City, for example, is a thriving city with stores and manufacturing and cultural affairs."

"I wouldn't know how to live in a place that had so much noise. I like the openness, the freedom, of this country where a person can be whatever she chooses."

"And there's California, still new and strange. There are entire communities of different nationalities. And there's the continent: England, France. Wouldn't you like to visit such places?"

"Visit, perhaps. But this is my home, the West, the mountains. I'm afraid that I would never be happy to leave them permanently. What about your home? Don't you want to go back there?"

"No. I watched it burn, watched the enemy rape and murder my sister when she refused to surrender the locket our father gave her. No, that part of me is gone forever. I have no wish to return to South Carolina."

"I'm sorry. I can't imagine watching my family die."

"But you did. Your father died before your eyes, and you were just as helpless to stop it."

"You're right. And I watched my mother die, and my stepmothers. I suppose that's why it's so important to keep my sisters safe."

"I hope you'll always be able to do that, Sabrina. But I'm not sure we can do much about the future. We have to take what comes and live with it."

"No, you're wrong, Colter. We can make things better. I believe that. Once we get the mine going, we can give my sisters the things they've always wanted."

"We?"

She blushed. Somehow he'd found a way into her plans. She didn't think she could mine the silver without Colter. And suppose her father had been wrong? Suppose there was no vein?

Sabrina closed her eyes, shutting out the brilliant blue sky dotted with little patches that looked like Lauren's whipped egg whites. How far did she want to go with the truth? Should she tell Colter that Papa found only two knobs of silver? Or that she'd hidden a chunk of rock with silver markings? They'd have to take samples into Boulder City to the assayer's office before they'd know. No, better still, they'd go to Denver, to the mint. Nobody would know them there.

"Yes, 'we.' *If* everything works out."

"Doubts? From Miss Sabrina Alexander?"

"I'm not always confident, Colter." She ran her fingers through her hair, trying unsuccessfully to untangle the long strands. "There are times when I'm very uncertain of what to do."

"I know. I have great doubts myself. I think it's the loneliness, not being able to say you don't have all the answers, that you're afraid. There are times when I just want to put it all behind and go."

Sabrina felt a twinge in her heart. Suppose, when they returned to the cabin, he did just that? They had four horses now for four men. Suppose they rode away and returned to their lives as Confederate soldiers? Suppose he forgot his promise to help her?

Down deep she acknowledged for the first time that it wasn't entirely for her sisters that she needed him to stay. The truth was, her sisters didn't care about the mine; they were ready to leave the valley and find normal lives for themselves. Except for Raven, who seemed to belong here. Sabrina was no longer sure of her direction. Was she following Papa's dream for him, or for her sisters?

Or for herself?

And what about the man she was involving in their lives? Colter wasn't a man to change. He had accepted a mock marriage ceremony in order to protect his men. Yes, he'd kissed her, and she'd felt the wild yearnings that kept her rest disturbed and her mind in jumbles. But she'd heard enough of Papa's stories and seen enough of the way men acted when she was following Papa around the mining towns to know that a kiss didn't mean anything.

Colter wasn't interested in her, not any more than he would be interested in any woman. He wasn't her husband. And she was beginning to understand that a silver mine wouldn't keep him. Once all this was over, he'd be gone. Maybe sooner. What did she have to lose in telling him the truth?

"Papa always expected to find gold, Colter. Instead he found silver. I don't know its value, but I'm prepared to divide. If you help me bring it out, you can share in the profits like any other—partner."

Colter raised up on one elbow and glanced at Sabrina in surprise. "Partner?"

She felt the heat of his gaze. An involuntary stir started behind her knees and shot up her body, magnifying that ever-present sensation. She felt as if she were a part of a meteor shower in a midnight sky, fragmenting from the heat. "I'm prepared to offer you a partnership in the Silver Dream, if you'll help us."

"A partnership in a silver mine," he murmured. "Nothing more?" His question slipped out before he'd been aware that he was thinking it.

Confused, she turned to face him, then wished she hadn't. He was too close, too real, penetrating her with eyes of silver. "What—what more would you want, Colter?"

"I don't know. I haven't cared about anything for so long. I don't think I have any feelings left inside me. I guess I want, just for a moment, to feel something other than emptiness."

His voice was low and raspy, as if it were forcing itself between lips long sealed in place. As if he were at war with that dark emptiness and unable to hide inside it. The sun splattered light across his face, catching his eyes, exposing the deep pain inside.

Dear God, Sabrina had never felt such darkness. She made an involuntary move toward him, finding his cheek with her fingertips. "I'm sorry," she whispered. "I wish there was something I could do, some way I could take the pain away."

At her touch his gaze seemed to melt, turning from icy silver to molten promise. Sabrina let out a gasp, her lips parting from the intensity of that gaze. She was caught by it, pinned to her blanket as a shiver of icy heat permeated her very skin.

From the moment he'd admitted to the emptiness inside him, she'd realized that she understood that emptiness, that need to share the pain. The feeling was new and terrifying, for once it was let free, she knew that her solitary life would never be the same. Could she take a chance on letting herself care?

"Colter . . . I feel so strange. I can't—"

"I know. It's something neither you nor I can stop. God knows, I've tried. But your passion is melting me, Sabrina Alexander," he said roughly. "The fire of your hair. The intensity of your gaze. The touch of your lips, like wildfire, ready to explode. You're lighting that darkness, and you don't even know it."

"I think I do," she said in a whisper. "But I don't know what to do to stop it. It's splitting me into little pieces."

"If you know what's good for you," he growled as he leaned closer, "you'll get on that horse and ride away, leave me here where I can't reach you."

"You said neither of us could stop it, Colter. Why do you want me to go?"

"I can't let go of the killing and the pain. I don't want to feel—not now—not here."

"Why? What's wrong with feeling?"

"Feeling is only the beginning. It leads to want and need, and it's been so damned long since I've let it happen. I might hurt you, Sabrina."

"Let what happen, Colter? I don't understand."

The tension arced between them like lightning. Sabrina couldn't have moved if she'd wanted to. The sun beamed down, the heat burning into her, smoldering, fusing with Colter's anger, holding her captive where she lay.

"You know this can't be," he said.

"I know. I don't want it to be."

"Yes, you do, Sabrina. Just once in your life I think

you want to be a woman. You want to let go of the weight of responsibility and feel for yourself, experience the joy of life tugging at you. Admit it."

"Yes!" she finally said, and moved into the crook of his arm. Then, wide-eyed and frozen by the brazenness of her behavior, she held her breath.

"God help us both," he rasped, knowing that the only way to resolve the potency of their desire was to satisfy it once and for all. He fell across her, slashing her lips with his own.

Sweet, hot fire ignited her and she parted her lips. She'd never known such feelings as she felt where their bodies touched. When his hand slid across her waist and jerked her even closer, she groaned.

This wasn't pretend. This was real, and Sabrina let herself reach out for what her body seemed determined to find. His beard was surprisingly soft, like golden silk caressing her rough fingers. She felt his cheeks, his ears, and finally his neck as he deepened the kiss. Now he was sliding his leg across her body, and she felt his hard maleness rocking against her.

There was nothing tender or soft about what he was giving and nothing hesitant about her response. She'd never expected to know a man, never allowed herself to think about such things. But not thinking didn't stop the deep yearning that seemed to rush toward this man like the floods after a thaw. That was Sabrina Alexander, a distant, snow-covered mountain, being melted by a heat greater than that of the sun.

Forced to draw back to breathe, Colter finally pulled away, gazing down at her from behind eyes glazed with need. "Are you sure? Once done, you will never be the same again."

"Neither will you," she said, pulling his lips back to hers.

Colter knew he was lost, as was she. So be it, he decided. Raven was right. There were some things beyond man's control, some things that shouldn't be controlled. His fingers moved up, cupping a surprisingly full breast. She stilled her movement for a second as he unbuttoned her shirt and the long underwear beneath.

"First time I ever made love to a woman wearing wool underwear," he said, moving down her chin and kissing the hollow of her neck.

Love? Sabrina didn't know whether it was the word, or the touch of his mouth on her nipple that took her breath away. This wasn't love. This was some wild physical need, like the way Papa felt when he drank his Irish whiskey. She was satisfying some unstoppable urge that had taken over her senses and was carrying her along in a rampage of desire.

His mouth was hot and wet and she pressed herself against it, twisting and turning, trying to get closer. Then she was touching his chest with her fingers, feeling the massive hard planes of a man's body.

Her shirt was wide-open, as was his, exposing her body to the sun and to his sight. Colter pulled back and let out a deep sigh. "Beautiful. Your breasts are beautiful. Why in God's name do you go around looking like some prospector when you have this to give?"

"I never wanted to give it before. It seemed simpler to cover myself."

Colter took the tangled strands of her hair and pulled them down across her breasts, playing lightly back and forth across her, rubbing her nipples and watching them pucker in response.

"Your nipples are like the cherries that grew on the tree by the barn back in Carolina, full and inviting. I knew you'd look like this, all swollen and ripe. Let me see all of you, Sabrina, please?"

"But I'm so tall and gangly," she protested. "Not at all beautiful like Isabella, or lovely like Lauren."

"No, you're not at all like them. You're the orange sunrise against a calm gray sky. You're all fire and ice, and I'm drowning in want."

He unfastened her belt and unbuttoned her trousers and her wool underwear, his lips following his fingertips as he slid her clothing down her legs and tossed them away.

She shivered, not from the cold mountain air, but from the twitching that had her body writhing beneath his gaze.

"You're cold," he said, tenderly drawing the blanket over them both.

"Yes! No! I don't know what I am, Colter." There was no keeping still. The shiver turned into a rumbling warning, like the earth just before a landslide. "But whatever it is I am feeling, you're going to feel the same."

Colter helped her as she removed his clothing, sliding his trousers down his legs as far as his boots, where they hung and remained, ignored as he lowered himself against her. Instinctively she spread her legs, allowing him to nestle his organ in the hot, wet place between them.

"Oh, please, Colter. I—" She lifted herself against him. But it wasn't enough. His mouth closed on her nipple again, pulling, sucking, as if he wanted to draw the fire from inside. Instead it only increased the heat. Now he was moving against her, lifting himself as he slid his male part back and forth across the crevice beneath. She was burning.

Sabrina's fingers dug into his back as he moved. The blanket slid lower. He raised himself over her, teasing her with his movements. She lowered her eyes so she could see that part of him which was tormenting her. There was a magnificence about him that caught her breath. No man had ever interested her before, and she knew now it was because none of the rare visitors to the valley were worthy of being compared to Captain Colter.

Her cheeks were flushed with fire. Her eyes burning. Her skin glistening. He caught a handful of her hair and jerked her head back so that he could claim her mouth again, savagely, with no holding back. If this was to be, he'd give this wild woman with her silver dreams whatever he had left in him to give.

"I tried to tell you," he growled. "Now it's too late."

"Nobody tells me anything, Colter."

"So be it." He slipped his hands beneath her hips, catching them and lifting her. Poised over here, he held back, telling himself that he could still end this madness, knowing that it was not true. He could no more stop than he could stop breathing.

"I want to be inside you. I need you so damned much," he said, and plunged into her fire.

Both were seared by the implosion. Colter felt her wince as the barrier gave way, then meet him lunge for lunge as he tried to reach the depths of her being. She was tight and hot, and clung to him like a velvet glove. Suddenly he felt a great weight fall away. He was free, free to feel what she was giving, free to give in return. Two equals meeting, joining, becoming, for that one second in time, one complete being.

Like the lava in the ancient volcano that created the very earth on which they lay, they were swept to the summit, caught in the primitive dance of passion that erupted in fiery splendor. He spilled himself into her in one long, last heated shudder. She rippled beneath him, still holding tightly to his body, then gradually relaxed in the aftermath of her own release.

He slid off her, his arm cradling her head, aligning his bare body against hers as if he couldn't yet separate himself. For a long time they lay, breathing deeply, then more lightly as they came down from the summit of their mating.

For Colter regrets came rushing back. What had he done? Making love to Sabrina was akin to opening the door to the dove trap and allowing the birds to taste the freedom of flight. The birds might return at nightfall, but their lives would never be the same again.

Sabrina and he had tasted the magic of making love, and it had been more than he'd ever dreamed. What would he say to a woman who had every right to expect more? How could he tell her that what she'd shared with him was all there could ever be? No words came.

Sabrina shrugged her shoulders and sighed. "I feel like butter," she said. "No—honey. Warm honey dripping straight from the comb."

Colter's body reacted instantly to that image, reacted as strongly as it had the first time. Now he was as hard as a rock and being pulled back to Sabrina with every part of his body. He groaned and clenched his fist.

"Did I say something wrong?" Sabrina rose, leaning forward so that she was half lying over him. "I don't know much about this kind of thing. Maybe the woman isn't supposed to speak?"

"No," he said tightly. "You didn't say anything wrong."

"Then why are you angry?"

"I'm not angry." But he was. Not at her, but himself. He knew that he'd tasted the forbidden fruit. He was the snake in the Garden of Eden, and he wasn't sure he could leave.

Sabrina leaned closer, examining his face and chest. Her fingertips ranged across him, memorizing what she felt so that she could keep it with her long after he'd gone. "I think you are hurting. I'm sorry that you didn't enjoy it as much as I." With exaggerated innocence she voiced the same statement he'd made that first day in the cave. "Your mother would kiss it and make it better."

She began to lower the blanket.

"Hellfire, woman!" He grabbed the blanket and jerked it back over his chest.

"Don't you want me to look at you? Are you very ugly down there?"

"No! I mean yes. I'm ugly as sin." He groaned even louder. "Sin, Sabrina," he said, grasping for a way to stop her. "That's what this is, Sabrina. Surely you realize that what we just did is—a sin!"

"Oh, no," she whispered, taking his nipple into her mouth. "This can't be a sin, Captain Colter. We're married, remember?"

Colter tried to stand. He really did. Then he caught sight of the amusement on Sabrina's face as her hand found his erection and he fell helplessly back to the ground.

Hell! That's where you're headed. "Just cut off my hair and call me Samson," he muttered as Sabrina slid over him.

"If that's what you want," she whispered between kisses. "But could we do the haircut later?"

The sunlight speckled them with gold. The very earth beneath them was soft and welcoming. The breeze from the lake died, and the day seemed to hold its breath.

Then Colter took her bottom in his hands and lifted her high enough so that his member teased her, nudging impatiently forward.

And then he was inside her and all thought of guilt vanished. Like Colter, Sabrina rode her lover, giving and demanding in return. She flung her head back, letting her hair fly across her shoulders.

"I don't feel like butter anymore, Colter."

"How do you feel?"

"Like the yeast in Lauren's dough. No, like the fizz on Papa's homemade wine, just before it blew its cork. Oh, Colter, I never knew."

Sabrina didn't believe that anything could feel so good. Always a very private person, she couldn't believe that she would ever feel so free, so abandoned, so wild. Deeper and deeper he went, holding her hips so that she took every bit of him inside her.

Her hands were clawing his arms. Her legs curled around his thighs. With nipples standing erect, her breasts bounced up and down, teasing him until he leaned forward and captured one in his mouth. Forced to lean closer, she almost pulled away from his manhood, hearing the sucking sensation as he threatened to slide out.

"No," she cried, collapsing on him. He quickly turned her over on her back, never losing his encasement. "Kiss me, Colter. I want to feel your mouth on mine."

Her soft cries of passion sent him over the edge. The world began to spin. The sun wrapped the lovers in gold and touched their bodies with its heat, burning away the darkness within.

At last they slept, a healing, gentle sleep.

* * *

It was late afternoon when they awoke, their bodies entwined, their clothes strewn across the bank of the lake.

Colter sat up, taking a careful survey of their surroundings. "You know that was a mistake," he said.

"Probably. But it happened, and I'm not entirely sure that I regret it."

"You will if you expect it to change anything."

"I don't. You're still my prisoner," she said, not entirely sure what she'd expected him to say, knowing only that tears licked the back of her eyelids. He was no longer her prisoner; after today she was very much afraid that she was his.

"A while ago you said I was your husband."

He stood, gloriously and unselfconsciously nude. At some point he'd removed his boots. He threaded his muscular legs back into the rough fabric of his trousers, pulling them higher, adjusting his body so that he could button the fly. His boots followed. Once dressed, he pulled a bandanna from his pocket and started toward the lake.

Stunned by the abrupt change in his manner, Sabrina sat up and began to dress. Before she finished, he was back, handing the bandanna to her.

She looked at him and back at the red handkerchief, her puzzlement etched across her face.

"To—to clean yourself," he said, dropping the wet square, and turned away.

Sabrina felt her face flame. She'd been condemning his cold behavior when he'd been doing something kind for her. She cringed. Being with a man was difficult. It was just as well that they would be back at the cabin tomorrow. She didn't know how to face him now, and the stiffness of his manner hurt.

By the time he returned with an armload of firewood, she was dressed and preparing their food.

He dropped the wood and began to rebuild their fire. "I figure it's better if we don't try to get back to the cabin tonight. We'll camp here and get an early start."

Another night together? Sabrina dropped the sack of flour she was holding.

"Careful," Colter said sharply, catching the flour in midair, inadvertently touching Sabrina's extended hand.

She snatched the flour away, then swallowed hard. "I'm sorry. I feel very odd, being with you now. I expect that feeling will go away, won't it?"

"It damned well better. Hell, woman, you know we aren't really married. We just got caught up in a moment. It happened. That's all. Don't make more of it than it was!"

"I don't intend to," she said. "Women have their moments, too!"

Why, then, did she feel like a bride, the morning after her wedding?

13

"I don't understand how you know when I'm here," Dane said as Gray Warrior walked his horse quietly from the woods to the cedar tree where Dane waited.

"I know. What do you want of me?"

"I want to know about the missionaries. Have you found them?"

Gray Warrior peered at Dane through narrowed eyes. "No."

There was never a change in his expression. There were times when Dane thought that the Ute warrior wasn't telling him everything. But short of chancing a break in the relationship, he didn't dare challenge the savage.

"I thought you knew everything that happened in these mountains."

"We share this land claimed by the Arapaho, but my people live to the west. The mountains hide the secrets from those who do not belong. Like the white man."

"You will continue to search?"

Gray warrior grunted his consent.

Dane studied the taciturn man, trying to decide how much he really knew, then decided that he had no choice but to voice the second question. "I want to know about that miner Alexander who prospects in the mountains. Can you tell me?"

"Alexander is dead, beneath the earth."

"Dead? But there are others in his family?"

Gray Warrior nodded.

Dane gave a low curse. Why was it so hard to deal with the Indian? They'd had a relationship for months, each dependent on the other, each profiting from their ventures. Still, he had to draw out the facts one question at a time. "Tell me about Alexander's son."

"No son. Only women. Live in high valley with old man, who digs for gold."

"Have you seen them?"

"I see." He smiled broadly and rocked back and forth on the balls of his feet. "They had fine horses. Gray Warrior take."

"But what about the woman's husband? Tall, blond hair, beard, mustache. Silver eyes?"

Gray Warrior studied Dane shrewdly. "One man has silver eyes."

Dane tried to conceal his excitement. It had to be Colter. "The prisoners, from the prison wagon, are they there?"

"There are four men, yes."

It was Colter and his misfits. Dane had found them. They were still here. They could ruin everything. Why hadn't they kept going? Now Dane would be forced to do something he didn't want to do—get rid of them.

"I have another job for you, Gray Warrior. Take your men and capture the prisoners."

Gray Warrior feigned indifference, but his question was anything but. "The shadow soldiers?"

"Shadow soldiers?"

"They hide in the night, wearing another man's skin."

"You mean they're spies. Yes, they are. But how did you know they were soldiers?"

"Gray Warrior sees much. He knows when they came from the land in the south. He watched you turn away from them and become the man in the blue uniform. It is better that you now deal with Gray Warrior. Pay him in whiskey."

"Fine. I'll pay you. Just get them. Otherwise they can cause trouble for me. You wouldn't want to end our little raids, would you?"

"I will think on it."

Dane was surprised. So far Gray Warrior had never backed down, never shown any sign of fear. Rather, he'd seemed to relish the battle almost as much as the spoils. "Is there something you aren't telling me? Something that keeps you from attacking these men?"

"They are under the protection of Flying Cloud. Gray Warrior would risk war with his brothers, the Arapaho. Not good."

"Surely you aren't afraid of the Arapaho? Not Gray Warrior, the most fierce warrior in the Colorado territory."

He drew himself up and glared at Dane. "Not afraid. Will think."

Dane knew he was losing his leverage to a man who could bring the future plans down around them both. Dane searched for an answer. "What if the army went with you? Could you do it then? Nobody needs know that the prospectors were kidnapped by Indians, only that you're guiding my troops to the Alexander mine."

Gray Warrior grunted and nodded once more. "Tomorrow at midday. We meet at the cedar tree by the stream."

"No, not me. I can't be involved. I'll send Sergeant Nealey."

Gray Warrior nodded once again; then he was gone.

Dane let out a long, ragged breath. No matter that it was to the Indian's advantage to join up with Dane, Dane was never sure that he could trust Gray Warrior.

He might be willing to kill, rob, do anything to the whites, but he rebelled at declaring war on another Indian. Dane would have to come up with something else to make sure Gray Warrior would comply.

Still, Dane had found out what he wanted to know. The Alexanders had given refuge to Colter and his men. In order for Dane to survive, the misfits had to go. Tomorrow he'd bring a selected number of soldiers to the tree Gray Warrior had chosen. They'd go after the men they believed to be the murderers of the detachment of federal troops transporting the paymaster with the payroll. If tomorrow brought casualties, Dane wouldn't be responsible, and the end result would be the elimination of any connection between Dane and the robbery. Then Dane and Lieutenant Littlejohn, the man he'd become, would disappear—a rich man.

Colter and the others had had the choice to leave. They hadn't. Now it was Dane's life or theirs. This was war. For a smart man who knew how to take advantage of an opportunity, life was good.

"So what happened to the missionaries, Lieutenant Littlejohn?"

Dane, finally comfortable with his new name, put a troubled expression on his face. "There was no trace of them, Captain. I've even had the Ute looking for them. Is Sergeant Nealey back?"

"Not yet. Where is he?"

"I sent him to the trading post to ask more about the Alexanders, the miner and his wife who were on the trail behind the missionaries. Perhaps they have information."

The commander folded his fingers into a tent on the desk and tapped them together. "Good idea, Littlejohn. When Sergeant Nealey returns, take him with you to question them."

"Eh, yes. I thought I'd take some of the Ute along."

"Fine." The captain took a sheet of paper, dipped

his quill into the inkwell, and began to write. "And while you're about it, take this invitation to the Alexander family. They might enjoy a visit to the fort on Sunday. I know Mrs. Holland would like some civilian company. We'll have a dinner party."

"Are you sure that's wise, Captain?" Lieutenant Garland, the captain's aide, asked. "I mean, there is much unrest with Gray Warrior's raids and the war. You know those Johnny Rebs could still be around."

"All the more reason to have a party. A little social gathering is exactly what we need now, Garland, to calm the situation. Who knows? There might be a pretty young lady for you to dance with. Issue the invitation, Littlejohn."

Dane left the captain's quarters with a different kind of worry. Having Colter to dinner wasn't what Dane had in mind. And he wasn't certain he could avoid delivering the invitation.

Dane frowned. This would take some careful planning.

Maybe he'd use this trip to reconnoiter, just take a few men. Yes, that would work. He'd stay back and watch, let Nealey be the point man, check out the Alexanders and issue the invitation. If Colter was there, Dane could find some excuse to avoid the dinner party. Then, as the Alexanders' returned from the fort after the dinner, he'd have to make his move.

People were frequently attacked when they traveled without the protection of a wagon train. Look what happened to the real Lieutenant Littlejohn. Dane would simply tell Gray Warrior that the Alexanders carried whiskey. Maybe he'd even plant some whiskey in their travel bags as an additional incentive to the renegade Ute.

Dane began to whistle. Whiskey. That sounded like a good idea. He needed a drink. He deserved a little celebration.

Sabrina winced the next morning as she mounted her horse to follow Colter back to the valley. The tenderness she felt between her legs was a constant reminder of what had happened between her and Colter the afternoon before.

His aloofness was a reminder of the estrangement that fell between them later when they laid out their bedrolls on opposite sides of the fire. She hadn't known what to expect, but the icy countenance he assumed soon told her that he intended to treat their foolish coupling as singularly unimportant, an event relegated to the past, with no promise of a future.

So be it, she decided as they rode. She'd had her one moment of womanhood, and she wouldn't lie about it. It had been glorious. But she'd never begged for anything, and she refused to let Colter know how much his coldness hurt her. What had she expected? He'd told her from the beginning that he had a job to do, that he had nothing to give.

He was wrong about that. She'd felt his pain and his need, and for those glorious moments she'd filled his darkness.

What was more earth-shattering was that he'd touched her with fiery longings, and then he'd taken her to a place of wonder she'd never hoped to know. But that was over. Like Papa said, she'd kissed the Blarney stone. Now it was time to get back to life as it was.

The Silver Dream had to be mined. She'd brought back four prisoners to work it, and that's all they were—prisoners. That's all she would think about. That was all that was important. A new life for her sisters.

Fulfilling Papa's dream.

As they rode back down the mountain, she tried to leave the memories behind her, knowing that her life below would be one of misery if she didn't. She turned her attention to the blue smear of fir trees nestled against a saffron sky. The sun shot the red walls of rock with gold that blinked in the distance like candlelight on the gemstone Papa had found in a mountain stream. Once a violet gloom settled over them as they passed through a stand of pines, then disappeared again as they rode out into the sunlight.

A soft wind whispered through the trees, caressing the boulders and tugging at their clothing. Sabrina felt a fullness in her chest. It rose, tightening in some frantic need to escape. She wanted to cry. Then, half-afraid that she would, Sabrina unwisely urged her horse into a gallop and crashed through the brush to pass Colter and the horses Flying Could had given them.

Seconds later Colter was behind her, taking the reins and tugging her horse to a stop.

"What in hell do you think you're doing?"

"In hell?" she asked, looking around. "I don't think so, Colter. This place is as close to heaven as you'll ever come. Too bad you can't tell the difference!"

She jerked her reins from his hand and rode away, leaving him thoroughly confused.

It was nearing midday when Colter pulled up. "Stop!"

"What's wrong?" she asked.

"Listen."

She grew still and listened. Movement. Horses, somewhere in the valley below. "I hear it, Colter."

"Wait here. Let me check it out," he said, turning his horse toward the sound.

She didn't wait. Instead she fell in behind, urging her horse forward until it was almost touching Colter's mount.

From a spot above the trail running through the valley, they were able to see the company of blue-uniformed men and Indians moving below.

"Where do you think they're going?" she whispered.

"I don't know."

Then Colter saw the sergeant from the fort and the familiar face of another blue-uniformed officer beside him. Dane in a Yankee uniform. That made no sense. Unless—

"Dane, you son of a bitch. You're still alive. It *was* you who betrayed us. I knew it!"

"Who is Dane?"

"Dane Beckworth, the turncoat responsible for our being captured." Colter started down the trail.

"Wait, Colter. What do you think you're going to do? We have a pistol and a rifle. There must be fifty men down there."

He cursed again and stopped. "You're right. Let's cross the valley behind them and see where they're going."

They cut through the boulders, making their way quickly down the mountain and across the creek to the other side. Moving at twice the speed of the troop, they caught up and found a spot high enough to follow their movements.

"Colter," Sabrina said, her voice suddenly fraught with urgency. "Look, they're turning. They're headed for our valley."

Colter immediately urged his horse into a run. "We've got to get there first, hide my men. You know this territory better than I, Sabrina. Get us to the cabin!"

Riding hard, they reached the cabin, turning the horses into the barn and closing the door. A quick check of the shed showed it was empty.

"The cabin," Sabrina said, running toward the door just as it opened.

"Brina, you're all right?" Lauren hugged her sister and let out a sigh of relief.

"Quick, where are my men?" Colter asked, coming to a stop as he looked around the empty yard.

"They're up at the mine. I hope it's all right, Brina, but they're clearing away the rest of the cave-in."

"Good," Colter said. "I'll warn them." He turned a concerned look on Sabrina. He didn't want to leave her, but he had no choice. "Can you handle the soldiers?"

"Yes." She was already shoving him through the door. "Hurry."

He took a step, then came back and put his hands

on her arms, holding her for just a minute. "Be careful," he said in a hoarse voice. Then he turned and
slipped out the door.

Sabrina brushed aside her sister's curious expression. "Lauren, where are Mary and Isabella?"

"They've gone for water at the spring."

"Go after them, keep them away. Soldiers from the
fort are on their way here. I don't know what they
want. But we have to make them believe that everything here is as usual."

"Where did we get the extra horses?"

"From Flying Cloud. Damn! There ought not to be
extra horses here if we're alone. And they'll see that
the animals have been ridden hard. I'll tie them together. Take them with you, Lauren."

"Fine. Don't worry, Brina. We'll be all right."

Lauren was barely out of sight when Sabrina heard
the sound of hoofbeats down the valley. She calmed
her breathing, picked up the rifle, and started back to
the cabin.

The man at the head of the detachment was Sergeant Nealey. The officer in blue, the one Colter had
cursed, was nowhere to be seen. That worried Sabrina.
She didn't know where he might be.

"Afternoon, Mrs. Alexander," Sergeant Nealey
said, and dismounted.

"Good afternoon, Sergeant Nealey. What can I do
for you?"

"We're looking for Brother Seaton and Brother
and Mrs. William. I left them broken down on the trail
and now they've disappeared. Have you seen them?"

"Why, yes. My—Mr.—Alexander and I found
them and brought them here."

"Good. I'm glad to hear it. In that case we'll escort
them on to the fort."

"They aren't here anymore."

"Oh?"

As they talked, two of the Indians had casually ridden closer to the barn, coming alongside the corral.

Sabrina lifted the rifle. Without making it obvious they were carefully reconnoitering the area, one man even peered into the house before disappearing behind it.

The sergeant took a step closer. "Where are they?"

"Mr. Alexander and my sister Raven took them to the Arapaho encampment."

"I see. I'd like to talk to your husband, ma'am. We still haven't found the four prisoners who murdered their escorts and escaped. Maybe the Arapaho have seen them."

Murdered their escorts? "He isn't back yet."

"I don't suppose you've seen the prisoners, have you?"

"No. Why should we?"

"Because they're wounded, ma'am, and in need of shelter. And," he added, giving her a look of warning, "they're even more dangerous than we'd thought."

"Oh? Why is that?" She tried to put a casual tone to her voice.

"Not only did they steal supplies bound for the fort, but the detachment was carrying the fort payroll and two pack mules transporting newly minted gold coins from the mint in Denver. After they took the money and the gold, they killed every man in the unit to cover their crime."

"That's terrible. But if they killed every man in the unit, how'd you find out?"

"One of the soldiers lived long enough to tell Lieutenant Littlejohn that the Rebs did it. Captain Holland is concerned about the settlers in the area. He thinks you might want to come to the fort for protection."

Lieutenant Littlejohn? Maybe Colter had been wrong about the officer's identity. It didn't add up. But where was the other officer now? Sabrina felt a sudden shiver of cold sweep over her, and this time it wasn't the temperature. What if the Indians decided to search the mine?

At the same time another thought make her stop. Colter had said his men had been after supplies, that the Indians had taken them. He couldn't understand why they'd been set up, or why everyone had been killed. Sabrina guessed that stealing the fort payroll and the gold was reason enough.

"I appreciate your concern, Sergeant, but we're so far up in the hills that nobody is likely to bother us. But please give your commanding officer our thanks."

"I will. Oh, he asked me to give you this invitation." The sergeant took a folded note from his pocket and handed it to Sabrina. "Even if you won't come to the fort to stay, he'd like you and your family to join him for dinner. Likely there'll be a dance after. The men don't get to see many white women out here."

"Dinner?" That was the last thing Sabrina expected him to say. And the last thing she would consider doing. Papa had kept them away from the fort, and she didn't plan to change that.

"Yes, ma'am. When will Mr. Alexander get back?"

"I'm not sure. It depends on where he finds the Ute. They move about, you know."

"And your hired men?"

This time Sabrina couldn't conceal her surprise. "What hired men?"

"The Indians said there are a couple of strangers around here. I figured you must have had to take on some help since you lost your husband's father."

He knew about that, too. "Eh, yes. Well, we have drifters from time to time, old stagecoach drivers who knew my—Mr. Alexander."

"But they're not here now?"

"No," she admitted, then wished she hadn't. By protecting Colter's men, she'd let the troops know that they were alone. "But thank you for your concern, Sergeant. Tell Captain Holland that we won't be able to attend. Perhaps another time."

"I'll do it, ma'am. And if you change your mind, just come along. We can always accommodate extra guests."

Sabrina watched the sergeant mount his horse and lead his unit back down the valley, the Indians falling in behind. Once they were gone, Lauren came out of the woods. She'd obviously been listening.

"A party, Brina?"

"You heard Captain Colter and his men weren't just looking for munitions, they were going to hold up the troops and steal the payroll and the gold. You can tell Mary and Isabella that it's safe to come back now and we're not going to the party."

"I don't believe they are thieves, Sabrina, and you don't either. And even if they were after gold, we know they're not killers."

"I know. Or maybe I don't, Lauren. I just wish I'd never brought them to our valley. I wish we could go back to the kind of life we had before."

"And we'd die."

Sabrina jerked around to face her sister.

"It's true. Once Papa died, our lives were changed forever. We have no money, no supplies, and no real way to get any."

"Oh, yes we do, Lauren. We have the mine."

"There's nothing in that mine, Sabrina. You and Papa might have believed in finding the mother lode, but we're not fooling ourselves any longer."

"Lauren, listen to me. That's what killed Papa. He found it. Finally, after all these years of looking, he really found his pot of gold."

"Gold?"

"No, not gold. Papa found silver. If he was right, and I think he was, we're rich."

"Oh, no!" Lauren frowned. "And I sent the men up to the mine to clear out the rest of the debris. You told me to keep them away from Mary and Isabella. I couldn't seem to find a way, so I put them to work. What if they find the silver?"

But Sabrina was already running up the mountain.

She didn't know where the Union officer was, but the Silver Dream was Papa's, she told herself, and she would keep it safe.

And Colter, too.

14

From a spot where he could remain hidden, Dane watched as Sergeant Nealey delivered Captain Holland's party invitation, then remounted his horse. Gray Warrior's men rode around the cabin, then followed the soldiers away from the house and back down the valley.

Dane didn't move.

Once the soldiers could no longer see the cabin, the woman wearing men's clothing and carrying the rifle moved quickly up the mountain, eventually disappearing into a hole high up the side of the ridge.

Dane waited patiently as the afternoon shadows lengthened. The wind whistled through the rocks, bringing the sound of musical notes.

Something wasn't right about the scene he'd just observed. Where were the men? Where was Colter? Dane knew that Colter would never leave his men, and this was the perfect place to hide them away. Dane was prepared to wait until he had an answer.

* * *

Sabrina ducked into the tunnel, colliding head-on with Colter, who stood just inside, and Tyler, who was holding a large rabbit.

"You're all right," she said breathlessly. "I was afraid—"

"For now," Colter cut her off. "I guess you know that you just gave away our location." His voice was sharply critical as he drew her deeper into the darkness.

"How could I? They're gone." She stepped around him, attempting to put some distance between them before he realized the extent of her concern. "They don't know I'm up here."

"You mean Nealey and his men are gone. But what about Dane? The other officer wasn't with Sergeant Nealey. He's out there somewhere, watching. Dane's too good an officer not to observe."

Sabrina forgot her relief at finding the men safe, and her concerns about the silver, as the realization of what she'd done swept over her.

"You're right. But the Ute were wandering around. I was afraid they'd see something. I couldn't wait. I needed to know you were safe."

Colter replayed her words. *I needed to know you were safe. Needed to know.* Her distress was overwhelming, as was her appeal. He took a step closer, ready to put his arms around her when Tyler cleared his throat.

"Captain, you don't suppose he'd do something to the women, do you? What can we do?"

"Nobody is going to do anything to any of you," Colter said, his eyes never leaving Sabrina's. "Sabrina is going to turn around and walk back down the valley as if nothing has happened. No, better still, she's going to go behind the boulders where she can't be seen and fire the rifle."

"Why? Won't that call attention to me? I mean, even if someone was watching, he might not know where I am."

"He knows. You're going to hide this rabbit that Tyler trapped beneath your jacket, and when you come back into view, he'll see it and think you were hunting."

Sabrina was subdued when she asked, "And what will you do?"

"We'll wait until it's dark and then we'll come down. By that time I'll know whether or not we've been discovered."

"Discovered?" She didn't want to know what that meant.

"Don't worry," he said, adding *"wife,"* softly. "There are more of us than there are of him. If he decides to investigate, we'll be ready for him. But I'd rather not have to kill him. He might deserve it, but that would make us murderers. I'd rather expose him."

Sabrina didn't want to leave. As long as she was here with Colter, she could protect him. Then she gave a silent laugh. She was holding the gun, but it was Colter who was the caretaker. She'd been so concerned about this man she'd made love with that she'd lost her normal sense of caution.

There was no concealing the truth any longer. The prisoner and she had reversed their positions. And both knew that it had happened long before they stopped by the lake. Sabrina lowered her eyes, drew the pistol from her pocket, and handed it to Colter.

"It wouldn't be murder, Colter, it would be self-defense. We'd all swear to that."

"Swearing wouldn't make it so, Sabrina. I'd know and that would be enough. Now go. I'll—we'll be back tonight."

"Be careful," she whispered, and swung around, taking the rabbit and slipping it under her coat.

A few minutes later the rifle shot sounded loud, echoing down the valley. Sabrina prayed that Lauren wouldn't come to find out what was happening. As Sabrina retraced her steps to the cabin, she tried to study the surrounding ridges. Brilliant pink clouds shifted, sending bright rays of the setting sun through a slit in their cover. Then she saw it, the quick reflection of light down the valley, sunlight flashing off shiny metal—a gun barrel, probably. And then it was gone.

Colter had been right. The missing Yankee must have been out there all along. He'd watched her enter the mine and leave again. She could only hope that he could see the rabbit she was carrying in front of her like a shield.

Otherwise she'd betrayed the men she'd rescued.

Lauren met her on the porch.

"I heard a shot."

"I got a rabbit," she said in a loud voice. "Have Mary and Isabella prepare it for our supper."

"But where—"

"Inside! We're being watched," Sabrina said under her breath, pushing Lauren inside with the rabbit. As her sister caught the sense of danger Sabrina was exhibiting, she accepted the animal and called over her shoulder, "Mary, look what sister has brought. Isabella, build up the fire!"

Mary took the rabbit. "There's no wound."

"No, Tyler trapped it."

"But the shot."

"I fired by accident."

Isabella started toward the door, about to open it when Sabrina caught her arm and shoved her aside. "No. Stay away from the door."

Isabella rubbed her arm. "What's wrong, Brina? Where are the men?"

Sabrina fought her natural tendency to conceal problems from her sister and explained. "Colter is afraid that the soldiers may not have left, that someone may still be watching. They will wait until after dark."

The three women, suddenly aware of the inherent danger, followed Sabrina's directions. They skinned and cooked the rabbit. For once Isabella's concern for Carl overrode her squeamishness about the furry animal. Mary chopped wild herbs. Lauren cut the animal into pieces and dropped it into the cook pot. They waited, Isabella pacing, Mary busying herself preparing the remainder of the meal, and Sabrina sitting at the window in the late-afternoon shadows.

Finally she stood, pulled on her coat, and moved

toward the door. "I'll check the animals. I didn't like the way those Indians looked at the horses."

"Oh, Brina, are you sure it's safe?" Mary asked.

"I have the rifle," Sabrina answered with more confidence than she felt, and opened the door. Carefully and slowly, she moved down to the barn. Darkness still came early and she was glad. The sooner Colter and the others came down the valley, the sooner the pain around her chest would let go.

What if the watcher hadn't believed her?

What if he'd waited until dark and made his way to the mine?

She hadn't heard any gunfire, but that didn't mean he wasn't waiting for Colter and his men to step out of the cave. He could be waiting, and they could be captured before Colter could act.

Sabrina couldn't bear to think about that. Instead, she forced her mind back to the afternoon before, when they were at the lake, when Colter had taken her, like a lover, like a husband. No, that memory was almost as painful as considering Colter's capture. She should have done something to throw the sergeant off the trail. At the corral, as she leaned against the post, she heard the rattle of paper inside her shirt.

The note from the captain at the fort. She gave a cynical laugh. The one thing she couldn't bring into focus was her attending a dinner party with Colter.

But just for a moment she allowed herself to imagine how it might feel—how it might be to be a wife, to lie with a man every night, to feel what she'd felt—forever.

A sound came from the barn.

Someone was there.

Sabrina lifted the rifle, checked to make certain there was a cartridge in the chamber, then, following the shadows around the edge of the barn, made her way to the door. Taking a deep breath, she pushed it open, trying to adjust her eyes to the darkness before she stepped in.

"Who's there?" she said in a low voice.

Her answer was a hand that took the rifle away

and pulled her inside, against a firm chest, into two strong arms that she recognized even in the darkness.

"Colter—"

"What are you doing out here?"

"I couldn't stand the waiting any longer. I came to check the animals. Where are the others?"

"In the shed, waiting for me to scout the cabin."

His arms pulled her closer, his hands closing around her with fierce tension.

"I don't think that's what you're examining," she said in a voice thick with need, with newly learned, newly admitted wanting.

Somehow the rifle was on the ground and his hands were on a mission of reassurance that quickly became a reawakening. "Sabrina! I was so worried." All the fear he'd bottled up inside had dissipated when he felt her lean against him. "I'm sorry. I said that I wasn't going to do this!"

"And I asked why."

"Because I never meant you to think that I—"

"Would stay? I didn't."

"But you hoped."

"Only because I needed you to—" The rest of her remark, "help in the mine," was lost in his kiss. And she knew as she opened her mouth to take him inside, that it wasn't the mine she needed him for—it was for herself.

Hot, sweet excitement filled her instantly, as if she were constantly simmering, ready for the smallest touch to bring her to a boil. And this was no small touch. Colter's mouth probed, his hands caressed, and he whispered words that were smothered by their kiss.

And then, slowly, he stopped, stilled his mouth and his hands, and finally, letting out a long sigh of pain, rested his forehead on hers and waited.

"Damn! Damn! Damn! Why do I keep doing this? Why can't I get close to you without kissing you?"

"I don't know," she answered, and stepped away. They were racing down uncharted waters now, with no familiar rules forcing them to keep their emotions in check. "What does a woman do when a man touches her and she melts at his touch?"

"Women are different. Some back away from their feelings. Some allow themselves the freedom to make love to the man. Though I warn you, there can be risks, consequences."

"Consequences, yes. I can see that. I wouldn't want Mary and Isabella to be with a man the way we were." *They would be crushed if you left them.* "But the truth is, I can't believe that what we did is wrong. Though I have little experience with that sort of thing."

Colter was a man who never made resolutions. He was what he was, and he had no intention of changing. Yet in the span of a few days he'd changed from a man of resolve to a man who wanted what he could not let himself have. He swore again, then moved to the door and looked out.

"Have you seen or heard anything, Sabrina?"

"No. Maybe you were mistaken about your friend."

"No. It was him. Something brought Dane here. He will be back."

"Oh, this is what the sergeant brought." Sabrina reached inside her shirt and brought out the invitation.

"What is it?"

"We've been invited to a dinner party."

A chortle of disbelief slipped out before Colter could stop it. "A dinner party? Us?"

"Well, Cullen Alexander and his wife and family. Captain Holland has invited us to the fort. Of course, I told them we wouldn't be attending. You'd better not mention this to my sisters, or they may decide to go alone."

Colter started to laugh again, then swallowed his chuckle. "Wait a minute. Maybe that's not a bad idea. Yes. The more I think about it, the better it sounds."

He walked slowly back and forth, his movements more a stealth than a pace. "Yes, that might work. We'll take the bull by the horns. When is the party?"

"Next week. What are you thinking, Colter?"

He slapped his hand against the wall. "Yes, by damn. We'll do it. We'll go to the fort to the party."

Sabrina stared at her pretend husband with unabashed horror. "You can't be serious. You intend to walk into the fort, where you'll surely be captured and put in prison? Or worse?"

"Who is going to arrest Cullen Alexander's son?"

"Well, if you were right about the man you call Dane he'll arrest you the minute you show your face."

"On what grounds?"

"Because you tried to hold up the paymaster wagon. You took the gold and killed the escorts."

"We didn't kill anybody. Dane can't say that we did unless he admits that he was in on the raid."

"No, I guess not."

"Right. So if I walk into that fort openly, he'll have to keep quiet or confess to his having been a member of Colter's misfits."

"So how will that help you?"

"I don't know yet. But we didn't know about any gold, and we didn't take it. If we didn't and the Indians didn't, that leaves only Dane."

"I don't understand," Sabrina said. "Another officer happened along. He said that one of the dying soldiers blamed your men. But that can't be true. They were *all* dead, I'm sure of it."

Colter turned to Sabrina and held out his arms. "I think I'm beginning to. I feel like going to a party. Will you do me the honor of this waltz, madam wife?"

"Oh, Colter, I'm sorry. I don't know how to dance, and there is no way I'm going to a dinner party."

"Why not?"

"Even if I wanted to, and I don't, I don't even own a dress. Besides, Captain Holland wouldn't believe for a minute that a man like you would be married to a clumsy Clementine like me."

He lifted one eyebrow. "Clementine?"

"Wearing boxes without tops, or however that song goes."

"It just goes to prove that you can't tell what's hidden beneath those clothes, wife. And the song goes like this." And he began to whistle as he slipped his arm around Sabrina and whirled her around the empty barn. " . . . my darling, Clementine."

Lauren stepped into the barn and came to an abrupt stop. Her sister was being danced around the barn by Captain Colter.

Sabrina, her head flung back, her auburn hair flowing across her shoulders, was smiling in a way Lauren had never seen her. For a moment she just stood, captivated by the lean, scruffy man holding her sister as if she were some plantation beauty in a hoopskirt and lacy drawers.

"Sabrina!"

"Oh," Sabrina came to an abrupt stop, tangling her feet and almost falling as she realized that they had an audience. "Captain Colter was teaching me how to dance. He thinks—I mean he says that we're—"

"Going to a party, Miss Lauren. Do you think you could find your sister a dress to wear by next week?"

"At the fort? You're going?"

"We're all going, Miss Lauren. At least you and Mary and Isabella. I don't think it would be wise to take my men along. What about that dress?"

"Well, yes. Of course. There are some of my mother's gowns in a trunk in the loft. Papa always thought she was beautiful, but my mother was a tall, large woman. I think I could cut something down to fit Sabrina."

"Good. In the meantime, I think I'll move the men into the cabin. Unless your hands return Dane will surely find a fire in the storage house suspicious. Besides, for the next few days we'll be safer if we all stay together."

Sabrina felt a lump the size of Mrs. William's frying pan form in her chest. "Stay together?" she whispered.

"Don't worry, Brina," Colter reassured her. "We'll put the women upstairs and the men by the fire. You and I will take the bunks by the door. We'll make sure that nobody gets out of line."

Sabrina didn't answer. She didn't know how Colter thought he could keep Tyler and Mary apart. He didn't seem to be able to stop himself from kissing her every time an opportunity presented itself.

Tyler and Mary. Dear God, suppose they had—no, that couldn't be the case. Tyler was a gentleman and Mary was pure and good. And what about Lauren and Irish? They were perfectly well suited, Irish with his boisterous voice and shy nature, and Lauren with her quiet need to mother. Sabrina didn't want to think about Isabella. Of the three men, Carl seemed the least admirable. Colter might give his word that her sisters would be safe from Mr. McBride and Mr. Kurtz, but Mr. Arnstine was another story.

And there was Isabella, who'd never backed down in her life from going after what she wanted. Seeing the look in Isabella's eyes every time she saw Carl re-inforced Sabrina's fear. Her sister had fallen in love with a scoundrel, and nobody was going to change that.

A scandal, a real scandal was in the making, and there didn't seem to be a way in the world that she could avert it. A brewing scandal in Alexander City— fate was hurtling them all down that uncharted river as fast as a leaf caught in a flood.

Oh, Papa, Sabrina thought. *Where are your little people? Send me a sign. Send me a miracle. Send me tiny feet and a party dress.*

As if in answer to her plea, the sound of bells echoed down the valley, over and over again, like scales being played on the rocks by some mystical force that could only be heard. And then, beneath her feet, the earth trembled again, only once, and then it was gone.

"I'm glad Raven isn't here," Lauren said softly.

"Why?" Colter asked from his position by the open door.

Sabrina found the words to answer. "Because she'd say we've been sent a message."

"From who?" he asked curiously.

"From the mountain spirits who allow us to dig in their earth. From the Earth Mother, who shares her wealth with us."

Colter studied Sabrina. "And do you believe all that?"

"I don't know. Didn't you ever ask the land for something and have it answer?"

Colter considered his answer, allowing his mind to range back to one night when he had run his fingers through Carolina soil for the last time. He'd drawn it to his mouth, to his nose, where the burned smell of parched dirt filled his nostrils.

Moe had stood beside the man who'd been his master and let the tears roll silently down his cheek. "Don't take it too hard, Mr. Quinton. Dirt is just dirt," he said. "The wind and the floods scoop it up and carry it off to the good Lord only knows where. It ain't the dirt that makes the difference, it's the heart of the man that plows it."

But Moe was gone, killed in a battle fighting the army who claimed to want to free him and those like him. And it had been Colter's fault. He should have forced Moe to go back home, to find his people and stay. But he hadn't. He'd wanted to take a little piece of his life with him. Then Moe had been killed and Colter knew that his death was the last pain that he would ever allow himself to feel.

Until now.

Until Miss Sabrina Alexander.

He risked one last glance at the woman he'd made his physical wife, if not his legal one. "A green dress," he said to Lauren. "Can you make it green?"

15

Captain Holland kept Dane from returning to the Alexanders. He also provided a reason for Dane to miss the dinner party. Since the payroll was lost, the men were growing more and more belligerent. To prevent a mutiny, Captain Holland was sending a detachment, with Dane in charge, all the way to Fort Laramie to escort the new paymaster.

Dane hadn't actually seen Colter at the Alexander cabin, but he was certain that the man Gray Warrior and Sergeant Nealey described was the captain. Colter had apparently settled in there to hide. Leaving Gray Warrior to keep watch, Dane followed orders and headed for Fort Laramie. Mrs. Holland cautioned him privately to be careful with the case of French champagne that was being delivered.

If one bottle disappeared along the way, the captain's wife would never know. One thing Dane had learned to appreciate at West Point was the finer things of life enjoyed by the sons of the wealthy planters. He'd been lucky. The war came along just in time to keep him from being discovered as the mastermind behind the examination-selling scheme. The commandant had already known how it was done, he just didn't know who was responsible. Determined not to return to the life of a merchant like his father, Dane withdrew from the academy and joined the staff of a government mapmaking expedition.

But the expedition ended just as the war began, and Dane, riding the wave of adventure, accepted a commission in the most elite regiment in Virginia. But he soon discovered that wars killed and that the pay of an officer would never provide him the money he wanted. After being assigned to Colter's secret mission, Dane saw a way to make his past experience with the Indians pay. So began his double life as a scavenger, both for himself and for the South. The first thing he bought was the pair of fine leather gloves that he never went without.

With his own coffers full, he had a fancy to travel, and California was the nearest port. Now that the war was drawing to a close, his means of escape was at hand. He'd already amassed a small fortune in his partnership with Gray Warrior. The shipment of gold had been the icing on the cake.

Colter wasn't going anywhere, and if he did, so be it. Dane left Fort Collins with no worries. He'd avoid confronting Colter until he was ready to leave, and he would toast his departure with French champagne.

Isabella didn't try to conceal her pique as she watched Lauren unfold their mother's dresses, searching for the best one for Sabrina.

"I don't see why Sabrina gets first choice," she said peevishly. "She won't know how to act in a dress anyway."

Mary cut a hard look at her sister. "Shame on you, Isabella, after all Brina has done for us. Of course her dress must be special."

"What's she done for us that we couldn't have done for ourselves?"

Lauren found the gown she'd been looking for and glared at her sister. "For one thing, you ungrateful child, she brought help for us. If it hadn't been for Brina, we wouldn't have—Captain Colter and—his men."

"Yes," Mary was quick to agree, "and we wouldn't be going to the social."

"But—Carl—and Mr. McBride won't be going," Isabella said with genuine unhappiness in her voice.

Lauren stood, shaking out the dress she was holding. It was worse than she'd expected. The lace was tattered, and there was a spot on one hip that looked like grease. But the color was a rich, dark green, and Captain Colter had asked for green. She'd repair the lace and find some way to conceal the stain.

"Lauren," Isabella began, "I don't understand why we've never worn Mama's dresses before. I think it was mean of you to keep them hidden."

"I've been saving them for a special occasion."

Mary looked at the dresses and beamed. "They're so beautiful. Where did Mama get such gowns?"

"She was the daughter of one of the men who was building the railroad from California. Papa met her and swept her off her feet. Papa said she was an angel sent from heaven. She used to look at herself in this mirror and say that when Papa found his gold we'd all wear diamonds and pearls." Lauren held out a silver hand mirror with a crack across the glass.

Mary's eyes filled with tears as she took the treasured looking glass and studied herself. "And he brought her up here? I hardly remember her."

"You were too young, Mary. I barely remember her myself. I remember her laughing—and crying. I think she loved Papa, but this life was hard for her. After she died, Brina packed these things up and gave me the key. I was to save them until the right time." Lauren glanced from one sister to the other. "I think that time might be now."

She repacked the mirror and plowed through the remaining gowns, pulling out a soft-blue print and studying Isabella. "Isabella, I think this will do nicely for you. If you help me, you will all have new dresses to wear. Just think, there will be plenty of young men at the party who haven't danced with a girl in months."

Isabella's pout turned into a smile. "There will be?"

Lauren could see Isabella's mind begin to work. "Of course."

"But what about Carl? He won't like it if I—"

Mary stood up and danced around the room, holding the gold-colored dress that Lauren had selected for her. "Isabella, just think of it as ministering to the soldiers. They've been away from their families for a long time. It would be the Christian thing to do, giving them a bit of happiness in the midst of a long war."

Isabella held the blue dress to her body and thought for a minute. "You're right, of course. Those poor, lonely men. I shouldn't be selfish with my attentions. I'll go."

"I thought you would," Lauren said under her breath, and considered the battle before her. Telling the captain she'd find a dress for Sabrina didn't mean that Sabrina was going to cooperate with her attempt to make the dress fit.

"Can we get the dresses done in time?" Isabella asked.

"With Mary's help in the sewing and your help doing the housework, I think so." Lauren started replacing the dresses and closed the trunk.

"But what about you, Lauren?" Mary asked.

"I'll not be going. Someone has to stay here with Mr. Arnstine and Mr. McBride."

"But, Lauren," Mary argued, "that won't be fair. I'll stay."

"You'll go, Mary. Captain Colter is taking Mr. Kurtz. He said he'll explain that Tyler is the hired hand Sergeant Nealey already believes we have. You don't want to miss a waltz with Mr. Kurtz, do you?"

Mary's heart skipped a beat as she realized what her sister was saying. Then her shoulders sagged. "I can't go."

"Don't be silly, Mary," Isabella said. "Why wouldn't you want to go?"

"I don't know how to waltz."

Isabella pursued her lips and narrowed her gaze as she considered the problem. "I know. We'll have Captain Colter teach us both."

Mary asked her question guardedly. "What makes you think he will?"

"Because," Isabella said confidently, "he wants Sabrina to go to the party, and if we don't go, she won't."

Mary sat down on the trunk, a new concern digging at her. "Lauren, do you think the captain likes Sabrina?"

Isabella laughed. "Of course he does, silly. Why else would he still be around? Besides, I saw him kissing her."

Mary gasped. "When?"

"After the sergeant left, the night the captain came back from the mine, in the barn. And she let him. I watched them."

"Isabella!" Lauren took the blue dress from her sister's hands and frowned. "You were spying. Shame on you. That was a private moment."

"And another thing," Isabella added, "she married her captain. I don't know why she's being so hateful, claiming the others are criminals. I don't believe for a minute that they did anything really bad, and neither do you."

Lauren wrung her hands. She didn't know how to argue with Isabella. Her own thoughts were running along the same line. Still, as the elder sister, she felt compelled to defend Sabrina's actions.

"Isabella, you don't know the truth. Sabrina may be doing what she has to do to take care of us. With Papa gone things are different. I don't want you behaving like some hoyden. Papa would expect you to be a lady."

Isabella turned a hard look of honesty on her sister. "Papa is dead, Lauren. Everything is different now. We have to think about our futures, and I, for one, don't intend to stay here for the rest of my life scratching in the dirt."

Suddenly, for Mary, the joy had gone out of the plans for the dinner party. "But what about the silver in the mine, Isabella? Don't you want to be rich?"

"I'm going to be rich," she declared. "I just don't know yet how I'm going to do it. All I know is that it won't be here on this godforsaken mountain."

Sabrina, standing in the cabin below heard the last of their conversation and blanched. Because of her childish behavior, Isabella had always been the sister who gave Papa the most reason for concern. Her flaxen hair and blue eyes set her apart, as did her bright smile and good heart. But something about her words chilled Sabrina. Isabella had grown up. She wanted to leave and she was planning her escape. Would the saloon keeper be her way out?

Sabrina shivered.

Everything was changing too fast.

She'd just come down from the mine. Colter was moving the last of the cave-in away. By afternoon the knobs of silver would be exposed. They'd learn whether the vein Papa had predicted was there. She might as well get on with her task.

"Lauren? Colter sent me to bring food back to the mine. He intends to keep working."

"It's ready, sister. Look at what I found, the green dress the captain asked for."

Sabrina looked at the limp garment and shook her head. "I think he's going to look a little odd wearing it, but if that's what he wants."

Mary laughed and followed Lauren down the ladder. "Oh, Brina. The dress is for you, not the captain."

"Don't waste your time." Sabrina's voice was razor sharp. "I have no intention of going to a dinner party, and I'm certainly not going to wear that dress."

"Of course you are," Lauren said, placing bread and meat in the basket. "And you're going to be beautiful for the captain."

"I'm going to stay here, with Mr. McBride and Mr. Arnstine," Sabrina said, gathering up the food. "You and Mary and Isabella can go in my place, that is, if Mr. Kurtz gets the wheels put back on the wagon."

"But, Brina," Mary argued, "won't Captain Holland find it odd for Colter—excuse me, I should say, Cullen Alexander—to bring three women when none of them is his wife?"

Lauren took the coffeepot from its hook in the fireplace and handed it to Isabella. "Go with Brina. She can't take it all. But don't tarry. As soon as they're done, you get back. You're going to have to prepare the evening meal if Mary and I are going to get these dresses done."

Sabrina left, sharply protesting that she wasn't going to the fort and they could just forget it. Isabella followed, carrying the coffee, ignoring her sister's comments. "Don't be silly, Brina. You're going. You know very well you aren't about to let me and Mary go to the fort without you along to make sure we don't have any fun."

That stopped Sabrina short. Isabella was right. She couldn't allow her sisters to go without supervision. But it would be Lauren accompanying them, not Sabrina.

Going to a dinner party was out of the question.

Sabrina Alexander was a miner, not a socialite.

Sabrina Alexander wore her father's clothes, not ball gowns.

Sabrina Alexander had no intention of accompanying her husband; she didn't have one.

Late that afternoon, after Colter had sent the men back to the barn with the rescued wagon wheels, they unearthed the vein to which the silver knobs were attached.

Colter folded his arms across his chest and leaned back against the rock wall that Cullen had blasted. "Well, Sabrina, there it is, your mother lode. You and your sisters are rich."

Sabrina had a lump in her throat the size of a hen egg. "I never really believed it would happen," she whispered. "Poor Papa. He looked all his life and he isn't here to see."

As if in answer there was a quick wisp of wind outside the mine and the muted sound of musical notes.

"Are you sure he isn't watching?" Colter asked.

Sabrina felt a tear slide down her cheek. "I hope so. I hope he knows. He made it possible for Lauren and Mary and Isabella to have a better life."

"I suppose. What about Raven?"

"Raven never cared about gold *or* silver."

Colter asked the question that he'd been wrestling with ever since they cleared the last of the debris. "What about you, Sabrina?"

"Me? Why I'll mine the silver, of course. I mean— we'll mine the silver and we'll—"

"What will we do?"

She looked up at the man who'd stepped into her life and changed it forever. "I don't know. I never thought that far. For so long it was all a dream. Now that it's happened, I don't know. First, I guess, we'll go to Denver to the assayer's office."

Colter shook his head. "No, Sabrina. I can't do that. You forget, I'm a wanted man. There's a price on my head."

"But surely we can prove that you didn't kill anyone. You have me as a witness."

"And how safe do you think you'll be when the real criminal finds out there was a witness?"

"Oh. I hadn't thought about that." She thought about it now. If she came forward to clear Colter and his men, she put her sisters in danger. If she remained silent, he could be hanged.

"You see, it isn't that simple, *wife*."

"Don't call me that!"

"Sorry. I was beginning to get used to the sound of it. But of course, it isn't true, is it?"

There was something about his voice that was different. He wasn't the officer in charge. He wasn't the man who'd dropped his guard long enough to tease her by calling her "wife." He was just a man who was as vulnerable as she was in a situation that neither knew how to deal with.

"No, Colter. You're a man who can't stay, and I'm a woman who doesn't want to leave this place. Even if we were—interested in more, it wouldn't work."

"I know. It's hell isn't it, finding there really is a snake in the Garden of Eden?"

"No," she said softly, "it isn't hell at all because you aren't a snake. You're a very nice man, even if you think you aren't." *The hell comes when you leave.*

Colter knew he wasn't a nice man. He didn't know what kind of man he was. He had spent little time worrying about that sort of thing since the war started. Learning that Sabrina thought he was nice disconcerted him.

For the next few days he threw himself into helping his men shore up the mine, cutting trees to be used for support and for fuel. They worked nonstop, as if they knew that their stay was about to end and they wanted to leave the women provided for. Carl was almost back to normal, and Irish had put aside his crutch.

The night before they left for the fort, Mary made it a point to encounter Colter as she was throwing out her dishwater. She shyly whispered her question. "Captain Colter, I—I mean Isabella and I wondered if you would . . ."

Colter, his arms filled with cut wood, waited for Mary to finish her sentence. He had become fond of the Alexander women, especially Mary, who so obviously cared for the studious Tyler.

"What would you like me to do, Mary?"

"Could you—do you think that you could teach me to dance?"

Colter hadn't known what she was going to ask of him, but giving dancing lessons was a real surprise. Then, as he reflected on their upbringing, he realized how many of the things they'd missed growing up in this wilderness.

"I'd be delighted, Mary. Of course it's been a while since I've done any dancing, but I'm willing—if you can talk Irish into playing his harp."

A short time later, with lamps lit, they trooped out to the barn, everyone except Sabrina.

Nobody insisted that she join them, so she didn't. Learning to dance was a frivolous pastime anyway. Except for that one night when Colter had whirled her around the barn, she'd never even thought about dancing.

But now, alone in the cabin, she heard the sound of Irish's mouth harp, and she felt a twinge of pain in her chest. Though she tried not to let her mind wander, she felt a strong, undeniable urge to move her hips in rhythm.

"Stop this foolishness, Sabrina Alexander!" she told herself, and began banking the fire for the night. Then her leather boots needed a good cleaning. And finally, unfastening the cord with which she'd tied back her hair, she began combing out the tangles.

But her feet refused to remain still.

The memory of being held, of moving in tandem with a man, allowing the natural body rhythms to merge and become one. It had been like making love, except she hadn't let herself think about it. But now those internal forces seemed to take control. Before she knew that she was moving, she was halfway across the yard.

Colter knew the moment she stepped into the doorway. His senses seemed fused with the sound of music, with the touch and smell of a woman—of Sabrina. As he moved Isabella gracefully through the steps of the waltz, he changed direction, finding himself at the barn door, opposite Sabrina as Irish's melody ended.

With a laugh Isabella stepped back and bowed. She flung out her arms and whirled back across the floor, to where Carl was sitting morosely viewing the dancers.

He drew her down beside him. "There are masked balls in the East where you don't learn who your partner is until the stroke of midnight. Or there used to be."

"Oh, I'd love to go to a real ball," she said. "I'd go as a unicorn, with a white horn on my forehead."

"Be a little hard to dance," Carl observed with a grin.

"What would you be, Mary?" Tyler asked as he, too, slid to the barn floor beside where Mary had stopped.

"I don't know. Perhaps a character from a fairy tale."

Irish, wetting his lips, glanced at Lauren, who was sitting on the milking stool at his elbow.

"My ma used to like music. That's why I learned to play. But she never heard me."

"Why?" Lauren asked.

"She was gone by then. But I liked to think that the music went up to heaven. I guess it was the way I talked to her."

"I'm sure she knew. Dance with me, Mr. McBride," Lauren surprised herself by asking.

"Oh, no. I'm afraid I have two left feet."

"Which will match very nicely with my two right feet," Lauren said, rising and holding out her hand. "Irish, I don't know how either, so I won't know if you do it wrong. We can learn together."

Still Irish hesitated. "But the music?"

Lauren smiled at him. "Couldn't you sing?"

"Aye!" Taking Lauren's hand, Irish began to sing, hesitantly at first, then with more confidence.

The song was an Irish lullaby, sweet and moving. It seemed, to Lauren, that the words "loving child, sleep, to wake as loving woman" seemed beautifully appropriate. If, as they moved about the floor, they were clumsy, neither noticed.

The lamps flickered. Those dancers watching from the other side of the barn grew quiet. Colter held out his hand and, drawing Sabrina close, danced in the darkness beyond the barn.

"Sleep now, loving child, sleep. Wake as loving woman."

* * *

The next morning a strange mood had settled over the group.

Mary, to her surprise, was looking forward to making the trip to the fort. Her dress was the most elaborate gown she'd ever worn. There were no hoops to hold out their skirts, so they had to shorten their dresses considerably. Mary used the fabric cut from the bottom to trim her cape. Carefully, she packed the dress and donned her regular skirt and overblouse. By the time she'd dressed her hair and climbed down the ladder, she was nearly sick with fear.

Tyler would surely see how out of place she was going to be. He'd finally see that his vision of her was simply that, his imagination. She was what she was, a simple woman, not someone who could travel to England.

Isabella, excited beyond reason, was showing Carl her new dress. She was torn between the promise of her first social event and leaving the man she'd nursed, the man who'd daily turned more sullen and silent as the time of the dinner party grew nearer.

When she'd come down the stairs, dressed in the blue gown—looking like the angel he'd thought she was that first morning when he woke and found her smiling at him—he'd actually hurt.

"Carl, what's wrong with you? Don't you want me to go?"

"You can do whatever you like," he said. "I have no claim on you. Just as you have none on me."

"You're right of course," she said with an unexpected catch in her throat. This wasn't working out as she'd imagined. She'd expected Carl to tell her she was beautiful, to be worried. She'd thought he'd ask her not to go. She had her argument ready: He'd been so many places and done so many things; this was her first time to go.

"Isabella," he said instead, "be careful. There are men out there who won't appreciate your innocence."

Carl grimaced. Now, where did that come from? He sounded like a father, repeating the warnings he'd so often urged a woman to forget. Too many times he'd vanquished that innocence with false promises and kisses that turned a woman's head.

But Isabella was different. She was too good for him. He couldn't take advantage. She was the kind of woman whose honor a man defended. She was the first woman he'd really wanted, and this was the first time he'd held back from talking his way into a woman's bed.

Now she was going out into the world, to blink those blue eyes at men who hadn't seen a woman this beautiful in months. He'd better talk to the captain. If Carl wasn't along to protect her, he wanted to make sure that someone did.

The ache in his gut rapidly overwhelmed him. He groaned and sat back down in the pallet where he'd been sleeping.

"What's wrong, Mr. Arnstine?" Isabella, her face full of concern, dropped down beside him, all thought of wrinkling her gown gone from her head.

"Nothing, just a pain. I'm all right," he managed to say. "Don't muss your skirt. You want to make all those men at the fort ready to fight a duel for your favors."

Isabella bit back a rebuttal. Suddenly the enthusiasm went out of the day. She didn't want to leave Carl. She was finally going to a real party, and now she didn't want to go. What was wrong with her?

"Maybe I ought not to go," she said.

"Of course you should go. Why not?"

"Because you don't look very well. Suppose you're suffering a relapse. I mean, you might need me."

Carl couldn't hold back a groan. Need her? She didn't know how much he needed her. And that was the problem. He didn't want to need a woman. Women were for bedding, entertainment, a good time.

And he didn't want to know what was holding him back from enjoying Miss Isabella Alexander. Now she was about to dive headlong into a nest of vipers, and it was driving him wild. He didn't want her to be hurt. He didn't want her to learn the harsh realities of life.

For the first time he wanted to protect a woman.

It had to be his injury, inactivity, being laid up.

Being trusted.

Being cared for.

"Get out of here, Miss Isabella. Have a good time, and come back and tell me all about it. I'll be waiting."

"All right, if you're sure. Can I bring you anything?"

Carl thought a minute, then searched his mind for something to request, something she would have to think about. He liked that idea, that she'd have him in her mind while she was away.

"Yes. If you could find a deck of cards, I could teach you how to play poker."

"But isn't that gambling?"

"If you want it to be."

"But I don't have any money to wager."

Carl let out a deep breath. "Don't worry, Isabella, we'll think of something."

"Go upstairs and change into your other clothes, Isabella," Lauren said. "If you wear that dress to travel in, you'll look like a kitchen maid by supper time."

"I will, sister. I just wanted Mr. Arnstine to see my dress. I mean, he knows how women in the outside world look."

"Go. I hear the wagon. They'll leave without you and then it won't matter."

Isabella flew back up the ladder.

Lauren caught the look in Mr. Arnstine's eyes and decided that sending Isabella to the dance was a wise move. She wanted her sister to learn that there were choices to be made.

If a woman wanted to look.

From beyond the cabin she heard the slap of the ax and the plop of the wood accompanying the sound of an Irish ditty.

Lauren smiled.

* * *

Colter, already mounted, waited impatiently for the party to move out.

Sabrina was the last one to appear, walking up from the barn, leading her horse.

"Brina," Lauren said in shock, "surely you aren't going to wear Papa's clothes. I laid out my black serge skirt."

"I told you, I'm not going to a party. I wouldn't know how to act. I'm simply going along so to keep an eye on Mary and Isabella."

Tyler drove the reconstructed wagon to the house and climbed down. "Miss Mary, may I assist you?" He held out his hand to the plump, red-haired woman on the porch.

"Thank you," she managed to say, but remained where she stood. She simply couldn't force her feet to move. They felt as if they were nailed to the floor.

"Mary, you goose," Isabella said, "get in the wagon. You may help me, Mr. Kurtz." She held out her arms and was rewarded with assistance up to the seat.

Woodenly, Mary forced herself to take the few steps from the door to the wagon and allowed Tyler to lift her. With the two women on either side of him, he clucked to the two Indian ponies that had been a gift from Flying Cloud and was rewarded by the wagon moving forward.

"Here, wrap yourself in these blankets," Lauren said, coming out of the cabin. "And put Sabrina's dress under the seat, just in case she changes her mind."

"I won't," Sabrina said, and climbed onto her horse.

"She will," Colter corrected, crosser than he had any reason to be. He took his place at the head of the traveling party and rode out of the yard, a slow fury at Sabrina's stubbornness beginning to boil.

Sabrina, her hair tucked beneath her cap, was wearing her customary trousers and sheepskin-lined canvas coat. A casual observer wouldn't know that she was a woman. But Colter knew.

Even in her father's clothing her curves were evident. After their moonlight dance, sleep had been a long time in coming. When Irish and Lauren had finished dancing, the evening had ended, everyone quiet, everyone thoughtful, as they walked back toward the house.

The others must have seen Sabrina, but wisely they'd made no comment. Now, in the light of day, the lessons weren't mentioned. It was as if everyone wanted to pretend last night had never happened. As if he and Sabrina had never made love.

No, that was a lie. He couldn't forget what they'd done, and if her short temper and sharp words this morning were any indication, she was having a hard time closing out the memories as well.

Now they were on their way to the fort. Carl and Irish were still grousing about being left behind. They were worried about their captain as well as about the women.

Colter was worried, too. His recent choices had been long shots, gambles that might or might not work. Making love to Sabrina had been a foolish deed, but probably not a fatal mistake. Facing Dane tonight was either smart, or the dumbest move he'd ever make. Time would be the judge of both matters.

Mary was completely tongue-tied, Isabella was chattering like a magpie, and Sabrina, in the rear, rode as solemnly as the lead rider in a funeral march.

But in her mind she was humming an Irish lullaby.

16

It was midafternoon when Fort Collins came into view. The rough board buildings were spread across the flat landscape like oddly shaped game pieces on a crudely carved chessboard. In the center, flying high above the tall whitewashed building, was an American flag.

"It looks like it's waving at us," Mary whispered.

"Buildings! People!" Isabella cried out. "Look, there are men marching back and forth."

The fort was still new, its raw wooden logs still light in color, its one lone tree standing by a ribbon of water in the distance. With the Laramie Mountains behind them, they rode across the brown grasslands on a road well-worn by the presence of wagons and horses.

A bugle sounded as Colter came to a stop at the hitching post outside the camp store.

"We're looking for Captain Holland," he said to the junior officer, who hurried toward them.

"I'm Lieutenant Garland. Please follow me, sir." The young officer headed toward a smaller wooden structure with a shingled roof that extended past the building to shelter a wooden walkway. "Captain Holland's quarters, sir."

A number of soldiers encircled the wagon, greeting Mary and Isabella in undisguised excitement. They paid little attention to the odd-looking woman on horseback beside the wagon.

Sabrina dismounted, tied her horse to the hitching post, and watched as her sisters, with unabashed astonishment, accepted the attention being offered.

Tyler climbed down and was in the process of helping Mary from the wagon when the door opened and an officer stepped forward, rubbing his hands in glee.

"Greetings. I am Captain Lucius Holland. Welcome!" He extended his hand to Mary, who stared at him in awe. When he saw that he'd overwhelmed her, he gave a sharp bow, clicking his heels together, then turned to Colter as he dismounted.

"And you must be the Alexanders," he said. "Mrs. Holland will be so pleased that you've come."

In the meantime Lieutenant Garland assisted Isabella from her seat in the wagon. He continued to hold her hand as he stood and looked at her.

"Mrs. Alexander," the captain said to Isabella.

"Captain Holland," Colter corrected, taking Sabrina's arm and folding it over his own, "I'd like you to meet my wife, Sabrina."

To give him his due, the captain tried to conceal his surprise, covering it by giving a second click of his heels and a bow. Sabrina had no idea how to respond, so she did nothing.

"Of course," the officer went on, recovering himself. "Please, step inside my quarters. I'll have rooms prepared for you and the ladies immediately. You must be cold and hungry."

Colter gave one final glance around the parade ground. Since entering the gates, he'd searched the crowd for Dane. He wasn't there, at least not where he could be seen. Colter didn't know whether he was glad or disappointed. Instinctively, he supported Sabrina as she stepped up on the walkway and moved stiffly inside.

"Lucy! Lucy! Look, we have guests," Captain Holland called out.

Moments later a thin, smiling woman swept into the room, the hoops on her skirts hanging momentarily on the rough sides of the door frame as she came in.

"These are the Alexanders," Captain Holland said. "And this is Mrs. Holland—Lucy."

Lucy looked from Mary to Isabella and then in astonishment at Sabrina. For a moment her eyes widened; then, remembering her manners, she gave a half curtsy.

"Welcome to our home. I'm sorry it isn't more comfortable, but when your husband is in the military, you have little to say about your quarters."

From Sabrina her attention turned to Colter. "And you, sir, are . . . ?"

"Sorry, ma'am. Your presence has left me speechless. I'm—I'm—Cullen—"

"Cullen Alexander," Tyler said. "This is Cullen's wife, Sabrina." He inclined his head toward Sabrina. "The—Alexander sisters, Mary and Isabella. And I'm their hired hand—Kurt."

"Of course," Lucy said, obviously finding it difficult to connect Sabrina with Colter. "Sergeant Nealey said you wouldn't be able to come. We're so glad you changed your mind and decided to join us for dinner and entertainment."

Colter stepped forward. "And where is Sergeant Nealey?"

"After he and Lieutenant Littlejohn returned from delivering your supper invitation, I sent them to Fort Laramie for—supplies," Captain Holland answered.

Lieutenant Littlejohn? Colter thought quickly. The officer with Sergeant Nealey was Dane. Obviously he'd taken a new name along with the new uniform. "Will Lieutenant Littlejohn be joining us for supper?" Colter asked casually.

"He should be back in time," Lieutenant Garland said.

Colter gave Tyler a puzzled look. How had Dane, Confederate soldier, become Lieutenant Littlejohn, Yankee officer? At least Captain Holland's assignment explained why Dane hadn't returned to the cabin. Colter would find out soon enough. In a few hours they'd be face-to-face.

"Lieutenant Garland, get their luggage," Mrs. Holland was saying. "Captain, please inform the cook that we're having four more for dinner. Ladies, for now I'll share my sitting room with Mary and Isabella. Mrs. Alexander, you may use our guest room. Please, follow me."

Sabrina decided that it was Mrs. Holland who deserved the salute, not her husband. As Mary and Isabella followed Mrs. Holland, Sabrina turned to go outside, where Tyler and the lieutenant were unloading the wagon.

"Where are you going, Mrs. Alexander?" Colter asked under his breath.

"I'm going to see to the horses," she replied, concealing her unease with a toss of her head.

"I don't think that would be wise. You're on a post with a hundred men, men who haven't been around a beautiful woman in months. I don't think you'd be safe."

She looked at him in disdain. "You don't think I'd be safe? Look at me, Colter. Nobody is ever going to pay attention to me."

"*I am*," he said with a look that disrobed her and made her remember how well he already had.

Sabrina gasped. "But you—you've—that's different."

"Exactly my point. As my wife, you'll be expected to let me see to the horses. Unless you want to arouse suspicion, you're going to have to behave like my— Mrs. Alexander."

"But—"

"I've ordered hot water and something cool to drink for your sisters," Mrs. Holland said, reappearing behind Sabrina. "If you'll come with me, I'll show you to your room. While we're having dinner, I'll have sleeping pallets prepared in my sitting room for your sisters."

"That won't be necessary," Sabrina said, "they can share my room. Mr. Alexander will be happy to sleep in the barracks."

Colter didn't argue. It might even be easier to keep the three women safe if they were together. He didn't intend to sleep anyway, not with Dane nearby—at least not until he'd had a chance to study the situation.

"Fine," Mrs. Holland agreed, leading the way down the corridor to a room at the end of the hall. "But they're already undressing to rest before the evening's activities. I have to speak with the cook and see to the table arrangements. You'll be able to use your room undisturbed."

The look she bestowed on Sabrina said that she feared the odd-looking woman might contaminate her sisters.

Sabrina was too tired to argue. Perhaps she *would* rest. The journey had been tense, and she hadn't slept well since their return from Flying Cloud's encampment.

Mrs. Holland waited for Sabrina to enter the room, then closed the door, leaving her alone in the late-afternoon shadows. Sabrina walked around the room, feeling a little like a child being punished. The room might be sparse by Mrs. Holland's standards, but she'd never stayed in such quarters.

There was a real bed, with a crocheted spread. White lawn curtains hung at the windows. Woven rag rugs covered the wood floor. There were candles on the mantel over the fireplace, and a warm fire had already been lit.

Wearily she warmed her hands, shedding her jacket and leaning against the mantel. She didn't know what she was doing here. She ought to be back in the valley working the mine. A miner was what she was, what she'd always been, not some fancy woman attending a dinner party.

Giving a sigh, she turned to sit on the bed, then rose quickly as she realized how dusty her clothing was. She couldn't even sit without soiling the spread, and there were no chairs. The dinner party wouldn't commence for at least two hours, and until then she was stuck there. Uneasily she stripped off the offending clothing and dropped it on the floor by the door. Wearing only her long underwear, Sabrina pulled back the spread and sat.

The bed was unbelievably soft. The room was growing warm and she was tired. Her eyes were closed almost before her head hit the pillow. While she slept, unseen hands removed her dusty clothing, unpacked the parcel Lauren had packed, and shook out the wrinkles in the green dress.

By the time Mary and Isabella knocked on Sabrina's door, it was almost time for dinner. She sat up, her mind fogged with sleep. The sky through the window was black. The fire had died down.

"Damn!"

"Brina, you aren't even dressed," Isabella said.

"Get up, we'll help you," Mary promised as she pulled the curtains and lit the oil lamp on the table beside the bed.

"I don't need any help," Sabrina said crossly, glancing around for her clothes. They weren't where she'd left them. "Where are my things?"

"Mrs. Holland is having them washed. They'll be dry in plenty of time for us to leave tomorrow," Mary explained, testing the pan of water by the fire. "Hurry, your water is almost cold."

Sabrina sprang to her feet and moved toward the door. "I want my own clothes."

Isabella stepped in front of the door. "I don't think I'd go out in the hall dressed like that, Brina. This is an army post. The captain's servants are enlisted men."

"Then I'm not leaving this room," she announced, sweeping the green dress Mary had laid out off the bed and onto the floor.

Mary picked it up and held it against her bosom. "Brina, I'm very worried," she said shrewdly. "Tyler thinks you ought to be there. He's afraid they could be arrested."

"Fiddle! Nobody is going to arrest the captain," Isabella said. "But this is our first dinner party, and I won't have it spoiled." Isabella took her sister's hand and squeezed it. "Please, Brina."

Sabrina didn't care two hoots in hell about spoiling a dinner party, but she couldn't take a chance on something happening to Colter because she wasn't there to intercede.

"All right, but you're going to have to help me. I don't know anything about dressing my hair. I don't even have bloomers and—"

"Yes, you do," Isabella announced, producing the necessary undergarments and stockings. "You even got the fancy shoes. Mama must have had extraordinary feet. None of us could wear these."

Sabrina stared at the shoes with the red heels. "I won't be able to stand up in those," she gasped.

"Yes you will," Mary said, drawing her sister to the washbasin. "You've been wearing Papa's boots. These heels aren't any higher."

Taking care that their own gowns weren't disturbed, Mary and Isabella urged and harassed until Sabrina was washed and into her chemise and drawers. When Mary produced the corset, Sabrina announced that she'd had enough.

Isabella was losing patience. "But, Brina, you have to let us lace you in. Otherwise the dress won't fit you properly in the waist. I'll have to go back to the store and buy you one of those shapeless things they sell the fort washerwomen."

"You've been to the store, Isabella?"

"I have. Lieutenant Garland escorted me. I had to make a purchase."

"What on earth did you buy?" Sabrina listened, expecting to hear her sister describe some bit of lace, or ribbon.

"A deck of playing cards." Isabella's reply surprised Sabrina. "Carl's going to teach me how to play poker."

"And how did you pay for them?" Sabrina said

angrily, tugging at the corset. "You don't have any money."

"That's right. The lieutenant paid for them. Take a deep breath, Brina."

Sabrina gave her sister a look of disbelief and jerked the offending garment away. "If the dress won't close without this thing, then it will just have to gape open."

"Fine," Mary agreed, tired of arguing. "Step into it and we'll button what we can."

With a flounce of independence Sabrina stepped into the dress and drew it up her body.

"Where is the rest of it?" she asked, tugging unsuccessfully at the shoulders.

"There is no rest of it," Mary said as she pulled the fabric together across her sister's bosom. The top two hooks beneath the lace fastened, but the buttons weren't going to reach. She stepped back and turned Brina toward a mirror over the chest by the door. Isabella held up the lamp.

"I don't think it's going to work, Sabrina," Isabella observed. "I know you don't care about fashion, but you can't go out like this."

Sabrina stared at her reflection in the looking glass. For a moment all she saw was her bare shoulders and the curve of her breasts at the top of the gown. She looked—like a woman. Then her eyes fell, caught by the gaping opening between her breasts and her navel.

"Why did you let Lauren do this?" she said, leveling a malevolent glance at her sisters. "You knew what would happen. You knew I wouldn't wear that—that thing."

"Oh, Brina," Isabella snapped, stamping her foot, "put the corset on and let's go. I don't want the dinner to start without me."

"Then you go on. I'll figure out something. If I don't, I'll just stay here."

Isabella glared at Sabrina. "Do what you want," she said, whirled around, and left the room.

"Brina, I don't think we ought to let Isabella go

out there alone. The corset won't be so bad, and besides, nobody will know. I think we need you."

Sabrina knew she was beaten. She unhooked the dress and stepped out of it. "Fine, put the damned thing on me. If I have to go to hell, I might as well feel the devil's pinch." She realized, exasperated, she was beginning to sound like Colter.

Finally she was in the corset. She couldn't complain. She couldn't even breathe. If this was what it took to be a woman, she'd just stay a—whatever she was.

Mary went to work on her hair, brushing, combing, arranging. "What happened here? Looks like some Indian tried to scalp you."

"It—I cut it. Just let it go!"

With an odd look Mary finished dressing Sabrina's hair, then stepped back. "All right, take Mama's mirror and have a look." She handed Sabrina the silver hand mirror and stepped away so that she could use it to see the back.

Sabrina followed her sister's directions, not believing the vision she was seeing. "Now," Mary directed, "step back into the dress and let me fasten it." This time the dress buttoned.

When Sabrina looked into the large mirror again, she blinked. Once, twice, then again. She didn't recognize the person looking back at her. She was a stranger, a woman, a lady. "Oh!" was all she could say.

"I think that Captain Colter is going to say a lot more than that," Mary said softly. "You're beautiful, Sabrina. Tonight, just for once in your life, be beautiful for him."

"Nonsense," she contradicted. "This isn't me. Anybody will be able to tell that. Even Papa knew that you can't judge a mine site by the look of the dirt."

"No, but the look can draw you in with its false promise, if you don't take care. One more thing," Mary said, reclaiming the silver mirror and pulling a fluff of lace from her pocket. "Put on these gloves."

"Gloves? Why? I won't be able to eat wearing gloves."

"They were Mama's, and they'll make your hands look like those of a lady."

Sabrina took the gloves and pulled them on her work-worn hands. Nobody would see her healing blisters now. She'd covered all her scars, all the things that said what she was. Glancing once more into the mirror, she felt a strange quiver. She'd eliminated the woman she was, and she didn't know the one she was looking at.

Mary opened the door and stepped aside, waiting for Sabrina to lead the way. "The dining hall is at the end of the corridor, Sabrina."

Swallowing back one last sigh of uncertainty, Sabrina followed the sound of conversation, marching down the corridor and into the dining room. She paused, uncertain of what to expect.

The room beyond was rife with laughter, bright with candlelight.

All eyes turned toward the door.

All conversation ceased.

17

At the hush of conversation Colter looked up, caught sight of the woman in the doorway, and felt his whole body tighten like a sun-dried strip of leather tied in a knot.

He'd known that Sabrina was naturally beautiful, that she concealed her lush body beneath her father's shapeless clothing. But the woman he was seeing was more than beautiful—she was spectacular. Even Isabella's golden hair and fair skin paled in comparison.

Like the heat of the sun, Sabrina radiated.

It took him a moment to realize that her aura came from fury. She was about to lash out, revealing her displeasure with the entrance she was making. He found himself moving toward her.

"Brina—" Isabella gasped. "You look—"

"Beautiful," Colter said, brushing her cheek with his lips. "Smile," he ordered, "don't do something to give us away." Then he pulled back and gave her a long, admiring look. "You are exceptionally lovely this evening, darling." He took her arm, hooking it beneath his and clasping her hand with his own.

Sabrina might have jerked away, had she not been struck temporarily speechless by the sight of the man standing before her. Captain Colter was no longer a drifter, wearing denim trousers, scuffed boots, and a scruffy beard. He was clean shaven, his blue eyes dancing with restrained merriment, his lean body encased in a black double-breasted jacket and a white shirt with a starched collar and a red tie.

Stunned, not only by the overwhelming physical presence of the man, but by the flash of fire that his touch ignited, Sabrina found herself complying with his request. Then, feeling like the fool she was, she wiped the smile from her face and tried to free herself from his clutches.

Tried unsuccessfully.

"Where'd you get the clothes, Colter?" she asked under her breath.

"Won them in a little poker game with Lieutenant Garland, the captain's aide. Seems he and our Isabella made a little excursion to the general store for playing cards, *wife*."

"Don't call me that!"

"I can't seem to think about you any other way. Odd how clothes are sometimes more exciting than the lack of them."

"Don't be foolish!" she said, knowing full well the power of the man wearing dress clothes.

"You've totally addled my wits, *Mrs. Alexander*."

"Mrs. Alexander," the captain said, coming forward in welcome. "Would you care for a glass of wine?"

"No!—No thank you," she added as she felt Colter jab his elbow against her rib cage. Then her mind went flying off in an entirely different direction when his arm ranged upward, much too close to her breasts. She gasped audibly, drawing air into her contracted lungs.

"Perhaps a glass of punch," Captain Holland suggested, indicating to one of the uniformed orderlies that he should serve their guest.

Sabrina had no choice but to accept the cup of punch. She should have sipped it slowly. It would have given her something to do, to cover her awkwardness. Instead, more nervous than she'd ever been, she turned up the cup and swallowed it all in one gulp.

"Thirsty, darling?" Colter said, taking the cup and returning it to the orderly with a shake of his head. "Come, I'm sure you'd like to speak with our hostess. We're awaiting the arrival of Sergeant Nealey and the lieutenant. They've returned from Fort Laramie early."

Grateful for the chance to escape the center of attention, Sabrina nodded her approval. "Yes, I would like that. I don't suppose she's in the stable?"

"No such luck, darling." He came to a stop before a red velvet sofa where the captain's wife was holding court. "Mrs. Holland, my wife and I want to thank you for having us in your home."

He gave a slight bow and nudged Sabrina forward.

"Yes, thank you," she managed to say.

"Please, come and sit beside me," Mrs. Holland said, sliding to the end of the cushion to make room for Sabrina.

"I don't think so, ma'am. I can hardly breathe standing up. If I sit, I'm sure to pass out and embarrass my—" She cut a quick gaze at Colter and said with a certain amount of glee, "My husband."

Mrs. Holland allowed herself a genuine smile. "My dear, I can't imagine your embarrassing anyone."

"Oh, but I would. You see, he comes from a very distinguished old family, and I'm afraid I grew up in a mining camp. I've never even worn a dress like this before."

"Well, you should have," Mrs. Holland said. "But I know just what you mean about being strapped up like a corpse. Myself, I came straight off a farm. Had a devil of a time learning about the proper fork to use. As for serving tea—well, if the captain hadn't had an orderly who was the soul of discretion, I'd be plain old Lucy Jones, working in the fields."

Sabrina doubted that Mrs. Holland would ever be plain, but she had, with her honesty, restored Sabrina's confidence. And for the next few minutes they conversed about the problems of living in such isolation.

For a time Colter remained by her side, playing the role of an adoring husband too well. When he leaned over, squeezing her arm affectionately for the second time, Sabrina wanted to scream. He was too close. Instead of being reassuring, his presence was unsettling. Just when she was ready to bolt, the door opened and another blue-uniformed officer came in.

From the tightness of Colter's touch, Sabrina knew the man they'd been waiting for had arrived. She turned slightly to view the proceedings, watching the man salute the captain, then turn to survey their guests.

The newcomer studied the guests until his gaze landed on Colter.

Sabrina concealed her smile of satisfaction as she watched the confrontational expression on the lieutenant's face. What would happen now?

He stepped forward, addressing Colter, and held out his hand. "David Littlejohn here. Nice to see you, *Mr. Alexander*, is it?"

Colter nodded, slowly extending his hand in return. "Good evening, Lieutenant."

Sabrina held her breath, waiting for Dane's next move. It was hard to believe that this man was responsible for the killings attributed to Colter and his men. What would he do now? Would he identify Colter as the leader of the Confederate guerrillas?

"I understand you rescued the missionaries and escorted them to the Indian camp. We appreciate your help."

"Glad to do it. How long have you been at the fort, Lieutenant?" Colter asked smoothly.

"Not long. I've been on a western mission, only just recently transferred to Fort Collins." A cat-and-mouse smile tugged at Dane's mouth. He'd planned to skip the dinner but Lt. Garland had sent an escort to meet them and he hadn't been able to delay their arrival. "How long have you been in the valley, Mr. Alexander?"

"I too only recently returned—when a business venture went sour—so to speak." Colter drew Sabrina forward. "Have you met my wife, Lieutenant?"

Dane looked surprised for a moment, then held out his hand, lightly clasping Sabrina's fingertips and planting a feathery kiss on them.

"Mrs. Alexander." He lifted his eyes, staring at her in unconcealed amazement. Then, realizing that the silence was deafening, turned back to Colter. "I trust you delivered our Shepherds without any trouble?"

Colter nodded.

"Thank you. I don't suppose you happened to see anything of our escapees along the way, did you?"

Colter had wondered how Dane would handle the situation. Not head-on, it seemed, as he continued to play his game of verbal tag. "What escapees?" he countered.

"Four Confederates tried to take a supply train. They were captured."

Colter lifted an eyebrow. "Four? I heard there were five."

"The Boulder City livery-stable operator who housed them said four."

"But they escaped?"

"They escaped."

"And stole the payroll for the fort," Sabrina interjected. "Pretty big gamble."

Dane nodded. "A very big gamble. They killed the guards. It was—unnecessary."

"Sounds like it," Colter said. "I knew the Rebs were good, but that sounds extraordinary for four unarmed men. They must have had help."

Why was Colter going along with this playacting? If this man was Dane why didn't Colter just accuse him straight out? Colter must have sensed her frustration, and with just a slight shake of his head he let her know that she wasn't to say anything. But she couldn't resist asking one question: "Why would men take such a chance under such odds? From what I heard, they were outnumbered."

Dane ignored Sabrina, speaking directly to Colter. "Sometimes they get enough of losing and find a way to win. You never know what a man can do when he has to—even a Reb."

"Oh, but I do," Colter countered, reclaiming Sabrina's hand beneath his arm. "And sometimes what you win is something you never expected."

Sabrina felt Colter's anger and searched for a way to diffuse the growing tension. She caught sight of Lieutenant Garland, who was listening to the exchange between the two men with an odd expression on his face. "Did you get the supplies you went after, Lieutenant Littlejohn?" she asked.

The lieutenant took a quick look at Colter, then nodded. "Yes, ma'am. This time our mission was uneventful."

"I don't think you've met our hired hand, Kurt." Colter inclined his head toward Tyler, who was standing by the back door, ready to take whatever action might be indicated.

"Kurt, is it?" Dane said, holding out his hand.

Mary, hanging on to Kurt's arm, stepped forward, ready to shield him with her body if necessary.

Instead, Dane, trailed by Lieutenant Garland, shook Tyler's hand. The men exchanged pleasantries with Mary and Isabella, who suddenly appeared by Tyler's side.

Short of pushing the women aside, there was little Dane could do except follow Colter's lead. Lieutenant Garland's expression said clearly that he sensed something wasn't right, but he couldn't fathom the underlying tension.

It was Mrs. Holland who brought the awkwardness to an end by announcing that dinner would be served. They were directed to the table. "Mrs. Alexander, you'll sit here by my husband, with Lieutenant Littlejohn on your right. Mr. Alexander, please take the seat by me. Kurt and Mary will fill in that side. Isabella and the captain's aide will sit beside Lieutenant

Littlejohn. I'm very sorry that we don't have another woman on the fort to make our table even, but I'm certain we'll manage."

With surprising ease the guests were seated and the orderly began serving the first course. Sabrina was glad that there were no hoops to contend with, for they were seated much too close for the large skirts to be manageable.

What was worse, she soon discovered, was that sitting made her dress fit even tighter. There was no pulling the top up, but she tried, until she saw Mary frowning at her attempts and Colter laughing.

Fine, she decided, if they thought she ought to expose herself before God and everybody, so be it. She might even get a little revenge. With that in mind she leaned forward to speak to Dane, pausing a long moment so that he was rewarded with an even closer look.

Colter's smile disappeared.

His half movement to rise was brought to a stop by the appearance of the waiter.

A thick soup made from potatoes started the meal, followed by a huge roast of beef, more potatoes, stewed apples, dried beans, and finally apple dumplings.

Through it all Captain Holland tried diligently to draw Sabrina into the conversation. But after her one attempt to play the coquette, she drew back. That sort of behavior wasn't like her, and she had no intention of pretending to be someone she wasn't. Kurt was left to answer for her. Colter glared at her until she thought her skin was on fire.

When Dane attempted repeatedly to rekindle her interest, she pretended indifference. Still, with him beside her, Sabrina found it impossible to eat, and for the first time in her life her voice literally deserted her. The emotional level of the dinner seemed unusually intense, though Sabrina had no experience by which to judge. She just wished it would end.

Not so for Isabella, who innocently focused all her attention on both the turncoat Confederate soldier and

Lieutenant Garland. She needed no instruction in the art of flirting, and chattered incessantly.

"Lieutenant Littlejohn," she said, "have you seen much of the world in your military career?"

"A good portion of the West. I was assigned to help survey it."

"How exciting. I've never been anyplace exciting."

"Are you're not going to," Sabrina snapped. "Isabella—"

"Have you ever been to Brooklyn?" Mary interrupted. "To a ball game?" Mary's eyes turned warmly toward Tyler.

"No, ma'am."

Isabella leaned forward, trying to reclaim the soldier's attention. "Where are you from originally, Lieutenant?"

"Good question," Colter broke in casually, forcing his attention away from Sabrina and back to the table. In that one simple answer to Isabella's question, he'd learned a great deal. His mapmaking experience accounted for the ease with which Dane had appointed himself the point man. That kept him separated from the others and concealed his nefarious activities. No wonder Dane had been able to establish contact with Gray Warrior.

"Do I detect a hint of the South in your speech, Lieutenant?" Colter couldn't keep himself from asking.

"No! I mean, yes. My roommate at West Point was from the South," Dane explained. "I may have picked up some of his speech patterns. You know how easy that can be."

"After so long?" Tyler asked. "I wouldn't think that the southern influence would be so lasting."

"Why, it's as if you were around them more recently," Colter observed dryly. "Odd, how influences linger."

Isabella glared at Colter, then turned back to the lieutenant. "You attended the military academy." She made no attempt to conceal her admiration for the swarthy young officer. He wasn't as much fun as Carl, but he was the best of the available men there, other than Colter, who had already been claimed by Sabrina.

Colter could have added to Dane's discomfort by asking which regiment he'd joined, but he decided that his barbs would be better served by going in a different direction. "About those Rebs, Lieutenant—do you think they're still in the territory?"

"I'm certain of it," Dane answered.

"Then why haven't we found some trace of them?" the captain asked.

Dane pursed his lips as he considered his answer. "They obviously have some contact here, someone who has taken them in, someone assuming the risk of arrest by harboring a fugitive from the United States Army." He turned his attention to Mary. "Would you have any idea who that might be?"

Mary upset her water glass, watching the liquid puddle across the crisp white tablecloth. "Oh, my goodness. I'm sorry," she whispered in embarrassment.

"Never you mind," Mrs. Holland interjected. "No more talk of Rebels. This is a dinner party. Serve the dessert, Raymond."

A short time later she was directing the men outside for cigars and the women into the parlor for coffee and sweets. Sabrina followed, grateful to be standing. Surely the evening was about to end. She wished that she was on the porch and Colter was inside with these women.

"Now, my dear," Mrs. Holland said, handing a small after-dinner cup to Sabrina. "How long have you and Mr. Alexander been married?"

Only because of Mary's steadying her elbow did Sabrina keep the cup from falling to the floor.

"Not long," Mary answered for her.

"Years," Isabella said at the same time.

"What my well-meaning sisters are trying to do, Mrs. Holland, is to say that Co—Cullen and I only recently went through a religious ceremony, when the missionaries came through. Our arrangement is very new."

Mrs. Holland looked stricken for a moment, then

smiled. "Of course. I understand that ministers out here are sometimes hard to locate. But you are married and I think you make a splendid couple."

"Thank you," Sabrina responded after Mary gave her a poke in the back.

In the corner of the room three soldiers began to tune up their instruments. A fiddle, a banjo, and a harp were to accompany the dancers.

"Would you like to freshen up before the dancing begins?" Mrs. Holland asked.

Isabella and Mary nodded, and the three women followed their hostess from the dining room now being emptied and readied for dancing. Sabrina felt a great weight in the pit of her stomach. She was swimming in deep water here, and she'd never before done more than wade in the creek.

Outside, the men were standing beneath the overhang smoking their cigars. The number of men was slowly increasing, as those who'd been invited to join the officers at the dance began to arrive.

Colter slowly managed to work his way out of the group, his movements designed to place him between Dane and the others.

"Join me for a short walk, Lieutenant Littlejohn?" he said.

For the first time Dane looked uneasy, then nodded and moved away from the officers' quarters.

"All right, Dane," Colter demanded without slowing his walk, "what the hell is going on?"

"I'm afraid you're mistaken, sir. My name is Littlejohn."

"Yeah, and my name is Alexander. Cut the lying, Dane. We both know we're dancing around like actors on a stage. What I want to know is why."

"Why? Because I'm tired of busting my backside trying to be somebody and getting nowhere. I never intended for anybody to be hurt, and I'm sorry it happened. But it happened, and I don't intend to let you or anybody else keep me from taking advantage of a lost cause."

"Why'd you kill those men?"

"I didn't, Captain. It was the Indians, a renegade band of Ute."

"And you set it up."

"Maybe, but you can't prove it. You can't even accuse me, for if you do, I'll name you and the others as the Rebs we're looking for."

"And I'll tell them that you were one of us."

"Me? Lieutenant Littlejohn, fresh from a secret mission in the West with orders straight from General Grant? I'm set to take over the fort when Captain Holland finishes his tour of duty. Who do you think they'll believe?"

"At this point, you low-down Yankee turncoat, I'm not sure I care. I almost think I'd take the risk to expose you. You don't have any more proof than I do."

"What about the livery-stable operator who turned his storeroom into a jail? He can identify you."

"And Sabrina—" Colter broke off. He was about to reveal to Dane that there was a witness to his dealings. But he couldn't do that.

"Ah, Colter, yes. About the ladies? I don't think you want to bring them any harm, do you?"

They glared at each other in the moonlight, lips tightly drawn, eyes narrowed in defiance. Finally it was Dane who turned and strode away, disappearing into the darkness.

Colter watched for a time. He didn't know where Dane was heading, but it wasn't back to the dance. That seemed suspicious. Why wouldn't Dane want to keep an eye on Colter, unsure of what he might say to the captain? Dane was heading somewhere else, and Colter wondered where. He'd follow him.

Dane's trek took him toward a small unmarked building near the captain's quarters. Colter watched as Dane unlocked the door and slipped inside. Moments later he reappeared, carrying two pouches. Hugging the shadows of the buildings, Dane dashed furtively down to the stable, opened the door, and crept inside.

The stable door fastened from the outside, so Colter was able to follow. He found a darkened stall where he could watch his former comrade's strange actions. Dane was in Sabrina's wagon, working at a board underneath the driver's seat. Once he had it off, he shoved the pouches inside, replaced the board, and piled the lap blankets against it. Moments later Dane left the stable, fastening Colter inside.

Colter waited for Dane to get out of range, then checked the wagon. Whatever he'd hidden couldn't be found by anyone who didn't know where to look. But what was in the pouches, and why did Colter get such a bad feeling about what he'd seen?

He was about to open the space and examine its contents when he heard someone outside the stable. Colter barely got out of sight as three men came through the door.

"This ought to do," one said.

"Yeah, if we can't go to the dance, we'll have our own party," another added. "You bring the whiskey, Snake?"

"Whiskey and cards. All we need is women and we're good for the night. Ain't nobody going to come looking for us."

Colter's heart sank. He'd already been gone far too long. If he didn't get out of the stable while they were setting up their card game, he'd be stuck. God only knew what Sabrina would do if he disappeared. Quietly, as the gamblers set up their table and lit their lamps, he made his way out the door, gambling that they weren't watching him. As he hurried back to Captain Holland's quarters, the stable door closed, sealing off light from the lanterns the men had lit.

As he reached the building, he saw Sabrina through the open window. She was striding across the floor, escape clearly on her mind. Dane cut off her attempt to sail out the door as Colter stepped inside.

"In the absence of your—husband," Dane was saying, "I claim the first dance with his lovely wife." He held out his hand.

"Ah, no," she stammered. "Where *is* my husband? I'm worried about him."

"He stepped down to the store for cigars. He must have been detained."

That information brought a frown to Sabrina's forehead. She doubted the store was open. "In that case I believe I'll just see if I can find him." She attempted to go around Dane.

"I insist you dance with me, Mrs. Alexander." With a smile on his face, Dane caught Sabrina roughly by the arm, turning her to face him.

"But, Lieutenant, I don't dance."

At that moment Colter stepped forward. "Except with her husband," he said. "Shall we, *wife*?" He led her away from the still smiling Dane.

"Don't 'wife' me. Where have you been for so long?"

"Relax, darling. You wouldn't want folks to think we're quarreling, would you?"

As they walked across the floor to the open space before the musicians, she snarled through clenched teeth, "Where, Colter?"

"I just wanted to see what the sergeant knew about his new officer."

"And what did he know?"

"Nothing, or at least if he did, he wasn't talking." Colter caught sight of Dane leaning against the wall, still watching with a satisfied smile.

Colter didn't return his smile. The situation was a powder keg, ready to explode. It was up to him to see that it didn't. Clearly, Dane wanted whatever he'd hidden in the wagon to leave the fort with Colter. Unless he was ready to accuse Dane—and he couldn't do that yet—examining the pouches would have to wait until they got back to the valley.

Colter forced himself to push the exchange with Dane to the back of his mind. They were safe for the moment. If Dane had intended to expose them, he would already have done so. Clearly, whatever plan he had wouldn't take place tonight.

Colter felt Sabrina's concern and knew she could sense his. "Is everything all right?" she whispered.

He looked down at her and felt the tightness in his

chest loosen. He'd waited all night to put his arms around Sabrina, and he could satisfy that need with everyone watching. He let out a long, deep breath and said, "Everything is fine now."

And suddenly that was the way he felt. He'd known she was beautiful. He'd known she was genuine and caring. He'd seen her nude body and felt it accept him, willingly, joyously. And he'd known that his pledges to turn away were weak. He just hadn't known *how* weak, until he'd seen her standing in the doorway like some jeweled lady in the candlelight.

Sabrina didn't need jewels. Jewels and laces would only have diffused the radiance of the woman.

His woman.

Tonight, his wife. Tonight, for a time, life was good.

The music started. Colter opened his arms, and Sabrina felt the remaining air in her lungs whoosh out. Before she could protest, Colter had put one foot between hers and pulled her so close that she had no choice but to move when he did.

"It's me or Dane," he said in her ear.

It wasn't the little people who made the floor move. It wasn't the wind that made music in the room. But Sabrina Alexander was beginning to understand why her papa had been married three times, and why each of his wives had loved him with abandon.

There was something inherently wild and primitive about the feelings that answered a man's touch. And Sabrina had inherited more than one thing from her father: Along with his love of mining, she had inherited his passion for life.

The difference between them was that Cullen had allowed his emotions free reign; Sabrina always held hers in tight control—until Colter had entered her world and set it in motion. She didn't have to be told. She didn't have to see herself in the looking glass. She had only to look into Colter's eyes. Tonight, for just a few short hours, she was beautiful. She was a woman, and she felt the shimmering glow that told her she was.

Tomorrow, she decided, could take care of itself. Tonight Sabrina Alexander would be the red-haired colleen her father had always said she was.

"Dance? I think we shall, *husband*."

And dance they did. The poorly trained musical group became the most exquisite musicians, and the rough floor beneath the rag rugs became the finest ballroom in the finest palace in Vienna.

Sabrina and Colter danced, dipping and turning like the figures on a music box Sabrina had once seen as a child, like the spirit figures Raven described late at night when she told the tales of Mother Earth and Father Moon.

"I don't believe it," Isabella said, her eyes wide in wonder.

"Why?" Mary asked. "You said you saw her with her hair down, dancing in the barn. You said that Colter kissed her."

"But Sabrina?" Isabella's disbelief was tinged with envy. Never before had she been eclipsed by any woman, certainly not by an older sister who'd previously concealed her womanly attributes beneath Papa's old clothes.

Dane appeared at Isabella's side, catching her and Mary alone for a rare moment. "Mrs. Alexander is lovely, but she doesn't compare with the angelic beauty of her sister—or is it her sister-in-law?"

"She's my sister," Isabella snapped. "I—I mean my sister-in-law."

Dane nodded. He's known they were sisters, but he'd simply wanted the fact confirmed. Captain Colter was masquerading as Cullen Alexander's son to conceal his true identity. It hadn't occurred to anyone else that the women were Sabrina's sisters, not Colter's. Apparently that charade had begun with the encounter with Nealey at the trading post. The ruse hadn't been questioned because the Alexanders lived such an isolated existence that nobody knew the truth. For now he was content to leave things as they were.

"Would you care to dance, Miss Isabella?" Dane asked.

Preening under the attention of the junior officer, Isabella allowed herself to try the waltz, deciding from the warm look in Dane's eyes that she was as adept as Sabrina.

Mary accepted Tyler's invitation, and they moved slowly around the room where the dining table had stood a short time ago. She felt awkward and uncertain, and continually looked at her feet.

"Mary, just like in the barn. Relax."

"But, Tyler, that was different. I'm so clumsy."

"You're beautiful, Mary, and I don't care if your feet move in opposite directions. I just like holding you."

She raised her gaze and saw the warmth in his. Confidently, with one hand firmly placed at her back and his other clasping hers, he moved to the beat of the music.

Suddenly she was dancing, smiling, feeling as if she were the most cherished woman there.

"She walks in beauty, like the night," Tyler whispered. "My Mary."

My Mary. Mary felt as if her heart would swell up and burst. She couldn't speak. Instead she allowed herself to be caught up in the music and knew she never wanted to be anywhere else.

Finally the waltz came to an end, and the dancers slowed their steps. When the captain started toward Sabrina, she panicked. "Save me, Colter. I can't do this with the captain."

Colter let out a deep breath and willed his body to restore itself to a respectable state. "I certainly hope not. I never want you to do this with anyone but me."

"Mrs. Alexander," Captain Holland said, "will you do me the honor of the next dance?"

The music started again, this time to a different beat. "Oh, Captain, I'm afraid that I don't know how to do whatever you do to this music."

"It's called a Virginia reel. Mr. Mark Twain, the writer, once described it in battle terms in his newspaper, *The Territorial Enterprise.* He said that we form ranks in two lines, one line facing the other. The call to battle is sounded and the skirmish commences. Then the rest of the troops join in along the line. Once the ladies' battalion is engaged, you just step back and pick one out and swing her around. Best thing about this battle is that nobody loses and the injuries don't signify."

With that he whirled a startled Sabrina around and deposited her in the line opposite where he was standing. In the next few minutes Sabrina was swung around by every man there. In the absence of enough women to fill out the women's line, some of the men took the places of women and in good-natured fun danced with each other.

Toward the end of the musical piece, Colter claimed Sabrina again, and she let out a sigh of relief. Though they were barely touching, the instant awareness flared once more. Each time they touched, the sensation became more intense, the danger magnifying.

As the fiddler drew his bow across the strings in the last note, Sabrina started toward the door.

"Where are you going?" Colter asked, refusing to allow her to cast off his hand.

"Outside," she gasped, clutching her throat. "I can't breathe in this devil's harness. And I can't continue to act like some idiot without air. Let me go, Colter. I need—"

Colter opened the door and followed her out. He knew that she was on the verge of losing control. For twenty-eight years Sabrina Alexander had been in control. Now, suddenly, her boundaries had been changed, her parameters expanded, and she was awash in a sea of pure emotion. She was vulnerable and he had no right to take advantage.

For a long moment he walked along beside her on the sidewalk adjacent to the captain's quarters. He continued to hold her hand without speaking. They left behind the squares of light spilling through the windows and moved into the darkness. The cold night air quickly dried the sheen of perspiration he'd worked up during the dance. Sabrina shivered and tried to cross her arms across her chest.

Letting her hand go, he removed his coat and placed it around her shoulders, backing her against the rough wall. "Thank you, Sabrina, for not giving us away to the captain."

Sabrina didn't answer. She couldn't. There was a pumpkin stuck in her throat. She knew now that she would never survive this trip. Someone or something was conspiring against her. Death by self-strangulation was at hand, and she couldn't seem to find a way to stop it.

His hands were still on her shoulders. His face close to hers in the darkness. She was shaking, and it was no longer from the cold.

"Don't, Colter. I want—"

"What do you want, Sabrina? Stop pretending, stop holding yourself back. What do you want?"

Colter felt his insides twist. He couldn't seem to stop himself from running his fingers through the cache of hair caught behind her ear, from caressing the back of her neck or allowing his eyes to fall to the bare skin above the neckline of her dress.

"Do you know that you've been driving me to distraction all night? Every man here has feasted his eyes on your face, on the sight of your breasts." His fingertips ranged lower, running across her nipples, ranging down inside the fabric until he could touch the hard knots now barely covered by the skimpy green fabric.

"Don't, Colter. It isn't fair."

"Why?" His own breath had turned ragged. "Because it's wrong for me to want you? To need your body next to mine? I don't know anymore what is fair and what is not."

"Because I don't know what to do. You've destroyed me, Colter, and I don't know how to put me back together."

She was clinging to him now. "What do you want, Sabrina?"

"I want—I want—ah, hell!" Then her arms slid around him and she lifted her face to meet his lips. "I can't put out the fire. It's burning me alive."

"I know," he answered, and captured her lips with

his own. His mouth demanded. The top buttons on her dress were opened, and he was hiding her breasts in his hands.

With a cry of anguish he let go of her breasts and slipped down to clasp her bottom, lifting her into his arousal, pinning her against the wall. Sabrina moaned. In another minute Colter would have her skirts pushed up around her waist and he'd be inside—

She gasped and tore her mouth away from his.

"Colter! Stop! We can't do this!"

Dazed, he pulled back. "I'm letting my feelings for you interfere with my mission and my judgment."

"I know."

"There are others depending on me. All I can think about is you and what I want to do to you. It closes out everything else. Wanting you is making me crazy."

"I know."

"Now there's Dane who can destroy us all."

"I know."

"Damn it, you can't know how I feel, what you've done to me!"

"I think I do," she said softly, reaching out in the darkness to touch that part of him that still throbbed. "Before, I didn't understand about the want between a man and a woman. Now I do."

"Don't do that, Sabrina. A man can only take so much."

"Colter, I didn't mean that it couldn't happen. I just meant that it couldn't happen here."

He swallowed hard. "What do you mean?"

"I mean I understand now that you don't care about Papa's Silver Dream."

Her hand didn't move. He felt as if he would explode. "I promised to help you, Sabrina. I'll keep my word. I just didn't know it would put you in danger."

"And I promised to pay you for your help. I'm just changing the terms of our agreement."

"I don't understand."

"You want me, Colter; I want you. There's no point in lying about something that is obvious to us both." Her logical words and terse voice turned whispery as she felt his pulse in the male part of him she was holding, felt her own pulse quicken in response.

"Yes."

"Then you may have me, Colter. The world believes that we are married. Come to me tonight. Come lie with me, Colter. Let me be what you need."

"What about your sisters?"

"I'll tell Mrs. Holland to prepare the pallets in her sitting room. It's on the other side of the building."

"You're sure you want to do this?"

"Yes."

He took her hand away and held it for a long time, then tucked it beneath his arm and started once more to walk down the sidewalk. When the cold finally accomplished what his mind couldn't, Colter turned, and they started back to the party.

"You know, Mrs. Colter," he said as they reentered the room, "you are the belle of the ball."

Sabrina cast her eyes on her sisters, each dancing with a soldier, and shook her head. "Only in your eyes," she said.

18

Another hour passed while Sabrina, for the first time in her life, played the part of the belle of the ball. She soon discovered that it made no difference that she couldn't dance. The men were so grateful to be with a woman, nothing mattered. Finally, as the candles burned down, Mrs. Holland brought out a bottle of French champagne.

"This just came today from Laramie. I thought we might enjoy a toast."

The orderly managed to uncork the bottle and poured the bubbling liquid into an assortment of punch cups. When everyone had been served, the captain raised his cup. "To the end of hostilities and the healing of a nation."

"To families," Mrs. Holland said, "and children, and lives that offer everyone an equal future."

Colter raised his cup. "And to the courageous people who will make it possible for all to survive." They drank the champagne as the musicians played one last tune, then gathered up their instruments and left the room.

"Oh, Sabrina," Isabella said, wiping her limp curls from her forehead, "I've had such a gay time. I can't imagine why Papa wouldn't let us come to the fort before."

"Because," Tyler said as he deposited Mary beside the two sisters, "he knew that every man there would desert their posts once they'd seen the two of you."

Mary was beaming. Isabella was ecstatic, and Sabrina's nerves were drawn to the breaking point. Colter hadn't danced with her again, but she'd been conscious of his eyes following every move she made. Only once had he relinquished that hold, when Dane had come to stand beside him. But that had lasted only a few minutes, and Dane had disappeared.

Now the evening was ending and Colter was approaching.

"Thank you for a lovely evening, Mrs. Holland," Colter was saying as he claimed his spot at Sabrina's side. "My family has been too isolated for too long."

"That isolation is over, Mr. Alexander, as, regrettably, is this evening. Come, Mary, Isabella. Your cots have been set up in my study. You'll be more comfortable there than the three of you trying to share one room."

This time Sabrina didn't protest. She turned away from Mary's questioning glance. Moments later her sisters were gone, leaving Sabrina and the captain in the hallway. Sabrina hesitated, then straightened her shoulders and started forward.

Colter followed behind.

Sabrina took a deep breath and opened the door to the bedroom. Her heart was thundering in her chest like the pounding of Papa's pick against a granite wall. How could she have thought that she could invite him into her room, into her bed?

You ninny, he's already been there. Not in a bed, of course, but he knows more about your body than you do.

She heard the door close behind them.

Sabrina unlaced her shoes and pulled them off. With shaking fingers she began to unhook her dress. She felt awkward, inexperienced. What did a woman do when she'd invited a man to make love to her? Did she ask him to excuse her while she removed her clothing? Did they talk?

Before Colter came, she'd had the security of knowing that her actions were following a pattern, the pattern set by Cullen Alexander. Now she was charting new territory.

In the silence she heard Colter take off his coat.

No, there would be no talking. Colter wasn't the kind of man to talk, though he had, that one afternoon. Silly little things that might have come from Papa when he was trying to impress a lady. Gentle, loving caresses that needed no words. Dark, wicked glances that made her toes curl and her heart skip.

The dress was unbuttoned now, and sliding down her hips to the floor. By the light of the fire she glanced down at her body, her breasts pressed upward by the corset. Even in her state of uncertainty, Sabrina relished the moment to come when she would be free of that instrument of torture. She wished she'd paid more attention when Mary was lacing her into it.

There seemed to be no discernible opening. After a frustrating attempt to free herself, she swore under her breath, then felt Colter's fingers moving hers aside.

"I guess you know more about these things than me," she said breathlessly.

"I guess I do. Suck in a deep breath."

"Say something else funny." She tried, and was rewarded with a partial freeing of the stricture.

"I think now that all I have to do is loosen these," he said, his own voice as tight as the strings in her corset.

Seconds later the awful thing was gone, and Colter's arms were around her waist, his hands cupping her breasts. His mouth found the tender spot behind her ear and planted hot little whisper kisses there.

"Are you more comfortable now?" he asked.

"Not much. Something seems to be taking my breath away."

The thundering sound inside her chest intensified.

"Colter, I—" Her voice squeaked as Colter's finger slid across her upper lip.

The pounding of her heart seemed to have turned into a hammer of destruction, echoing through the entire room.

It took her a moment to understand the pounding was coming from the outside door, not from her heart.

As the knowledge stilled her trembling, a man's yell split the air.

"What the—"

Colter whirled around, grabbed his coat, and stepped into the hallway. Captain Holland was already at the outside door. "Who is there?"

The door swung open, allowing Lieutenant Littlejohn to come in. He had a worried look on his face. "Captain, the new payroll, the greenbacks are missing! We opened the paymaster's box and it's empty. The money is gone."

"How can that be, Lieutenant?"

"I don't know, sir. It was there when we left Laramie. On returning to the fort we moved the pouches into the safe and locked it. After the dance, when we opened the knapsacks to begin parceling out the wages, we discovered that newsprint had been substituted for the money."

"You think it was done here?"

"I'm afraid so, sir."

"Sound the alarm! The fort must be searched."

"Damn!" Colter muttered under his breath. "So that's what he's up to."

Sabrina, standing out of sight by the door, studied Colter's expression. He was worried. "Do you think the lieutenant is involved?"

"Of course he is, but I'm not going to let him get away with it this time." Colter turned toward Sabrina, let himself take in the flushed cheeks and the pearly glow of her skin, and groaned. He couldn't stop himself from taking her chin in his hand. "Sabrina, I'm sorry."

She trembled. "You're leaving?"

"Yes. Perhaps it's for the best. Perhaps we aren't to be, Sabrina. Involving you in a scandal was wrong from the beginning."

"But—"

"Reality is never what we want, Sabrina. In my fantasy you'd wear a silver ball gown, and nothing at all underneath."

Colter leaned forward, touching his lips to hers for a long, regretful moment; then he was gone, following Captain Holland and David Littlejohn out into the night.

Long after they'd gone, Sabrina stood at the window looking out into the darkness.

At that moment a shooting star crossed the horizon. A shooting star—a promise of good luck—a silver wand in the night sky. An omen.

Sabrina sat down on the bed and leaned back against the pillow. One thing she'd learned from Papa was when to admit defeat and when to be bold.

Colter had been ready to cut his losses too soon.

Maybe the time had come to be bold.

The firelight flickered, shooting streaks of light onto the green dress. That gave her an idea. She was a wealthy woman now, just how wealthy she didn't know. But the time had come to do a bit of prospecting on her own. For that she needed the right equipment.

For that she had to go to Denver. As soon as they'd mined a good sample of ore, she'd have it assayed. Then she'd implement her plan. She wasn't quite sure how, but she intended to put a permanent stop to Captain Colter's roving.

First she'd buy a new dress.

A silver dress.

A scandalous silver dress.

A dress beneath which she'd wear nothing at all.

As if she'd known that Lauren was alone, Raven returned the day after the dinner-party guests had left for Fort Collins.

"I'm glad you're home, Raven," Lauren said, hugging her younger sister. "We were worried about you. Is your grandfather well?"

"He is growing older," she said. "His spirit is troubled."

"His spirit?"

"Yes. As a boy he went into the mountains alone, fasted, and waited for the vision that would gave him his name."

"You don't mean visions like Papa had when he'd had too much Irish whiskey?"

Raven let a rare smile part her lips. Lauren caught her breath. Her youngest sister was beautiful. There was something ethereal about her deep, dark eyes and ebony hair. There were times when Raven's eyes were old, or stormy even, as if she could see things that no one else saw.

"Perhaps," Raven answered. "When Grandfather was a boy, his people had journeyed to lands in the South, the lands of the sandstone hills and deserts. His journey into the mountains took him to a different place from his ancestors. For days he waited, until finally he saw the night people, people who entered the mountain and joined with the sun."

"I don't understand."

"Grandfather said that, suddenly, dark clouds flew across the moon and the vision vanished. The wise man of his tribe said Grandfather was to be called Dark Flying Cloud."

"Dark Flying Cloud?"

"When he became chief, the tribe omitted 'dark' and shortened his name to Flying Cloud. But I worry about my grandfather. I think he needs me with him."

"Oh, Raven," Lauren said, hugging her sister again, "we need you. You can't leave us now. Sabrina would be very upset. You know how determined she is that we stay together."

"I know. That is why I have returned. To be with you while she is away. Grandfather says that trouble is coming and you will need me more."

Lauren glanced out at the peaceful scene beyond the cabin walls. The snow on the canyon floor had melted, leaving the brown grass waving in the sharp wind that always blew down the valley. She could hear the sound of the pickax hitting the hard wall of the mine. Its rhythm gave her comfort, knowing that Mr. McBride and Mr. Arnstine were nearby. Unaware of her own expression, she smiled.

Raven's attention was directed not on the valley, but on the single rider on the ridge across the open range. He sat astride his horse, not moving, watching, like a predator waiting to swoop down on his unsuspecting prey.

Gray Warrior was waiting.

"I don't like it. I don't like it at all," Carl grumbled as he loaded the rock into the crude wheelbarrow. "I can't see him, but I know that Indian's up there somewhere. Being spied on is getting me real rattled."

Irish swung the pick even harder. "Simmer down, Carl. The captain knew he'd be there. He said for us to go on as if nothing had happened."

"But what's going to keep him from storming down that hill and overrunning our position anytime he gets ready?"

"Not a blessed thing. So keep working. What worries me is that Miss Lauren's down there in the cabin all alone."

Carl looked up at the big man with a grin. "I think everything about Miss Lauren is worrying you, Irish. The way you two tiptoe around each other is enough to make a man want to shake you both."

Irish blushed. "I don't know what you mean."

"I mean she's sweet on you, you big dunce."

"Ah, Carl. Don't tease me."

"And you're worse than an old hound dog sniffing around a lady dog. Except sniff is all you do."

"What do you expect me to do?" Irish demanded. "Miss Lauren is a lady."

"So? Even a lady expects her beau to court her, hold her hand, steal a kiss."

Irish laid down his pick and walked toward the

opening to the mine. "I don't know beans about court-
ing a lady, Carl. I never had a chance. Tell me what to
do."

Carl looked at his friend. "I don't know if I can.
I'm having something of the same trouble myself. Isabella likes to flirt and pretend she's a little wild, but the
truth is, she isn't one of the saloon girls I usually fool
around with. I like her, Irish, and I shouldn't."

"Why not?"

"Because I'm not good enough for her. She deserves a man who can take care of her, give her a fine
home and pretty dresses, and—"

"Children?" Irish finished Carl's sentence, and the
two men looked at each other, the pain of their dilemma
crashing over them.

Then Carl glanced past Irish toward the cabin below. "Look!" he said, and shoved past the startled
Irishman.

Irish turned to follow.

The Indian rode his horse slowly down the ridge
toward the little house. Irish and Carl dropped their
mining tools and hurried toward the cabin as fast as
their healing injuries allowed them to do. But Gray
Warrior still reached the dwelling first. By the time
they arrived, the Indian was holding out his hand for
the sack that Lauren was handing him.

"Wait a minute!" Irish said, coming to stand beside Lauren.

"No!" Carl said to Irish, and stepped in front of
the man who was ready to defend Lauren.

"Wait," Lauren said. "He only asked for food.
We're always willing to share what we have with those
who ask."

"Yeah!" Irish grudgingly agreed.

Carl didn't comment.

The warrior looked from one man to the other,
grunted, and turned away. The three watched as the
Indian rode slowly down the valley.

"What was that all about?" Carl asked. "Has he
been here before?"

"Not like this. Months ago he came one night, or

at least a party of his braves came, and took our horses. But we never saw him again until today."

Carl allowed himself to slump slightly and brushed the dust from his trousers. "I think he was just reminding us that he is watching."

Lauren turned back toward the house. "Wash up and come in for supper. If he'd wanted to hurt us, he could have."

Irish knew she was right. She wasn't afraid of Gray Warrior. He was once again taken with her courage—this woman who quietly went about her life with little fuss.

"Go with her, Irish," Carl said, and headed toward the barn. "I'll settle the animals down for the night."

"Tell Raven to come in," Lauren called over her shoulder. "She came home while you were in the mine."

Irish was halfway to the house when he realized that the only animals to be settled were the cow and that calf who'd rather follow Carl than stay in the corral.

Detouring by the water barrel, Irish washed his face and hands, dried them, then stood outside the door for too long. Finally Lauren opened the back door. "Mr. McBride? Mr. Arnstine?"

Irish stepped forward into the kitchen, closing the door behind him.

"Where's Mr. Arnstine?"

"He's still in the barn."

"I have beans and bacon for supper."

"Sounds good."

"Is something wrong, Mr. McBride?"

"I—I don't know. I mean, I think we need to talk—to—" Irish forced himself to walk to a spot directly opposite Lauren. "Miss Lauren, I don't know much about this kind of thing, but I want to say—"

Lauren waited, the look on Irish's face holding her still. His gaze was open. It was filled with honest need. It was too full, and she dropped her chin, shielding her eyes with lids that fluttered closed, lest he see her answering need.

"You don't have to say anything, Mr. McBride."

"That's good, because I don't speak so good."

"It isn't what a man says that counts, it's what's in his heart." Shyly, she reached out and touched his arm, then slid her hand down to hold his more boldly than she'd ever thought she could do.

Irish took her small hand in his large, rough one. He looked at the two, twisting them back and forth. "You're so small. I'm afraid you'll be hurt. I just want to be certain that you're kept from harm."

"Life doesn't seem to work like that. I wish it did. If we could be certain, Papa would have found his pot of gold long ago. You would never have been captured. But if that had happened, we would never have met."

He wanted to kiss her, but he couldn't. He wasn't bold.

He didn't have to be bold. Lauren raised herself to her tiptoes and pressed her lips against his cheek. "I wouldn't have liked that very much," she said.

They were standing by the fireplace, holding hands, beaming shyly at each other when Carl and Raven came in. At the sound of their entrance, Lauren blushed and turned toward the stove. Irish didn't move. He simply stood, watching her, a silly look on his face.

Carl stopped inside the door. "Shall I leave and come in again?" he asked.

"Of course not," Lauren said. "Have a seat, supper's ready. Raven, pour the coffee."

The men ate. Lauren and her sister cleared the table, and they sat before the fire long into the night, each lost in her own thoughts, each waiting for tomorrow and the return of the party-goers.

The bugler sounded general quarters, calling the men to muster in the open area of the fort that was the parade ground. Captain Holland assigned men to begin a search. Even before daylight they reported that there was no sign of the missing payroll. The only thing they'd learned was that in addition to the money, a few bottles of French champagne were missing.

Colter waited with Captain Holland and Lieutenant Garland, standing silently in the background as Dane directed the search. Colter considered his options. How could he use this? How could he expose Dane as the thief without involving the women or revealing that his men were the Rebs being hunted? Apparently Dane intended to allow the money to leave the fort in their wagon. Which meant that at some point he had to retrieve it, and blame Colter for the theft. Colter had to do something.

But damn it, he couldn't.

There was Sabrina to think of, her safety and that of the others.

Finally Captain Holland directed Dane to send a messenger to Fort Laramie for information. There was the possibility that the payroll had never left Laramie.

Dane gave Colter a hard look and left to follow orders.

Colter debated only a minute, then made his decision. Dane wasn't going to get away with this. It was now or never. "Captain Holland, may I speak with you in confidence—quickly? I may be able to solve the mystery."

The captain glanced around. Only his aide remained in the office. "By all means. But Lieutenant Garland is privy to any knowledge I have. Go ahead, Alexander. Do you know something about this?"

"First, I'm not Cullen Alexander. My name is Quinton Colter, captain, Confederate States of America. And I do know something about all this. I only hope I can make you believe it. If you'll bear with me, I think I can prove my claim."

Captain Holland's eyes narrowed. He reached into the drawer of his desk and removed a pistol, sat down, and directed it at Colter. "Go ahead, Captain. I'm listening."

Colter told him about his assignment from General Lee, about what happened when his men were captured, and described the events leading up to the massacre.

"And you never saw this man called Long Rifle who was directing the raid?"

"No, I didn't. But as his part of the robbery he took the pack mules carrying the payroll and the gold."

"And how do you know this if you were left in a wagon away from the campsite?"

"Sabrina Alexander watched the whole thing. She didn't know we were prisoners. Being a compassionate woman, she rescued us and helped us get away before the Indians could kill us too."

"And why didn't she come forward and tell us what happened?"

"Because it would have meant our arrest. And the Alexander women badly needed our help to bury their father."

Captain Holland shook his head. "You realize that this is all very convenient, Colter. Even if I did believe you, which I have no reason to do at this point, you still haven't explained how the murder of the men escorting the first payroll ties in with this payroll."

"The same man planned it. I watched him tonight as he took the pouches containing the money and hid them. If you'll agree to go along with me, you'll have the thief."

"And who is this man, Captain Colter?"

Dane would return any minute. Colter had no more time to waste justifying his plan. He simply looked at the captain and said, "The man is Dane Beckworth."

"And who is Dane Beckworth?" Lieutenant Garland asked.

"The Confederate soldier I knew as Dane Beckworth is the man you call Lieutenant Littlejohn."

The captain came to his feet with a roar. "I don't believe it. Littlejohn is a man with impeccable credentials. This is all some kind of lie to protect yourself and your men. I'm placing you under arrest, Colter."

"I can prove it, at least part of it. I don't know

how Dane came to be Littlejohn, but I can prove that he's responsible for this theft. It's up to you to link him to the massacre."

Captain Holland was ready to have Colter taken away when Lieutenant Garland walked around the desk and leaned forward, speaking quietly to Colter. "How do you expect to prove this?"

"Dane hid the payroll beneath the seat in our wagon. The thief is the only one who knows it's there. He thinks I'll keep quiet about what happened to the escorts to protect our identity. But he can't be sure for how long. Once the money is moved out of the fort, he'll come after it, kill us, and nobody will be alive who knows the truth."

"And why should I believe you, Colter? You could set up my officer, find a way to make him go for the money and incriminate himself. Then you'd be off the hook."

"Then I wouldn't have told you who I am, would I? By telling you the truth, I've incriminated my men. Whatever happens, we'll be arrested. I just want you to protect—my wife. I'll expect you to do that when I'm gone."

Garland leaned back, deep in thought. "He's right, Captain Holland. By admitting that he's the leader of the guerrillas who've been playing cat and mouse with us for months, he's turned himself in."

"Maybe this is an elaborate scheme to blame Littlejohn for the massacre," the captain blustered, still unwilling to accept the truth. "Why should we take the word of a confessed Rebel who only stands to gain?"

"What harm can it do to go along with him, Captain Holland? We keep both Colter and Littlejohn under surveillance and see what happens."

"All right, Garland, but I'm taking no chances on losing the money a third time. The payroll stays here if I have to hide it in Mrs. Holland's petticoat drawer. Find something to substitute for the greenbacks. Get Nealey—"

"No!" Colter snapped. "I think Nealey may be involved with Dane. I don't mean that he was in on the massacre, but I'm not sure you want to trust him."

Captain Holland looked as if he wanted to argue, then clamped his mouth shut. "Anybody else I shouldn't trust, Captain Colter?"

"I don't know, sir. But the fewer men who know what you're doing, the better."

"Then you're confined to your quarters until morning, Colter. I'll have someone watching you and Kurt, so don't try to leave."

A somber Colter went to Sabrina's room. He didn't intend to tell her what was going to happen. For now Dane didn't know there'd been a witness to the massacre. So long as Sabrina didn't give that away, she was safe. He regretted the need for dishonesty, but he couldn't be certain that she wouldn't try to involve herself in the ruse.

She was asleep, still wearing the same chemise she'd been wearing when he'd left, her hair a raging blot of red on the pillow in the gray morning light. The fire had burned down, crackling now and then as he stood at the foot of the bed and watched her sleep.

He could feel it between them, the sizzle, even with her asleep—but never had it been more potent. Neither had the danger.

He'd set the plan in motion, putting both his men and the women at risk. Either it would work, or he would have endangered the people he cared most about in the world. And he was ready to admit it. He cared about Carl, Tyler, and Irish. But more, he was in love with Sabrina.

Other than his family, the only other person he'd ever cared about was Big Moe, who had followed Colter into the war, first as a freed slave, then fighting by his side. They were inseparable until the day another soldier challenged Moe's sharing the captain's quarters, wearing Colter's clothing, and eating meals in the officer's tent.

Colter had seen the pain in Moe's eyes and realized that it didn't matter that Moe was a free man—he would always be a slave, subject to the taunting of those who couldn't understand genuine affection and respect between a black man and a white. Moe deserved to be whatever he was without challenge. That night he'd given Moe money and a paper proclaiming he was free. He'd sent Moe away, to the West—to a place where, if he died, he would die as a man, not as a slave.

The next day he found Moe hanging from the limb of a dying apple tree, his feet bare and his hands tied behind him.

Colter cut him down and buried him, along with the last of his own compassion, and replaced it with anger. Caring was a risk. The person who cared was in danger because his actions might jeopardize the very one he loved.

Now he'd placed Sabrina in the same situation.

God help him, and her, he'd allowed himself to care again. To love another human being.

Sabrina knew he was there long before she spoke, testing her tight throat, her voice a husky whisper. "Did you find the money?"

His reply was hoarse, almost gruff. "No, of course not. I didn't expect that we would."

"Dane?" she said, shifting beneath the sheet, vividly conscious of the feel of her skin against the coarse fabric.

"Yes."

"What are you going to do?"

"I don't know," he lied, and wished there were another way. "He's practically daring me to accuse him."

"Why don't you?"

"I can't. Not until you and your sisters are safe."

"Can we go home now, Colter?"

"I hope so." That was Colter's plan: take Sabrina and her sisters home, set up the mine so they would be able to live on the ore, and prepare for his arrest.

"You're leaving, aren't you?"

He didn't answer. She already knew. She just didn't know yet where he was going.

Then she was on her knees, holding out her hand.

"Colter, don't go. We can find an answer. I'll talk to the captain. He'll listen."

"No, Sabrina. Let me handle this. Promise me, don't tell anybody what you saw, not yet." He took a step forward.

She inched her way toward him, leaning against him as she slipped her arms around his waist. "All right, but give me this last time with you, before you go."

Colter took a deep breath, trying desperately to quell the hunger, the need, the overwhelming need he had for this strong woman who had the courage to ask for what she wanted, even if it meant flouting convention.

"Let me make love to you, Sabrina," he said.

She tilted her head to look up at him in the gray, shadowy light. "Loving has never been easy for me, Colter. When Mama died, there was no one, just the men in the mining camp. I had to be strong for Papa. Sometimes—sometimes I was so afraid. I learned to keep everything inside. I think you're like that, too."

"Yes. Loving is hard."

"I didn't even allow myself to feel. To feel was to hurt, and somebody always needed me to be strong." She pressed her face against Colter's midriff, hugging him close, as if she were the one asking for help and comfort.

Colter knew this was the first time in her life that she'd reached out to someone. She needed him. She needed to be allowed to be afraid, to be cherished as a woman. Just for one moment he could give her that.

"To hell with being strong," he said, and backed away, peeling off his clothes. He lay down and reached for her. When she moved into his arms, he gasped. Now she was nude.

"You almost put me in the brig tonight," he said, pulling her close.

"How?"

"I wanted to black the eyes of every man at the dinner table." His hand found her breast and clasped it possessively. "I didn't want them to see you."

"You didn't?" His statement filled her with pleasure.

"No. I felt like any husband whose wife is exposing her body to other men. These—your breasts—are
mine, for my eyes, for my hands to touch."

Any husband. The warm glow that had started the
moment she heard him enter the room skipped up her
body, flooding her breasts, her neck, and her face.
"They are yours, Colter. I'm yours. For one night or a
lifetime, you're my husband—the only one I'll ever
have."

A shuddering sigh escaped him as his hand left her
breasts, ranging lower, across her ribs, into the thick
curls that hugged her woman parts.

"Are you sure—" he began.

"Hush, Colter. I'm sure, and if you don't hurry, I
shall surely scream out and wake the others."

Colter was helpless to resist her. He came to his
side, then slid over her, kissing her lips, caressing her
body with his own. She rewarded him by parting her
legs, eagerly, hungrily.

With a hoarse cry of desire, he plunged inside
her. God help them both, for neither was strong
enough to turn away. And he loved her. He loved every part of her, touching, caressing, claiming, until at
last he could feel the quivering signal of her release.

"Oh, Colter," she whispered. "I love you. I love
you. I love you."

Then his own tumultuous response came, hot and
wild, like a prairie fire caught by the wind. His whisper, "I love you, too," was lost in the frenzy. Over and
over again the pent-up passion of his release expended
itself, until finally he collapsed over her.

Sabrina reached over and pulled the blanket across
them, unwilling to allow him to move. It was almost
daylight. This moment would be all she'd have, and
she didn't want it to end.

19

She was alone when she awoke the next morning. At first she stretched and lay there in the covers, smelling the scent of him, remembering the night and the way he'd touched her.

The last time had only been a short while ago, when he'd turned gentle and unsure, when he'd seemed, just for a time, to go away from her, back to that dark, lonely place where he'd been before. She'd sensed that he'd wanted to talk, but he hadn't, not with his voice. He had raised himself over her, cupping her face in his hands, staring down at her in the darkness.

"Colter!" she'd whispered in a husky voice.

He'd entered her, slowly, with such exquisite hunger that he took her breath away. And what happened was wondrous. She couldn't understand the endearments he uttered under his breath, but she didn't have to. He might never tell her that he loved her—he might not even know—but he did. She was sure of it.

Then later, when he pulled away and held her

tightly in his arms, she understood that he, too, was trying to hold on to something that would be gone in full light. She tried to stay awake, unwilling to lose a moment, wanting desperately to see his face come into complete focus, hoping to read the truth in his eyes. But she hadn't.

Now he was gone.

And somehow she knew that he wouldn't be in her bed again. Once they left the fort, she wouldn't be Mrs. Quinton Colter anymore.

As they saddled the horses the next morning, Colter told Tyler what he'd seen and what he'd done, voicing his concern. "If I'm wrong, we could be in trouble."

"When have we not been in trouble, Captain?"

"This is different. We may have exposed Dane, but in doing so, we've admitted to being the unit scavenging for the South. Suppose Dane doesn't come for the payroll? I've sacrificed you for no good reason."

"You had no choice. Dane will come for the money."

"I hope to God you're right, and I hope General Holland is keeping watch on him."

"Those hills are going to get pretty crowded with Gray Warrior watching us and General Holland's troops watching Dane."

Colter nodded. "Just so long as Dane doesn't get spooked." At that moment Sabrina came out the door to the captain's quarters. Her glorious hair was hidden beneath the worn felt hat, and she was pulling on her gloves. He hadn't known he'd made a sound, but he had, for Tyler looked up.

"You care about her, don't you, Captain?"

Colter watched her walk, seeing now the feminine curves beneath the trousers and bulky jacket, feeling his loins tighten at the sight of her. "Yes, Tyler, I care. God help me, I care."

"Have you told her?"

"No, and I'm not going to. That's madness and I

can't allow her—us—to hope for—expect anything. Whatever happens with Dane and the army, we're going to be arrested. Sabrina isn't the kind of woman to accept anything she doesn't want to, and I can't let her get involved."

Tyler smiled inwardly. The captain was right about Sabrina. She'd already kidnapped Colter once, because she needed him. If she wanted to keep him, there was no telling what she'd do. But the captain must know that. Tyler turned his comments to another matter that had been nagging at him. "I don't understand how Dane got Littlejohn's papers."

"I've been thinking about that," Colter answered. "Wiley said they'd found a drifter on the trail, dead. There was an army mule in the woods nearby. I'm wondering if that man might have been the real Lieutenant Littlejohn."

Both men grew silent, considering the situation. They had all become more and more involved in the lives of the Alexander women. Though they had not been unwilling, the involvement was weighing heavily on their call to duty. They had their orders, and no matter what they wanted, the soldiers fighting with Lee and Johnson desperately needed supplies. Still, the women needed help, and that need had served the wounded men well. But now they were facing the possibility of leaving, and Tyler had admitted to himself that Mary's affection was something he didn't want to leave behind.

"Good morning," Sabrina said as she approached the wagon. She couldn't bring herself to call Colter "husband." He was no longer "Cullen," and "Colter" didn't feel right. She flung her clothing into the back of the wagon.

Her horse was already saddled, as was Colter's. Mary and Isabella walked toward the barn, several uniformed men following along, prolonging their departure with one last word, one last smile.

Tyler helped the girls into the wagon and climbed up on the long wooden seat beside them, clucking to the horses and driving them away from the scattering of buildings.

Captain Holland saw them off, bidding Sabrina and the others to come back for a visit. Dane was nowhere to be seen. Only Lieutenant Garland gave any indication that their status had changed. He shook Colter's hand. "Be careful, Captain," he said, oblivious to the fact that he was giving voice to his acceptance of Colter's story.

With the fort behind them, and the mountains to the side, they began their return trip. March was almost over. The wildflowers of April would soon sprinkle the grassland like colored bits of ribbon waving in the breeze. The trees dotting the mountains already seemed greener, and the snow dripped down the stark, bare peaks like icing on a layer cake.

But Sabrina had a hard time seeing the beauty. She knew that everything was changed, she just hadn't known how much it would hurt. The ride home was strained. Once Sabrina folded away her ball gown and pulled on her normal clothing, it was as if she'd rolled up inside her dress and packed away the night she'd spent with Colter.

Now she rode alongside the farm wagon while Colter rode on the other, the memory of their night together riding with her. But little by little she began to draw inward, building soft, insulating walls around the memory, directing it to a place where it would remain, a place away from reality and whatever was ahead.

Isabella, still overflowing with the excitement of the dance, chattered gaily as they rode. Mary sat quietly in the middle. Neither Tyler nor Colter spoke.

Along the trail they ate the lunch Mrs. Holland had packed for them as they rode. Suddenly everyone was ready to get to the cabin. By midafternoon they took the turn off the main trail and rode up the valley.

With every step Sabrina's heart grew heavier. She'd been brave last night when she'd told herself that being with Colter one last time would be worth the pain of his leaving. She'd lied. Just a glance over at his stiff posture told her that this was no easier for him.

He hadn't made any kind of committment. In fact, he'd continually said that the relationship was wrong; that it shouldn't be allowed to happen; that they were wrong for each other. But neither had been able to resist the other. Neither had been able to say no.

At least they were riding away from the people who might arrest Colter and his men. For now everything was temporary, and with every step nearer the cabin, everything that had happened seemed more important, more painful, more hopeless.

As they rode into the yard, Lauren and Raven came out of the house.

"We're home," Isabella said, sliding from the wagon seat before Tyler could climb down to help her out. "Where's Carl?"

"Hello, Isabella," Raven said in mock reproach. "He's in the mine."

"I'll just go and let them know we're back," she said.

"No!" Colter stopped her. "Let's get the wagon unloaded. Then I'll go speak with Irish and Carl. You can tell them about your dinner party at supper."

Moments later the clothing had been taken inside, and after unharnessing the horses, Colter and Tyler were hiking up the valley on foot.

"I don't see why I couldn't go," Isabella said as she went into the house.

"Because you are going to tell Raven and me about the dance," Lauren said, gently diverting Isabella's attention to a topic she knew her sister would be interested in. She gave Sabrina a long look, wondering why she wasn't charging up the valley with the men. Remaining behind, giving way to Colter, was unlike Sabrina. But something had changed. Lauren had only to look into her sister's dull eyes to know.

Lauren felt a shiver ride across her shoulders. She wanted to see Irish and hear him tell her not to worry. But he too was gone. There were only the five women in the cabin, as they had been when Papa died. Except that now, like the pussycat Papa always referred to when he teased Sabrina, her sisters had "been to London to visit the queen."

For the next half hour, as the shadows lengthened across the floor of the valley, Isabella and Mary described every detail of their trip to the fort. Sabrina restlessly paced the floor, wondering why she was staying instead of following Colter.

The Silver Dream was her mine. It would be up to her to mine it after the men were gone. She wondered when that would be.

"The saints preserve us," Irish said, wiping his forehead with a scrap of cloth that had once been Lauren's apron. "You mean it was Dane who got us shot?"

Colter let out a long breath. "I don't think he meant that to happen. He only ordered the Indians to capture us. He figured that we'd be taken to Union headquarters and held as prisoners of war."

"That lying son of a—" Carl was less kind. "And I'll bet he sucked up to Isabella like a cur dog turned in with the hounds. I'll kill him!"

Tyler could have pointed out that there was a time before Isabella when Carl might have been accused of the same approach to women. "At any rate, the military knows where we are now, and whatever happens, it's only a matter of time before we're arrested."

"That'll mean the women will be left unprotected," Irish observed.

"True," Tyler agreed, "but once Dane is caught, they won't be in danger anymore."

"There's still one problem," Colter said. "Gray Warrior."

Carl slammed his pick into the wall of the tunnel where they'd been digging and walked toward the entrance to the cave. "Flying Cloud will take care of the women."

The men agreed that he would, if the women would go to his camp. They also agreed that Sabrina wouldn't.

"You know, Colter," Irish chided, "she isn't likely to leave the Silver Dream. Mining this silver was what she was about from the beginning. So far as I know, nothing has changed."

The three men studied Colter, waiting for some acknowledgment that their lives *had* changed directions, that they'd become something more than soldiers, that this land was theirs now and the future it offered was what they would protect.

"No," Colter finally said, "nothing's changed."

Tyler dropped his head. "Fine, Captain. What do we do now?"

"Tonight we watch the barn. I'm guessing that Dane won't take a chance on leaving the money in the wagon long. He can't be certain that we won't find it."

Carl said, "Tonight?"

"I think so." Colter nodded. "Now, let's set up a schedule for watch. Two men, I think, in four-hour shifts. We'll have one in the barn and one in the trees down the valley."

"How will we signal the house?"

Colter looked puzzled for a minute, until Carl came up with the answer. "The calf. Whoever waits in the trees will keep the calf. Once we see somebody, we'll turn it loose. It'll head for the barn, lickety-split."

Irish wasn't sure. "Don't we stand the chance of getting the little thing shot?"

"Yeah, I guess you're right," Carl admitted sheepishly. "And Isabella would shoot me if anything happened to that animal. How about lighting a candle?"

"Too obvious," Tyler countered. "Maybe some kind of vocal signal, like an owl. Surely we can all hoot."

Carl laughed. "But who'd believe we were owls?"

"Nobody," Irish agreed. "But it's the only thing I can think of. Do it like this—whoo who, whoo whoo." He gave a soft, muted sound that might be suspicious, but at least it wasn't obvious.

"So it's settled," Carl said, moving out of the tunnel. "Captain Colter, you decide who gets which watch. Right now I've got a real urge for a roof and a fire."

Irish chuckled. "And the company of a good woman?"

"You're damned right. Only I wish she weren't quite so good. She's more frustration than satisfaction."

"No, Carl," Tyler said as they followed Carl. "I think what you're figuring out is that she's more permanent."

"Getting married ain't such a bad thing," Irish said. "If you find a good woman."

"No!" Colter snapped. "Don't start thinking about that. We're all going to be arrested. Until this is behind us, we don't know when, or if, we'll ever see this valley again. Don't make these women a promise you can't keep."

In spite of the pending confrontation with Dane and the Union Army, supper was a gay affair. Isabella insisted on teaching Carl the dance steps she'd learned. Even Mary joined in, dancing first with Tyler, then with Irish and Carl. They seemed unaware that Colter had slipped out of the cabin and hadn't returned.

Sabrina, restless and worried, finally justified her following him with her need to know what was happening. She found him near the barn, where they'd shared Papa's whiskey that night. It seemed like a hundred years ago, instead of merely days.

"What's going on, Colter? Why are you out here?"

"I just wanted to smoke the cigar the captain gave me." He pulled a cigar from his pocket, thought about Dane, and stuck it back into his pocket.

"Why don't I believe that?" she said.

"Because you believe little of what I tell you?"

"Because you don't tell me anything, Colter. My sisters are inside that cabin, and I know something is going on. The men inside have never seemed so relaxed and happy. But you, you're about to explode."

He hadn't fooled her by keeping his distance. From

the first they'd been connected somehow, able to sense the currents of emotion that flowed between them. He'd hoped that she'd believe his preoccupation was due to his feelings for her. But he could tell from the bulge in her pocket that she'd brought her pistol—that she'd sensed more immediate danger.

Unless he could divert her attention, she'd be caught up in what he was expecting to happen. Dane would think nothing of using the women for his own purposes. They could be hurt. Sabrina could be hurt.

He had to do something.

He kissed her.

Sabrina was caught by surprise. She hadn't expected the urgency, the hunger, the deep need. With total abandon she responded, taking his tongue into her mouth, working the sides of her jacket apart so that she could press herself against his hard body.

Moaning softly, then more desperately.

His hands were cupping her bottom, pulling her close. His mouth was attacking her savagely. His blood was hot and rushing through his body on a wild trip that carried him beyond knowing. He'd intended only to divert her attention. He'd never meant to cloud his own.

He was supposed to be keeping watch, and he almost didn't hear the intruder's approach. A horse's nervous neigh was the sound that finally broke through, alerting him.

Instantly, he slid his hand over Sabrina's mouth and shook her. When she finally understood that he was trying to get her attention, she stilled. Someone was coming. Someone Colter had been watching for, someone coming silently in the darkness. He had one hand on her mouth and the other inside her trousers, cupping her bare bottom, and there were footsteps cautiously moving toward the barn.

Sabrina slipped her hand inside her pocket and pulled out her pistol.

The barn door creaked. The intruder was going into the barn. Sabrina didn't understand. Who? An Indian, perhaps, trying to steal the horses? No, they were in the corral.

Colter's hand slid down her body, giving a reluctant caress to her breast as he removed his hand from her trousers and turned her so that he could move around her. His mind was on the money now. Had Dane come alone?

He had no need to go inside the barn to know what Dane was doing. There were shuddering sounds when he climbed into the wagon, followed by the muffled noise of the board being ripped away.

Two thuds, then more creaks before silence was regained. Thank God Sabrina had the sense to remain behind him as he waited outside the barn. Colter strained his eyes, peering into the darkness. Nowhere could he see any sign that they were being watched either by Gray Warrior or by General Holland's troops.

Even the misfits weren't standing ready.

It was too early.

Nobody expected Dane to come immediately after darkness had fallen. Midnight, maybe. Or just before dawn, when the world was sleeping, but not now. Colter tried to tell himself that General Holland and the army were out there, watching. But even so, Dane could slip away in the darkness and escape. He was smart. What he'd already pulled off was evidence of that.

A bitter taste filled Colter's mouth. With Sabrina behind him he didn't dare try to stop Dane here at the house. The most he could hope for was that he could follow him, and if the army wasn't where it was supposed to be, he could capture Dane and—

But Sabrina didn't see any need to wait. This was her property, and the intruder, now visible in the moonlight, was taking something from her barn. Colter was letting him walk away from the barn, where their ore was stored. The thief was carrying bags, heavy bags from the look of his posture.

Colter wasn't stopping him. He was letting someone steal her silver.

"Stop where you are!" she said, and stepped out into the barnyard, gun drawn, ready to fire.

"Damn it, Sabrina!" Colter shouted, shoving her aside as Dane fired his own pistol.

Moments later the door to the cabin burst open, spilling Irish, Carl, and Tyler into the yard. Simultaneously three Ute braves rode in, surrounding Dane, now lying on the ground. Behind the braves came Gray Warrior, wearing full war paint and emitting an eerie war cry that split the night.

Colter lifted Sabrina and pushed her against the side of the barn. "Stay put before you get killed. And give me that gun." He wrenched it from her grasp and started toward the melee, which had turned into hand-to-hand combat.

"What is it, sister?" Mary peered from the window, watching as the Indians and Dane fought with Colter and Irish.

"It looks like that Indian who asked for food," Lauren answered. "And Colter and a Union soldier are fighting. Irish is slugging another Indian, and Tyler and Carl are being held in the center by more Ute on horseback. Every time they try to break out, a brave rides between them."

"It's Lieutenant Littlejohn!" Mary grabbed the skillet and flew out the door, slamming it against the head of one of the Indians heading for Tyler.

"Run, Tyler," Mary said desperately, holding her skillet high. "I'll keep them covered while you get away."

"No, Mary, you don't understand!" Tyler called out as he saw that Mary was trying to protect him from capture. "We expected this. It was all arranged."

At that point the sound of a bugle rent the night, and Lieutenant Garland, followed by Captain Holland, rode into the yard, leading the charge of soldiers.

The action quickly came to a stop as the new soldiers circled around Gray Warrior and his band, bringing the fighting to an end. Flares were lit and weapons were collected by the newcomers.

"Captain Holland," Dane said, struggling to his

feet. "I'm glad to see you, sir. I think I've just found the thieves. See? The payroll. They had it here."

He held up one of the pouches. Unnoticed by Dane, the other had come open, scattering cut-up newsprint across the yard.

"This man who calls himself Cullen Alexander is an impostor. He's really—"

"I know, Lieutenant, he's really Captain Quinton Colter of the Confederate States of America. An army for which I'm told you recently fought."

"But you're wrong, sir. I'm David Littlejohn. These men are responsible for the massacre of our troops at Cedar Bend."

Captain Holland slid from his horse and walked toward Dane. He studied his junior officer with sadness and anger. Then he moved his attention to Gray Warrior, the Ute Indian leader of the renegade band who'd killed and looted the settlers and stagecoaches for months. His gaze traveled down to the Indian's feet.

Boots. Leather boots—not military issue, but custom-made. Even in the flickering light of the flares, they looked familiar. He'd seen boots like that before—he just couldn't remember where.

"What's going on, Captain Holland?" Sabrina burst into the circle and planted herself in its center.

"We followed Lieutenant Littlejohn tonight, straight to your cabin. We watched him slip into your barn and were prepared to arrest him when he removed the payroll from your wagon. You nearly ruined our stakeout."

"And you almost let my husband get killed."

"Sabrina, get to the house!" Colter ordered. "This has nothing to do with you."

"Please, do as he says, Mrs. Colter," Captain Holland asked. "Nobody is going to kill your husband." He turned back to the man she was trying to protect. "Colter, you know what this means, don't you?"

"Yes."

"We're prepared," Tyler answered as he and the other two men joined Colter in the circle of light.

"Arrest them all, Garland," Captain Holland directed.

"All of them?"

"Yes. Littlejohn, Gray Warrior and his men, and Captain Colter and his men. We'll take them back to the fort and await General Schumacher's arrival from Laramie."

Garland snapped handcuffs on Dane and, with assistance from his troops, Gray Warrior. The other Indians had their hands tied securely behind their backs. From somewhere in the darkness Sergeant Nealey was being dragged into the light. In spite of his protests, his hands were also bound.

"Let him ride with Littlejohn," General Holland directed. "The big man can take Nealey's horse. The rest can ride double with one of you. I don't want to take the women's horses and wagon."

"Please don't take the men, Captain," Isabella pleaded.

"They haven't done anything that your soldiers haven't also done," Mary sobbed.

The captain walked over to the women standing by the door to the cabin. "I'm sorry, ladies. If it were up to me, I'd forget I ever saw them. But it's out of my hands."

"Will you least allow us to tell them good-bye?" Lauren asked quietly.

"Yes, but don't try anything. I'm bound to take them back to the fort, and I will. I'll give you a few minutes."

Tyler walked over to Mary. She put her arms around him and laid her head on his chest. Nobody but Tyler knew that she was crying. Nobody but Tyler felt her strength as she forced herself to stop and pulled away. "I intend to see England," she said, and turned back to the house.

Carl's farewell was strangely silent. He didn't tease. He didn't flirt. He simply backed Isabella against the wall of the cabin and kissed her, deep and hard, in a way he'd never kissed a woman before. Then, just as silently, he turned away and allowed himself to be helped into the wagon the soldiers had pulled out of the barn.

Irish was the last to make a move. He walked slowly over to Lauren, ducking his head so that he couldn't see the unspoken question in her eyes. "Take care of yourself, darlin'. Don't let the little people trick you out of your treasure."

"Irish McBride," Lauren said in a low voice, "I think it's time you admitted that you love me. And even if you don't, I'm waiting right here until you get back. Don't be long, you big Irishman."

Irish raised his head. "What are you saying, Miss Lauren?"

"That I love you and I intend to be your wife. A farm along the Rio Grande sounds very grand to me." Then Lauren kissed him soundly, whirled around, and dashed inside the cabin.

With a stupid grin on his face, Irish turned back to the others, pausing as he came even with his captain. "I don't know what's going to happen to us, Captain, but I'm thinking that it will go a lot easier with a good-bye kiss. Go get yours, sir."

But Colter didn't move. Every time he kissed Sabrina, he lost control. He had no intention of doing that in front of his men and his captors.

He didn't have to. Sabrina walked toward him, coming to a stop and standing there for a long moment. "You knew the payroll was in the wagon, didn't you? You were waiting for Dane to come for it, knowing that it would mean your arrest."

"Yes."

"Words don't come easy to me, Colter, but this once I need to say them. I never expected to need a man, and I know there's no future for us, but I want you to hear me say what I feel. I love you, my husband, and if you ever get out of this and want a partner, I'll be waiting."

She turned and started to join her sisters.

"Sabrina." His voice was so husky that she could barely hear him. "Wait." Even then he didn't say the words. He simply kissed her. His kiss was brief and sweet, full of regret and pain. And she knew then that he didn't expect to return.

Finally he drew back, his final words almost lost in the tightness of his control. "Good-bye, my wife. I don't think I'll ever find warm rain at midnight. But I came close."

20

Inside the cabin her sisters were waiting for an explanation. "Why?" Lauren asked.

"Captain Littlejohn was a traitor," Sabrina explained. "He was one of Colter's men. He's the one responsible for both holdups, and the massacre of all those soldiers. The men set a trap for Dane, knowing they'd be arrested as escaped criminals."

Mary and Isabella were crying softly. Sabrina looked at her sisters and felt a coldness settle in her chest. She couldn't make this right.

From the first she'd known that Colter would leave. She'd thought she was prepared. She'd expected it, but not this way, and there was no way to stop the hurt. Loving Colter had torn down her walls, opened up her heart, and let the pain flow in. Now Colter was gone.

And worse, because of her, her sisters were unhappy; their lives were being destroyed. She had to do something, for them, if not for herself. There was no Papa to step in, no little people and no miracle to be handed out. It was up to Sabrina, just as it always had been.

"Hellfire!" Sabrina swore. "We're acting like the world has come to an end. It hasn't, not yet. What we have to do is find a way to free them."

"Do you really think we can?" Mary asked, swallowing her sobs.

"Of course I do," Sabrina said. "We needed a man to help us, and I went out and found one. An Alexander never quit before, and we aren't going to start now."

Isabella held on to Mary, who'd begun to stop her sniffling. "But you aren't an Alexander anymore, Sabrina. You said you're Mrs. Colter."

Sabrina gave a hollow laugh in a desperate attempt to relieve their despair. "So I did. You know the hell of it? I wish I were. In fact, when we get this straightened out, I intend to be Mrs. Colter."

"Why do you keep saying that?" Mary asked.

"Saying what?"

"Hell, and hellfire. You never cursed before."

Sabrina swore again. "I just found out that Colter was right all along. Colorado Territory is another name for hell—or heaven, depending on where you are."

"Or," Mary said softly, "who you're with."

"Go to bed now," Sabrina directed. "In the morning we'll start to make plans."

Sabrina twisted and turned for most of the night. By morning she was hollow-eyed and she had no plan. As Lauren made coffee, the others prepared the bread, waiting in silence for Sabrina to share her ideas.

Finally Isabella could wait no longer. "What are we going to do, Brina? We have to get them out."

"I don't know," she admitted. "I'm afraid that Dane will figure a way to blame this robbery on them and hang them before they have any kind of hearing."

"The way I see it, Sabrina," Lauren said, "is that

you have to talk to Captain Holland. You'll tell him that you were there. That you saw what happened."

"Ah, but the question is, will he believe you?" Mary asked. "I mean, it sounds like he believes that you and Captain Colter are married. Any woman would protect her man, even if it meant lying."

"But I was there!"

"But," Lauren agreed, "you were the only one. Without someone else to corroborate your story, he isn't going to buy it."

"I'll just have to try. I can't let him—them die."

Raven walked toward the fire. She stared at the flame for a long time, then turned. "You weren't the only one there, Sabrina. There was Gray Warrior."

"That's right," the others agreed.

"That's not going to work," Isabella said. "Gray Warrior is under arrest too. He's not going to confess to the captain that his men killed the escorts and blamed it on the Rebels."

"You're right," Sabrina agreed. "And even if he did, how will that save the men? They've become prisoners of war, charged with crimes against the Union."

Sabrina rubbed her hands, still tender from the healing blisters and the abuse she'd put them through. Suddenly, mining the silver seemed unimportant.

Raven felt her heart fill with pain. She'd thought they were safe when Flying Cloud sent her cousins to watch over the valley. In spite of their protection, trouble had come, just as her grandfather had predicted.

Finally Sabrina reached for her sheepskin-lined jacket. "I'm going to the fort to talk to Captain Holland," Sabrina said, pulling on Papa's felt hat.

"Is that safe?" Mary asked.

"I don't know. I just know that I have to go." There were dark circles under Sabrina's eyes. She felt as if she were being shattered into a million pieces. Loving Colter had changed her, and she didn't seem able to reassemble the pieces to bring the old Sabrina back.

"We're coming with you," Isabella said.

"No! There's no point in putting you in danger.

Besides, what could you do? You need to stay here with Mary and Lauren."

"We can't stand by and do nothing," Mary said sharply.

"What I'd like you to do," Sabrina said, "is pack up the best of the ore samples and gather feed for the animals. I'll talk to the commander and make certain that the men aren't hanged. Then we'll go to Denver to find out how much our ore is worth."

"Of course. That way we can repay any losses the captain and the others are being charged for," Mary said.

Spirits lightened immediately.

"Why not?" Sabrina said. "Greed, that's what started all this. A silver mine ought to be worth something."

Lauren studied her elder sister. "You'd be willing to give up Papa's mine to save the captain and his men?"

"I would," she said, and hugged her sisters goodbye. "I'll be back late tomorrow. We'll take the silver knobs and the last of Papa's gold nuggets, and we'll go to Denver."

Isabella lifted her golden lashes in question. " 'We'?"

"All of us," Sabrina said. "I might need some help."

"You finally need us to help?" Mary's voice chronicled her disbelief.

Though nothing had really changed, those left behind in the cabin felt renewed hope, not so much because Sabrina had always found solutions to their problems in the past, but even more because she seemed to need their help now.

It became immediately apparent that the captain had no intention of seeing Sabrina.

"The captain is very busy taking statements and handling the investigation, Mrs. Colter," Lieutenant Garland relayed the Captain's reply.

"But Captain Holland needs to know that my husband had nothing to do with killing those men, no matter what kind of report he got. I was there. I saw what happened."

"I told him. But it seems Captain Colter refutes your claim. He warned Captain Holland that you'd do anything to protect his men."

"But that isn't true. I swear."

Lieutenant Garland gave a patient smile. "At the proper time, I promise, Captain Holland will listen to what you have to say. Truly, it would be better if you were to return to your cabin. He'll send for you when you're needed to testify officially."

"Not until I see Captain Holland."

Garland shifted uncomfortably. "I'm sorry, Mrs. Colter, but I'm afraid you'll have a long wait."

Sabrina thought quickly. "All right, but perhaps I'll visit with Mrs. Holland before I go. Is that possible?"

Lieutenant Garland might have refused, but Mrs. Holland, always aware of the happenings inside the fort, burst through the door and clasped Sabrina's hands. "You poor dear," she said, "I heard what happened. Come inside and let me make you a hot cup of tea."

Sabrina found herself in Mrs. Holland's quarters by the fire, a cup of honey-sweetened tea in her hands.

"Now, tell me, how did that money get into your wagon? My husband doesn't seem to want to tell me about this trouble. Probably because he knows I would never believe that your captain could kill an entire company of men in cold blood to steal a payroll. There has to be another explanation."

"May I tell you the truth, Mrs. Holland?"

"I wouldn't expect you to do less, Sabrina."

"It's Lieutenant Littlejohn who is responsible for all the trouble. His name isn't really Littlejohn, it's Dane Beckworth. He was one of my husband's men. He and Gray Warrior plotted to steal the first payroll and the gold from the detachment. Gray Warrior's men killed the Union soldiers. I saw it all. I was there. Please believe me!"

"Of course I believe you, Sabrina. All you have to do is tell my husband, and he'll let Captain Colter go."

"I wish it were that simple. They're still Confederate soldiers who've been stealing from the Union: horses, munitions, medicine. They're prisoners now, and they'll have to stand trial for their war crimes, if not for the payroll robberies. Besides, Colter has already told your husband that I wasn't there. He thinks he's protecting me."

"From what? Being implicated in the robbery? Of course. That's it. If you were both involved in the robberies, your testimony wouldn't hold much water."

"But it was Lieutenant Littlejohn. He hid the money in our wagon. How else would he have known it was there? The Union soldiers caught him taking it out. He's trying to blame Colter by pretending that he just discovered the pouches."

"And I think that's the problem, my dear. General Holland is having a hard time believing that the lieutenant is a thief. Lieutenant Littlejohn reported with a glowing recommendation from General Grant. In fact, he was to take command of the fort on our leaving. Are you certain you aren't just trying to divert blame from your husband? I truly wouldn't blame you."

Sabrina took a deep breath. "He isn't my husband. We are not really married." She couldn't keep the tightness from her voice. "I—I wish we were."

"Oh, dear. I think you'd better start at the beginning."

Sabrina did, telling Mrs. Holland about Papa and the Silver Dream, about going into Boulder City to find a husband, about overhearing Gray Warrior and Long Rifle, and finally, about rescuing and hiding the prisoners.

"And the men were wounded?"

"Yes. When the Indians attacked the guards, I knew that the prisoners would be next. I couldn't let them die. One of them was an Irishman, like Papa. I rescued them."

The afternoon slid into evening. Still, Mrs. Holland listened.

"I took them to our cabin in the valley. Since I'd gone after a husband, my sisters thought I'd found one, Captain Colter. They assumed the other men were for them."

"Sounds like divine intervention," Mrs. Holland observed. "What happened then?"

"Colter and I went to Wiley's Trading Post for supplies. That's where we ran into Brother and Mrs. William and Brother Seaton. They got the idea that Colter and I were living in sin, and Brother Seaton insisted on marrying us."

Mrs. Holland couldn't hold back a smile. "Then you are married?"

"Hell, I don't know," Sabrina said, then realized what she'd said. "I'm sorry. I seem to have picked up Colter's habit of swearing. You see, it got all mixed up. Brother Seaton married Cullen Alexander to me."

"Who's that?"

"Cullen was my papa. At the trading post they thought that Colter was Cullen. That's what we called Colter when Sergeant Nealey came along, to protect his identity."

"So he married you and the captain, he just married the wrong names."

"Yes, ma'am." Sabrina let out a deep sigh. What had made her think that Mrs. Holland would have an answer? There was none.

"I can see where you have a problem, my dear, but how can you connect the payroll robbery to Lieutenant Littlejohn? Did you see him at the site of the massacre?"

"No, I never really got a good look at the man called Long Rifle. But I'm certain it was the man you call Lieutenant Littlejohn. And I'm just as certain that there was no dying soldier who accused the prisoners of that horrible crime. Dane was lying."

"I'm afraid that wouldn't stand up in an inquiry. Captain Holland is very taken with the lieutenant. I'm sure he would require proof."

"I know. And I don't have any. I know you can't do anything. I just wanted to be sure Colter was all right."

"That I can assure you. The captain would never let anything happen to a prisoner. I still don't quite understand why your Captain Colter and Mr. Kurtz came to the fort. Didn't the captain know the danger he would be in?"

"I think he wanted to confront Dane. Colter figured the only way Dane could accuse him of a crime was by admitting to his own part in the attack."

"But you were there. You could have cleared that up."

"I wanted to, but Colter said that once I told Dane I was there, Dane would have to kill me to protect himself. Colter thought if we came to the fort and Dane didn't give himself away, we'd all be safe."

"But he wasn't," Mrs. Holland said. "I'm so sorry."

"No," Sabrina said with a catch in her voice. "They all ended up in the brig, charged with stealing from the Union Army."

"I'm afraid the outlook is pretty grim, my dear. Stealing the gold from those escorts involved murder. Perhaps it would be better if they were charged with stealing the pouches, as Lieutenant Littlejohn claims. At this time it's not a hanging offense."

Sabrina stood and walked toward the window. "I don't think Dane will ever let him go to trial, Mrs. Holland. Dane can't afford to let that happen."

"But Dane, I mean Littlejohn, is behind bars, too. The old guardhouse and the new one are filled with prisoners. Oh, dear. Let me think about this, Sabrina," she said. "In the meantime I'll have some supper brought to your room, the one you shared with Captain Colter. And maybe I'll be able to arrange for you to see him."

Sabrina felt her heart leap. "Do you think you can?"

"I'm sure of it, first thing in the morning. I promise."

* * *

For safety's sake Colter was being held separate from his men, in the old brig, the same building where Gray Warrior and his men were locked up. Colter's cell was dark and cold. Sabrina was glad for the privacy, though for all the warmth of Colter's greeting, he might have been a stranger.

"What are you doing here?" he asked.

"I came to see the captain. I wanted him to know the truth."

Only a grimace gave evidence that he'd even heard her.

"I'm not going to stand by and let them charge you with a crime you didn't commit."

"They aren't. I've been arrested for stealing from the Union Army. I did."

"But you didn't have anything to do with those murders, and if Dane has anything to say about it, he'll see that you are blamed for them."

"I don't believe it will come to that, Sabrina. Holland is a fair man."

"I know, that's why I told Lieutenant Garland the truth. Why did you tell him I would lie to protect you?"

He didn't even turn around.

"Give it up, Sabrina. They won't believe you."

"Then I'll find a way to prove it."

That's exactly what he was afraid of. "Go home, Sabrina. Look after your sisters and forget all about this."

"Can you?"

He didn't answer. There was nothing more to say. With her heart in tatters, Sabrina turned around and left the room. She'd thought she hurt before. Now she knew what real pain was, what Colter must have felt all the time. Losing Papa was the worst thing she'd ever known, until now.

"I'm so sorry," Mrs. Holland said as Sabrina was leaving. "I tried to talk to my husband, but I've never seen the man so stubborn. He absolutely refused to listen, said that Captain Colter was the head of a Confederate guerrilla team that had been stealing from his troops for months."

"He was," Sabrina said. "He never denied that."

"The only thing I could do, my dear, was convince him to conduct a full investigation of the entire matter. He's waiting for the general from Laramie to oversee the hearing. I'll send word as soon as it's arranged."

"Thank you," Sabrina said. "I'll be going now. I have to get back to my family."

"Captain Holland has assigned two men to accompany you. He doesn't think it's safe for a woman to ride alone. There's been another Indian attack on the mail train. Two settlers were killed, and their horses were stolen."

Mrs. Holland watched the tall red-haired woman leave, shoulders slumped, head bowed. It was hard to believe that this was the same vivacious dancer from the dinner party. She hadn't told Sabrina, but the one thing that the captain had agreed to do before he turned over his command was send a telegram to the Department of the Army requesting information on Lieutenant David Littlejohn.

That was the best she could do to keep Captain Colter safe until a trial could be arranged. In the meantime, she'd set her orderly to do some private investigating. There were always things the enlisted men knew that the commanding officer never learned. Mrs. Holland meant to find out whatever she could.

Sabrina rode listlessly, replaying the events of the day over and over. After her visit with Colter, the captain had escorted her from the guardhouse and bade her farewell, apologizing for what had happened and assuring her that Colter would get a fair trial. He would keep her informed as to when and where. And he'd have his men keep watch over her and her sisters.

Back in the valley her sisters shared the disappointment. "Don't worry, Brina," Lauren said. "We'll figure out what to do."

"Sure we will," Isabella agreed. "We'll take these two silver knobs into Denver and find out that we're filthy rich. We'll be wealthy enough to bribe the guards at the U.S. mint in Denver. Money always opens doors."

Doors, maybe, but not prison walls. Still, Sabrina forced herself to pretend that she was confident. Sufficient feed was left for the cow and calf, and for Colter's horse. Nobody suggested that Sabrina wear a dress for the trip, and nobody advised her to give up her horse and ride in the wagon. At the last minute Raven decided to stay behind with Flying Cloud. Sabrina watched as she was joined at the top of the ridge by a rider on a horse. Raven climbed on the back of the pony, then turned and waved.

On the journey down the valley Sabrina rode ahead of the wagon in silence. She filled her mind by trying to figure out the best way to mine the silver. Irish had explained that first they'd need to reroute the creek that ran down the valley and ended beyond the cabin at the edge of the woods. Then they needed a stamp mill to crush the ore.

It wouldn't be wise to tell anyone the location of the mine yet. Without men around to protect them, they offered too good a target to claim jumpers. She didn't know how pure the knobs of silver were, but Papa said they were beacons, placed there by the little people to mark their treasure. She didn't know about beacons, but she knew enough about mining to know that silver doesn't usually announce itself that way.

Still, freak occurrences did happen, and the two knobs appeared to be the beginning of some kind of vein of silver streaking through the mountainside. If Papa was right, the silver knobs ought to provide enough money for their needs now. The rest of the vein could wait.

While making camp that night in the cave where she and Colter had slept, Sabrina was unapproachable. Even Lauren, who always shared Sabrina's deepest fears, was unable to get past her wall of silence. They ate quickly and the party turned in. Traveling alone to Denver wasn't like having Colter's men as escorts.

The cold, subdued travelers rode past Wiley's Trading Post the next morning, stopping only to water their horses. Sabrina allowed the wagon to move ahead, then turned back to question the trader about the war.

"The Union troops have captured those Confederate soldiers," she said, hoping for some positive response from Wiley.

She was disappointed when he said, "Too bad. What'd they do?"

"They've been accused of murdering all those Yankees and taking the fort payroll and some gold they were carrying."

"You don't say. How'd the military learn that? I thought all those Yanks were killed."

"A Lieutenant Littlejohn was reporting for duty at the time. According to him, he came along just after the attack, and one of the dying soldiers blamed the massacre on the prisoners they were transporting."

"You don't say. How'd the army find the prisoners?"

Sabrina looked at Wiley for a long time. She didn't know what she'd expected, but the man obviously didn't know anything. "They were betrayed by one of their own, a man called Dane, who was really the thief. They're all at the fort, under arrest. Any good news on the war?"

"Depends on which side you're on, I reckon. Then again, I guess it don't matter. Without a miracle it's over for the Rebs."

"Maybe that's good. No point in any more people being hurt. What do you think will happen to the prisoners when it ends?"

"I don't know, ma'am. I'll—I'll ask some questions. Maybe there's something I can do."

On that odd note Sabrina left, catching up with her sisters down the trail. By noon they were pulling into Boulder City.

"It isn't much of a town," Lauren observed as they rode down the main street.

Isabella defended the stark wooden buildings. "Papa said it started in fifty-nine when some miners formed the Boulder City Town Company to lay out a town and sell lots."

From one of the saloons came the sound of tinny piano music. The song was a popular one, "Sweet Betsy from Pike." Lauren felt a deep sense of longing for Irish and his beautiful voice. She wished he were with them; she'd even be willing to have Carl swing down from the wagon and enjoy a hand or two of poker and a good stiff drink.

But the soft touch of Isabella's hand and her worried frown pushed Lauren's longings from her mind. "Look, Sabrina, an assayer's office. Looks like we don't have to go to Denver."

Mary, Isabella, and Lauren's attention was quickly diverted to the general store and the dressmaker's shop. Lauren stopped the team alongside the stores and climbed down, tying the horses to the hitching rail. Sabrina, still on horseback, studied her sisters for a minute. "I'll ride over to the assayer's office and have him take a look at the two knobs of silver. I'll catch up to you."

Isabella waited for the horses to be watered, then started off down the wooden sidewalk, oblivious to the curious looks of the townsfolk who studied Lauren and Mary.

Sabrina rode her horse down the street, tied him up at the rail, and pulled the saddlebags from his back. Inside the office a lone man sat behind a counter, transferring figures into a ledger. Behind him she could see a rough map of the territory. On the counter were a pair of scales and a mallet.

"Henderson Brooks, ma'am, can I help you?"

Now that she was there, Sabrina felt great concern over confiding in a stranger, even if he was a government official. She'd kept her own counsel for so long that telling anyone about Papa's mine was almost more than she could do. Then she remembered Colter and Tyler, and flung the saddlebag onto the counter.

"Mr. Brooks, I'd like you to take a look at these two ore samples."

Mr. Brooks opened the ties and pulled the two silver knobs from the bag. His eyes widened as he studied them, their shape and color. Then he used an eyepiece to study them closer. Next he took a small hammer and chiseled out a sliver of the silver and examined it again. After he smelled and tasted, he turned and submerged the silver into a liquid.

Finally he turned back to Sabrina and allowed a broad smile to widen his mouth. "I've never seen anything quite like this. Two knobs of pure silver. I'd say you've got the real thing here, Miss—?"

"Colter. Mrs. Sabrina Colter," she said, claiming a name to which she wasn't certain she had the right. Still, though her Papa had filed a formal claim to his site, there was no point in advertising who she was—not yet. "How much is it worth?"

"Well, I can't say for sure, until I do some further testing, but I'd say that if there is more like this, you're a very wealthy woman. Have you staked a claim?"

"The silver is mine, Mr. Brooks."

"And where is Mr. Colter?"

"He's away just now—at the mine. I also have some gold. Where can I trade this for money?"

"Yes, ma'am. I'll just lock this in the vault and walk down to the bank with you. I'm certain that Banker Calhoun will be glad to trade greenbacks for this. He's even been known to advance funds to a promising claim, on my recommendation, of course."

But Sabrina had no intention of sharing this claim with anyone she didn't have to. With Mr. Brooks standing behind her ore samples, Sabrina was suddenly being treated like the most elegant lady in town.

Banker Calhoun exchanged Sabrina's silver ore for more than she'd ever expected. In the end she didn't even have to give up all her gold nuggets. Mr. Brooks personally escorted her to the mercantile store, where Lauren and Isabella were admiring shawls and ready-made shoes, and introduced her to the proprietor before excusing himself to return to his bank.

"Oh, Brina, look at this." Isabella was holding a bolt of burgundy-colored material beneath her chin. "Isn't it the most beautiful material you've ever seen?"

"It certainly is. I think you ought to have it. In fact, I think each of you ought to pick something you want. It looks as if we can buy almost anything we want now." She turned to the proprietor. "I'll settle the bill when they're done."

"Yes, Mrs. Colter," he agreed, and hurried to assist the women with their purchases.

"Mrs. Colter?" Lauren questioned.

"I thought it better not to use Papa's name. There are some who would know Cullen Alexander, and I'd like to keep the mine's location secret as long as I can."

"Then it assayed out?" Mary asked.

"Looks like it. Mr. Brooks and the banker would like to give us the town. Get what you want," Sabrina directed, and handed her sister some money. "This ought to be enough to take care of it. I have an errand to run. But first"—she turned back to the store owner—"is there a lawyer in Boulder City?"

"No, ma'am. But if you need some legal work done, Mr. Brooks usually handles it." Sabrina thought about that, then decided that Tyler would be as good at lawyering as Mr. Brooks, and he already knew the case.

"Thank you, I'll take care of that later." Sabrina darted out the door and into the dressmaker's shop beside the general store. She discussed her request with the seamstress, paid for her order, and left before she had time to question the absurdity of her action. By late afternoon she was sternly refusing Isabella's request to spend the night in a real hotel, and loading the wagon for their return trip.

They were at the edge of town when they heard pistol shots. The men in the saloon came running out, firing wildly into the night sky.

"It's over!" one man shouted. "The war is over!"

"Lee has surrendered to Grant at a place called Appomattox," a man wearing a white shirt and armbands on his sleeve said, fluttering a piece of paper in his hand.

Mr. Brooks ran into the street. "How do you know?"

"A telegram. It just came from Washington, from President Lincoln."

The men began to dance in the streets.

Lauren looked at Mary. "It's done," she said. "Lee surrendered."

"Let's get out of here before they decide to start celebrating. You know how men are when the music and the drinking starts." Lauren urged the horses into a trot.

Back at the fort the celebration was louder. A twenty-one-gun salute echoed across the plains. In recognition of the occasion, the soldiers serving time in the brig were released—all but Dane, Gray Warrior and his band, and the southerners.

Lee had surrendered, Colter heard the shouting. He hadn't known how he'd feel. He'd thought his loyalty was long gone, that all he'd feel was regret for the waste. But he was sad. Not at the loss, but because so many had fought so long and for so little.

If only the news had come a month ago, before the ambush, before Sabrina. He'd half expected her confession and had attempted to head off any involvement on her part by telling the captain that she would make the claim that she'd been there. He'd simply nodded. It was not only reasonable, it would be expected that a wife would try to protect her husband.

Foolish, loyal, beautiful Sabrina—the one good thing to come out of a desperate war. He'd had one last chance at happiness only to have it taken from him by one of the men he'd trusted, one of his own.

In the end it was probably just as well. What in hell made him think that he'd ever make any woman a husband? Mining silver was about as practical for him as thinking he could protect his family, protect Moe. At least he'd kept Sabrina from being involved.

The day after Sabrina left, Colter was reunited with his men in one large cell. Apparently they'd found somewhere else to house Dane. Colter hoped it was a room with bars. If the military didn't take care of Dane, he intended to do it for them. One way or another.

"At least nobody is paying any attention to us," Irish said. "I was afraid that a hanging might be part of the celebration."

"Does that mean we'll be freed, Captain?" Carl asked.

Colter wished he knew more about the law. "I doubt it. We confessed to the theft of army property. That charge probably won't change, even if the war is ended."

Conversation was limited to the two men for a time. "Captain, maybe if one of us could get out of here and go back to South Carolina, we could get proof that Dane was part of our unit."

"Who'd believe us? If they don't believe that Dane is a thief with his holding the stolen pouch in his hand, they aren't going to believe us. No, we'd be better off to stay put. They'll have a hearing of some kind. Tyler's used to talking; he has the schooling to represent us. We'll come up with a way to get off."

"I may be able to debate an issue, but that's a far cry from knowing anything about the law," Tyler protested. "We need a real lawyer. Maybe we can find one."

But Irish was all out of confidence. "And if we don't, what kind of sentence will we get?"

"We didn't do anything that the Yanks didn't do," Carl argued. "We'll serve some time in prison, maybe. Maybe only a lashing."

But nobody really believed him.

"I don't see why we have to sleep on the ground when we're wealthy now." Isabella complained as they left town. "We could have stayed at the hotel and left in the morning instead of driving in the dark."

"Now, Isabella," Lauren was saying. "Raven would say that the spirits of the mountain will protect us under the stars. Back there in Boulder City, who can say?"

Isabella gave one last look behind her, then forced a smile. She didn't mean to sound petty. She was just worried about Carl, and she didn't know how to talk about that. He was worldly and exciting, the kind of man she could only have dreamed of, and he was interested in her. Oh, he hadn't said anything before she'd gone to the fort, but she'd known. And she'd lost him before she'd ever had a chance to know.

Now she filled her mind with the promise that one day soon she would try out one of those rooms, she and Carl. Once all this mess was over and they were on their way to California.

Sabrina urged her horse into a gallop. Being away from the valley was a risk. Introducing her sisters to the luxury they could now afford was an even greater one. She could already tell that Isabella was eager to move into town. Lauren was less readable. She still did the mothering, but more and more it became apparent that Lauren wanted and needed a home of her own.

The cabin was cold and lonely looking when they returned the next day. Quickly they built a fire and unloaded the wagon, but nobody was anxious to talk. Food and supplies were replenished. The weather was abating. For now, until she heard from Captain Holland, she intended to mine the Silver Dream.

Her family had to come first.

But it was hard to hold her heart in check. It hurt.

21

For two weeks Sabrina dug ore from the mine with a fury.

And waited.

Raven had returned, announcing that the missionaries were being accepted by Flying Cloud and the Arapaho. In fact, on learning of Colter's arrest, they wanted to journey to the fort to intercede in his behalf. Flying Cloud had considered the situation and decided that the plan was a good one.

In three days they'd arrive at the cabin. If Sabrina and the others wished to accompany them to the fort, they would be welcome.

"I intend to go," Lauren said. "I want to be sure that—the men are being treated well."

"Me too," Mary added. "Tyler will need fresh clothing. I will find something of Papa's." She glanced anxiously at Sabrina. "That is, if you don't mind."

"No, I don't mind. We should have thought to buy new clothing for the men when we were in Boulder City."

Isabella frowned. "Don't we have time to get it before the missionaries arrive?"

"Of course we do," Sabrina said, arousing herself to action. "We still have money. I'll ride into Boulder City and buy what they need."

"We'll go with you," Mary said.

"No, I can make the trip on horseback faster. You look after things here, and I'll be back by the time Flying Cloud and the missionaries arrive."

Going into Boulder City to buy clothing for Colter and his men wasn't all Sabrina had in mind. She'd been considering the trial and their plan to use the silver to repay any losses the U.S. Army blamed on Colter's misfits, and she'd decided that they'd need proof of this ability to cover the thefts. Henderson Brooks could prepare a paper certifying the worth of the mine.

And, she thought as she galloped her horse south, there was the matter of the dress she'd ordered. It would be ready. Though she had no idea that she'd ever wear it, it had been her private promise to Colter, and she intended to find a way to make it come true.

She bypassed the cave where she and Colter had camped, driving herself until she was beyond exhaustion. Even then she barely slept. She couldn't forget the night she'd burned her hands on the skillet, when Colter had taken those hands in his. That was the night he'd wished for a place where there'd be warm rain at midnight.

Though they had shared the cave less than six weeks ago, it seemed so much longer ago than that.

The next morning she left before full light, riding past Wiley's Trading Post without stopping, arriving in Boulder City before midday, where Henderson Brooks obligingly prepared the document she needed. He mentioned the report in several eastern newspapers that President Lincoln favored freeing the Confederate soldiers to return home without punishment. Nobody was certain that Lincoln's wishes would be followed.

Disappointed, she made her way to the general store, where she picked up ready-made clothing for the men. Her last stop was the dressmaker next door, where she paid for her special purchase.

The trip back seemed interminable. After a few hours' sleep she was up and riding again. By the next day she was making her way up the trail to the cabin, while Flying Cloud and the missionaries arrived from across the mountain.

Sabrina greeted her sisters and handed over the clothing, keeping her own parcel. They took the garments inside the cabin while Raven went to meet Flying Cloud and the Arapaho, now visible on the trail down the valley past the mine.

More tired than she'd ever been, Sabrina swallowed back the growing feelings of discomfort she'd fought all the way home. She unharnessed the horse, patted him down and fed him, then turned him into the corral. The bacon she'd bought in Boulder City must have been tainted, she decided as she left the barn, beginning now to feel sick. Flying Cloud was riding into the yard behind Raven, who'd already slid from her pony and started toward Sabrina.

"Mrs. Alexander," Brother Seaton called out, then corrected himself. "I mean, Mrs. Colter, I'm so sorry to hear about your trouble."

"Thank you, Brother Seaton," Sabrina said, reaching an unsteady hand toward the wall of the cabin. "Please come in . . . Raven . . ."

Like a flower wilting in the desert heat, she slowly and gracefully collapsed at her sister's feet.

Lauren, who was in the process of opening the door, frantically called out to the others. "Come quick, Sabrina's fainted."

In a matter of minutes Sabrina had been carried inside and laid on her cot by the door. With a damp cloth Mary was wiping her face and Isabella rubbing her hands.

"Dear, dear!" Mrs. William observed as she stood to the side. "She looks very pale, Lauren."

Mary answered. "Sabrina has just made a trip to Boulder City and back. She always pushes herself too hard."

"I think she would do better if you all moved away," Lauren said, giving a quick tilt of her head to the other sisters. "Why don't you help Mrs. William make some coffee? I expect our guests are cold and in need of food."

"Yes," Mary agreed, rising and leading the way to the fire. "Isabella, you and Raven fetch fresh water. Mrs. William, there is bread in the cupboard."

Sabrina opened her eyes. She was disoriented and confused, lying on her bed with Lauren looking down at her. "What happened?"

"I think you fainted, sister."

"Nonsense. I've never fainted in my life. I must have looked like some fool woman out in the sun too long."

"Well, you've fainted now, and I will say that you managed to do so beautifully."

Sabrina raised up, felt her stomach turn over, and swallowed hard. In another minute she wouldn't have to worry about that bacon anymore. Unless she got out of there quick, she was going to do more than faint.

"Help me up, Lauren. I need to get out into the air."

"But—"

"Quick!"

Lauren helped Sabrina to her feet, and before the women knew what was happening, they were out the door and around the corner of the house.

For the next few minutes Sabrina wished she'd never cooked the bacon, wished she'd never gone to Boulder City, wished she'd never seen the missionaries in black.

Finally, resting her hand against the cabin, she drew in several long, cold breaths and wiped her mouth on her arm. "Forgive me, Lauren. I don't know what made me do that. It must have been the bacon I ate last night."

Lauren took a long look at her sister. "Maybe," was her only comment. "Do you feel like coming back inside?"

"I suppose."

"I'll tell the missionaries that they'll have to go ahead. We'll come along later, when you're ready to travel."

Sabrina swallowed hard and stood up. "I'm ready. If we leave now, we'll arrive at the fort before midnight."

"No, you won't. If you insist on going with Flying Cloud, we'll leave in the morning. You've already made a long ride; one more day isn't going to matter."

Sabrina finally nodded. "But I'm not going back in there and have everyone fuss over me. I'll make a bed in the shed."

"Fine. I'll send you some supper."

"Forget food!" Sabrina snapped. "I'll just wait on breakfast."

But at breakfast all she ate was dry bread.

As they loaded the wagons, Sabrina listened to her sisters explaining what had happened at the fort and how Captain Holland had caught Lieutenant Littlejohn removing what he thought was the stolen money from the Alexanders' wagon.

Brother William was stunned. "And you're certain this man called Littlejohn is really an ex-Confederate soldier who was responsible for an entire detachment of Union soldiers being killed?"

"Oh, yes," Isabella answered. "He was a member of Captain Colter's unit until he turned into a traitor. Now we have to find a way to prove that he's responsible."

"But Captain Colter was a soldier following orders," Brother William argued. "I mean, we don't hold with killing, but those Yankees did bad things too. Are they going to build enough prisons to hold all the soldiers who fought each other?"

"Of course not!" Mrs. William announced. "It's time to mend wounds, to send all the men home to farm and work in the factories. There are children who need their fathers and wives who need their husbands."

"That's it!" Sabrina said. "Children need their fathers! Mary, Isabella, go fetch the pillows and bring towels. We're going to a trial. If the army doesn't give us back our men, we're going to send in a better negotiator."

"What on earth are you talking about?" Lauren asked as Mary and Isabella hastened to follow Sabrina's orders.

"I think I have an idea. What if—"

But she didn't get an opportunity to explain, for it was then that they saw the dust kicked up by the rider in the blue uniform.

"A Union soldier," Lauren said, her heart suddenly filled up all the space in her throat.

"It's Lieutenant Garland," Sabrina said, suddenly afraid to hear what he'd come to say.

"Mrs. Colter, Captain Holland wants you to come to the fort. The general is on his way from Fort Laramie to hear the evidence against—your husband and his men."

"Only my husband? What about Lieutenant Littlejohn?"

"Yes, ma'am, him too."

"That's good," Sabrina answered. "As you can see, we were already loading up to come. When does the general arrive?"

"Tomorrow afternoon."

"That's perfect," Sabrina said, nodding her head. "Is everyone ready?"

Flying Cloud and the Arapaho were mounted and ready. The missionaries climbed into their wagon and pulled in behind the Alexander sisters. With Sabrina in the lead they headed down the valley toward the trail to Fort Collins.

"What are we going to do with the pillows?" Isabella whispered under her breath to Lauren.

"I have no idea, but I think Sabrina is back in charge."

Mary beamed and settled into place on the bench. "I feel much better about everything now, don't you?"

It was then that the wind kicked up and bounced

off the rocks, singing as it danced down the ridges along the valley.

"Music," Raven said. "The mountains are speaking."

"Not the mountains, Raven," Sabrina corrected. "Bagpipes. It's Papa's little people. I know. I've heard them before."

Colter came quickly awake. It was a trick he'd learned during the war, this half sleeping that kept him always on guard. Only recently had his sleep become confused—only since Sabrina.

The air in the guardhouse was cold. It seemed that he'd been cold for so long. Only when he was with Sabrina did the cold go away, and for a time he could be warm, as he'd been as a child in the Georgia sunshine.

Quietly, he came to his feet and walked toward the barred window. From where he was, he could see the mountains, the tops catching the early-morning light like beacons in the darkness. Behind him Carl and Irish were still sleeping, but Tyler soon joined him at the window.

"You think this is the day, Captain?"

"I think so. Holland said two weeks. It's been more."

"What will the general from Laramie do with us? The war is over. Will they keep us in jail?"

Colter didn't know and he said so. "I'm not sure it matters. Out here we're the enemy they fought, and the rest of the world probably doesn't even care about four misfits in Colorado Territory. Then again, maybe we'll be sent back to the South."

"Like the women of the Sabine," Tyler said in a low, pained voice. "History in reverse."

"What?"

"In the Roman myth Romulus went into the land of the Sabine and stole women to become wives to his men, who were establishing what we know as the city of Rome. Sabrina called her valley the site of the future City of Alexander."

"I remember. Sabrina talked about that. Her father must have been an unusual man. An educated dreamer, like you, Tyler."

"Perhaps, Captain."

"So what happened? I forget. Did the women marry the men of Rome?"

"They did. And finally, one day, the army of the Sabine defeated their enemies and came to take the women home. But the women refused to go. They'd fallen in love with their captors."

Colter turned to look at Tyler. "Are you in love with Mary?"

"I think I am. Even if General Lee came riding through the yard to take me away, I'd stay."

For a long time Colter stared out the window, watching full day break through the square that connected him to the outside world. It mattered little what answer he gave. They weren't going anywhere, he was convinced of that. What would he do if he was given the opportunity to go or stay? He honestly didn't know.

Damn Dane! Damn the war. Damn his heart for letting down its guard.

Sabrina lost her breakfast. Nobody knew but Lauren, and Lauren didn't question her about the cause. As the one sister who'd never dreamed about husband and family, Sabrina had never given one thought to having a child.

But she'd been there when her father's wives had exhibited all the symptoms. She'd held their heads and emptied the buckets as they'd thrown up. The one thing she'd never anticipated had happened: Colter had given her a child.

The knowledge was there, held close and secret. She wasn't ready to examine her feelings yet, nor share her news. It wasn't shame that held her back, though that would come. Her secret remained secret because it was hers and she didn't want to share it yet.

And there was the matter of her marriage. In her mind she and Colter were married. They had been from the first. It wouldn't have mattered whether they'd had the words said over them or not. That Brother Seaton had, only made the commitment more binding.

Still, Colter was leaving. She'd accepted that from the beginning. It would be as if he were tearing her apart when he left, but she'd survive. And he would never know about the child. She refused to use that as a lever. For she understood that, underneath it all, Colter was an honorable man.

Colter had become a soldier to defend his home and his people. From the beginning, when he could have escaped without harm, he'd put the welfare of his men first. Then when he'd learned about the trouble she and her sisters faced, he'd assumed responsibility for them. Until the time the soldiers came from the fort to make the arrest, Colter could have taken his men away. But he hadn't.

And if he learned that she was carrying a child, he'd assume that responsibility too.

Even now she could see him, that lean, proud face looking down at her, holding back his emotions when his body refused to hold back its need.

"Beautiful," he'd called her. She'd known better, but she'd loved him for thinking that she was, for burying her father, and for understanding her need to follow his dream. She hadn't understood in the beginning what it meant to love a man. Even when he'd kissed her, she'd been slow to know. Then by the lake he'd loved her, before he'd seen her in a dress, before he'd known that she could be a woman.

Quinton Colter hadn't cared about what was on the outside. He'd needed her, and she'd given herself to him because she'd needed him, too. For all her life someone had needed her and she'd given. But Colter was the first to understand and give back.

Oh, yes, she was Mrs. Quinton Colter. She knew,

even if the world didn't know. And she'd carry his child and love it. They'd mine Papa's silver and use that silver to make the world bright and shiny and new.

At noon the next day Sabrina reined in her horse by a clear running stream and announced that they were stopping for a meal. Somewhat surprised, the women quickly prepared the bread and meat they'd brought. On finishing, Sabrina turned to face her little band, surprised to see that somewhere along the way, Flying Cloud had disappeared.

"Is something wrong, Mrs. Colter?" Lieutenant Garland asked, coming to stand beside her.

"No, I'm fine. But I would ask you for your help, Lieutenant Garland. Will you go to the fort and take Colter and the others the fresh clothing we've brought? We will follow slowly, waiting just out of sight of the fort until you send word that the proceedings have begun. I don't want us to arrive before the judge convenes the hearing."

"You understand that this isn't a trial, but a hearing. Even so, you may not be able to attend the proceedings. Military matters are not normally open to civilians."

"I understand," she said over the anguished protests of her sisters.

"Well, you may not be able to see the prisoners," Brother Seaton said, "but we can. Any prisoner is allowed the privilege of spiritual counsel. We will come with you."

Garland looked helplessly around. He didn't know what Sabrina was up to, but he was certain she was up to something. He was equally certain that Captain Holland wasn't going to be pleased. Still, he thought of Colter and his men with genuine regret. They were to be made scapegoats for the entire Confederate Army. He'd sensed it from the beginning, and nothing had occurred to make him change his mind.

Maybe whatever Mrs. Colter had in mind would

work. He and Mrs. Holland certainly hadn't come up with a solution. Even finding Littlejohn with the payroll hadn't completely satisfied the captain. Littlejohn's contention that he was following Colter's party only to look for the missing money was as reasonable a story as Colter's that Littlejohn was an impostor and a thief.

What Garland hadn't said was that civilians who were a party to the proceedings would be called to testify. And even though Colter had disavowed her claim, Mrs. Colter, by her own admission, was a party to the massacre. Garland would do what she asked. After all, it would be better if the men at the fort made a good appearance.

Once the missionaries and Lieutenant Garland were out of sight, Sabrina turned her attention to her plan. "Sisters, this is what we will do. I want each of you to take a pillow and stuff it under your dresses, except for Raven, of course. Where is Raven?"

Mary answered. "She went with Flying Cloud, to watch from a safe place."

"Watch what?" Isabella said crossly. "Watch us poke pillows under our skirts?"

Lauren pulled the pillows from their storage place in the back of the wagon. "Don't be silly, Isabella. Flying Cloud thinks there could be trouble from the Utes."

That was news to Sabrina. "Why?" She answered her own question. "Of course, he thinks that even though they don't approve of Gray Warrior, they may try to rescue him." That was one thing she hadn't counted on, an Indian attack. Maybe that wouldn't happen. After all, Gray Warrior had been held for two weeks and they hadn't tried anything, so far as she knew. Sabrina considered the ramifications of a Ute attack and discarded them. She couldn't worry about that now.

Mary was trying to insert the pillow under her skirt. "Why are we to keep the pillows under our skirts, Sabrina? Are you worried that someone might take them?"

"No!" Isabella snapped. "We're going to sit on them and hatch baby pillows."

"You're both wrong!" Sabrina said, unbuckling her belt and poking the pillow inside before she fastened it again. "Mary, use the waistline. Tie the pillow in place with your apron or your bonnet strings."

"I won't do it," Isabella said. "It makes me look fat."

"That's the idea, sisters. We are all fat. We are all with child."

The three women gasped collectively, then asked, "Why?"

"Because the only chance we'd have at getting soldiers released from prison is because President Lincoln thinks they need to get home and work the fields and take care of their wives and children."

"But we aren't wives," Mary said in bewilderment.

"We know that and the men know that, but the general from Fort Laramie won't know that. Do you think you can act as if you're with child?"

Lauren cut a sharp look at Sabrina. "From what I've seen, I think that calls for us to look a bit green about the gills and throw up our food, doesn't it?"

Sabrina didn't trust herself to answer.

"Of course we can do that," Mary agreed, with a twinkle in her bright eyes. "Am I having a boy or a girl? I think it will be a boy, a tall, studious boy with dark eyes and hair. I'll call him Tyler, Junior, maybe Ty for short. What about you, Isabella?"

"Oh, mine is a girl. She'll have blond curls like mine and big blue eyes. And we'll have a fine house in San Francisco, and a carriage and attend the circus. And I'll call her Regina. That means 'royal.' Papa told me."

"And what about you, Sabrina?" Lauren asked quietly. "What will your baby be?"

"Loved," was her answer. "Now let's look at each other. Do we look like mothers to be?"

Mary giggled. "We do. But, Brina, do you really think they'll believe that we're in the family way? I mean, we didn't look like this at the dinner party."

"They can't be sure. Besides, we were wearing corsets, weren't we?"

"That's true," Mary agreed. "But I never saw a woman with child wearing pants."

"Well, you have now," Sabrina said, and climbed back onto her horse. "Let me do the talking. We're going to tell the judge that our husbands couldn't possibly be guilty of any crimes because they've been with us for months."

Lauren reclaimed her seat and the reins, giving a flick to the horse's backside. "I only hope they believe us, Sabrina."

"They will," she said with a great deal more confidence than she felt. "Because," she said under her breath, "it's the truth. Papa wouldn't want me to lie."

With their first shave in more than two months, and clean clothing that had been delivered by Lieutenant Garland, Colter decided his misfits looked almost human again.

It was midafternoon when Garland opened the cell door and directed them to the captain's quarters, where the hearing was to be held. Escorted by three men on either side, they marched across the compound, wrists handcuffed in front, loaded guns pointed at their backs.

Inside the room where they'd danced, a desk had been set up, behind which Captain Holland and a tall, gray-haired man with whiskers and a tired face now sat.

"Please come forward," the stranger said. "I am General Roger Schumacher, the commander of all the armies in the Colorado territory. I've been sent to hear the charges and make a determination whether or not you will be taken to Fort Leavenworth to stand trial. First, you must swear to tell the truth."

Lieutenant Garland produced a Bible and administered the oath, to which the men pledged their honor.

The general went on. "Please state your name, rank, and your purpose in being in the territory."

"Quinton Colter, captain of the Confederate States of America. These men are a part of my unit, assigned to find weapons, money, and medicine for our troops."

The general made a notation on the paper before him, then lifted his gaze to the other men. In turn each stated his name and assignment, echoing the words of his commanding officer.

"You admit that you were under orders to take supplies, yet you deny that you had anything to do with the massacre of Union troops escorting the payroll from Denver to Fort Collins?"

"We do, sir. We were at that time captured prisoners of war, wounded and bound to a wagon from which we could not escape."

"I see," General Schumacher said. "And you also deny any knowledge of the theft of the second payroll, hidden in your own wagon?"

"We do, sir!" Tyler answered for the others. "And we believe that the facts will prove our story to be true."

Captain Holland intervened. "Mr. Kurtz will be acting as their lawyer, sir."

"Fine. Be seated, and I will hear your testimony one at a time. We'll begin with the first robbery. Captain Holland?"

"Now, Captain Colter. You believe that your man Dane Beckworth, masquerading as Lieutenant Littlejohn, was the man known to Gray Warrior as Long Rifle?"

"I do," Colter, the last man to testify, said firmly. "He spent considerable time in the territory mapping the West for the railroads before the war. He knew Gray Warrior then. In his assignment as point man for our unit, he roamed the area looking for places where we could lie in wait for our prey. He very often disappeared for days before the mission and after. It seems that he was doing as much procuring for himself as he was for the South."

"So you believe that he set up your men to take the blame. Why would he do that?" the general asked.

"He admitted the night of the dance that he was tired of war. We all were. He wanted to go to California, and he thought he had enough money to do it."

"That was the night you contend that you followed him, watched him take the payroll and hide it in your wagon."

"Yes, sir." Colter was beginning to have a bad feeling in the pit of his stomach. What had made him think that anyone would believe him? The truth was that he *could* have set Dane up to be the guilty party. By telling the captain what he'd seen, he hadn't proved Dane's guilt.

"Do you have any questions you'd like to ask?" Captain Holland asked Tyler.

Tyler walked toward Colter, praying that he could find something to support their story. "Captain, let us go back to the massacre for which we were blamed. How did we escape from the wagon? I had a head wound and could barely stay conscious. A bullet passed through Irish's thigh, and Carl had been shot in the shoulder. Except for you, we were all wounded."

"We—I managed to untie the ropes holding me. Then, while the shooting was going on, we climbed the mountain and hid in a cave. The Ute never found us."

"You did all that, Captain, freed four wounded men by yourself, without help?"

If looks could have turned into ammunition, Colter's eyes would have pinned Tyler to the wall and set a barrage of fire through the man.

"I did."

"That's a lie!" A woman's voice contradicted Colter. The general looked up. The room grew silent. All the men were stunned at the sight of four women entering the general's quarters, four women who appeared to be in the family way. It was the auburn-haired woman, wearing the odd-looking man's clothing, who seemed to be speaking for the group.

"I see, and who are you, madam?"

"I'm the person who overheard Long Rifle and

Gray Warrior plot the massacre, and I rescued these—our husbands from the wagon and took them home."

"I'm Mrs. Tyler Kurtz," Mary said, coming to stand beside Tyler, her round little figure even rounder.

Isabella found her spot next to Carl. "And I'm Mrs. Carl Arnstine."

"And I'm Mrs. Irish McBride." Lauren joined the others, her hand cupping her stomach tenderly.

"And you, madam, the angel of mercy who braves the wilderness and snatches wounded men from the face of death, your name is—?"

"I'm Sabrina Alexander Colter. Captain Colter is my husband. We are prepared to make good on any monetary losses the U.S. Army may have suffered. I submit this letter of our financial worth, and I'm here to plead for his release for the sake of his unborn child."

22

Irish couldn't hold back a choked denial. "Captain, I swear, I never touched her. I mean, once I kissed her, but—"

"I know," Colter answered, his own heart thudding with emotion. *With child.* They were all claiming to be with child in order to save his men from prison.

"And you never saw the man called Long Rifle?" the general continued to question Sabrina.

"No, but I heard his voice, and later I recognized it as belonging to the man my husband knew as Dane Beckworth."

"Dane Beckworth," Captain Holland repeated, "Dane Beckworth isn't the man's name, and he's no Johnny Reb either. He's a highly decorated Union officer, the man who will replace me as commander of this fort."

"I'm sorry, Captain Colter," the general said with sincere regret in his voice, "but you understand that the testimony of a man's wife is not allowed in a military hearing. I'm afraid that, given the evidence, there are sufficient grounds to hold you for the possible theft of the second payroll, if not the cold-blooded murder of Union soldiers."

"But General," Sabrina interrupted, "we'll make good any of your earlier losses, and you still have the new payroll. The war is over. Surely you will adhere to President Lincoln's plans to put all the pain and punishment behind." She said a silent thank-you to Henderson Brooks for telling her what the president had suggested.

"These men," she went on, with a dramatic catch in her voice, "are the fathers of our children. We need them at home with us. Colorado needs them."

A pained looked crossed the general's face. "I'm sorry to have to tell you this, Mrs. Colter, but even if we agreed to your offer, President Lincoln is dead, assassinated by an actor called John Wilkes Booth. I'm afraid that our new president, Andrew Johnson, is not as lenient in his views."

A cry of dismay rang out, followed by a stunned silence in the courtroom.

"An actor killed the president?" Isabella finally asked.

"Son of a —" Tyler swallowed his words and looked at Colter.

Sabrina sank down in the nearest chair. She'd lost. Colter had lost. She might not have totally agreed with Lincoln but he was a wise man. Now the men she'd captured would never become husbands. They would be returned to the land from which they had come. They were no longer prisoners of the Alexander women, but prisoners of the army. And it was all her fault for asking them to stay and help her and her sisters. If they'd gone as soon as they were able, none of this would have happened.

Colter stepped forward. "If we are to be tried for a crime we did not commit, I believe it is my right to see my accusers face-to-face."

"You are being accused by the U.S. Army, Captain Colter, and I represent that army," the general said.

"No. It's Dane Beckworth and Gray Warrior I

want to see. I want to look at Dane and have him tell you that I killed those men. It is my right to face him."

"I assure you, Captain, I know nothing about Dane Beckworth. This is highly irregular," the general protested.

"This war was highly irregular," Captain Holland said. "I can't see why we can't honor his request. After all, Lieutenant Littlejohn is still technically under house arrest for the possible theft of the payroll. We don't have to enter his accusation and arrest into the records."

"Very well, Captain Colter. Lieutenant Garland, bring in the Ute and Littlejohn." There was a hint of a smile about the general's face as he waited, watching the door minutely. "I ought to be able to clear this up, once and for all. You see, I know David Littlejohn personally."

Sabrina couldn't pry her gaze away from the general, the man who held their future in his hand. Then, suddenly, the smile on his lips disappeared, and his face took on a look of pure ice.

"Come forward and identify yourself, soldier."

Dane glanced around, immediately picking up on the tension in the room. There were Colter and his men, clean shaven, looking as if they were ordinary citizens. And there were the Alexander women, very round, giving every appearance that they were with child. "What?" he said, frowning at what he was seeing.

"I said," General Schumacher repeated, "give us your name, rank, and unit!"

Sabrina couldn't understand the general's tone. It was as if Dane had suddenly become the accused instead of the about-to-be-released member of the fort's staff of officers.

"My name is Littlejohn, lieutenant, assigned to take command of Fort Collins on Captain Holland's reassignment."

"And where were you last assigned, Lieutenant?" the general asked.

"I was on a secret mission to the West. I am not at liberty to say, sir."

"Nonsense!" the general roared. "Your name is not Littlejohn, and you were not in the West. You, sir, are an impostor."

Dane gave Captain Holland a pleading look. "I don't understand, General. Of course I am. Captain Holland has my orders."

"Orders issued to Littlejohn giving him command, yes. I don't doubt that, for I issued them—not to you. Where is Littlejohn?"

"I believe I can answer that," a man standing in the doorway said as he came forward.

"Wiley! From the trading post," Sabrina whispered. What in God's name was he doing here? All they needed was Flying Cloud and Henderson Brooks, and the entire scope of her acquaintances would be present.

"Who in hell are you and how'd you get in here?" Captain Holland asked.

"I'm Wiley Smith and it wasn't easy," the man answered. "Your aides wouldn't even tell you I was here."

Lucy Holland joined Wiley in the doorway. "In fact, he had to come to me with his story. I thought you ought to hear it, so I brought him." They moved toward the general's desk.

The general stood. "Everybody step back. Give Mrs. Holland and this man room. I'm beginning to feel like I'm being smothered by people, Now, you, Mr. Smith. What can you tell us about this situation?"

"I operate Wiley's Trading Post. At the same time the troops were massacred at Cedar Bend, a body was discovered in the woods. The man was missing the last joint of one finger. Would that be your Lieutenant Littlejohn."

"It would," the general agreed. "Who killed him?"

"Since nobody saw it happen, I can't say for sure. But I do know that he was a stranger in the territory, and the man who is now impersonating him is not."

"You know this man?" The general inclined his head at Dane and awaited Wiley's reply.

"I do. He was a member of Colter's misfits, the band of Confederate guerrillas who had been operating in the West for several months."

"And how do you know this?"

"Because I was their contact in the territory. General Lee sent me here early on, to establish a supply line that could get goods back to the South. I am turning myself in as a Rebel sympathizer."

At that piece of information a silence fell over the room as its inhabitants looked at each other in disbelief. Now it made sense to Sabrina, why Wiley had been so generous in his prices for their supplies. He was helping his fellow Confederates.

The door opened suddenly and two soldiers entered, escorting Gray Warrior, who was shackled and handcuffed. The Indian, wearing blue uniform trousers and military boots, glanced around, then gave out a shriek of fury as he advanced toward Dane, grabbing him by the throat.

"Long Rifle, I curse you to a painful death!"

"Get him off me!" Dane yelled. "He's the one. Gray Warrior killed your escorts. He and his men, not me. All I wanted was the gold. I didn't mean for anybody to be hurt."

Even cuffed and shackled, it took four enlisted men to pull Gray Warrior away from Dane.

After order had been restored, Captain Holland walked over to Gray Warrior and studied him carefully, starting with his face and moving down to his feet, where his gaze remained.

"Of course. Now I recognize these boots. They belonged to one of the men guarding the payroll. Nobody else had engraved boots. Take him away."

General Schumacher and Captain Holland conferred for a moment; then the general turned back to face the prisoners. "Captain Colter, it appears that Dane Beckworth is Long Rifle, the man who directed the massacre. Whether or not he will be held responsible for the murders remains to be seen. Gray Warrior and his men will be imprisoned until we receive directions from Washington."

Captain Holland nodded as the general continued. "But we have decided that, in the absence of firm guidelines for the disposition of prisoners, and because there seems to be great doubt that your men are in fact guilty of any of the charges for which you were arrested, we are going to release all of you.

"And, since birth seems imminent," Captain Holland added, barely holding back a smile, "we remand you into the custody of your wives."

The decision was met with a scream of joy by Isabella, who flung herself into Carl's arms, a quiet smile of approval from Mary, and an awkward moment of waiting by Lauren before Irish held out his hand.

"There's only one thing wrong here," the Irishman said. "And I wouldn't want the rest of our lives to start out with a lie, General Schumacher."

"Oh? What's that—Mr. McBride, is it?"

"It's Irish, sir, and the truth is, we ain't married. It was just a plot, thought up by these colleens to get us off. It wouldn't be right to tell you that there's to be a babe if there isn't."

"Don't worry about that for a moment, Mr. McBride," Mrs. Holland said. "Come in here, Brother Seaton and Brother William. I've already had a talk with these men of God, and they're prepared to hold a wedding this very evening."

"No!" Sabrina said, coming to her feet. "No, this is wrong."

"Oh?" Colter stepped toward his wife. "Why would that be, *wife*? Don't you want your sisters to have a proper religious ceremony?"

"Of course, but it was wrong of us to try to keep you and your men. I formally release you. You are no longer my prisoners. You may return to the lives you left behind."

Colter continued to advance, Sabrina retreating with every step he made. "So you release us, do you? Do you hear that, men? You're free to go. Do you want to leave?"

"Me?" Carl said. "Not me. Isabella is still learning to play poker."

"Not me," Tyler said. "The trust my father left has mounted up in the months we've been at war. After I arrange for part of it to be used to restore our home, Mary and I will be off for England."

"What about you, Irish?" Colter said, his voice as cold and stiff as a weather vane in an ice storm.

"It's like this, Captain, there's the matter of the little people. They're waiting back there in the valley, and I have a hankering to hear their music again before Miss Lauren and I head for Texas."

"Sorry, Mrs. Colter, I guess none of the men are interested in returning to the land of their birth. You captured us, you're stuck with us."

"But—"

"Now, about that wedding, Brother Seaton," he went on, "do you think you could say the words again for Quinton Colter and Sabrina Alexander? I've got a hankering for any children we have to have the right name, my name."

Sabrina didn't remember fainting. She wasn't a wilting kind of woman, and she was certainly inexperienced in using feminine wiles to manipulate. In fact, in all her life she'd never considered that she even could. Now she'd already done it twice, and as she slid into that hazy, protective cocoon of escape, her last thought was that Colter couldn't possibly know the truth of what he was saying.

As Colter caught her in his arms, he knew that he wasn't going anywhere; he was home. All the pain and loneliness was gone. He'd been changed by this determined woman who, in the midst of a loving family, had created her own hiding place, who needed love as much as he. By giving to him she'd filled his emptiness with a sense of belonging that he'd never expected to feel again. As he looked down into her beautiful face, it came to him that, somewhere, somebody was playing bagpipes.

Colter smiled.

* * *

As it turned out, the wedding was postponed. Mrs. Holland decided that she needed time to prepare a proper banquet. Then the fort store had to be turned into a chapel, and the women had to have time to prepare themselves for the ceremony.

By two o'clock the following afternoon, the attendees began to assemble. There were the enlisted men and the laundresses, clean and starched and glowing, as invited guests. Flying Cloud and the members of his tribe arrived on horseback and on foot, wearing their ceremonial dress and bringing gifts.

Raven, the only Alexander sister not taking part in the joining, was wearing a creamy dress made of antelope skin, and a cape lined with the same white skin. On her feet were boots of white fur, embroidered with turquoise. On this day it seemed her transformation from her white family to her Indian ancestors was complete, and Sabrina knew that they'd lost her to her mother's people.

As the sisters dressed, Sabrina peered listlessly through the window at the landscape. A sudden warm spell had turned the mountains in the distance into carpets of blooming wildflowers. The sun, high in the sky for most of the morning, warmed the air. By noon the clouds began sliding over the mountain, swallowing up the brightness. The temperature rose and the air felt heavy.

"Oh, it's going to rain," Mary said, looking out at the sky.

"Not until after the wedding," Isabella said confidently. "I'm certain of it."

Sabrina turned to face her sisters. "Are you sure this is what you want, to marry these men?"

It was Lauren who took away the last of Sabrina's doubts. "Oh, yes, Brina. Don't you see, it was meant to be. Why else would you have found them? Brought them to the valley?"

"Because I wasn't thinking clearly at the time," Sabrina said harshly. "I still don't know why I did it."

Mary walked over to her sister and put her arm around her. "Ah, Brina, why do you make it so hard? No, you weren't thinking, you were feeling. For once you acted with your heart instead of your mind. Why are you fighting what you feel?"

"Because—because, I'm not sure. This is all very strange, very powerful, very frightening."

"Posh!" Isabella said, whirling around so that the skirt of her new dress twirled out, revealing her ankles and her new white leather shoes. "You're crazy about the man. He's crazy about you. And you can't tell me that you haven't already allowed him the liberties of a husband. It practically shows when you're together."

Sabrina dropped the hairbrush she was holding, splitting the silence with its thud. Isabella was right. She was crazy about Quinton Colter. Right now it was all she could do to keep herself from going in search of the man who called himself her husband.

Ah, Papa, what am I do to? Send me a sign. Help me!

"Rain," Raven said as she entered the room, slipping her robe from her shoulders. "Soft, warm rain. Flying Cloud says that it comes to clear away the spirits and kiss the flowers. Just for you, my sisters, to make your day new and clean."

And then Sabrina understood. Warm rain, falling on the prairie, in a place where life was demanding and hard. Warm rain, for Colter, to bring softness to his life—to their life.

She rose from her place by the window and retrieved her parcel, revealing the dress she'd ordered in Boulder City, the silver dress she'd wear for Colter.

"Sabrina!" Mary said in surprise. "You're going to wear a silver dress to be married in?"

"I am." She began to wash herself in the pan of water Mrs. Holland had sent. Finally, when she was satisfied that the scent of wildflowers anointed her body, she pulled on her stockings and shoes, then stepped into her drawers and her petticoat.

The sisters watched her odd manner of dressing in

amazement. "But sister," Lauren asked with worry in her voice, "what about your chemise, your—"

"I'm not wearing anything else." Sabrina stepped into the dress and motioned for Raven to button it. After years of wool underwear, the silkiness of the fabric felt strange against her skin. Moments later she was ready, turning to allow her sisters to see her wedding dress.

Isabella took in a quick gasp of air.

Mary shook her head in wonder.

Lauren didn't know what to say. "Don't you think that might be a little scandalous?"

"Absolutely," Sabrina agreed. "A scandal in silver, for the man who will mine the Silver Dream."

With her russet hair falling across her shoulders in a mass of wild color against the silver garment, Sabrina looked like fire and ice. Her sisters knew that she was even more beautiful than she'd been the night of the dinner party.

But it wasn't simply the dress—it was the sparkle in Sabrina's hazel eyes. They were almost green tonight, like the lichen-covered rocks beside the hot springs they'd passed once on their way across the Colorado mountains.

Finally Lauren said, "Colter will be speechless."

"No," Sabrina said softly, "Colter will be the father of my children, my husband. Husbands, the real treasure Papa sent us."

The rain had stopped. Now the grooms waited inside the store, dressed in their new clothing, on edge and ready for whatever was coming.

"Are you sure you want to marry Isabella, Carl?" Colter asked the saloon keeper nobody ever thought would settle down.

"Got to, no choice. I owe her too much money."

"Owe her too much money?" Irish questioned. "How's that?"

"When I said I'd teach her how to play poker, I didn't know she'd be better at it than me."

"I saw you playing last night," Tyler said with a grin. "It wasn't skill, it was that low-cut dress that did you in. That and a few kisses that might have gone just a bit too far."

"You're wrong," Carl protested. "I've looked at more women's bosoms than you'll ever see, in many towns, in many card games. This woman is special, and nobody is going to play with her except me."

Irish chuckled. No matter what Carl said, he knew that the man was head over heels in love with the beautiful Isabella. She'd likely lead him a merry chase, but Carl would go willingly.

Marrying Lauren was another story. He still couldn't figure how a petite, beautiful woman like Lauren would even consider an oaf like him. He'd spent most of the night worrying about it, fearing that she was going along with the ceremony to make certain that her sisters got their wishes. It wasn't until sunrise, when he'd finally walked down to the river that flowed past the rear of the fort, that he'd allowed himself to be convinced.

She'd followed him, and he'd been so deep in his thoughts that he hadn't even known she was there. "Mr. McBride? Irish?"

"What? Miss Lauren, what are you doing out here in your—your—"

"Cape and slippers? I saw you walk away, and I felt that you were troubled. I would not want to force you into an unwanted arrangement. If you want to refuse my wish to become your wife, you have only to say the words."

"Not want to marry you? Oh, Miss Lauren, you can't know how much I want to be your husband. But you must be certain. There are so many men who would better suit."

Lauren had taken Irish's hand and pulled him down on a grassy spot behind a clump of rocks. "I find that I'm cold, Mr. McBride. Will you let me sit close to you?"

Awkwardly Irish had slipped his arm around Lauren, catching his breath as she leaned against him, resting her head on his chest and pulling the cape across both their knees.

"Now, that's better. In fact, if you'd lean back and put your other arm around me, it would be just perfect."

She had reached for Irish's hand and pulled it beneath her cape, planting it squarely on her breast at the same time she maneuvered her bottom until she was sitting in his lap, the heat between her legs planted squarely against that part of Irish's body that was embarrassing him with its burgeoning response.

"Miss Lauren, what are you doing?"

"Don't I give you pleasure, Irish? I thought that you would like it. I do. I like it very much. I suspect that Sabrina and Colter have already sampled the marriage bed, and I envy her. Is it wrong for me to let you know that I find you desirable?"

All rational thought had flown from his mind, and there by the river, out of sight of the fort, Irish learned that when a woman makes up her mind, she always gets what she wants. The rest of the morning he'd gone around with a grin on his face that made kissing the Blarney stone seem like an everyday occurrence.

Tyler had seen Irish and Lauren as they walked back to the parade ground. There's been no mistake about the love in their eyes. He'd envied Irish his secret meeting with Lauren. He'd wished he'd been with Mary. But their time would come. Mary didn't know it yet, but he intended to show her the world. But he'd protect her gentle innocence. And when they'd tired of travel, he had a notion to return to his home along the ocean in Carolina. There was a country to rebuild, a wounded people to heal. With Mary beside him, to give him roots, he was considering doing what he could to make it right again. He could never have done that without Mary, without her firm convictions that he was a man of destiny. Today they'd be joined, and finally, for the first time in a long time, he'd have a reason to restore the life he'd once lived. Pain from the past and promise from the present. Tyler and Mary—the future.

Colter was the most nervous. He was about to take a step he'd never thought to do. Was it right? Was it fair? He'd paced for half the night, snapping at anybody who tried to ask what was wrong, finally resorting at daybreak to saddling a horse and riding out into the mountains, where he sat and watched the day and the night argue until, finally, the darkness slunk away behind the mountain ridge.

With the light came the sound of birds, the re-emergence of the prairie dogs on the plains beneath, and the movement of deer toward the river, where they would drink. The world was alive. And he knew that his decision was right. A sense of peace settled over him as he watched the day arrive, full and bright. In spite of war and pain and death, this proud land with its stark mountains and endless fields of waving grass endured.

Like Sabrina.

Sabrina, the woman he would join his life with, share his bed with and his sorrows. He'd always thought she was like the land, strong and determined. Now he knew that she was also like its storms—wild, passionate, and free. Marriage would never change that. He wouldn't want it to. Together they would bond, merging the power of their strength, allowing their desire to prevent the icy coldness of being alone ever to form again.

He'd thought they'd go to California, but he understood now, here on the mountain, that they were part of Colorado, this territory that had become heaven when he looked through the eyes of love.

The women remained inside their quarters for most of the day. Just before the ceremony the rain stopped, and periodically the sun peeked through the clouds. The time had come for the ceremony. Colter donned his new clothes, the vest of black with silver threads, his shiny leather boots, and his black frock coat. With the other grooms he filed out of the guard-house to the store.

Inside, Mrs. William was directing the service.

"Oh, Captain Colter, yours was our first wedding in this new land, and now you're repeating those vows again. It is only fitting. You will stand over here."

"Mrs. William," Irish said hesitantly, "I'm worried about saying my part right."

"Not Mrs. William," she said, "from now on I'm Mrs. Bartholomew, Grace Bartholomew, and don't worry, I'll help you."

Not only was this new land giving Colter's men a new life, it was giving Mrs. Bartholomew the courage to claim her own identity. But Colter wasn't certain that Grace would ever be known as anything but Mrs. William. Colter and Tyler were directed to one side of the draped packing crate used as an altar, with Irish and Carl on the other.

One of the soldiers began to play his mouth organ. Another fiddled a solemn tune as the ceremony was ready to begin. Outside, on the porch and gathered around the building, were the Indians, the soldiers, and the families who considered this wedding a part of all their lives. Inside were Flying Cloud, Raven, Captain and Mrs. Holland, Lieutenant Garland, and General Schumacher.

The first bride to appear in the doorway was Mary, in her dress of blush rose, holding a single flower tied with a rose-colored ribbon. Tyler met her halfway down the aisle and took her arm.

Wearing a white dress embroidered with blue and gold flowers, Isabella looked like an angel shimmering in the light that split the clouds and shone through the doorway. When Carl took her hand, an aura of happiness surrounded them.

Lauren was next, wearing a yellow dress with inserts of lace and roses. Beside Irish she looked little more than a girl. Irish held her carefully, still in awe of what she'd given him in the early light of morning, his face filled with love.

And then there was Sabrina, blinding the eyes of the guests in an outrageous dress of silver and pearls. She moved forward, with purpose in her step and merriment in her eyes. Gone was the indecision, the pale face, the uncertainty. Colter could only fill his eyes with her beauty, her strength, her passion.

Brother Seaton stepped forward, his Bible open to the scripture he'd chosen, which he read and followed with a prayer. His "amen" was echoed by Flying Cloud from his place by the door. As Brother Seaton concluded, not one of the couples could have coherently repeated what he'd said. To Sabrina it had been something about a burning bush. To Colter the minister had mentioned Moses leading his people. Isabella knew it was about a woman who followed her husband into a strange land. Only Mary knew the woman was called Ruth.

"Now," Brother William said, "repeat after me, using your own name. I *William*, take thee, *Grace*, to be my wedded wife ..."

Mrs. Bartholomew picked up the next vow with, "I, *Grace*, take thee, *William*—"

Brother Seaton ended the ceremony with, "I now pronounce you man and wife. You may kiss your brides."

Carl let out an exuberant cry of celebration as he swung Isabella into the air, then kissed her soundly. Tyler's compliance was soulful and sincere. Irish shyly planted his lips on Lauren's, then drew back at the smattering of applause. But it was Colter who held back nothing, hungrily capturing Sabrina's mouth and ravishing it without hesitation.

Afterward the couples and guests were served a banquet of wild turkey, rice, tender new greens, canned peaches, and cream. The wedding cake was unexpected, as were the tiny carved figures, a gift from Flying Cloud, adorning the top. Following the meal, the same orchestra from that first dinner party struck up the music, and before the night was over, every man in the fort who wished to do so had claimed at least one dance with a bride.

Finally, Captain Holland broke open the champagne and proposed a toast to "the four brides and the men they rescued and took to heart. May your lives prosper wherever life takes you."

Amid much laughter and backslapping, the couples were escorted to private quarters prepared for each of them. The party-goers carried on, the men dancing now with each other when Mrs. Holland and Raven finally pleaded exhaustion. The champagne was consumed. Fresh musicians replaced tired ones, and the night grew late.

Raven finally slipped away, finding her own sleeping place in the camp of her grandfather. She found him beyond the fort, standing on a ridge looking up into the mountains.

"What bothers you, Grandfather?"

"I am growing old. More and more I feel a pull to the lands of my father's past."

"I know. You have told me of your people and their journey to the lands in the South among the mountains. But you were just a boy."

"I know, my child. But there is a place I must tell you about someday, a place of great treasure. There may come a time when you will need to know, when our people will claim it again."

"Me, Grandfather?"

"Yes, you. I have seen it, my bird with wings to move through the darkness. Soon you will make a long journey."

Grandfather often hinted at a mysterious future. It was the way of the great chiefs, to interpret their dreams. This time, though the night air wasn't cold, Raven shivered. She believed in her grandfather's visions. She believed that there were times when the spirits sent their warm breath across the plains. Glancing up at the sky, she noticed that it was growing heavy once more with rain.

"Come, Grandfather. Let us go back. We must leave in the morning for the valley where our people camp."

"Yes," he said, and started down the hill. Then he stopped and faced the sky. "Look, Raven, rain falls across the moon, like streaks of war paint."

"Or tears," Raven said. "The heavens are crying tears of happiness."

23

"You were going to give up your mine to cover our thefts?" Colter's voice was low and tight. He stood just inside the door.

"If need be."

"Why?"

"Because we agreed, the four of us."

Sabrina walked to the fire and pretended to study the low flames while she waited for Colter to move closer, to say something to ease the tension. He didn't. She was suddenly uncertain, on edge, and she didn't like that.

"Couldn't we talk about that tomorrow, Colter?"

"We could."

He still didn't come any closer.

She had to do something to reach him, to get past the sudden awkwardness that had come between them. "Then would you mind stepping back outside for just a moment while I . . ."

Colter considered her request, then complied. He was still stunned by what she'd offered. She—no, they—were willing to give up the Silver Dream to secure his freedom, and his men's. He didn't know what to say. Maybe they both needed a moment. Though he and Sabrina had been as close as two people could be, he understood that a woman might have some feminine ablutions to make before a new husband was allowed in her bed.

Husband. That word took his thoughts in another direction. Maybe they'd moved too fast. Maybe he ought to go out that front door and just keep on going. Then he heard her moving about and knew that he couldn't leave.

He didn't want to go. And he had no intention of allowing her to give up her dream to protect them. If there were repercussions to his past deeds, he'd find another way to solve them.

Colter listened to the music still coming from the ballroom. He tapped his feet, both in impatience and in time to the music. With any luck nobody would enter the corridor and find him leaning against the wall like some nervous bridegroom waiting for his bride.

His bride. Colter smiled.

Inside the bedroom Sabrina quickly removed her drawers, her petticoat, and her stockings. She'd left off the corset and chemise when she'd dressed. Now she was ready.

"Come in, Colter," she called out.

Once more he entered and leaned against the door.

He hadn't known what to expect, but the silhouette of Sabrina's body outlined by the fire was a surprise. He couldn't move.

"Are you planning to stay over there all night?"

"I hadn't thought about it," he said lazily. "What did you have in mind?"

"Damned if I know!" she snapped. "I mean, hellfire, this is our wedding night. Don't you want to—I mean—I thought there were certain expectations of a bridegroom."

"Tsh! Tsh! Damn? Hell? You sound impatient, Mrs. Colter."

"Don't be silly. I'm just a bit overwrought, I ex-

pect. I never got married before. I mean not to anybody but you. And heck, that wasn't really a wedding."

"I'm very glad you never got married to anyone
but me."

She couldn't stop herself from looking at him,
from taking in the proud beauty of the man she'd just
promised to honor and obey. Standing there with the
firelight playing across his finely chiseled face, he was
the most noble man she'd ever seen. There was something heroic about him, much like the gods in those
myths Papa had always favored.

I'm very glad. Could he actually mean that?

"Would you like some more champagne?" he
asked, coming to stand beside a chest by the fireplace.
"To relax you."

"No, I'm afraid I've already had too much. Besides, it doesn't relax me, it only makes me feel giddy."

He turned so that he was facing her, their lips almost close enough to touch. "But no more fainting?"

She blushed and dropped her gaze. "No."

"No more swinging your skirts to show your legs
to the rest of the world?"

Sabrina gasped. "Does that mean I can never
dance again?"

"Only for me, Sabrina Colter, only for me."

She began to hum along with the sound of the har-
monica, swaying in time with the music.

"Damned right, only for me."

"Why, Captain Colter, such language."

She was driving him crazy. "Where are your petticoats, Sabrina?"

"I took them off. Haven't you noticed?"

He lifted her chin. "Of course I have. Was that
what you wanted?"

"No! I mean yes!" Blue eyes caught hers and
melded, holding her with such heated intensity that she
couldn't move. The room grew warmer. The haunting
tune swirled inside her head, adding a different kind of
heat.

"Why, Sabrina? You know how beautiful you are.

I've told you. There could be no misunderstanding about what's between us. Why the elaborate ruse? I'm ashamed of you, allowing your sisters to plead that they were with child."

"It seemed to be a good idea. I thought that Captain Holland was a reasonable man. He wouldn't want to be responsible for leaving four women alone at such a time."

"Of course not."

"And your men love my sisters, don't they?"

"We agree on that. But what does that have to do with what you aren't wearing underneath that dress?"

"I thought that you—that I—I wanted you to want me, Colter. You said you'd buy me a silver dress. I—I intended to make you stay because you really want to."

"I see. And was there more to this plan?" he asked.

"Only this," she said. She stepped back and began to unbutton her gown. Colter felt as if a red-hot poker had branded his manhood, eliciting frissons of heat that zinged outward through his body like fire.

He wasn't touching her, but his very skin was burning. His throat was parched and tight. His fingers formed fists, and his pulse was racing so fast that he could feel the thunder in his head.

Letting the front edges of the dress fall from her shoulders, she stood before him as it shimmered down her bare body like a sheen of mist falling away from the moon.

Sabrina Colter smiled at her husband and reached for his collar, unbuttoning and removing the offensive object. The buttons of his shirt were released, and moments later she peeled the trousers and his underdrawers down his legs, allowing his body the freedom to announce its desire to the woman who was kneeling only inches away.

"Sabrina—"

She brushed aside his attempt to lift her, instead planting her mouth across his stomach and down the taut muscles in his thigh. Slowly, with exquisitely sen-

sual nips with her teeth, and kisses, she moved down
his legs until she encountered the top of his boots.

"I want them off," she said, coming to her feet.
"Will you help me?"

He thought he agreed, though he couldn't be certain of anything except that he was on fire. Moments
later he was on the bed, his feet bare, his erection
throbbing painfully. Under other conditions he might
have tried to cover himself, to protect the lady from
the sight of that part of a man's body that might prove
offensive. But Sabrina was having no part of that.

After she'd satisfied her mouth and tongue on his
skin, she moved toward the source of his body's heat,
working her way around it with her fingertips as she
lowered her head.

"Sabrina," he groaned, "you shouldn't do this."

"Why? Are we not one being now? As the wife,
doesn't my body belong to you and your body belong
to me?"

"Of course, but I never knew a woman to take
that literally."

"You've never had a wife like me before, Quinton
Colter. And I intend to see that you never have another." She took him inside her slick, hot mouth, surrounding him with her scent and touch. And he knew
at that moment that she was branding him, she was
imprinting him with herself. He belonged to her for all
time, even if nobody but he could see the mark with
which she'd claimed him.

Then, just as he was ready to explode, she lifted
her head, inched forward and kissed him. He could
taste the musky sent of himself in her mouth, the soft
moisture that lubricated the shy intrusion of her
tongue. His hands found her nipples, now tightened
into heated beads.

Her wild mane of mahogany-colored hair fell
across him, teasing his skin as it shimmered against his
chest. Under such sweet torment Colter's body began
to move in protest, undulating against her, announcing
its need.

Then she drew back and gazed down at him, desire shortening her breath and turning her hazel eyes into piercing orbs of heat.

"*Mrs. Colter,*" she whispered. "I never thought to be married. I never thought to take a husband, never knew what it would mean to feel this overpowering need."

"Nor did I."

"But I thought that men—that you—"

"That we didn't fall in love? That we couldn't belong to one woman? You're wrong, my darling wife."

Every part of her throbbed, with pleasure, with pain.

Colter's fingers slid down between them, past his own insistent organ caught between them and nestled now in the vee between her legs.

As he sought and found the nub of her pleasure, she shuddered. "Colter?"

"It's only fair, darling. I want to give you a new life, a new world, pleasure such as you have never known."

Her thighs quivered and the slick dampness sucked at his hand, then opened wider to allow his long finger to enter. "Ohhh! Stop, Colter, stop before I—before it's too late."

"Then match your pleasure, take me inside as you have taken my fingers." He could scarcely speak, so tense was his body, so ready to explode. Then, as she understood what he was asking, she raised up and took him inside her, one pleasurable second at a time, until at last she was totally impaled.

She started to move.

"No! Stop! Don't move!"

Sabrina gasped and stopped her motion, holding herself in tight control. But squeezing back the spasms didn't halt the ripple of sensation that had already begun deep inside, that roiling upward like the rumble of a geyser that refused to subside.

"I'm sorry, Colter. I can't stop it. You too, together."

And Colter knew that was the way it would be. As he felt himself being torn apart by the power of his climax, he knew that was the way it would always be. Mindless shudders turned into waves of pleasure. Two strong people who'd never expected to find each other were joined equally in their hearts and with their bodies.

He lifted her and moved her beside him in the bed, taking her in his arms and holding her close. They lay in each other's arms, sated, drained, as if they were floating on clouds of velvet just above the bed for a long time.

"Tomorrow," he finally said, "we'll head back to the valley. We have to get the mine operating as quickly as possible so that your sisters won't have to wait for their shares."

"I don't understand, Colter."

"I'm afraid, my darling, that by bringing me into your life, you traded away your sisters. Irish has his heart set on a farm in Texas. And Carl and Isabella are headed for San Francisco. I'd hoped that at least one of them would stay, but Tyler wants to take Mary to England. That just leaves us to mine the Silver Dream."

"And Raven. The cabin in the valley is her home, Colter."

"Of course. But Raven seems to be destined for another kind of life. I have the feeling that she'll spend much of her time with her grandfather, Flying Cloud."

"She always has," Sabrina admitted. "But she'll be with us when she chooses, even if the others are gone."

"Will you hate losing your sisters?"

"I'll hate losing them, but I'll never hate finding you. But you'd better know, Colter, our silver is pure, probably the best find in the West since the Comstock Lode. We're going to be filthy rich."

"I can handle that, at least for now, wife. But I think you'd better know that I don't know a thing about mining silver."

"And I don't know a thing about having a child, Colter. I guess we both can learn." She grew very still.

"A child?" he asked, almost in a whisper.

"It's much too early to be sure. But Bessie had

what she called 'light-headed spells' when she was with
child, and her stomach was often unsettled."

"Then that's why you fainted."

"I did not faint," she protested. "I just wanted you
to put your arms around me and hold me close."

Colter tightened his arms around her, holding her
tight against him, fanning the ever-simmering heat in
his loins to new life.

"What about what we just did? It didn't hurt you,
did it?"

"Hurt? Heavens, no. It was wonderful." The room
was completely dark. Colter let her go, moved to his
feet, and padded naked to the fireplace. Taking a splinter of wood, he inserted it into the coals until it caught,
then lit the oil lamp by their bed.

"What are you doing?" she asked, making a move
to cover herself.

"No. I want to see you. I want to learn your body
so that I can know every change that will come." He
pitched the splinter into the fireplace, added a log, and
moved back to the bed, his eyes now a hot, smoky
gray.

Sabrina felt her muscles relax, and she uncrossed
her arms to give him free access to her body.

He knelt beside her, touching his hand reverently
to her stomach, then moved slowly up to her breasts,
clasping them gently in his hands. Her nipples, at first
relaxed in flaccid, dusky rose patches of color, puck-
ered, turning dark and hard under his gaze.

"So beautiful," he said, touching them gently with
his mouth.

"You don't have to say that, Colter. I don't need
compliments."

"But I need to give them," he said. "I need to let
it spill over, the feelings you've thawed, feelings you've
brought back to life. Can you understand that?"

"I love you," was all she said, her nerves dancing
like the flickering flames across the dry log Colter had
thrown into the fireplace.

He whispered an endearment that she didn't understand, then raised himself so that he could look

down at her. "I don't know all the right words, Sabrina. In fact, I'm almost afraid to speak for fear of saying the wrong ones, but I want you to know that I love you."

"I know. Words don't matter, Colter. We don't need them. Leave those to Tyler and Carl, who can speak their minds. Just share my life, Colter, be there for me, be my partner."

He kissed her breasts, allowing his tongue to work a busy little circle around her nipple, worrying it into a state of arousal. "Does this mean that you don't intend to obey me?"

"Depends on what the order is."

"No order, Brina—request. I love you, and I want you to always be beside me, in my bed, in my life. Just love me back."

Sabrina shivered and reached for Colter, pulling him over her. "Oh, yes. That's one request I approve of, husband." She felt him respond, throbbing against her. Sabrina ran her fingers down his back, relishing his firm body and his muscular thighs. They were so close that their mouths were touching, the hair on his chest caressed her breasts as he breathed. It was almost as if they were one person.

And then he was inside her and the joining was complete. He pulled back, heard Sabrina gasp, and felt her hands pulling him back again. This time he slid his hands beneath her and held her buttocks, moving her in unison with him until he felt her gasp and the muscles deep inside her tighten and begin a rippling dance of release.

"Oh, yes, Colter," she said in breathless spurts, "I like your requests."

"And I yours," he said in a low voice as he collapsed against her, "especially those that you make with your body."

"Will it always be like this, Colter?"

"Probably not. There'll be times when you'll want to kill me. You might even try."

She turned suddenly serious. "Papa said that sometimes we walk a fine line between love and hate. We just have to make sure our steps know which path to take."

"Then let's always walk toward each other, Sabrina Alexander Colter. We have silver to mine and a city to build."

He pulled her back into his arms and held her, pulling the covers over them. The wedding guests had long gone. The fort was silent. Then they heard it, rain splattering the roof and the windows.

"Colter," Sabrina whispered, "listen. Warm rain at midnight."

About the Author

SANDRA CHASTAIN is the bestselling, award-winning
thor of 32 romances. She lives in Smyrna, Georgia.

Next from Sandra Chastain—

THE REDHEAD
AND THE PREACHER

on sale in summer of 1995

The following is a preview of this
wonderfully entertaining new romance. . . .

Afterward, McKenzie Kathryn Calhoun consoled herself with the thought that she didn't intend to commit a crime the day she took part in robbing the Bank of Promise, Kansas.

But the morning it happened, it wouldn't have done her any good to claim innocence. It was far too late. The people in Promise had long ago given up on the rangy, red-haired girl who wore men's clothes, avoided town as much as possible, and called herself Macky. By that time she was considered as peculiar as her father and as wild and out-of-control as her shiftless brother had been.

Had she been anybody else, they might have shown some consideration over her having buried her father one day and learning the next that her brother Todd, hadn't shown up for the funeral because he'd dealt himself four aces in a crooked poker game. There was nothing unusual about that, except this time he'd been stabbed to death by the man who caught him.

Macky could have told them that she had had to sell her father's horse to pay for his funeral and her own horse to pay for her brother's, but nobody asked. All she had left the day of the holdup was a worthless farm with the mortgage due. Her plan that morning to confront the banker might fail, but it was the only one she had.

The year was 1860. The month was April, the time of year when spring crops were planted, though not on Calhoun land in Promise, Kansas. It's fitting, Macky thought, that snow fell last night, scalloping the prairie with white ruffles like the fading memory of frothy waves back home in Boston Harbor. Like everything else in her life, even the earth seemed to be moving away from her. She closed her eyes for a moment, stilling the spinning in her mind.

It was easier to wear the clothes she'd need than to

carry them. She rolled up her only dress in her bedroll, along with the last of the cheese and bread.

Then she donned a pair of Todd's underwear that she'd cut off and hemmed, two of his shirts, his trousers, and his work boots, stuffed with rags so that she could keep them on. Instead of the braid she normally used to restrain her unruly mass of red hair, she tucked it beneath the felt hat that Papa had worn since the day he left his job as a schoolteacher back east.

Macky never had cared much about looking like a woman, but today even Papa wouldn't have recognized the washed-out shell of a person she'd become. With her mother's cameo tucked into the pocket of Papa's coat, she mounted the mule and started into town.

As she rode away she looked around. There was nothing else of value left to be disposed of; no more livestock, no food supplies, nothing except a run-down house ready to collapse in the wake of the next windstorm. If her father hadn't died of heart problems, he'd have died of starvation, for there was no money left for seed that wouldn't grow.

The only thing that gave her pause was leaving her father's books. Carrying them would have been a sentimental gesture only, for she'd memorized them all long ago.

Today was Friday, payroll day for the banker's cowhands. She had better hurry if she was going to catch the man before he left for his ranch. As she rode she rehearsed her plea to the smart-talking moneyman who'd sold her gentle, scholarly father a worthless piece of land where nothing would grow but rattlesnakes and sagebrush.

If the banker-turned-land dealer refused to buy back the land, Macky would sell her mother's cameo for enough money to buy a ticket on the noon stage heading for Denver. The brooch was the last thing of any value, that and a mule so ornery no one would buy him.

Macky gave little thought about what she'd do next, other than going west. Denver had to be better than Promise, Kansas. She would sign on as a farmer, or maybe a miner. Anything physical that would take away the pain of remembering.

About a mile outside of town, a hawk swooped down, clasped a frightened jackrabbit in his talons, and flew away. The sound of his wings spooked the mule, which stepped into a gopher hole, and bolted. He deposited Macky in the middle of the trail and, braying at the top of his lungs, took off with her bedroll, bellowing his displeasure

Macky let out an oath, ending with, "The Lord giveth and the Lord taketh away." She was still cursing when four hard-riding men crested the hill and came to a stop where she'd fallen. One man was leading a horse with an empty saddle.

"Looks like you got trouble, boy!" The stranger who seemed to be the leader glanced at the disappearing mule, then moved closer. He hadn't shaved in days, but the beard didn't cover the fresh wound that ran from his hairline across his forehead to the top of his ear. His ugly face was going to get uglier if the wound healed and left a scar.

Boy? One look at the cold expression in his eyes made Macky decide that being a boy at this point was much safer than being a girl. She nodded and came to her feet.

"What's your name, son"

"McKenzie," she answered in the deepest voice she could manage.

"Heading to Promise?" another asked.

"Yep."

"Folks there know you?" the leader asked.

Once again she nodded. They knew her, but that wasn't likely to do these men any good if they were looking for someone to put in a word for them.

"How'd you like a ride the rest of the way to town, pick up a dollar or two? We got an extra horse." The leader nodded at the black horse trailing behind them. "One of my men had a little accident a way back and—stayed behind."

Macky would have said no, but walking would make her miss the noon stage. Somehow, catching that stage had become the most important thing she'd ever done. She studied the man making the offer. She had nothing for them to steal and as long as they didn't know she was a girl, accepting his offer was less likely to give her away than refusing. Besides, Promise was only a short way down the trail, and once she reached town she'd separate herself from these rough-looking men.

"Much obliged."

Macky climbed on the horse, kicking him into a steady gallop to keep up with her new companions. She wondered where they'd come from. The horses had been ridden hard; their coats were icy with frozen perspiration. Why were they heading for a town that had little claim to fame other than the attempts by a few homesteaders to raise crops in an area where the only year-round water belonged to one man?

The leader slowed his horse, allowing Macky to come abreast of him. "Is there a bank in Promise, kid?"

"Yes, sir."

"Good, you can show us where it is."

That hadn't been part of Macky's plan. The bank was to be her first stop all right, but not in the company of these men. At the moment, however, she couldn't see a way out. Maybe it wouldn't matter. The bank, standing between the blacksmith's forge and the dressmaker's shop, would be clearly visible as they rode in. They'd see it.

They did, pulling up their horses in front of the rustic building and sliding to the street, which was mushy with melting snow. Macky, anxious to separate herself from the men, stopped her horse in front of the smithy's shop. She was already in enough trouble with the town; riding in with a group of men would only make matters worse. She'd just tie the horse to the hitching rail and disappear.

She soon found *that* wasn't going to work. "Watch the horses, boy," the man she'd mentally called Scarface said as he climbed down and dropped the reins to his horse.

Two of the riders stationed themselves beside the front door of the bank while the leader and the other man went inside. Before Macky could figure out how to get away, gunshots rang out.

As if he'd been waiting, the sheriff's deputy stepped out from between the bank and the blacksmith's shop, catching the strangers as they ran out of the bank.

"That's far enough, Pratt," the deputy shouted out.

"Throw down your guns," the sheriff called out from where he was hiding behind a water barrel in the alley between the bank and the blacksmith's shop. "We got word from the prison that you were heading this way. You'd better just let me have the money."

The deputy, out in the open, didn't have a chance. The outlaw leader whirled and fired. The deputy fell, but not before he'd wounded one of the robbers. The sheriff fired as Scarface mounted his horse, grazing its haunches. The animal reared up. In his attempt to stay on his horse, Pratt lost control of the flour sack he was carrying, flinging it behind him toward the startled Macky, who instinctively caught it.

Pratt? The sheriff had called the man Pratt. Everybody in the West knew about the infamous Pratt gang. Scarface finally slid from his horse, holding his shoulder, and began firing at the sheriff. Macky, paralyzed by what was happening, suddenly realized that the sheriff would step out from the alley and see her. With the money in her hand, he'd believe that she was part of the gang.

Macky kicked her horse into action. She'd come to town to ask the banker for money and she'd been caught up in a holdup.

Desperately, Macky rode into the blacksmith's barn, slid to the ground, and slapped the horse on the rear, peeling off her hat and coat as she watched him gallup out the back.

A moment later, Macky followed the horse out the back door. She didn't know what would happen, but being accused of involvement in the bank robbery was the last thing she needed. She could only hope that nobody had noticed her in Papa's coat and hat. No matter; her chance of selling her brooch had been all but ruined and it was almost time for the stage.

Perhaps the dressmaker would be interested in buying the cameo. Macky knocked on the shopkeeper's back door, found it open, and slid inside.

"Did you need something?"

The woman facing her did so with distaste and disbelief. Macky had never visited this shop, and nobody knew that better than the proprietor.

"Yes, I wonder if you can help me." Macky started to reach in her pocket and realized she was still holding the flour sack full of money.

"I doubt it, what are you looking for?" the seamstress asked icily.

"I'd like—" Macky reached for her cameo, heard the sound of coins jingling in the sack, and stilled her movements. There was no reason for the seamstress to question her, but after what her brother had done, the sheriff would never believe that she was an innocent pawn. She could be in even bigger trouble with the outlaw Scarface, who was sure to come after his money.

Then it came to her. She didn't have to sell the cameo now. She had money for her ticket if she wanted to use it. Granted, it wasn't hers, but she'd been handed a means to administer justice to a man who seemed untouchable, the man who'd cheated her father and so many others. She'd take the money her father had been cheated out of, plus interest. Later, she'd figure out how to return the money that wasn't truly hers.

Macky considered her next move calmly. The sheriff hadn't seen her, only the outlaws and the deputy, and from what she'd seen the deputy's wound looked fatal. There was no reason for this woman to know anything, for her window offered no view of the front of the bank. If Macky was lucky she still might make it—if she didn't miss the stage.

She made up her mind. Providence had provided.

"I'd like to buy a dress and a bonnet and cape. Quickly, please. I must make the noon stage, so I have to hurry."

The stage driver cast a dubious eye on the odd-looking young woman who boarded his coach at the last minute looking behind her as if she expected to be called back at any time. Her clothes didn't fit and her manner was a bit rough, but she was determined to get to Denver.

Ordinarily he'd worry about a young woman traveling alone, but he was already behind schedule and with the recent increase in Indian attacks, he had other things to worry about. Besides, she wouldn't be alone. She ought to get on well with the passenger inside. He was polite, well-mannered enough, a preacher, so he claimed. But most preachers didn't wear fancy clothes and carry a Bible in one hand and a gun in the other.

And most preachers didn't wear a black patch over one eye.

Anyway, the gold with which he'd purchased his ticket was real, and if he looked like the Devil instead of a messenger of the Lord, so be it.

The stage was due in Denver by the next day, and

there was Indian country to get through first. Indians and the Pratt gang who'd broken out of jail and robbed the bank in Promise only minutes earlier. The deputy had been killed, but the sheriff had caught two of the outlaws and wounded another. Pratt and a young boy who'd been riding with them had escaped and were likely heading west.

The driver opened the stage door and assisted the young woman inside.

John Brandon didn't move as the new passenger boarded the stage. He continued to lean his head against the back of the seat, his face covered by his hat. He'd learned long ago that his senses could discover much without the aid of his eyes.

He'd had to learn. A cold-blooded killer had taken the sight of one eye.

He wished he hadn't been able to see or hear the night the thieves pretending to be Indians had swooped down on his family's small homestead along the Mississippi. An arrow had lodged in John's eye, convincing the outlaws that the eight-year-old boy was dead. They'd forced his father to hand over the money from the sale of a year's crop of indigo and skins. Then they'd murdered everyone but John.

To cover his failure, the commanding officer at the fort nearby put the blame on the Indians instead of the river pirates he'd been sent to restrain. Eight-year-old John had tried to explain that the men who killed his family were white, but nobody had believed him. Alone and filled with anger, he'd run away from the authorities, who were no better than the thieves.

The Choctaw Indian tribe who'd taken him in and saved his life had called him Night Eyes because they thought he had special powers; they thought he could see in the dark.

Later, he'd accompanied the tribe west to the lands they were assigned in Oklahoma. Along with his Indian brothers he'd attended the missionary's school, where he studied the white man's Bible, the same one his mother had read to him as a boy.

His eye healed after fashion, but nothing healed the scar in his heart. As he grew into a man he made a vow that if it took the rest of his life, he'd find the outlaw responsible for murdering his family.

Fifteen years ago he'd shortened his last name, Brandon, to Bran and begun wandering across the country, looking, searching, hiring himself out as a private avenger of evil. As a gunfighter, he'd found crooks guilty of every kind of crime, found and punished them. But the man who'd given the order to murder his parents was still out there. Finally he had a new lead in a little mining town called Heaven, just outside Denver in the Kansas Territory.

Now he waited quietly, listening, feeling, allowing his mind's eye to discover the identity of his traveling companion.

Female. The driver had called her miss.

A good build and firm step, because the carriage had tilted as she stepped inside, and she'd settled herself without a lot of swishing around.

Probably no-nonsense, for he could see the tips of her boots beneath the brim of his hat. The boots were worn, though what he could see of the clothing looked new. The only scent in the air was that of the dye in the cloth.

Practical, for she'd planted both feet firmly on the floor of the coach and hadn't moved them; no fidgeting or fussing with herself.

Deciding that she seemed safe enough, he flicked the brim of his hat back and took a look at her.

Wrong, on the last couple of counts. Dead wrong. She was sitting quietly, yes, but that stillness was born of sheer determination—no—more like desperation. She was looking down at her hands and holding onto her portmanteau as if she dared anybody to touch it. Her eyes weren't closed, but they might as well have been.

The stage moved away in a lumbering motion, picking up speed.

The woman didn't move.

Finally, after an hour of hard riding by the horses pulling the stagecoach, she let out a deep breath and appeared to relax.

"Looks like you got away," he said.

"What?" She raised a veil of sooty lashes and uncovered huge eyes as green as the moss along the banks of the Mississippi River where he'd played as a child. Something about her was all wrong. The set of her lips was meant to challenge. But beneath that bravado he sensed an uncertainty that threatened to soften the lines in her forehead.

"Back there you looked as if you were running away from home and were afraid you wouldn't escape," he said.

"I was," she said.

"Pretty risky, a woman alone. No traveling companion, no family?"

"Don't have any. Buried the last—companion back in Promise."

Macky risked another look at the man across from her. He was six feet of black, beginning with his boots and ending with the patch over his eye and a hat that cast a shadow over a face etched by a two-day growth of beard. She received an impression of quiet danger from the casual way he seemed to look straight through her as if he knew that she was an imposter and was waiting for her to confess. "What's wrong with your eye?"

She hadn't meant to ask. Asking questions would be considered bad manners. In the past, manners were something in which she'd never taken much stock. Now she was no longer what she had been and she was still uncertain about the person she had become. The memory of the dressmaker's frosty glare made her suddenly aware of her ill-fitting lady's dress and bonnet.

Skirts and petticoats didn't make a lady; she'd already reverted back to her old way of saying what she thought without regard for the consequences.

"I'm sorry. *A fool uttereth all his mind.*"

Bran surprised himself by responding in kind. "*Answer a fool according to his folly.* Don't have but one."

She looked at him in surprise. "Plato?"

"No, Proverbs. The quotation, I mean. I buried the other eye a lot of years ago."

"Forgive me. Your eye is none of my concern."

Bran wouldn't normally have continued the conversation, but he couldn't resist the impulse to learn more about the woman. "Do you have a name?"

"Yes. Do you?"

"Indians call me Night Eyes."

Macky noticed he had a way of clipping off the first word in each sentence as though he were rationing them. "Why?" she asked.

"Thought I could see in the dark."

"What do *other* people call you?" she asked.

He frowned. "Depends."

"Fine, it's your business," she said and pressed her lips firmly together. She didn't have to talk to him. She'd learned early on that people didn't invite conversation from an outcast. Once her brother started hanging out at the saloon in town, the people back in Promise were quick to let her know that they'd done their Christian duty in welcoming the Calhouns, but that that welcome had come to an end. Since then Macky had avoided the town.

Across the carriage, Bran felt himself giving the girl a reluctant grin. She was a feisty one, his peculiar-looking companion with the cool green eyes and wisps of hot red hair trying to escape her odd little hat.

If the Indians who'd named him Night Eyes had been giving her a name they'd have called her Frozen Fire. She might have herself dressed like some dowdy schoolmarm, but there was more to her than her appearance indicated. In fact, he doubted that she cared much about clothing. And she damned sure didn't know how to buy a hat.

"I'm called Bran," he said slowly, in a low, gravelly voice that gave the impression he didn't talk a lot.

Macky wished she'd never spoken to the man. She didn't want to encourage conversation. All she'd do was call attention to herself. But it was too late. He wasn't going to go back to sleep and he was bound to ask questions.

"What are you called?" he asked.

"Trouble, mostly," she said with a sigh that told him more than she'd intended.

"That's an odd name for a woman."

"That's as good as you're going to get," she replied, turning back to the window.

"Good? Good—a rare quality in my life and," he took a long look at her, "debatable at the moment, but I'm willing to reserve judgement."

He didn't know why he was continuing the conversation. He didn't usually talk much, but something about this young woman's demand for privacy was intriguing. "Truth is, I'm a lot more likely to appreciate a woman who's bad. Wake me when we get to the way station."

Macky's eyes flew open. She was ready to tell him where he could go, but the brooding one-eyed stranger had resumed his position beneath his hat. Macky hadn't had much experience with men, but she had the feeling that beneath his hat he was leering.

Well, two could play that game. Unless he had holes in the crown, he wasn't watching her. And no matter what the Indians thought about his sight, Macky had no belief in a person's ability to see through felt. She studied him more carefully.

His fine leather boots were splattered with mud as if he'd come a long way. She'd noticed a saddle strapped on top of the coach and a horse tied to the back. His black canvas greatcoat showed signs of hard use, but what she could see of his trousers was of fine cloth. His shirt was white, tied with a thin black ribbon tie, and the striped waistcoat looked like the one Papa always wore when he went into town.

Papa. A pang of regret pierced her. She'd left town so quickly that she hadn't even stopped by his grave to say good-bye. But he wouldn't have wanted her to grieve. His heart had said good-bye a long time ago. It had been dying inside for years. It just took his body longer to go.

Macky tried not to look at the long, muscular legs filling up the space between the seats, but her gaze seemed drawn to her companion. She focused on his hat, an expensive black Stetson. A jaunty silver feather had been pinned to the leather band. The feather seemed out of place on a man so totally devoid of warmth. A dandy who quoted scripture.

That was what was bothering her, she decided, the aura of danger he carried with him. It was distinct and impenetrable, and it was the only explanation she could think of for the uneasy feeling in the pit of her stomach. She tried to keep her breathing light in order to conceal her agitation.

But she soon decided that it wasn't only the lack of air that was bothering her. Her stomach was reacting just as oddly. Macky Calhoun was never sick, yet suddenly she felt an odd uncertainty in the area of her person where her portmanteau was resting.

Resolutely she pulled her attention away from her companion's hat, allowing her gaze to fall once more on the seat across from her.

Beside him, on the hard leather bench, was a black object, an object that, after a moment, she recognized. A Bible. The man was carrying a Bible. What did that mean? Was he some kind of missionary? He'd said something about Indians. Maybe he'd been sent to convert the heathens.

Heathens.

Outlaws.

Bank robbers.

Sinners.

McKenzie Kathryn Calhoun, on her way to hell, was traveling across the prairie with a man of God. No wonder he'd seemed so remote. The Lord had sent an escort to make sure she got what she deserved.

If you loved SCANDAL IN SILVER, don't miss

REBEL IN SILK

A Once Upon a Time Romance

by Sandra Chastain

"*Rebel in Silk* is a sinfully funny and emotionally riveting novel, the usual Sandra Chastain masterpiece of entertainment. This delightful author has a tremendous talent that places her on a pinnacle reserved for special romance writers."
—*Affaire de Coeur*

Dallas Burke had come to Willow Creek, Wyoming, to find her brother's killer, and she had no intention of being scared off—not by the roughnecks who trashed her newspaper office, nor by the devilishly handsome cowboy who warned her of the violence to come. Yet she couldn't deny that the tall, sun-bronzed rancher had given her something to think about, namely, what it would be like to be held in his steel-muscled arms and feel his sensuous mouth on hers....

Don't miss these fabulous Bantam women's fiction titles

On Sale in November

ADAM'S FALL

by *New York Times* bestselling author
Sandra Brown

Blockbuster author Sandra Brown—whose name is almost synonymous with *New York Times* bestseller list—offers a classic romantic novel that aches with emotion and sizzles with passion.
❑ *56768-3 $4.99/$5.99 in Canada*

PURE SIN

by nationally bestselling **author**
Susan Johnson

From the erotic imagination of Susan Johnson comes a tale of exquisite pleasure that begins in the wilds of Montana—and ends in the untamed places of two lovers' hearts.
❑ *29956-5 $5.50/6.99 in Canada*

ON WINGS OF MAGIC

by award-winning author
Kay Hooper

Award-winning Kay Hooper offers a passionate story filled with all the humor and tenderness her fans have come to expect—a story that explores the loneliness of heartbreak and the searing power of love.
❑ *56965-1 $4.99/$5.99 in Canada*

THE VERY BEST IN HISTORICAL WOMEN'S FICTION

Iris Johansen

_____	28855-5	THE WIND DANCER ....$5.99/$6.99 in Canada
_____	29032-0	STORM WINDS $4.99/5.99
_____	29244-7	REAP THE WIND $4.99/5.99
_____	29604-3	THE GOLDEN BARBARIAN $4.99/5.99
_____	29944-1	THE MAGNIFICENT ROGUE $5.99/6.99
_____	29968-9	THE TIGER PRINCE $5.50/6.50
_____	29871-2	LAST BRIDGE HOME $4.50/5.50
_____	29945-X	BELOVED SCOUNDREL $5.99/6.99
_____	29946-8	MIDNIGHT WARRIOR $5.99/6.99

Susan Johnson

_____	29125-4	FORBIDDEN $4.99/5.99
_____	29312-5	SINFUL $4.99/5.99
_____	29957-3	BLAZE $5.50/6.50
_____	29959-X	SILVER FLAME $5.50/6.50
_____	29955-7	OUTLAW $5.50/6.50
_____	56327-0	SEIZED BY LOVE $5.50/6.99

Teresa Medeiros

_____	29407-5	HEATHER AND VELVET $4.99/5.99
_____	29409-1	ONCE AN ANGEL $5.50/6.50
_____	29408-3	A WHISPER OF ROSES $5.50/6.50

Patricia Potter

_____	29070-3	LIGHTNING $4.99/5.99
_____	29071-1	LAWLESS $4.99/5.99
_____	29069-X	RAINBOW $5.50/6.50
_____	56199-5	RENEGADE $5.50/6.50
_____	56225-8	NOTORIOUS $5.50/6.50

Ask for these titles at your bookstore or use this page to order.

Please send me the books I have checked above. I am enclosing $ _____ (add $2.50 to cover postage and handling). Send check or money order, no cash or C. O. D.'s please.

Mr./ Ms. _____

Address _____

City/ State/ Zip _____

Send order to: Bantam Books, Dept. FN 17, 2451 S. Wolf Road, Des Plaines, IL 60018

Please allow four to six weeks for delivery.

Prices and availability subject to change without notice.   FN 17 - 7/94